I DREW HIM
FROM THE
WATER

ADVENTURE, MYSTERY, INTRIGUE

CECILE LONG

WESTBOW
PRESS®
A DIVISION OF THOMAS NELSON
& ZONDERVAN

Copyright permission provided by:
Kathy L. McFarland and Joanne Holstein, Becker Bible Ministries
and
behindthename.com.

WestBow Press books may be ordered through booksellers or by contacting:

WestBow Press
A Division of Thomas Nelson & Zondervan
1663 Liberty Drive
Bloomington, IN 47403
www.westbowpress.com
1 (866) 928-1240

Because of the dynamic nature of the Internet, any web addresses or links contained in this book may have changed since publication and may no longer be valid. The views expressed in this work are solely those of the author and do not necessarily reflect the views of the publisher, and the publisher hereby disclaims any responsibility for them.

Any people depicted in stock imagery provided by Thinkstock are models, and such images are being used for illustrative purposes only.
Certain stock imagery © Thinkstock.

ISBN: 978-1-5127-1112-7 (sc)
ISBN: 978-1-5127-1114-1 (hc)
ISBN: 978-1-5127-1113-4 (e)

Library of Congress Control Number: 2015914376

Print information available on the last page.

WestBow Press rev. date: 10/13/2015

Dedication

With love, I dedicate this book to Brittany Bublitz, whom I owed a story.

God is in charge of this book **I DREW HIM FROM THE WATER**. My prayer is that whatever he has planned for this book may take place. Adapted from Proverbs 16:3 (Message Bible). This book was put together by a three-stranded cord and shall not be broken. Adapted from Ecclesiastes 4:12 (Message Bible).

Contents

Third Group of Three Plagues:

The Final Plague:

Preface/Acknowledge

This book came to be through the desperation of a dear friend of mine, Pastor Elisa Thibodeau. Pastor Elisa is a children's pastor for a local Assembly of God church. She mentioned needing to find a way for her children to learn about Moses and the ten plagues. After about two months of writing, a children's play came to life. I have written and performed other plays and skits in the past, but nothing on this large of a scale.

Each child participated in this play that took twelve consecutive Sundays to perform. Because the children performed this play in children's church, the parents were bummed, at not seeing it. They asked for something else—unable to turn it into a two-hour play—people encouraged me to turn it into a book. After some time of pondering and prayer, I felt prompted to give it a try. This book is full of ancient times and traditions mixed with modern times and technology. Although this is a work of fiction, this was a real life story that took place thousands of years ago; for this reason, some of the character's names are real.

I wish to give thanks to my husband Mark, for his many hours of support, missed dinners and for listening to my frustrations in writing this book. The following people sacrificed hours to help me with this book. Kami Burke, Janice Sanford, and Pastor Elisa Thibodeau. To Paul Bauer, I thank you for sacrificing time spent with your wife and letting me have her for this book. Vicki Bauer you have been a Godsend for your help on this book, and I cannot begin to thank you enough. May God bless each of you with joy, happiness, and abundance of life in life's purest form.

I pray that any person who touches this book by reading it, hearing it read or touching the pages, experiences a new way of living by becoming a new creation in our Lord, Jesus Christ.

I thank everyone, my friends and family, you know who you are, for your much-needed encouragement and support in this project. Those who showed interest gave me encouragement and listened to my forever talk about the excitement of writing this book. Last but not least, I give thanks to The Holy Spirit, if not for the Holy Spirit's help this book would not have come to fruition.

History of the Israelites

Once upon a time centuries ago, there was a young man named Joseph. As Joseph grew, his father showed more love for him than his half-brothers, causing a hatred to build that would one day cause their father's grief. When Joseph was seventeen, his father sent him to check on his brothers, who were tending the sheep.

His brothers saw an opportunity to get rid of their pesky little brother. They bound Joseph up and sold him to a caravan of Ishmaelite cousins coming from Gilead heading to the market in Egypt.

Despite the hate they had for him, Joseph was destined to become second in command in the kingdom of Egypt under Pharaoh someday. Taking life's events as they came, he received from God, the God of the Israelites, favor and grace in every situation—which helped him to overcome even the harshest of circumstances with love and not hate for those around him.

There came a day that Pharaoh the ruler of the kingdom of Egypt due to a dream, called for Joseph. Joseph was the only one able to interpret Pharaoh's dream was ordained as the second in command of the kingdom under Pharaoh. Knowing that there was to be a seven-year drought, as it was part of the dream, Joseph became overseer of the food supply in all the land of Egypt. He kept food on the tables and made sure all was safe in the kingdom for the Pharaoh of Egypt.

In the middle of that famine, Joseph's brothers came looking to trade for some food. Joseph recognized his brothers; however, his brothers did not recognize him. So for good measure he gave them a hard time. When they came to the reality of who he was, they fell to their knees and asked his forgiveness. Joseph forgave them and then instructed them to bring his family to live with him at the palace.

Pharaoh, wanting to show his appreciation to Joseph, gave Joseph's people the land they came to call Goshen. The people lived in the luxury of what Joseph had done for Egypt for years to come. Then all too soon came the day when the great Joseph went to sleep with his ancestors, and a new Pharaoh came to reign in the land of Egypt.

The new Pharaoh, not knowing Joseph, became intimidated? by the massive tribe of Israelite people. Concerned, he declared that the people of Goshen, the Israelites, would now become slaves to Pharaoh. As slaves, they would not be able to revolt or cause trouble to his country.

So life has now become as a bed of roses for the people of Goshen. Why roses you ask? Roses have roots that run deep into a soil that is fertile and well drained. Roses also require hours of sunshine to grow and stay healthy. Attached to the Rose are long stems that have thorns, prickly and hard, but serve a purpose in the life of the rose.

The life of the Israelites had become like the thorns of the rose. A life that had once been comfortable, pleasant, and enjoyable, overnight became uncomfortable, harsh and miserable. Pharaoh decreed them his slaves, forced to make bricks used to construct cities the royal family would use to store their wealth in, was grueling. However, they still had hope that their God would hear their cries and would one day rescue them from the hands of the evil Pharaoh.

Just like a rose, the Israelites' roots run deep in their God. The Israelites are a fertile people—even under the harshest conditions of life they have endured and produced children.

Unknown to the Israelites, they are part of the rose that will very soon show himself as their hero from on high. The rose has watched them daily and fed them the sunshine required to keep trudging on with life.

The Rose is about to provide them the nourishment that would cause the weakened, unhealthy and exhausted thorns to become once again invigorated, healthy and unwearied.

What is this just around the corner? What is to happen next? As the story unfolds, we'll meet a wicked Pharaoh, a princess who rescues a baby, a murder, a fugitive, a news anchor eager for fame. How and where will this all end? Who are you rooting for: the Ruler of Egypt, the one the Egyptians call the ruler of the world? Maybe the God of Abraham, Isaac, and Jacob, the Creator of the world, the ruler of all?

Prologue

Who is this man Moses? Egyptians call him by the name of Moshe (mo-SHEH). We hear the Israelites call him Moshe Rabbenu, meaning: "Moses Our Teacher." Some people just call him Moses. Whatever name you call him, one thing stays the same: everywhere you go; people seem to be fascinated by this man called Moses.

Let me introduce myself, my name is Marinda. I am a great, great, great niece of the news anchor in this story; her name is Marissa. My Aunt Marissa requested that the story I am about to tell you, be passed down from generation to generation. This story is full of bravery and our beloved Pharaoh. Pharaoh was the victim of Moses and his God.

My Aunt Marissa, was assigned to do what was supposed to be a straightforward documentary, about this Moses. This story turned out to be more than any of them could have ever imagined. Aunt Marissa's encounter with this man called Moses, would not only change her life, but that of all humanity forever. From here on, for the ease of my readers, I am referring to Moshe as Moses. Pharaoh was also called different names by the people; the Egyptians called him "God of the Earth," "Lord of the Two Lands," or "High Priest of Every Temple." For easier reading, with a few exceptions, I am referring to him as Pharaoh.

Dear readers, here is the story of my Aunt Marissa, and how she got more than she ever dreamed of—the day her life collided with the life of a man called Moses.

Chapter 1
Marissa

"Hello, you lovely people of Egypt. My name is Marissa. I am Egyptian by birth and a news anchor for *The Egyptian Times News,* or ET NEWS, as the local people know us.

My story begins with a committee meeting I attended in one of the ET NEWS conference rooms. Our news team had gathered together to discuss topics for our next documentary. As we spent time together and later spoke with people on the streets of Egypt, we soon realized that everyone was talking about a man named Moses.

One of our reporters heard, on the street, that this Moses is a man who has just arrived in Egypt. He has not even announced himself to anyone yet, so what is he doing here? Moses seems to be spending most of his time in the land of Goshen. Why would anyone be spending time in Goshen?

It was also reported to us that some people were saying that this was the Moses of old—the man who ran away after killing one of his Egyptian people, in a fit of rage.

Some thought that he might be someone sent here simply to stir up trouble, to call the slaves to revolt against Pharaoh. However, why come back now? The leaders of the community said that forty years ago the Moses of old left Egypt and was presumed dead.

We came to the conclusion that ET NEWS would do a documentary on Moses; that way we could get to the bottom of all the talk that is going on about him.

We then needed to decide who to interview. Would Moses have family or friends in Goshen willing to speak with us? What would interest our audience the most regarding the life of Moses? How much time should we set aside for the documentary—four or five days?

Where would this documentary be filmed—in Goshen or Rameses? There was a lot to do and no time to do it in—always the life of a news anchor.

The team picked me to host the documentary, and I needed to pick my co-anchor. Research showed that Moses was both an Egyptian and an Israelite; born to Israelite parents, but raised as an Egyptian prince—as the son of Princess Bithiah—to be more precise. For that reason, I assigned one of our male Israelite slaves to be my co-anchor.

Abdullah was purchased by me when he was a young boy. I have used him at ET NEWS to help me with whatever needs done at the news station. Occasionally, I lease him to ET NEWS for whatever project they see fit for him to do.

None of us at the time had a clue that this would be a life-changing year. Not just for the Israelites or those of Jewish or Hebrew descent, but the Egyptians as well. No one, except maybe Moses himself, had a clue about the drama that was about to unfold. The Egyptians knew, all too well, that the Israelite people are always causing trouble. The trouble I am speaking of however was of a *"different kind."*

We would be experiencing something that had never been seen before and hopefully, would never be seen again. When the Egyptian "slash" Israelite, known as Moses, and our Pharaoh met... let me put it this way.

I remember when a stray dog found his way into my living room. What was the problem with that, you ask? My living room is where my precious cats live; that is what was wrong! What a mess! That dog wanted nothing more than to find his way out. My cats immediately went to war, letting him know he was invading their territory.

My house was a mess, and it took the servants a week to get it back in order, not to mention to get my cats to settle down. My cats are territorial, and when that dog came in, uninvited, and tried to take over—that was not going to happen without a fight. That is the way it was the first time Moses had an audience with Pharaoh.

After much discussion about who to interview for the documentary on Moses, where to find these people, scheduling the broadcast dates, and numerous other tasks, the day came to do our first of four live interviews.

We planned to speak with Jochebed, Moses' blood mother; Miriam, Moses' Israelite sister; Aaron, Moses' Israelite brother and then Moses himself.

That was the plan, but as one learns in the world of reporting, you can make all the plans you want, but learn to expect something to go wrong. While going over the plans for the documentary, my colleagues and I decided that, if indeed, this is the Moses of the past, then he came only for one thing—to start trouble.

We normally broadcast our shows once a week. However, due to the circumstances of this situation, my colleagues and I, decided that we needed to do this particular documentary as a four-day special.

We needed to get the dirt on him, to let the public know that Moses was up to no good before he could start something that would make us all look foolish. Let me take you back to the broadcast as it happened."

Chapter 2
Jochebed

We are on in 5, 4, 3, 2, 1, Action.

ET NEWS: PRESENTS: "Who Is This Man Called Moses?"

"Hello to everyone in Pithom, Rameses, and Succoth, I am your Host, Marissa. I hope you stay with us the four days that we investigate Moses. Our documentary, "Who Is This Man Called Moses?" shall prove to be most intriguing. Moses is a man who mysteriously entered Goshen, and has avoided introducing himself.

Who would come to Goshen and then stay hidden? The only reason a person remains hidden is because they are here to cause us trouble. Is this 'the Moses' that our Princess Bithiah found in a basket in the Nile River some forty years ago? Is he the infant she took pity on and brought home with her to be raised and groomed as the next Pharaoh?

Is this 'the Moses' who understood that Hebrew blood ran through his veins—not the blood of the royal family?

Is this 'the Moses' that killed one of his Egyptian relatives and then left the country in an act of, dare I say it… fear?

Is this 'the Moses' who ran like a coward instead of facing Pharaoh and explaining his actions and possibly being acquitted of his crime?

If indeed he is 'that Moses,' why has he come back after all these years? Rumor has it that Moses has a relationship with the Israelites' God.

The facts need to be made known and these questions need answers. As Abdullah and I investigate this man, you'll see us report to you the clear, uncut story.

I promise you, in the next four days you'll find out the truth, and nothing but the truth, about this mystery man that came uninvited into the land of Egypt.

I hope you stay with us as we interview Jochebed, Moses' birth mother. Tomorrow's interview shall be with Miriam, Moses' Israelite sister. Wednesday we are with Aaron, Moses' Israelite brother, who is said to be assisting Moses with whatever it is they have planned.

Thursday is the final night of our documentary on Moses and Moses *himself* is making an appearance. I promise you that this is to be the most insightful and entertaining documentary I have done to date.

You are watching us live, people, something we do not normally do for our documentary series. However, the owner of ET NEWS felt that this documentary series on Moses required particular attention.

They want you informed, able to hear and see the moment of truth as it is happening. In this way we can verify that the speculations about this Moses are false.

We would like to thank, ahead of time, all the people that are allowing us into their homes and lives while we film this documentary. So, thank you! Abdullah is in Jochebed's house ready to speak with her. Abdullah, are you and Jochebed ready?"

Abdullah: "We are ready. Hello to all of you wonderful people out there watching us. I am in Jochebed's home, she is the woman that gave birth to Moses'. Jochebed how are you today?"

Jochebed: "My God blesses me. Thank you for coming to my home."

Abdullah: "To help us better understand Moses bloodline, would you give us a little background on you and your husband?"

Jochebed: "Moses' father's name is Amram. Amram's father is Kohath, one of Levi's sons. Amram was destined to start the Amramites' family tribe.

5

They were assigned to become a priestly tribe, to take care of our God's Holy Place. That is why his name means 'exalted nation.' Sadly, Amram is no longer with us, his bones rest with those of his ancestors..."

Marissa: "'God's Holy Place' indeed, the God of your imagination is more like it... People of Egypt, do not forget that these Israelites are our slaves. What kind of a God watches over slaves?"

Jochebed: "A God who is loving and kind; a God, who cares about his people." Jochebed was not surprised by Marissa's anger.

Marissa: "Loving and kind? Ha! How loving and kind can this God of yours be when you are no more than slaves? What kind of God allows his people to live as slaves and then says he cares about them?

Your people live and work like dogs. You lack common sense and have no idea how to act in a civilized manner. Loving, kind and caring! Right."

Jochebed: "Marissa, I realize you do not understand our God. However, I can say that you'll live to see our God's loving-kindness for his people. May I finish answering Abdullah's question? (Marissa silent Jochebed continued.)

My parents are Levi and Melcha. My father, Levi, is one of Joseph's brothers. Joseph was second in command to Pharaoh and was responsible for all the food and security of the country at the time of the great famine. Amram and I come from the same Levite tribe."

Abdullah: "I understand your marriage was not an arranged marriage, and yet you come from the same bloodline, interesting. Ah, you have two other children besides Moses, is that correct?"

Jochebed: "We have three children: Miriam, our daughter, is the oldest; Aaron is our middle child; and Moses is the youngest. During the time of Moses' birth, Pharaoh ordered the midwives to throw any male children born, to the Israelite people, into the Nile River—thus causing the river to run red with the blood of those babies. The blood of the babies cried out from the Nile River to our God for righteousness..."

Marissa: "'Causing the river to run red with their blood? The voice of the babies' blood cried out to their God'? Really! Jochebed, I want you to know that *those* babies did not count for anything, *those* babies were no better than a lamb!"

Jochebed: "They were *human babies*, Marissa! Babies are babies, no matter what blood line they come from!" Filled with indignation at Marissa's lack of compassion for human life, Jochebed continued: "In the years following Joseph's death, a new Pharaoh came to rule Egypt. Having never met with Joseph personally, the new Pharaoh, and his men became concerned about the large Israelite population.

The Israelite people were growing larger in numbers than the Egyptians themselves. Watching the Israelite people, Pharaoh, and his men came to the conclusion that if anyone ever declared war upon them, my people would probably side with Egypt's enemies. In doing so, they would leave the country or possibly revolt and take Egypt as their country."

Abdullah: "How would things have been different if the new Pharaoh had met with Joseph before he died?"

Jochebed: "Had Pharaoh and Joseph met, Pharaoh would have realized he had nothing to fear from the Israelite people. We were comfortable and had made Goshen our home. We had no reason to want to cause trouble for ourselves or anyone else..."

Marissa: "You had food and land because of who Joseph was, and because of what he Joseph had done to Pharaoh. When Joseph died, you had no guarantee of food or land anymore. Speak the truth, Jochebed."

Jochebed: "When Pharaoh found out that Joseph's family was here from Canaan looking for a place to live and setting up our tents in Goshen, Pharaoh was delighted. He asked the elders, 'What do you do for a living?' The council elders answered, 'We are shepherds looking for somewhere to pasture our livestock.' Pharaoh replied, 'You may have the land of Goshen.'

Marissa, you know that shepherds are disgusting people in the eyes of the Egyptians. So letting us live in Goshen separately from the Egyptians was a pleasing solution. Pharaoh wanted to honor Joseph and keep the peace with his people at the same time. Why should that be taken from us just because Joseph went to sleep with our ancestors?"

Marissa: "Why should the Israelites be allowed to have a free ride when the one whom Pharaoh respected was dead? Pharaoh and his council of wise men knew what they were doing. Shepherds were disgusting to our people then, and they still are today. Why people need to stay out with stinky sheep and smell that way, I shall never understand."

Jochebed: "Everyone has something that they are good at, Marissa, which they can do better than others. You enjoy eating the meat of those sheep from time to time, would you have that pleasure if there were no one to take care of those sheep?"

Marissa: "We have livestock of our own, we do not need yours!"

Jochebed: "That is true, however, did you know that Pharaoh asked Joseph to assign someone from his Israelite family, to care for Pharaoh's Palace livestock? He did that because he had no one that could take care of the sheep as well as we could."

Marissa: "Pharaoh's Egyptians are a first-class people. Of course, we were not made to raise *sheep!* Pharaoh was probably relieved when Joseph's people came to take care of our sheep for us."

Abdullah: "So, Pharaoh and his officials decided the best thing to do was have the all the male babies, born to Israelite women thrown in the Nile River."

Jochebed: "Not at first. Shiphrah and Puah, heads over the midwives of the Hebrews, were ordered to kill each male baby born at the birth stool of the Israelite women. They could not bring themselves to do such a thing, and did not instruct the other midwives to do so either.

Pharaoh was furious when he found out that the babies were not being killed by the midwives as he had instructed. When Pharaoh asked them why the male babies were still alive, they explained that the Israelite women were much stronger than the Egyptian women and had their babies before they arrived.

Pharaoh then ordered all his people to throw any male Israelite child they found into the Nile River, but he allowed the female babies to live. For a season, Pharaoh attempted to have all our male children killed; however, our God had other plans for one special baby boy born during that time."

Marissa: "What do you mean your God had other plans? How is it that any God has plans for his people?"

Jochebed: "Our God, the God of Abraham, Isaac, and Jacob made each one of us. He knows the very thoughts of our hearts. Our God knew that Shiphrah and Puah would not kill the babies for fear of their God.

He knew that they would leave it up to the parents to choose what to do with their babies. What parent is going to throw their son willfully into the river to drown because of a decree by the ruler of the country! The babies were still alive. Our God blessed Shiphrah and Puah for not killing the baby boys."

Marissa: "These women did not kill the babies! Why would your God bless these women?" They disobeyed a direct order from Pharaoh!"

Jochebed: "As I said before, our God, the God of Abraham, Isaac, and Jacob is not like any of your Egyptian gods. Our God sees, hears, and feels. Our God cares about his people. At the time, Shiphrah and Puah had not been blessed with children so later, God blessed them both with children and made their families prosperous."

Marissa: "Blessed them? Prospered them?"

Abdullah: "So Jochebed, when you brought Moses into the world, you were afraid of losing him to the Nile?"

Jochebed: "What parent at that time would not have had a concern about their child's life? At Moses' birth, he had a glow about him we had never seen before. Beautiful is what it was, so we called him Beautiful. That beauty gave us a peace that I cannot describe to you. Not sure what to do with our new little bundle of joy, Amram and I prayed that God would spare our baby Beautiful's life."

Abdulah: "You said you prayed that God would spare the life of your son. You prayed that Moses, I mean Baby, Beautiful, would not fall victim to the Nile River. How did you see this prayer answered?"

Jochebed: "Again, after praying for many days, Amram, and I felt that God had something special planned for our son. So after talking it over, Amram and I decided we would hide him.

Unfortunately, the Egyptian people decided to conduct searches for any male children that the Israelites might be hiding in or around their homes. They wanted to make sure that none of the children escaped the death that Pharaoh had placed upon them. As they searched our homes, the Egyptians told us they wanted no part in a judgment placed upon them by their gods, because of one failure to carry out a decree from Pharaoh.

When Baby Beautiful turned three months of age, we realized we could no longer hide him. Frustrated, we asked each other, 'What are we to do? How are we going to keep the baby safe?' Abdullah, what would you do? Amram and I spent time in prayer and felt led to make a basket to place our son in. Our heart's desire was that our God would safely deliver baby Beautiful from harm's way.

That night after we completed our basket, we prayed once again to our God, and asked for guidance and the security of our baby. Because of that basket, he had a chance to float safely through all the hazards in the water. Remembering that Princess Bithiah had a bathing spot along the Nile River, we pointed the basket in that direction. We knew that God had a plan to keep Beautiful, safe—whether or not the plan included Princess Bithiah, we did not know."

Abdullah: "How did you make a basket that kept your son safe from the elements in the Nile?"

Jochebed: "Miriam and I built the basket with papyrus plants and coated it with pitch and tar. That made it strong enough to hold any baby."

Abdullah: "You had friends and family who lost their baby boys to the Nileand yet your son lived to see another day, how did that make you feel?"

Jochebed: "For some time that question haunted me. Why did so many other babies have to die, and yet my son was allowed to live? Continually, I questioned that... It was not fair, yet I was desperate to do anything to keep him alive-he was my son! I did feel such sadness for the others... In my old age, I have grown to understand that sometimes things happen, and they are not for us to understand.

We are supposed to accept that there are times when things happen to us, and the reason these things happen to us, we are not always able to comprehend. We must not ponder long on them; otherwise our sorrow and unanswered questions may turn into anger and bitterness—and for what? What shall that accomplish? Will anger and bitterness help us to gain understanding? I have not seen anger and bitterness help anyone to acquire knowledge in all my years of life. Instead, I have learned to live each day looking for the beauty of God that is around me.

Does that mean that I have no sorrow for what has happened? No! It means that I *choose* each day to trust my God with what is going on each moment of that day. I elect to have faith that God is right beside me, and he is helping me to overcome any hardships that come my way."

Abdullah: "You said you chose to trust your God to overcome any hardships that came your way. However, I think you and your family were fortunate not to have had the hardships that many other Israelite families suffered."

Jochebed: "Abdullah, you have not visited your homeland of Goshen for some time, so I see how you would come to think that way. We did not suffer the hardships of some other Israelite people, however, are you saying that we suffered no hardships? In many different ways, we have suffered hardships. If you will, but ponder for a moment, shut your eyes, relax, and listen to this story:

There once was a couple who became the parents of a beautiful baby boy. The new parents' excitement quickly turned to concern. The ruler of their country had given an order that all newborn, male, Israelite babies, were to be taken and offered as a sacrifice. These tiny humans were to become living sacrifices to the water gods and goddesses.

The kingdom council became intimidated by the growth in numbers of this tribe's people and believed it was better to have the male babies drown in the Nile than to risk the males becoming a threat to them later. Anyone loyal to the ruler was commanded to throw the newborns into the Nile River immediately. The parents had a decision to make: Do they succumb to the ruler's order and let their newborn son drown, or do they risk keeping him alive and hide him from the world?

As they held their new bundle of joy, they felt a violent anger rise up inside of them. How dare anyone command their son drown! Are they the type of parents who are going to turn a blind eye and have their son succumb to a watery grave—just to be obedient unto the ruler of the country?

With God-given determination their decision was made. They would hide the baby from the world. In the meantime, they would pray and ask their God to show them a way to keep their new bundle of joy alive and safe. After three months, it became impossible to hide him anymore. Feeling that their God had directed them through prayer, they made a basket and placed him into it, so that he might float to safety in the same river in which he was supposed to have drown.

It was time to put the baby in his basket, close the cover over him and gently push the basket out away from the Nile River's shore. They knew they must do this, and they knew their God would take care of him, yet their heart ached for the little one they could no longer keep. With every ounce of strength they had, they trusted in their God and let the baby float down the river. In faith they trusted their God with their baby's future.

With heavy yet hopeful hearts, the parents began the lonely walk home, leaving their daughter to watch over the baby from afar and let them know when he was safe and sound.

Meanwhile downstream, the royal princess, along with her handmaidens came to the river, intent on enjoying a time of bathing and worshiping the gods. Arriving at the spot reserved for the women in the royal family, they came to a brick laid patio area equipped with lounging chairs and tables for times of refreshment. In the hot sun two eunuchs fanned the princess with large ostrich feathers, as she lay on her lounge. The maidservants took turns cooling off in the river.

At the same time the basket—holding the baby—weaved in and out of the bulrushes along the river's shore. Splashing and cooling herself, a maidservant noticed the basket, turned to the princess, and pointed her finger toward the basket saying, 'My Princess, I believe I see a basket floating in the reeds.'

The Princess walked over to the maidservant and followed her finger, 'There is something floating in the river, go and bring it to me!' commanded the Princess. With the basket in the hand of the maidservant, the Princess looked at it and motioned her to place the basket on one of the tables for her. A group of curious maidservants, and two eunuchs, surrounded the princess to see what was in the basket.

As the Princess slowly opened the lid, she saw a baby boy with eyes of green—that same sparkling green you see when the sun hits the waters of the Nile. The baby did not cry and scream, as one might expect. He merely smiled and cooed at the princess with a sound that went straight to her heart. Unwrapping the diaper, she saw it was a boy; the Princess spoke with a smile on her face and joy in her voice: 'This baby is one of the Israelites that was to drown.'

The servants were surprised at the princess's reaction—they expected her to refuse this baby. The Princess herself should have ordered him drowned, but instead she was touched with a longing for this baby to the very core of her being.

The sister, who saw what was happening, bravely made her way to the princess and asked; "Would you like me to find a wet-nurse from the women of his tribe who'll nurse the baby for you?" To which the Princess replied, "Yes, child, that would be nice of you—now go."

Back at the house the mother's mind was traveling, mixed with thoughts of what might be happening, when suddenly she heard her daughter calling to her: 'Mother, Mother!" Excited to hear about her son she asked, "What is it my daughter? Who has found the baby?"

"Mother, the pharaoh's daughter has found the baby! She has asked me to find a wet-nurse for him, will you come?" Out the door and on her way to meet the princess, she found herself in shock. Her mind was not able to comprehend the miracle that had taken place. How is it that when you, in your soul, believe in something so deeply, and you know that your God will produce the miracle for you, that when it happens your mind can't comprehend the miracle?

She prayed, "Dear God, please do not let me make a mistake, please do not let our son show any sign of recognition when he sees me. Cover the eyes of all involved to blind them of who I am, that we may have our son back in our home. Amen."

Upon being introduced to the princess, and after a brief conversation with her, the Princess declared she was the one to take care of the baby until he no longer was in need of a wet-nurse, making the people with her swear to keep quiet about this matter. The Princess made arrangements for the provisions of the child to be brought to her once a week.

She was charged with the baby's care, keeping him away from people, giving him only the necessities of life. The Princess declared she would make sure that her family received everything they needed for the household until the day she delivered the child to the palace where he would live permanently as her legal son.

She walked home, with baby Beautiful in her arms, and found herself thinking about all that had just happened. God had chosen her to take care of her own son and to return him to Pharaoh's daughter! He would be adopted, educated, branded as a family member of the royal family of Egypt. For the next six years, her family will live close to their God; no one could ever know that the baby was hers by blood.

During those precious few years she would have with him, she trained him to know who his God really was. She taught him these truths so that the false gods and goddesses of the Ruler could not steer him wrong when he left. She taught him and told him stories about his bloodline as much as she could.

So soon, time runs out, how can it be time for the child to leave? She hoped and prayed that as parents, he had been prepared, equipped, and nurtured enough for the adventure that lay ahead of him.

His father prayed a blessing over him, 'May the Mighty One of Jacob, give you blessings from the heavens above. May the Almighty One give you strength and courage, may the God of our Father's gift you with boldness and wisdom to complete the journey that he has planned for your life. Amen.' With that, she and her daughter left for the royal palace to deliver him to his new home.

As the Princess approached and took this precious little boy away, she steeled herself as, not to show the emotions that were screaming from inside. The Ruler's daughter thanked her for the care and attention she gave to her son these past six years, then dismissed her from his life as if she never existed. As she walked away with him, her heart longed to say, "Good-Bye my son, Mommy is coming back to get you soon."

For six years, she had had this child as her flesh and blood, and yet not once did he call them mother or father—for the princess and another were to be his parents. For six years, she had called him one name; and now upon arrival at the palace, he was renamed by the princess—her Ruler's daughter.

Walking home, she had time to wonder how Beautiful was doing. The Princess, named him the moment she held him in her arms. She desperately wanted to remember that name so if she heard it in the future, she would know it was her son.

She constantly wondered how he was doing, but she couldn't go and ask. No one must ever know or suspect the circumstances surrounding this child. Now with your eyes tightly closed, imagine: 'This happened to *you*—this is *your* son, *your* family, *your* life!' Abdullah, we have had our hardships—different though they may be from other Israelites. I have been blessed to have cared for and raised Moses as my own *and* as the son of an Egyptian Princess."

Abdullah: "Wow! That's too much to think about right now. Let us just move on."

Marissa: "Wait a minute! What do you mean Abdullah, saying 'Wow! That is too much to think about'? What about Princess Bithiah? How do you think she felt when all this took place? Wasn't she taking an awful risk in bringing an Israelite baby into the palace?

Wasn't Princess Bithiah risking everything by letting this Israelite woman nurse her baby? The Princess was not spared suffering either, you realize that, do you not? You saw what happens when you trust an Israelite, right?

Princess Bithiah trusted this, this... woman with her son, with future royalty. What do you think she thought when she finally had her little Moses all to herself? Was she not also saying, 'I wonder what I can do to make my son forget his bloodline? From now on he is Egyptian Royalty, and I'll raise him as such.' Do you think she was not excited and a little nervous herself?"

Jochebed: "Princess Bithiah took on a significant risk; however, that was because our God placed it in her heart to take that chance. She was part of the plan God had for Moses. Moses knew who he was and where he came from when I took him to become a son of Princess Bithiah.

He also realized that he had now become part of the Egyptian

Royal Palace. He was too young to understand it all, but deep down inside Moses knew. Princess Bithiah raised Moses well for one not born in the palace. I am very fond of Princess Bithiah."

Abdullah: "You said you never gave Moses his name, did you know what the name Moses means?"

Jochebed: "That is correct. We never named our son officially; we called him Beautiful. Princess Bithiah gave him the name Moses; the name people have come to know him by. At the palace, as I handed him to her, she looked at the little boy and said: 'You, little one, I'll give the name Moses for I drew you out of the water.'"

Abdullah: "When you were back home and could no longer communicate with Moses, how did you and your husband feel?"

Jochebed: "We were delighted and grateful our son was alive. We knew our God had special plans for Moses. Had anyone found out that we were his blood family, the chance was good that Pharaoh would have had our heads chopped off, don't you think? So we gratefully let him go and prayed daily for him with the hope we would see him again someday."

Abdullah: "After all these years, and from the point of view of an Israelite mother, what can you tell us you have learned from your experience in bearing your children?"

Jochebed: "Child bearing is hard work; however, so is raising children. As much as we think our children belong to us, they do not. Each one of us is a gift from the God of the Israelites; and yet each one of us also belongs to the God of the Israelites. We as parents are not in control as we like to think.

By giving our children over to the God of the Israelites in prayer, we learn to enjoy our children more. The sooner we learn to give our children over to the God of the Israelites when things that concern us come up; the sooner we live with a whole lot less stress, and become wiser, kinder, and more patient parents to our children."

Marissa: "What is this you say? The God of the Israelites is the God of all? I think not! Your God did not create me or help my mother in child labor, and I certainly do not belong to Him!"

Jochebed: "What god brought you into this world, what god do you belong to now, Marissa?"

Marissa: "I am proud to say the goddess Heket brought me into this world. Heket is the wife of Khnum, the one who creates people on the potter's wheel. Once taken from the potter's wheel, it is Heket that gives us the breath of life as she places us in our mother's womb.

Like any pure Egyptian, I belong to and worship the many gods and goddesses of our country. Something you Israelite people do not seem to understand, but you will, yes, you will."

Jochebed: "We know about the Egyptians gods and goddesses, Marissa, and I pray we *never* come to understand them or fall prey to them."

Abdullah: "Can you tell us why, after all these years Moses has come back to Egypt? From the Egyptians point of view, the Pharaoh that was King when Moses was young is now with his ancestors. So why come back now?"

Jochebed: "Moses has been chosen by the God of the Israelites to bring forth God's people from the bondage of Egypt."

Abdullah: "What did you say?"

Marissa: "Did you just say that Moses is going to take the Israelite people out of Egypt?" Marissa laughed, almost to hysteria, and continued, "Jochebed, you are a fool! I told those in the conference room that something like this was coming. I hope they are watching this."

Jochebed: "Moses told this to the Council Elders of Goshen. He informed them that God had a message for them. The message was "I shall bring you up out of the affliction of Egypt and take you into a land of milk and honey. Moses is the chosen one to lead the Israelite people out of Egypt."

Marissa: "How does he plan to accomplish this? Does he think that Pharaoh or the Egyptian leaders are just going to roll over and let the Israelite people leave? You better be careful in what you are saying to the world, Jochebed."

Jochebed: "I speak only the truth."

Marissa: "Truth! Truth! You do not know the truth, but you will! Truth really?" Marissa proudly declared, "The world has yet to see what Pharaoh can do to harm Moses and his God!"

Jochebed: "Yes, Marissa, we'll all see the truth of God's plan."

Abdullah: "Okay...Ah, Thank you, Jochebed."

Jochebed: "You are very welcome, Abdullah, may our God bless you all."

Abdullah: "Marissa, back to you."

Marissa: "People of Egypt you have just witnessed some *outrageous* news. What do you think Moses and his God are trying to pull? What are your thoughts about Jochebed; is she a fool? Something *very* interesting is about to take place, and I can guarantee you we'll get to the bottom of this. We look forward to tomorrow when we interview Miriam, Moses' Israelite sister. Until then, this is Marissa with Abdullah for ET NEWS saying 'May the gods of Egypt protect you.'"

Chapter 3
Miriam

"Hello everyone, I am your host, Marissa, with ET NEWS. We are live with Part II of our four-part documentary series entitled 'A Man Called Moses.' In Part I, we interviewed Jochebed, Moses' birth mother. Jochebed told us that Moses had come back to Egypt to get the Israelite people released, from Pharaoh's charge.

Today we are interviewing Miriam, Moses' Israelite sister. What will she have to say? Will she be as intriguing as her mother? We are about to find out. Abdullah is at Miriam's house ready to speak with her. Abdullah, over to you."

Abdullah: "Thank you, Marissa. Thank you, Miriam, for allowing us into your home."

Miriam: "You are welcome in my home."

Abdullah: "How did you feel the day you found out you had another brother? Did you know he was supposed to become a sacrifice to the Nile gods?"

Miriam: "I was excited and happy when I found out I had another brother. Yes, I was old enough to realize that my brother was one of the many that were to drown in the Nile River. I was also mad, confused, and unsure what my mother and father would do."

Abdullah: "Were you there when your parents decided not to throw Moses into the Nile?"

Miriam: "My parents did not speak about this in front of us. However, I was not surprised when they told us that they would not be throwing our brother into the Nile. Understandably, they could not follow Pharaoh's decree.

At the time, I did not understand why Pharaoh was doing what he was doing, and I was angry with Pharaoh. I had seen many babies die because of his decree. I would do whatever I needed to keep him, and not have my brother thrown into the Nile."

Abdullah: "You said at the time of Moses, Baby Beautiful's birth, you were unable to understand why Pharaoh had the decree placed on the babies. Through the years, have you come to an understanding as to why Pharaoh put that decree upon the male babies?"

Miriam: "Over time and much prayer, I began to realize that my fear left, and my anger seemed to have disappeared."

Abdullah: "How can anger just disappear?"

Miriam: "With time God helped me to understand that bad things happen to people. Whether you are a righteous person or an unrighteous person. God helped me to understand that if I let myself feel the raw anger of the moment and just react to it, then I am as wrong as the person who has committed this wrong.

However, when I take that anger and give it to him, ask him what to do with it, then I see clearer and react justly to that anger. Pharaoh was not right in making that decree, but God had a plan to turn that bad into good; and I had to trust God to help me understand that.

Abdullah, it is my hope that someday you receive God's knowledge. That you may understand it is only when people finally come to realize that God is watching over us, and protecting us, that you receive freedom. The fear we had felt is no more. I now understand the way it feels when he is there to protect me and take care of me. He is protecting his people right now."

Marissa: "Abdullah, do not listen to Miriam; she is trying to confuse you. God as a protector... some protector! Look at how your people suffer! They suffer that way because they are a lower class people, with a lower level God. They suffer that way because, after all these years, they still haven't learned to appreciate the gods of Egypt!"

Miriam: "You'll soon see what the God of the Israelites will do to protect his chosen people!"

Marissa: "You are wrong! Crazy like your mother. Proving that the Israelites need to stay slaves, even the family of the so-called leaders, proves that they lack intelligence. Some of your people are not even intelligent enough to be slaves!"

Abdullah: "Ah... You knew that one day Moses would go to live in the palace and become part of the royal family. How did that make you feel?"

Miriam: "I was a young lady dreaming of her future, of course I thought of those things... I thought about all the pampering and all the attention he was going to get. I thought about all the food he would get to eat. How come he gets to live the life of comfort, in the palace without me? I should be able to go with him, as his nanny. Yes, I was a bit envious of him."

Abdullah: "When you saw Moses in a basket floating toward the Princess, how did you feel?"

Miriam: "How would you feel? I was scared to death and excited at the same time."

Abdullah: "What do you mean scared and excited at the same time?"

Miriam: "I was about the age of fifteen; a young adult with a large task to perform. Put in charge of watching over him; I was the one who had to see who would find my baby brother. That alone was enough to keep me scared and excited. If I got caught, then my brother would be killed. Perhaps my family and I would have been killed, or at the least severely punished. My mother gave me this assignment; she acknowledged the fact that I was now grown up.

Standing in the Nile River, thick with reeds, I kept a sharp lookout for a crocodile or a hippopotamus. When I saw the Princess and her servants come to the river, my heart started beating so loudly with anticipation that I thought I would be found out. I was praying hard that my God would protect us.

Before I knew what had happened, the Princess was opening the basket. Two of her servant girls held the basket as the Princess lifted baby Beautiful, ever so gently from the basket and took his wrapping from around him. As she examined the infant, she said, 'This little one has the mark of circumcision, He belongs to one of the Israelite women.'

I watched as he nestled himself into the arms of the Princess. She looked at him and said, "Do not worry, everything is going to be all right, I'll take care of you. Suddenly, I heard Baby Beautiful cry. It was one of his soft cries, almost more of a coo. He was letting the Princess know that he wanted her to become his mother.

I forgot about hiding and ran to the Princess and asked her if she would like me to find an Israelite woman to nurse the baby for her."

Abdullah: "To which she said yes. What caused you to ask the Princess that question, did you have that planned in advance? Did you and your mother make a plan in case certain things happened?"

Miriam: "I wanted to see what was going to happen to my baby brother. How was that going to happen if I did not go and see the Princess? I got there in time to hear her say the baby belonged to one of the Israelite women and that she was going to keep him as her child.

I wanted my brother at home, with us, where he belonged; why not ask the Princess if she wanted me to find her an Israelite woman to nurse the baby? What better way to get to know what was going to happen to my little brother? You would have done the same thing..."

Marissa: "That sounds just like you Israelites! You double-crossed the poor Princess, all for the sake of your brother."

Miriam: "As to a plan Abdullah, we had no plan, except to trust our God. My mother prayed a lot about this before it happened. I remember when Princess Bithiah said to go find her a nurse, I forget about everything except finding my mother before someone else came to the Princess with a nurse."

Abdullah: "How come the Princess did not find it strange that a young Israelite girl was in her bathing area?"

Miriam: "Her bathing area was close to where the Israelite women went to collect water for the bricks. So on occasion one of the Israelite girls would find their way to the Princess's bathing spot. Princess Bithiah was kind to all the children."

Abdullah: "How did you feel about being Moses' sister when growing up?"

Miriam: "Moses was only with us for six years. It went by fast and so slow at the same time. At times, I forgot that Moses would have to leave us and go live at the palace. I did not want him to leave.

However, we were raised to know that God had a different plan for Moses' life. We knew that he had to leave to fulfill the destiny God had for him. Remember, we never knew him as Moses, we called him "Beautiful." When Princess Bithiah named him Moses, she said it meant 'I drew him from the water'.

Mother prayed every day for Moses. We'd listen to what people had to say, in hopes of hearing any news of how he was doing. Funny how this all took place many years ago and yet it seems like it all happened yesterday. I remember how mother played a game of

24

sticks and stones with Moses and at the same time tell him stories. The stories passed down from generation to generation.

Living in Egypt as part of the royal family he would be taught to worship the false gods of Egypt. He needed to have a cemented foundation in our God; the God of Abraham, Isaac, and Jacob or he would drown in the false gods of Egypt."

Marissa: "Moses' brain was full of poison before he even got to Princess Bithiah! Is it any wonder that he killed an Egyptian man and ran? He was turned against his adopted people before he even got to meet them!"

Abdullah: "Thank you very much Miriam; it has been an informative evening."

Miriam: "You are welcome in my home. May my God, the God of the Israelites bless you and keep you."

Abdullah: "Now back to you Marissa."

Marissa: "People of Egypt, what are your thought's about tonight's interview? Contact our office at ET NEWS Station, News Street, Rameses, Egypt. On tomorrow's show, we'll have some of your response's. Until then, this is Marissa for ET NEWS saying 'May the gods of Egypt protect you.'"

Chapter 4
Aaron

"Hello everyone, I am your host Marissa with ET NEWS. We are live with Part III of our four-part documentary series entitled 'A Man Called Moses.'

Yesterday I asked you to contact our office with your thoughts on this documentary. The first response is from Karam of Pithom. She says; 'Thank you, Marissa, for asking our opinions on your documentary. I have watched the series from the beginning and let me tell you; Moses' mother is not all there. She needs to ask Seshat, our goddess of wisdom for help.

Moses' sister seems to be forgetting her place in our Egyptian society as well. She is nothing more than an Israelite and like her brother Moses, she could never become a good and upright Egyptian citizen. Keep up the good work, I am enjoying this documentary very much.'

Here is another response from Jalal of Rameses: 'This seems to be the same Moses that Princess Bithiah took in as a child. It saddens me to find that Moses is still as confused and as mislead as he was in his childhood.

I was hoping for our Princess Bithiah's sake that Moses would have found his way to the Egyptian beliefs by now. The royal family showed him so much kindness; we all had such high hopes for him. Excellent documentary, keep on with the series.'

Thank you to our viewers for the responses you sent to us. Please keep your responses coming to us; they help to let us know that we are conducting this documentary in a way that meets your approval. I wish we had more time to read all your responses to the audience, we do read them all at the office.

Abdullah is with Aaron in Goshen. Abdullah, are you and Aaron ready for this interview?'"

Abdullah: "We are; I would like to start out by saying thank you, Aaron, for agreeing to meet with us today."

Aaron: "You are most welcome."

Abdullah: "When you found out you had a new baby brother what did you feel? Did you understand all that was happening at that moment?"

Aaron: "I do not remember much about Moses' birth as I was only three at the time. I do remember being upset the day mother took Moses to the palace. Our parents told us that God had a special destiny for him and because of the way things were at the time, God chose to keep Moses alive by placing him in the palace."

Abdullah: "Did you want to go with Moses?"

Aaron: "What nine-year-old would not want to go and live in a palace with his brother? I was confused; I did not wish to leave home, yet I also wanted to be with my brother. My parents won out in the end."

Abdullah: "What have you been doing in the years since Moses left Egypt?"

Aaron: "I have been working in Goshen as a mediator, keeping the peace between our kinsmen."

Abdullah: "You are a peacekeeper? How does that work?"

Aaron: " When the men of Goshen have a problem with each other they come to me. I act as a mediator, helping them come to an agreement; helping them understand a situation or sometimes, giving them counsel on how to give a problem over to God."

Marissa: "Right, you just go in and act like you are their God, and everything's made right again. You people are something else, you know that!"

Aaron: "Marissa, it is hard for people from different backgrounds to understand each other at times. It is also hard for family members to understand each other at times.

That is where someone like me comes in. I am able to look at the situation from an outside view. I am able to talk with each side and bring out things that they were not able to see on their own. Frequently I am able to bring the people to a peaceful understanding."

Abdullah: "Interesting, I have never heard of such a thing before. Aaron, how did you and Moses become reunited, after all, these years?"

Aaron: "I was deep in prayer one day when God spoke and said; 'Aaron, I want you to travel to the land of Midian. I am sending you to Mount Horeb, once there you'll meet up with your brother Moses.'"

Abdullah: "Did you meet anyone besides Moses when you arrived at Mount Horeb?"

Aaron: "Yes, I did. It seems that Moses took a wife while living in Midian."

Abdullah: "A wife, what is her name? Do they have any children?"

Aaron: "Her name is Zipporah; she is the daughter of a priest who lives in Midian. Moses and Zipporah have two sons. I think their names are Gershom and Eliezer, but I cannot remember, for sure."

Abdullah: "We have no knowledge of Moses having a wife and family; did they come along?"

Aaron: "No, Moses sent them back to her father's to live until we are back in the Midian area."

Abdullah: "Why would Moses not let them come to Egypt with him?"

Aaron: "Moses having spent more time with God, realized that what God was asking of him would make it hard to have his wife and sons with him. He would be too busy to spend time with them.

After explaining to Zipporah his circumstances, it was decided that Zipporah and the boys would go back and live with her father. Moses told Zipporah that he would reunite with them when God brought them back to the area. Then he would be able to spend more time with them.".

Abdullah: "Do you know how Moses met his wife?"

Aaron: "You'll have to ask him. We have had little time for general conversation."

Abdullah: "Do you know what life was like for him when he lived in Midian? What did he do in the forty years he was there?"

Aaron: "He was a shepherd for his father-in-law."

Abdullah: "And how did you feel when you heard that Moses had fled the country all those years ago?"

Aaron: "How did I feel? I was shocked at first, how was I supposed to feel? I knew Moses would not have killed someone for the fun of it.

How many times have we all felt like killing someone for the injustice that they serve us day after day? I knew that he had no choice but to leave. I prayed to our God and asked him if he was still alive."

Marissa: "Your God answered you?" she chuckled in disbelief.

Aaron: "Of course, my God answered me. He said, 'Moses is alive and well.'"

Marissa: "You do not have a god that speaks to you! Gods do not talk to people unless they are priests!"

Aaron: "Marissa, I come from a family of priests, and yes, my God does speak to me. I was told to meet with Moses at Mount Horeb."

Marissa: "You are a fool, Aaron! A fool—just like your brother— your whole family is nothing but fools!"

Aaron: "I am not a fool, Marissa. I am an ambassador of truth for God."

Marissa: "Ambassador of truth? You would not know the truth if it was staring you in the face. You are helping us to understand what kind of person your brother is; I'll tell you that."

Abdullah: "Aaron, did Moses say how he came to get so acquainted with your God?"

Aaron: "I asked Moses the same question. He told me that he was watching the sheep at Mount Horeb, 'the Mountain of God,' looking around, he spotted a bush on fire that would not burn up."

Marissa: "Here we go again! A burning bush that would not burn up! Moses sat around all day drinking so much Zytum [see glossary] that he was seeing and hearing things. I am sure of it. Continue with your amusing story—I cannot wait to hear your answer for this one. Once again, we have proven that Moses is not an average man."

Abdullah: "A bush burning that would not burn up? Do you not think that might seem extremely strange to most people?" Said

Abdullah as he threw a look indicating that he was not comfortable with this conversation.

Aaron: "Yes, it seemed strange to me. Moses explained to me that the desert is an area that has many lighting strikes in a day. The heat makes some bushes just start burning all on their own.

To nomads it is normal, so they do not pay much attention to them. We are the same way with someone in pain; there is so much of it that unless it is extreme, we do not seem to see it anymore."

Abdullah: "Which means that this one had to be really different to have caught the attention of Moses."

Aaron: "Yes, however, I think Moses should tell you the story of the burning bush. All I can say is that God told Moses I was on my way to meet him."

Abdullah: "Was Moses concerned about Pharaoh and all the authorities that wanted to kill him?"

Aaron: "I asked Moses that same question. Moses said that God told him all those who wanted him killed were dead."

Marissa: "Makes no difference, our Pharaoh is finding a way to have Moses killed and soon!"

Abdullah: "So you packed up and left to meet Moses at about the same time that Moses packed his family up and headed for Mount Horeb?"

Aaron: "Yes, it seems so. Moses, who was adopted by his father-in-law, asked his permission to leave for Egypt. Having received permission, he then packed his family up and waited for me at Mount Horeb. While at Mount Horeb, God trained Moses in the skills needed to complete his assignment when he arrived in Egypt.

When I arrived at Mount Horeb, Moses explained to me all God had spoken, and then he trained me in all that God had taught him."

Abdullah: "Was it at this time that Moses decided his family should not continue to travel with him to Egypt?"

Aaron: "Yes, we helped Zipporah and the boys pack up and stood watch to make sure they were safely on their way back to her father before we left for Egypt."

Marissa: "Your story gets crazier by the minute. Schooled by this god of yours, I think not!" Marissa enjoyed the fact that Aaron was making a fool of himself and that she was playing a part in it.

Abdullah: "There you have it people, the facts, as given by those closest to this man called Moses." Feeling uneasy, he continued, "Marissa, I give it back to you."

Marissa: "Abdullah, this interview is not over yet." She was determined to catch Aaron giving her information that she could use to help Pharaoh build a case against Moses, should the need arise. "Aaron, will Moses be leaving soon for Mount Horeb?"

Aaron: "As soon as we have completed our assignment here in Egypt."

Marissa: "And that assignment is...?"

Aaron: "That is between God and Moses. Marissa, if you want to know, you'll just have to keep an eye on what we are doing and where we are going."

Marissa: "What kind of an answer is that? Scared to let me in on what you are doing? We know that Moses is here to free your people from Pharaoh. I know that is not possible, so why not tell me what you have planned?"

Aaron: "Marissa, we do what God tells us to do, when God tells us to do it. Follow us and see what he is doing! We do not know ahead of time every detail of what God wants us to do."

Marissa: "Trust me, I'll be following you and Moses. I'll show you for who you are!" Marissa's eyes, the window to her soul, showed Aaron, and the world, that her hunt for the truth was far from over.

Abdullah: "I hope you have enjoyed this time as much as I have." Hoping Marissa would take the hint this time he continued, "Aaron, I want to thank you for allowing us to speak with you. I look forward to seeing you another time."

Aaron: "It has been a pleasure talking with you, Abdullah."

Marissa: "Thank you, Abdullah. Tomorrow we will finish our documentary series with an appearance from Moses himself. Contact our office at ET NEWS Station, News Street, Rameses, Egypt. On tomorrow's show, we'll have some of your responses. I encourage you to contact all your friends and neighbors and tell them to tune in to ET NEWS to watch us live." Until then, this is Marissa for ET NEWS saying 'May the gods of Egypt protect you.'"

Chapter 5
Marissa and Jair

"Marissa, Jair is here," Kebi announced from her new intercom system. "Send him in," replied Marissa looking like a sly Egyptian cat prepared to pounce. Marissa's voice purred as he entered, "Jair, I need you to go undercover for me."

Jair looked around to see where Marissa had moved his favorite seat the seat that made him feel like a professional snitch. "You sent for me, so I figured you had another job-good I need the silver pieces. Where?" Jair spotted his favorite chair, the slab seat with a large blue silk covered pillow. He immediately headed over to sink into the luxury of the soft billowy pillow.

Marissa took her seat behind her desk and continued, "Goshen, it is where you live so no one will be suspicious of you. I want you to find out more about this Moses person. What is the real reason for Moses coming back? What is he doing behind the scenes? What people has he been talking to, and meeting with? I do not trust him!"

Unable to sit still any longer, Marissa got up and paced while continuing to give Jair his orders. "Jochebed said that Moses was sent by their so called God to free the Israelites from Pharaoh. Aaron talks like they plan on sabotaging Pharaoh. My reporter's nose tells me that Moses is a cupbearer about to put poison in Pharaoh's bedtime drink! I want the first-hand scoop on this secret Moses is trying to hide from me!

Our documentary is scheduled to finish tomorrow with Moses' interview. I want an ending that is a thriller, a shocker! I do not want Moses looking like a 'Hero'! I want Moses on *his* knees, kissing the toes of our Pharaoh! Do you understand? You will not fail me. When I receive my Emmy, you'll be amply rewarded. You have until tomorrow morning. Do what you must, I want that scoop!" Jair did not respond right away. Marissa stopped pacing turned and looked at him.

Musing to himself, Jair thought: "Marissa must want Moses on her silver platter. I am not so sure about being her mouse bait though. This job had better pay well..."

"Jair! Are you paying attention?"

"Yes, Marissa, how do I get the information back to you?"

"In the same way I sent for you, you'll also send the information back to me! You have until the morning to have it in my hand!"

Not in the mood to waste a minute of her time, Marissa walked over to her desk and spoke into her new intercom system, "Kebi! Since Jair is confused about how to get his information back to me, I need you to give him our contact information before he leaves. Escort him to your desk and then show him the way out."

"Yes, Marissa," Kebi answered as she rose from her desk and headed for Marissa's office.

As Kebi opened the door to escort Jair out, Marissa informed her, "I'll be at Ma'at's temple should anything arise." Jair, rose to follow Kebi saying, "I shall have the information for you sometime tomorrow morning." Marissa replied, "I expect nothing less from the best informant I have. Now let's hope all goes well for us in the morning."

With that, her office was hers again. Marissa grabbed her rainbow mystic quartz studded purse, turned and looked at her accomplishments. I have my own office, a respectable slab desk with traces of gold dust on the top. A few green and blue stones running up and down the legs. A comfortable desk seat, none of that old run-down-pillows-on-the-floor seating for me anymore...

Even my own little primping corner; very few anchors have an area where they can stand and look in a mirror to make sure they are presentable. Yes, in five years of blood, sweat, and tears, you have come a long way. She smiled to herself and said, 'now my dear

Marissa, I think it is time to go worship Ma'at. I want the truth about Moses, the truth that only comes from praying to my God.

Marissa, walking from her office continued talking to herself, "It is time that I help Pharaoh with these troublesome Israelites. Praying to Ma'at for protection from the stupidity of the Israelites, and for the protection of Pharaoh against the evil schemes of Moses cannot hurt. Oh, Marissa, you have been eating, sleeping and drinking your Emmy, but now is the time to taste the caviar of your Emmy."

Chapter 6
Moses and Aaron Meet the Council Elders

That night in Goshen, "How in the world am I going to accomplish this mission. 'You will not fail me,'" Jair said with the sassiness of a spoiled two-year-old. "Does Marissa think I am her little puppet on a string? Well, I am not! Think, Jair, think." With a snap of his fingers, he said, "I'll go over to Joshua's watering tent and see whom I can find. Someone is sure to have a loose tongue.

Marissa! She was strutting around like a cat today. I saw her trying to sharpen her claws on me! Ready to tear apart anyone or anything that gets in the way of her precious Emmy! Look past that Jair, after all, she does pay up with much silver when you need it."

Jair, heading over to Joshua's watering house, noticed men heading in the same direction. What would be going on this late at night he wondered? "Johnathan! Hey! Johnathan!" "What's going on? Where are all these men going?"

"Where have you been Jair? Moses and Aaron have called a meeting of the Council Elders, at sunrise. Thaddeus wants to see if the men think they should attend that meeting. So he has called for a meeting at his house, it should start anytime," answered Johnathan.

"Really? So Thaddeus is not sure if the men want to honor Moses' and Aaron's call for a meeting? Hmm, interesting, if Moses is the Moses of old why not go to the meeting?"

"Don't you remember? Moses killed an Egyptian and then went after some Israelite men like he was a judge over them. We believe he is Hebrew, but why should we believe he is someone special? The meeting will let Thaddeus know what the council's thoughts are about Moses and Aaron. I am going home. Tomorrow could be a long day. Shalom Jair."

"Shalom Johnathan."

"Wow!" Jair said to himself; 'I need to get over to Thaddeus' house and find a way to listen in on that meeting.' Walking just a little further, he found an acceptable spot, at the back side of the house. "It has a window; I shouldn't have a problem hearing anyone from here."

Thaddeus began to speak. "Order! Order! I call this meeting to order. We have been requested by Moses and Aaron to meet with them at sunrise. They have a message from God, our God. Moses and Aaron spoke to Dan, Asher and me along with a few others a couple of days ago.

We were told that our God has sent Moses to take us from Egypt and deliver us to the Promised Land. Now they have called for a general meeting. Do we as the Council Elders of the Israelite people go to the meeting or do we simply tell them to leave?"

The men respond, "Tell them to leave!"

"No, hear them out!"

"Tell them they have one chance!"

Thaddeus spoke, "We are the Council Elders of the Israelite people. Shouldn't we hear what God has to say? If we do not meet with Moses and Aaron, they may go to anyone who's willing to listen to them. We could have a mess on our hands. You know how easy it is to get the people all riled up."

"If we do not go and listen, then we could miss out on something God wants to give us," replied Asher.

"Dan, what do you think?" asked Thaddeus.

"I think as the elders of the community we at least need to hear them out."

Thaddeus called for a vote, "All those in favor of attending the meeting of Moses and Aaron at sunrise say 'yes.'"

"Yes!" was heard loud and clear.

"All those, not in favor of attending the meeting with Moses and Aaron at sunrise say 'no.'"

"No!" only a few responded.

"The yeses have it! Meeting dismissed, let us go and get some sleep, we'll need it!"

"Yes," Jair said to himself, "I better go get some rest, sunrise shall be here all too soon."

The next morning, Jair walked out to find a beautiful sunrise, a sign that it would be a good day. Jair wondered, 'How many elders are already in the Council tent? I better hurry, being seen heading that way on purpose would not be wise.' Looking around, he noticed that the street was empty. "I must have overslept, got to get to that meeting without being noticed...

Here is a spot to the north, no one should be able to spot me here. As he burrowed into the sand, he glanced over his shoulder thinking, 'I better get the information I need, Marissa is expecting to hear from me before the morning is over.'

The men were in conversation wondering what Moses and Aaron have to say. Thaddeus opened the meeting, "Quiet! Quiet! I declare this meeting open. Aaron, the son of Amram and his brother Moses, have called this meeting to share a relevant word from God, our God. So I shall turn this meeting over to them."

The room was open, a dirt floor with a few concrete slabs, and at the front with the leaders of the council sat Moses and Aaron. Aaron walked over and stood on one of the slabs with Moses standing next to him.

Aaron prophesied to the men. "Men of Egypt, Council Elders of the Israelite people, I have a message for you from the Lord God of our Fathers; the God of Abraham, the God of Isaac, and of Jacob.

The Lord has said, "I've clearly seen my people oppressed in Egypt. I've heard their cry of injustice because of their slave masters. I know about their pain. I've come down to rescue them from the Egyptians in order to take them out of that land and bring them to a good and broad land, a land that's full of milk and honey, a place where the Canaanites, the Hittites, the Amorites, the Perizzites, the Hivites, and the Jebusites all live."

Thaddeus spoke up, "Anyone can use a god's name. How do we

know that you are speaking of our God and not of one of the many Egyptian gods? We know that you hear from our God, Aaron, but we have to be cautious about these things when it pertains to us. Who are you to say that our God will take us out of this land?"

Aaron turned to Moses, who said, "Give them the name God gave to us to speak." Aaron looked at Moses and nodded, then turned to the Elders and said, "God has told me to tell his people; I AM sent me to you!" "I AM will be with his people!"

The name I AM showed itself when some of the men became paralyzed with reverence to hearing the name, I AM. Some of the men, who had not quite grasped the fullness of the name, became full of anticipation and joy. The name I AM also brought confusion and fear into the hearts of those men who had doubted the importance of Moses and Aaron calling this meeting.

Had they actually heard Aaron say that the name of their God is I AM? Is this name I AM the one that means I Am, Who I Am and What I Am? Could this be the name meaning I WILL BE WHAT I WILL BE?

The Council Elders were beginning to realize that their God, the God (who for years very few heard from), could be with Moses and Aaron, after all? However, it would take more than the name alone to convince some of the men in the council that Moses and Aaron represent their God.

Dan spoke, "Moses, you left Egypt forty years ago! Most people only know you through the stories told about you. You have given us a name—now show us a sign."

The men shouted, "Yeah, we want a sign!"

"God may have given you a name but honestly did he send you to take us out of Egypt?"

"You say God has plans to take us out of Egypt, prove it!"

Aaron asked, "Do you need a sign from God to believe on his word?"

"Yes!" was the response that came from six of the Council Elders.

Aaron spoke, "Take notice of my rod. Watch carefully, see what happens when I throw it to the ground." As Aaron threw his rod on the ground, it became a serpent, not just any serpent but an Egyptian Cobra.

The men were scared and trampled over each other to get out of the reach of this killer serpent. "Get rid of it!" The men shouted. "Moses, get rid of that serpent!" "Kill the serpent! Kill the serpent!"

"This serpent represents all divine power in Egypt and is the very symbol Pharaoh has on one of his many crowns. As a child of God, you men should know, that power of the serpent cannot harm you. God has all power, all authority over the divine false power of Pharaoh.

Watch now as I pick this serpent up by the tail." Aaron picked the serpent up by the tail, and it became the rod it was before he threw it on the ground. The men responded, "A rod!"

"It has become a rod again!"

"What kind of magic is this?"

Aaron spoke, "This is not the magic of the serpent. What you have just seen is the power of our God! Do you not understand that God is in control? The power you saw in the Egyptian Cobra is the false power of Pharaoh. The gods made of wood and stone are mere images, they represent the false gods of Egypt.

They cannot perform any miracle, and they cannot cause any harm! They are dead objects! What you see when you look at the gods of Egypt comes from nothing more than pure evil, the evil of the serpent, Satan himself.

God, our God, is the ruler over all! He has shown you his great power, and he'll show his great power again, his power over all!"

The men responded, "Even if God has sent you to us, just make our lives better here."

"We are not interested in leaving Goshen."

"We just want to live a better life in Goshen, like our ancestors before us, is that so much to ask?"

"Our families are here, our homes, and our lives are here in Goshen."

"We just need out from under the rule of Pharaoh, let God do that for us."

Having heard enough, Moses spoke, "You do not understand! It is not God's wish for you to stay here. If you were to stay here, you cannot have what God wishes to give you.

God wants to take you to a place where you are his and his alone, to a land that is full of all the riches of the earth. Where you'll not have to work so hard for your food.

A land where you'll have room to move, explore, or stay and feel comfortable; a land where you can talk with him and live a life of no hardship.

Do you not remember that God promised Jacob that he would bring his people back to the land he came from which they left? That is what God is doing right now; he is leading his people back to the Promised Land.

God wants you where there shall be no distractions from having a relationship with the One true God. God has called you to be his chosen people.

God has not chosen other people, he has chosen you! God has not chosen the Egyptians that follow Pharaoh and his ways; you'll be living a privileged life, I wish you could understand that.

However, to have that life you must leave here. Leave the bondage behind you. You must choose to leave all you have had in Egypt in the past. Trust in God and look forward to a new life ahead of you."

Asher asked, "How could we forget the promise God made to Jacob—we have heard it for years! What makes you think that God has picked now to be that time?

In order for me to become convinced that now is the time God has chosen to take his people to our promised land, I need another sign. I believe I speak for the men when I say I want a sign that no one has ever seen before, then I'll be convinced of all you say."

The men responded with mixed emotions, "Yeah!"

"That's right!"

"It'll take more than one miracle; we want two more."

Dan said, "I am not sure either, will you show us another sign from God?"

Aaron—remembering God warned him that this might happen—spoke, "Watch as God uses me to show you another sign." He purposefully placed his hand under his shirt and over his heart.

The crowd responded, "Let me see... what is he doing?"

"He put his hand under his shirt and over his heart!"

"What kind of a miracle will this be? Is he going to pull his heart out of his chest?"

"Hush! We want to see what happens."

Aaron pulled his hand out and stretched it up in the air for all to see.

"Leprous!"

"Leprous!"

"White as snow!"

"How is it that your hand is leprous Aaron?"

"What does this mean?"

"How is this a sign?" the men asked in a panic, for leprosy has no known cure.

"Our God, the God of our Fathers, is showing you his power. Our hand represents our work, our power. We all have things hidden in our heart. How many of us work hard every day for Pharaoh?

How many of us when we work, think in our heart how we would love to, just once, get even with those who treat us so cruelly? Those are deadly thoughts, represented by my hand being struck with the deadly plague of leprosy. The power of our hands comes from the thoughts in our heart.

Watch what happens when I put my hand over my heart this time." All watched as Aaron placed his hand back in his shirt and over his heart. As he pulled his hand out, he once again stretched it high for all to see.

The men responded, "Normal!"

"I want to see!"

"His hand is normal again!"

"What does this mean, Aaron?"

"The God of our fathers is showing you that right now we are all living in sin, the sin that we have hidden in our hearts. Our hands, representing our work, lets us know that we cannot get rid of that sin on our own. We need our God. He has shown you this by inflicting my hand with leprosy.

God is telling you that he plans to touch our hearts, make us whole again, and restore us to live with him in the land of milk and honey. He has shown you this by restoring my hand back to normal."

Dan spoke, "I believe that our God has sent you. Are there any of you out there that are still unsure?"

Some in the crowd responded, "We want another sign!"

"Just one more sign!"

Aaron, becoming frustrated, but again remembering God's warning said, "One more sign? You want one more sign. Then I'll show you one more sign. Thaddeus, I need one of your men to go and get me a jar of water from the Nile River."

Thaddeus shouted to Josephus: "Find one of the watering women and help her bring back a jar filled with water from the Nile."

"Yes, Thaddeus."

Thaddeus turned to Aaron and asked, "Why have you asked for water from the Nile?"

"When Josephus gets back, you'll receive one last sign. Then you'll know that God has sent us to you," replied Aaron. In the meantime, Moses and Aaron looked around and wondered how these men are apt to make it through all that God shall require of them.

Moses said to Aaron, "God said they might ask for three miracles, and then they would become convinced. We should have that much settled in their mind in the next few minutes."

"I hope so, we have so much more work to get done after they become convinced; I am tired just thinking about it."

Josephus walked in carrying the water, "Here's the water you asked for, Thaddeus."

"Thank you, Josephus."

Thaddeus walked over and informed Moses and Aaron that the water had arrived. Walking over to the water, Aaron once again called for the attention of the men.

"You have asked for a final sign, here is your final sign. Watch, take notice of what happens as I pour water from this jar onto the dry ground."

The men were curious, "What is he doing?"

"Let me see."

"What is happening?"

"Aaron is pouring the water from the jar onto the dry ground at his feet."

"So what?"

"The water... is not water!"

"What!"

"The water starts out as water, but as it pours out and hits the ground it turns to blood!"

Just as God had spoken, the men were made to see that Moses and Aaron were indeed there to represent God, the great I AM.

In reverence to the Lord the men fell to their knees saying, "We have been wrong!"

"The God of our fathers' has truly sent Moses and Aaron to us!"

"Aaron, what do we do now?"

"Help us to worship our God."

Moses said to Aaron, "Lead these men into the worship of God. We must worship and give thanks before we go to Pharaoh."

Aaron explained to the men that first they must sing praises unto the Lord and then he would lead them in a prayer of forgiveness. "I'll lead you in a song of worship in our Lord, for those of you unfamiliar with the words, I'll sing first and then you may repeat what you have just heard."

"Great I AM, Great I AM, Great I AM, He is the Great I AM, God of all creation. The I WILL BE WHAT I WILL BE.

God of Abraham, Isaac, and Jacob. You are the God that loves all Israel.

Sing Hallelujah, Sing Hallelujah, Sing Hallelujah, Sing Hallelujah.

He is the great I AM, God of all creation. You are the God that loves all Israel.

He is the great I AM, the God of Moses, The God of Aaron,

The God of peace, the God of righteousness, the everlasting God. He is the God, that... loves all Israel.

Sing Hallelujah, Sing Hallelujah, Sing Hallelujah, Sing Hallelujah.

He is the Great I AM, God Almighty; He is the God, that... loves all Israel.

Sing Hallelujah, Sing Hallelujah, Sing Hallelujah, Sing Hallelujah.

Worship complete, Aaron now turned his attention to leading the men in a prayer of forgiveness. Aaron said to the Council Elders, "Men repeat after me:

'You are the God of Abraham, the God of Isaac, and the God of Jacob. We are sorry for doubting you. You have opened our eyes, and now we see that you have come to rescue us from the hand of Pharaoh. We are thankful to you for sending Moses and Aaron to us. Amen.'"

The room turned quiet as the men were still in awe of what had just happened. At Moses' request Aaron once again spoke, "Attention! Attention Council Elders! God has instructed Moses and me to tell you that you are to come with us as a Council to request an audience with Pharaoh right now.

This is what you are to tell Pharaoh, 'The God of the Hebrews has met with us and instructed us to go three days' journey into the desert to sacrifice to him. Give us your permission to do so.' Thaddeus, Dan, and Asher you'll be the representatives of the men." Thaddeus asked, "Dan, Asher, what do you think?"

Looking at each other in agreement Asher said, "God has instructed us, so let's go with them."

Thaddeus said, "Let's go with Moses and Aaron to the palace to do as God has instructed us to do. Meeting adjourned."

Excited, Jair said, "I should receive a bonus for this information. I need to hurry, no time to lose."

Marissa was in her office pacing back and forth like a trapped cat wanting out of her cage. "Where is that man when I need him?" Opening the door, she yelled, "Abdullah!" As if on cue, Abdullah was standing right at her door.

"Marissa, how may I help you?"

"How may you help me? What do you mean, how may you help me? Where is Moses? I told Aaron yesterday we would be following him. How can we follow him if you do not know where he is?"

Abdullah feeling that familiar mouse trap squeeze replied, "I am not sure, what should we do?"

Seething, Marissa said, "What should you do? Is that what you meant to say!"

Abdullah, trying hard to stay out of Marissa's reach answered, "Yes, Marissa, that is what I meant to say."

"So Abdullah what are you going to do?" asked Marissa, trying hard to control her temper.

"I am going to find Aaron and hope I find him before 'we go live,'" answered Abdullah as he slowly backed away from Marissa's reach.

"You better or I am confident that you'll no longer be my co-host, understand? Azad, get the cameras ready to film whatever comes our way."

Almost running, to get away from Marissa, Abdullah said to himself: "Where would Moses be, think Abdullah, think? Would he just leave and not tell us? Where do I even start looking? Moses has been with the men in Goshen lately; I'll look there. Wait, is that Jair over there? Jair! Jair!"

"Who is calling my name?"

"Jair, I am Abdullah, Marissa's co-anchor."

"I remember you, why are you calling my name?"

"Marissa's fur is flying, we are trying to get the dirt on Moses and Aaron, but they have disappeared. Do you know where I can find them?"

"I know where Moses and Aaron are, and was on my way to inform Marissa. Take me to Marissa, I'll explain along the way."

A very relieved Abdullah said, "Thank you," as he led Jair back to find Marissa.

As they walked toward Marissa's office they heard her shouting orders and instilling fear in everyone around her. In the middle of her shouting one of her commands, Marissa turned right into Abdullah.

Abdullah proudly announced, "Marissa, I found Jair."

That was the match needed to strike the fuse, Marissa exploded, "It is Moses I need, not Jair!"

Abdullah unaware of her anger toward him replied, "He came looking for you, Jair knows where Moses and Aaron are."

"What!" shouted Marissa. "Where are they? What were they doing?"

Jair interrupted, "Marissa, listen to me, and I'll tell you." Marissa gave Jair one of her cat eye stares that said, "You are mine, now answer me."

"I was listening in on a meeting Moses and Aaron were having with the Council Elders of Goshen. It seems they have a message from their God to give to Pharaoh. The Council Elders have been instructed to go with them, to ask for an audience with Pharaoh. When I left, they were on their way to the palace."

Marissa could not believe her ears, "Moses and Aaron went to request an audience with Pharaoh?"

"They were headed that way when I left them," replied Jair.

"Abdullah, pick up everything—we are heading for the palace. I want the first-hand scoop on what is about to happen!" Jair stared at Marissa trying to get control of his anger. Who does she think she is, the Queen of Pharaoh?

Abdullah tried his best to get his legs to move, but the thought of the palace and Pharaoh made his brain freeze. Marissa turned around to find the two had not moved an inch, "Move!" That did it, fear of Marissa is enough to get anyone moving.

Arriving at the palace, Moses walked up and addressed the palace guards. "Excuse me, I am Moses, and this is my brother Aaron. We are escorting this group of Goshen Council Elders to the palace. We are here to request an audience with the Courtier."

"*Who are you*, to request an audience with the Courtier?" asked the guard. "I am not familiar with you! What makes you even think that the Courtier would address you, a commoner?"

"I am Moses, son of Amram and adopted son of Princess Bithiah. My Palace name is Senmut."

The guard still not convinced that this Moses is anyone of importance, casually instructed Kamenwati, "Go find Courtier Obaid tell him someone claiming to be Moses, and having the Palace name of Senmut, is here requesting an audience with him."

The guards turned their attention back to Moses and the men, "You, and your men, wait here; Kamenwati will return with Courtier

Obaid's answer. You give me any trouble and the only person you'll see is the prison guard."

Kamenwati, walking down the business section of the palace said to himself, "How am I supposed to find Courtier Obaid... What good fortune! The gods are smiling on me today, he's walking into that office." "Courtier Obaid! Courtier Obaid!"

From behind a closed door came the voice of Courtier Obaid, "Who is shouting my name? What do you want? We are about to open the court!"

"My Courtier Obaid, there is a man here who says he goes by the name of Moses. He claims he also has the Palace name Senmut, I think; he has requested an audience with you," answered Kamenwati.

"The adopted son of Princess Bithiah? Moses? I've heard stories about him when I was growing up. I wonder, could he really be the Moses from my childhood? No one else would know that name."

Back at the entrance to the palace, Thaddeus and Dan, along with Asher, strike up a conversation. "Do you think they'll let us in?" asked Dan.

Wringing his hands in nervous anticipation Asher answered, "Yes, but do you believe that we'll get out the same way we go in?"

Thaddeus whispers nervously, "Moses and Aaron had better be right, or we'll be feeling the whip!"

Dan said, "I am not going to Pharaoh's prison, daily life is prison enough for me."

Asher, looking nervously around him said, "How am I going to explain what went on here to the people of Goshen if this meeting goes badly?"

"Here comes the guard," replied Thaddeus.

"Abdullah! There you are, well? Get me over there before it is too late!" shouted Marissa.

Abdullah and Marissa shoved their way through the crowd, "ET NEWS, We are ET NEWS reporters! Let us through!" shouted Abdullah. " Marissa with ET NEWS, let me through!"

At the mention of her name, she gained the attention of people in the crowd. "Marissa? What's she doing here?"

"Yeah, something is up if Marissa is here."

"Let's go snooping."

"Aaron! Aaron!" shouted Abdullah, Marissa right behind Abdullah and eager to talk to Aaron.

"Abdullah, What are you doing here?" asked Aaron.

"You invited us to follow you around remember?" replied Marissa.

"I invited... (A smile came over Aaron's face). Yes, I did. I just didn't think about you following us to the palace."

Marissa put a soft purr in her voice and said, "You told me yesterday, that if I wanted to know what was going on, then I needed to follow you. So if it is alright with you, we'll go on the air, live right now, and let the people see for themselves who this man called Moses is.

Abdullah, you get the crew set up, and I'll let the guard know what we are doing here. Is this acceptable to you, Aaron?"

"First, let me introduce you to my brother. Moses, this is Marissa, the anchor for ET NEWS, you'll be interviewing with her and Abdullah this afternoon. Marissa wants to broadcast our message live here at the palace.

Please excuse us for a moment would you, Marissa?" asked Aaron. Leading Moses away from Marissa, "God did not say to hide what we are doing, do you think it'll be alright to let everyone see this as it happens?"

"By all means, Aaron, let her do her filming, God has nothing to hide." answered Moses.

As they met up with Marissa again, Moses spoke, "It is nice to meet you finally Marissa, I find it interesting that you are making a documentary about me. I am the least intriguing person around."

"The people disagree with you, Moses. You are quite the talk of the town. That is the reason we decided to do the documentary on you. Everyone seems to want to know more about you."

"I have to disagree with you. Is this Abdullah?"

Abdullah, squirming with excitement, shook Moses' hand, "Nice to meet you at last, Moses."

"You are an Israelite, are you not?"

"Yes, sir, I was born of Israelite parents."

Moses gave them a warning, "You, Abdullah shall witness something never seen before in the history of the world. Marissa, I warn you, you are in for more than even you could imagine."

Marissa's eyes squint with pride thinking, you have it all wrong Moses, and this shall not go the way you expect it to go. I can taste that Emmy of mine. In the middle of all the introductions, Kamenwati stepped up to speak with them.

"This man is the one who claims he has the Palace name, 'Senmut.' Sir, this is Courtier Obaid."

"Your name is Moses if I remember correctly. Pleased to meet you, after all, these years; I remember hearing stories about you when I was a little boy. We must leave the past for another time; I am due to open court very soon. Why have you requested an audience with me?" asked Courtier Obaid.

"We are here to speak to Pharaoh, we are to give him a message from our God," answered Moses.

"A message from your God? What God do you speak of Moses?"

"The God of our Fathers, the God of Abraham, the God of Isaac and the God of Jacob."

Courtier Obaid gave a chuckle and looked around at all the men with Moses, "Oh, that God... my, my, does it take all you men to give the message? Who are all of these men?"

"This is my brother Aaron, son of Amram."

"So you are Moses' backup. I understand that, why all these other men?" asked Courtier Obaid.

"These men are the Council Elders of the Israelite people in Goshen. They also have a request to make of Pharaoh."

"A request to make of Pharaoh is it? Kamenwati, keep a close eye on these men, I'll be right back. If they give you any trouble, do not hesitate to throw them in prison," commanded Courtier Obaid. "I'll go petition your request to see Pharaoh."

Moses replied, "Thank you, Courtier Obaid."

"Thaddeus, would you speak to Dan and Asher? Tell them they need to explain to their group of men what is happening," asked Aaron.

"Yes, Aaron I'll see to it." After doing as Aaron requested Thaddeus said, "If we get in to see Pharaoh, I hope we get out alive."

Aaron scolded, "Thaddeus, you are the leader of these men, you must not talk that way. Our God has sent us; all will be well with us."

Courtier Obaid, walking back into the palace, decided to go meet with Vizier Jibade to ask him how he would handle Moses and his men. "Thank the gods, there is Vizier Jibade talking with one of the men; he is not in court yet. Vizier Jibade! Could I speak with you a moment, please?"

"What is it Courtier Obaid, we are about to open court!"

"I know, I have a situation going on at the front gate and I need your help."

"My help? What would come up that you are asking for my help?" asked Vizier Jibade.

"There is a man at the palace entrance who claims to go by the Palace name Senmut and the name of Moses."

"Senmut? Moses ... you mean Princess Bithiah's adopted son, that Moses?" asked Vizier Jibade.

"That is exactly the Moses, he claims to be."

"Well! Well! We thought him dead. What does he want, after all these years, and why would he come back now? Is he coming back to try to be part of the royal family?" asked Vizier Jibade.

"No, he has brought his brother Aaron and the Council Elders of the Israelite people with him. He says that he has a message to Pharaoh, from their God," answered Courtier Obaid.

"A message to Pharaoh, from their God? What God is that?"

"You know, the one God that the Israelites claim as their God—they claim to serve just one God."

"Really?"

"Yes, really!"

"What about the other men, why bring them?" asked Vizier Jibade.

"They are the Council Elders of the Israelite people and they have a request to make of Pharaoh. Should we risk letting them see Pharaoh? What if they just make Pharaoh mad and we end up in prison by the end of the day?" asked Courtier Jibade.

"I want to see how Pharaoh reacts to seeing Moses and hearing this message from their God," replied Vizier Jibade. "I'll inform Pharaoh, and you tell Moses that he has permission to have an audience with Pharaoh, and then lead them up to the court area."

Aaron asked, "How long must we wait outside the palace? Since we have to go through this chain of command, do you think we'll speak with Pharaoh today?"

"We will wait as long as necessary. Aaron, God told us to do this today, so we will see Pharaoh today. As you spend more time with God, you'll gain confidence and understanding of who he is, and how he does things. I know that you'll have that opportunity," answered Moses.

ET NEWS: BREAKING NEWS: "Live At the Palace Court!"

"Hello everyone, this is Marissa for ET NEWS. Moses and Aaron, along with the Council Elders of the Israelite people, have requested an audience with Pharaoh himself.

We are here to see if they receive permission from Vizier Jibade to have an audience with Pharaoh. If granted permission, we shall follow along and take you for the first time into the palace court system.

What kind of trouble does Moses and Aaron plan on causing? I see Aaron, let's see if he would answer a few questions. 'Aaron,' Marissa with ET NEWS, 'what is the real reason you and Moses came to see Pharaoh today?'"

"You'll have to wait and see."

"What about all these men, the Council Elders, what kind of a request do they have to make?"

"You'll have to wait and see with the rest of us, now please we are busy getting ready to meet with Pharaoh."

"Aaron is reluctant to answer our questions; however, I see Courtier Obaid approaching Moses. Abdullah is with them."

Abdullah, "Marissa, Courtier Obaid is speaking with Moses."

"Moses, I have talked to Vizier Jibade, we are to proceed to the outer court and wait there with the others appearing in front of Pharaoh today. If you and your men would follow me, I'll lead you to the palace waiting area."

"As you heard Marissa, Moses and the men received permission, and we are walking to the outer court waiting to enter the court. Back over to you Marissa."

"We'll take a commercial break while Abdullah and I make our way over to the palace outer court."

As they walked down a very long hallway, the men were talking among themselves. "Look at the door, I have never seen another door so tall," said one of the men.

"Who cares how tall it is look at that gold covering it!" said another man.

"Thaddeus, is that colored stones and pearls inlaid with these stone floor tiles?" asked Asher.

"Wow, I think you're right," replied Thaddeus. Stopping at another tall door, they found an official waiting for them.

"You must be Moses; we have heard about you from our foremen. I am Vizier Jibade. Your men have a request to make of Pharaoh?"

"They have, Oh my Vizier," answered Moses.

"I have spoken to Pharaoh and he is very interested to meet you, Moses. He's interested to hear what you and your men have to say. Wait here until it is your turn to appear before Pharaoh. I'll see you in court."

"Thank you, Oh my Vizier."

This is Marissa; we have made our way to the outer court waiting our turn to make an appearance before Pharaoh. Earlier Abdullah took footage of the hallway as we walked through to get here. Abdullah would you run that footage for us?"

"Yes, as you can see the floors appear to be of marble stone with blue stones and pearls—very professional craftsmanship. One wonders how they put those stones in the marble like that. Maybe it is natural to the rock and cut just the right way to give the effect we see now.

Here you see the walls of the long hallway. The walls seem to have magnificent stones embedded in them, very intricate and technical work. I do not remember seeing work this precise before. Here we see the ceiling—it seems that you'll find yourself in the first heaven before you find the end of the ceiling..."

While waiting, everyone appeared to be noticeably nervous about appearing before Pharaoh. Dan, who was so nervous that he couldn't seem to think straight asked, "Aaron, are you sure that God told us to do this?"

"You should know that God cannot tell a lie. Do you think I would be here if he had not told me to be? Behave like you should, like our fathers of the past have behaved."

Asher asked, as if needing reassurance, "God said he will use Moses to lead us out of Egypt. So all we have to do is speak this message and all will be well, Moses, all will be well?"

"Asher, you have to learn to trust God. When God speaks, things happen. God cannot tell a lie. God would not lead us astray." Moses placed his arm around Asher's shoulder to reassure him. "You must show these men that you belong to our God and him alone. Stand up straight and rejoice in the fact that all of us shall be leaving Egypt and Pharaoh very soon."

"For those of you who have just tuned in, this is Marissa, I am in the palace with Abdullah. Moses and Aaron are here awaiting entrance to the outer court of the palace. They are to have an audience with the Pharaoh. We are here to let you see the news as it happens.

Presently, we are standing by a very tall door awaiting entrance to the outer court. We have been granted permission to film, but out of respect for the court proceedings, we will not provide commentary until later.

At this time you will have first-hand information as to how the court system operates. What a privilege to be the first news team allowed in the court arena! You'll see our great Pharaoh in action as he conducts his court.

You will not want to miss a minute of this historic event. So stay tuned, as together we shall see how Moses and the Egyptian court system flow. Oh, look, I see someone coming down the hall, it seems we are about to enter the court."

A palace guard walked over, and instructed Moses: "You and your men follow me." The men watched as the massive double doors opened. Upon entering the court arena, they found themselves needing time for their eyes to adjust from the bright sun that was hiding behind the massive door.

Whispering, "This is Abdullah, as you can see, there is a stone throne chair that sits high above the people. Pharaoh's seat looks to be a throne chair covered with red satin pillows, and each embellished with gold threads streaming down the side.

The men with Moses, are so consumed by the majestic royal presence of this open air courtroom, it looks like they have forgotten why they are here."

Marissa whispered, "The air here is so thick with the anticipation of our Pharaoh's appearance it is hard to breath. All eyes are on Pharaoh as he enters the court arena. My, Pharaoh is a majestic looking god."

The Vizier, sitting just a little lower than Pharaoh, stood and spoke: "Pharaoh, I present Moses, Aaron and the Council Elders of the Israelite people to your royal court."

With eyes fixed on Pharaoh, Marissa and the others watch for Pharaoh's reaction to Moses presence. "Moses, it has been a long time—forty years if I remember correctly. I remember the day you killed an Egyptian brother and then ran. Instead of giving a reason for killing one of our own, you ran—ran like a coward away from Pharaoh, your grandfather!

Why, after all these years would you come back and request an audience with me?" Not giving Moses time to answer, Pharaoh's menacing eyes scan the men as he asked, "Who is this standing beside you?"

"This is Aaron, my Israelite brother, and these three men, Thaddeus, Dan, and Asher, are Chief Council Elders of the Israelite people in Goshen. Our God has sent us to give you a message."

"What kind of a god do you have that sends messages to *me*, that thinks he can rule over my slaves? Moses, you know as well as I, that their god is just a simpleton, nothing for me to concern myself with."

Moses responded with a very defensive voice, "I would be very careful talking about the one true God that way, Pharaoh."

"Who are you to give me advice? Moses, you were a coward forty years ago, and you are a coward now. Bringing your Israelite brother and three elders—not to mention a bunch of other men who should be out making bricks—to back you up was not a smart move.

Why is this room so full of men? I refuse to conduct court with a bunch of uncivilized men in here. Maybe they are here to be witnesses to the other slaves when I crush you and your men into powder?"

Pharaoh stood up, stepped down and began pacing back and forth looking the men in the eye to let them know that he was the almighty authority in Egypt. "Or are they here to go out and tell the rest of the slaves to bow before Pharaoh as I am their god! Did you forget that they are *my* slaves, nothing more than spotted goats!

Go ahead, Moses, do what you are supposed to do; I am interested to see how amusing you and your men can be. I need a little laughter and you'll do as a court jester for now." Pharaoh then moved like a man of power and might as he walked back to his throne.

Turning, as he sat back down, he said with the authority of a god, "I warn you, if you provoke me you'll not like what happens. You have asked for an audience; you may make your request known to me."

Aaron prophesied, "Pharaoh, I have a message for you, 'Thus says the Lord; the God of Israel, Let My people go, that they may hold a feast to Me in the wilderness.'"

"Who is the Lord that I should obey his voice to let Israel go? I know not the Lord, neither will I let Israel go."

Dan and Asher stood beside Thaddeus, trying ever so hard not to show that they were about to collapse with fear. Thaddeus said to Pharaoh, "The God of Abraham, the God of Isaac and Jacob, has met with us and instructed us to go three days journey into the desert to sacrifice to our God. Otherwise, he may strike us with disease or death. Pharaoh, we ask you to give us your permission to go."

"Permission! Permission! Have I not just given my answer? No! Moses, forty years out in the desert has made your mind like that of a dog! Look what you have done! You have kept these lazy slaves from their work.

Can't you see that as the population of people grows, we need more work done, and you are keeping them from doing their work?" Pharaoh waved his hand and pointed his finger toward the door, "Go!"

Moses and Aaron turned and left Pharaoh's presence, with the Council Elders following close behind. Moses and Aaron were singing praise to the Lord, "Praise to God Almighty, you have given your people a new land. Praise to God Almighty for you keep us safe."

"This is Marissa, you heard what Moses and Aaron said to Pharaoh. I think they are asking to spend some time in prison chains. They got off lucky, if you ask me. As for the men of Goshen, the Israelite people, they still needed to be reminded that they are nothing more than slaves.

Pharaoh did well with them, wouldn't you say? Did you see how Moses and Aaron were singing praises to their God? Praising their God for getting them into enough trouble to be killed? They are crazy.

What do you good people of Egypt think about this Moses now? We are scheduled to interview Moses on the show later today. Contact our office at ET NEWS Station, News Street, Rameses, Egypt. We would like to have your input. Until then, this is Marissa for ET NEWS saying 'May the gods of Egypt protect you.'"

After signing off the air, Marissa went right back to work, "Abdullah, go find Jair, make sure he keeps an eye on Moses. We need Moses to be at the interview this afternoon."

"Yes, Marissa," replied Abdullah with a moan.

Palace

Later that same day, Pharaoh called the taskmaster and officers of the Israelite slaves to his court. Pharaoh decreed, "I say, you shall no longer give the people straw to make brick; let them go and gather straw for themselves.

I shall require from them the same number of bricks which they made before I took their straw away. For they are idle; that is why they cry, 'Let us go and sacrifice to our God.' Let us make their work harder so that they have no time to pay attention to Moses and his lying words. Now go!"

GOSHEN

Moses and Aaron were walking back to Goshen when Thaddeus, Dan, and Asher caught up with them. "Moses, what are we to tell the others after the meeting today? It was on live TV! The whole world saw Pharaoh as he called you 'dog brained,' and us 'a bunch of lazy slaves.' How do we continue to work and live this way?" asked Thaddeus.

Dan accused them both, "You said God had sent you to take us out of here—to a new and better land. Why has it not happened yet?"

"You said when God speaks, things happen; I don't see things happening. Not for the benefit of us, his people. The life here is hard, but at least we have a roof over our head and food to eat." observed Asher.

Not giving Moses a chance to respond to their anger, they quickly walked away in frustration. Moses said, "Aaron, I'll meet you later, I need to spend time in prayer and be ready for Marissa's interview this afternoon."

Aaron spoke, "Marissa is trouble for us, you know that. She seems to eat, breathe, and sleep thinking up ways to cause us harm and to make us look like fools."

"Aaron, when you work for God, people always try to harm you—but they cannot unless God allows it. Haven't you learned that people can always make us look like fools? It is how we carry ourselves with our God that counts; now I need to go spend time with God and prepare myself for that interview."

Chapter 7
Moses

"Hello everyone, I am your host Marissa with ET NEWS. Today is the conclusion of our four-part documentary on 'A Man Called Moses'.

For the convenience of our audience, tomorrow we will be airing a special show that we have pieced together with highlights of this documentary. Yesterday, I asked our viewing audience to contact our office with their thoughts on the documentary. Here are some of the many responses we had.

The first letter comes from Khayri of Pithom, it reads, "Thank you, Marissa, this has been a fascinating documentary so far. I have watched the series from the beginning, and I find it interesting how we, as Egyptians, seem to be fascinated with this Moses character and his family.

I agree with Jalal. I feel for Princess Bithiah, and I hope we all learned a lesson from her—to keep to our relationships with those in our own bloodline, and not to mix with those whose bloodline comes from different religious beliefs.

The way Moses treated our dear Pharaoh makes me mad. I pray to the gods of Egypt that he gets 'his' from Pharaoh very soon. Whether he is the Moses of the past or a new Moses remains to be seen. I will look forward to watching the final show tomorrow. I hope you receive an Emmy for this documentary."

The next letter came from Sahar of Succoth. "Marissa, thank you for taking the time to let us form an opinion on Moses. I have watched from the beginning, and I have often thought that you've shown great restraint when it comes to these foolish people. It is hard to believe that Princess Bithiah got involved with an Israelite child.

However, when any woman with a motherly instinct sees an abandoned baby, she does not think of them getting older—she just sees the cuteness of today. It shows us that we are a very compassionate people.

The Princess tried hard to take a lesser form of people and help Moses to rise to royal standards. Princess Bithiah's efforts failed, but she showed great courage to take on such a task. She has proven that you cannot take someone and make them something they are not.

We are a people born of Egyptian blood, grafted into royalty by Pharaoh, and ordained to be a superior people over the Israelites. I will look forward to the final show tomorrow. I have very much enjoyed your show and plan to vote yes, when the time comes to vote for your Emmy."

"I want to thank our viewers for the responses you sent in. I would love to have time to read them all on the air. They were all very thoughtful and encouraging, thank you.

We have the honor of Moses himself here with us today to complete our documentary on 'A Man Called Moses'. Moses is here to explain who he is and why he is here in Egypt.

For those of you who may have missed yesterday, we interviewed Aaron, Moses' brother. This morning we were live at the Palace with Moses and Aaron, where they had an audience with Pharaoh. Abdullah, are you and Moses ready?"

Abdullah: "Yes, thank you Marissa. Moses, thank you for making room for us in your busy schedule."

Moses: "You are most welcome, Abdullah."

Abdullah: "I would like to start out with your childhood. Do you remember Jochebed as a child?"

Moses: "I remember playing stones with Jochebed at a very young age. I remember the stories she would tell me. Jochebed is responsible for letting me know that I was a special child born with an assignment from our God."

Marissa: "Jochebed is the one responsible for brainwashing you, so that Princess Bithiah would not stand a chance of raising you as an Egyptian Noble."

Moses: "Jochebed is not the one responsible for my abandoning the Egyptian Religion. You feel you need to blame someone, I understand that. Jochebed raised me to know our God, the God of Abraham, Isaac, and Jacob.

She knew the importance of giving me a firm foundation in God before I was turned loose into a world filled with false gods. She knew I would have to be strong, so God could fulfill the plan he had for my life.

The rest of what you blame Jochebed for, Marissa, came from me. I made the choice at an early age to stay close to my God; no one could make that choice for me."

Marissa: "If Jochebed had not brainwashed you, then you would have turned to the way of the Egyptians. You know that as well as I do, Moses."

Moses: "I know that even if Jochebed had not done for me as she did, God would have found me and made a way for me to do what I have been assigned to do. As long as I say yes to God, then no one and nothing shall stand in the way. Ask any Hebrew, and they can tell you that whatever their God wants of them sooner or later they shall do it, no matter what."

Marissa: "Nice try Moses, you are going to have to prove to me that your god has that kind of power."

Abdullah: "Moses, I notice you call Jochebed by her name and not by mother, why?"

Moses: "As you already know, I was not allowed to call my parents by any name but their given name. They had to raise me as Princess Bithiah's son and not their son."

Abdullah: "Do you remember the first time you met Princess Bithiah at the palace when your mother brought you to stay?"

Moses: "I do, and I remember looking at Princess Bithiah and thinking she was a very kind and loving lady. I realized she must be the lady Jochebed told me about; I remember liking her very much from the start."

Marissa: "Well, that is a relief. It proves my point; you felt for her when you first met her. You would have worshiped her gods had Jochebed not interfered."

Abdullah: "How was it growing up in the palace? Did you have work to do?"

Moses: "It is not all fun and games; there was much work we had to do also. It was expected of us to be well educated. We were required to know three languages: Hebrew, Egyptian, and Arabic. We also were required to do Math, Science, Palace Management, and Sports.

We were expected to be well-educated above everybody else in the kingdom. We also had our fun times—sitting on grandpa's lap and hearing his stories is one of my favorite childhood memories.

Another fun time for me was playing the game *Senet* [see glossary] and beating Bithiah. She would always pretend to be upset when I would win the game. Pharaoh had fun pretending to be mad when I would beat him in a good game of *Hounds and Jackals*." [see glossary]

Abdullah: "You were raised to be a Prince of Egypt, what made you want to give that up?"

Moses: "I did not just wake up one day and say, 'I do not wish to be a Prince of Egypt anymore'. I was born to fulfill the plan God has for me, and I felt that I needed to help my people."

Abdullah: "So when you were forty, you decided to go out and see how your blood relatives were doing and what you could do to help?"

Moses: "I had a stirring inside of me that made me restless. I felt a need to go and see how they were doing. When I got there, I was appalled to see the abuse the Israelites were taking from the Egyptians."

Abdullah: "So what is your excuse for killing an Egyptian and running away from home?"

Moses: "I remember that day like it was yesterday. I was out walking around looking to see how I could help my people. I had a hard time seeing the injustices my people were suffering.

I asked myself, What can I do to change these injustices? What can I do to make this wrong right? The inhumanity and injustice had been going on for generations, and it had to stop! I had a belly full of the stench around me.

As I turned to walk away, frustrated with myself for not having an immediate answer, I saw one of the Egyptian overseers beating one of my Israelite relatives without mercy. Looking around and seeing no one, I saw red—then, in a fit of rage at the situation, I let that unfortunate man have all my frustration.

I never intended to kill him just knock some sense into that thick skull of his. I did not beat him; but with my fist I naturally gave him one good left hook to the face, and that's all it took. I was a fit young man back then...

When he fell to the ground dead, I was startled and panicked. My mind raced with desperate thoughts: 'Was I responsible for taking another person's life? What am I going to do? Pharaoh is never going to listen to my explanation.' I had to bury him in one of the sand pits, and because no one was around, there was no way anyone would ever find him!

That is what I thought at the time. So I went home convincing myself that all was well, and that I was in the right. After all, the Egyptian was bullying the other man for no good reason and deserved to be stopped by any means possible.

Feeling content that no one knew what I had done and that I would never get caught, I went back out the next day. That day taught me that no matter what one does in secret, when you belong to God, sooner or later your sin is exposed. In the same spot that I killed a man the day before, I saw two of my Israelite relatives arguing and then one hit the other.

Shocked and enraged at the brutality of my blood relatives, I walked over to them and said to the aggressive one, 'Hey! What do you think you're doing? Isn't it bad enough that the Egyptians beat you, why are you hitting one of your own?'

To which the man responded, 'Who appointed you ruler and judge over us? Do you intend to kill me the way you killed the Egyptian?' I was shocked, how could anyone know what I had done?

My thoughts raced, 'If people know what I have done, surely Pharaoh will want me dead! What do I do now, how am I going to help anyone if I am dead? Good job, Moses!

Dear God in heaven, what am I to do now?' I felt an urge to leave the country, and so I went out into the desert. I just left. The one thing I regret the most was not being able to say good-bye to Princess Bithiah."

Abdullah: "So you left taking the hopes, dreams, and possibilities for a better life for your people with you. Is that why you have come back, Moses, to make amends with us?"

Marissa: "Abdullah, I did not know you had it in you. Moses, do you see what happens when someone like you turns tail and runs? Just proves my point, right?"

Moses: "Abdullah, God has a plan for his people. Yes, he is using Aaron and me to restore the hopes of his people, to fulfill their every dream, and give them the gift of a better life."

Marissa: "Do not believe it, Abdullah—do not listen to a word of it."

Abdullah: "I hope so, Moses, I truly hope so. Where did you end up when you stopped walking?"

Moses: "I found a well in Midian, not too far from Mount Sinai. I stopped there to gather my thoughts and get refreshed."

Abdullah: "And...."

Moses: "There I found a new life. I was sitting there relaxing, when a group of girls came over my way."

Abdullah: "A group of girls, were you dreaming?"

Moses: "I thought so at the time, but no. Seven young women, daughters of a priest of Midian, by the name of Jethro, came to the well to water their sheep. I was busy taking in the beauty around me when suddenly some men came up to the well and started making trouble for these women."

Abdullah: "Trouble, why would they want to make trouble for these women?"

Moses: "The well is a community well, and these men decided that they wanted to water their sheep before anyone else. Not really wanting to get involved in another dispute, I watched for a few minutes to see how things were going to play out.

It looked like this had been an ongoing problem. The women had grown tired of them and decided to clobber the men. The women were armed only with their shepherd staffs. I could not watch the men overpower the women. Could I?"

Marissa: "Killed some more men did you?"

Moses: "No, Marissa, I did not. I stood up and told them to wait their turn."

Abdullah: "And they just waited their turn? I doubt that."

Moses: "No, however, one asked me who I thought I was. Laughed at me because I was a stranger getting involved in women's business. I explained to them that it is not who I think I am, it is who I am.

I kindly told them that it was not right for them to pick on women; not right for them to treat others of their belief with such contempt, no matter who they are. I also informed them that I would be watering the sheep for the women that day, so they had better wait their turn."

Abdullah: "These shepherds just waited, didn't give you any grief?"

Moses: "When I saw that they were going to need me to teach them a lesson, I took my walking stick, picked it up, and rendered the first one unconscious.

Two of the men came toward me, and that was it—those seven women were coming after them. I shouted 'Stop!' and everyone stopped and looked at me with the funniest expressions on their faces. I told them that if they insisted on acting like spoiled children, then I would deal with them as such.

One of the men, at about that time, came at me intending to cause me harm; and wham, I let him have it with my right hook to the jaw. I was a little more careful not to do damage this time. Without hesitation, I knocked him out cold.

Startled and unsure about this stranger that had come to the land, two of the men came and picked up their friend. I reminded these men that I would be taking care of the watering of the sheep for these women today.

Once again, one of the men decided he would show me who he was. As he came toward me, I let him have my left hook to the jaw and told the men to back off. I let them know I meant business and would keep this up as long as necessary. They scoffed and moved back until I had finished watering the sheep."

Abdullah: "How did these seven women feel about you after your encounter?"

Moses: "They were very thankful for what I had done and let me know it. When they left, I said to myself, 'Moses, you will be seeing those girls again.' Walking, not really sure where I was going, I looked ahead and saw a couple of the women coming back my way.

Leah, one of the sisters, said her father wanted to thank me and asked if I would come to dinner? Excited and looking forward to a good meal I said, 'Lead the way, young one.'"

Abdullah: "So you went for dinner and stayed?"

Moses: "When their father found out I was a stranger in a foreign land, he invited me into his home."

Abdullah: "Aaron told us you married one of the daughters?"

Moses: "Yes, I married Zipporah, the oldest daughter."

Abdullah: "You have children?"

Moses: "We have two sons."

Abdullah: "Could you be more precise? I am sure our audience would like to know their names."

Moses: "Gershom is my oldest. When I saw him, I said: 'I have been a stranger and a sojourner in a foreign land, and we shall call him Gershom.' When they put Eliezer in my hands, I said, 'the Lord gives help' so I named him Eliezer."

Abdullah: "Did you live in one spot in Midian during the forty years you lived in that land?"

Moses: "Jethro's people are tent dwellers, nomads, we move from place to place as we find new grazing ground for our sheep."

Abdullah: "What kind of work did you do for your father-in-law?"

Moses: "For Jethro, my father-in-law's name is Jethro. I was a shepherd for him until God told me to come back to Egypt."

Abdullah: "So how did your God ask you to come to Egypt?"

Moses: "God spoke to me through a burning bush."

Abdullah: "Would you explain what you mean by through a burning bush?"

Moses: "I was watching the sheep at Mount Sinai, the mountain of our God. Looking around, I spotted a bush on fire—nothing unusual—however, this bush was not burning up."

Marissa: "Burning bush! Moses, you sat around all day drinking so much Zytum that you were seeing and hearing things; that is what happened. However, go on with your amusing story if you must."

Abdullah: "Seeing a bush burning seems strange to me. How can we believe in a burning bush?"

Moses: "In the desert we have many lighting strikes in a day. It is also so hot that some bushes burst from spontaneous combustion. There are so many burning bushes, and it is so normal to us that we do not pay attention to them.

It is similar to you in that every day you see people in pain. Yet this has become so normal for your eyes that you pay no attention to them or their suffering.

It is only when a person is moaning with a sound that is different from the rest and acting so abnormal from the other people, that your eyes see that person. Only then, are you drawn to go see what is wrong with them."

Abdullah: "Which means this one had to be really different to have caught the attention of your eye!

Moses: "Your audience is not familiar with where we live. When one tends sheep, there is no one else around for a good walking distance. You cannot keep other peoples' sheep too close by, as sheep take one acre of land for every four head of sheep on the grazing ground we have in Midian."

Abdullah: "Did you not just tell us about encountering some men and their sheep at the watering well?"

Moses: "You can keep sheep close by for watering, but not grazing. That well is usually a good half-day walk to get to."

Abdullah: "You went over to see about this burning bush and ..."

Moses: "I went over to get an understanding of why this bush was burning, yet not burned up. As I was walking, I noticed it was glowing like a bright and shining light. I kept asking myself 'How can a bush be burning with such a bright flame and not be burned up?'

Then I heard a voice calling my name: 'Moses, Moses.' So I called back; 'Here am I!' The voice spoke and said; 'Moses, do not come any closer. Take your sandals off your feet, the place where you stand is *holy ground.*' I have to admit I was scared! God really spoke to me through this burning bush.

During our conversation, God told me that he had chosen me to bring the Israelites out of Egypt. I could not think straight, why had God chosen me? I learned that day when God wants you to do something, he will let you know it."

Marissa: "That is the wildest story I have heard in a long time. Have you gone mad? You think, Moses, that you and your God can conquer our Pharaoh? You have been in the sun too long. You think you can talk like that and our great king, our Pharaoh will let you get away with it?"

Moses: "You will see what our God, the great I AM will do if Pharaoh will not obey him."

Marissa: "Who do you think you are?"

Abdullah: "Moses, you worked for Jethro and you needed to get his permission to leave, didn't you?"

Moses: "He had adopted me as his son and I worked for him. Yes, I asked him to let me come back to Egypt and see how my people were doing."

Abdullah: "Did you tell him why you wanted to go and what God said?"

Moses: "Jethro is a man that has wisdom and integrity; I needed not to tell him and he asked no questions."

Abdullah: "Had you ever planned on coming back to Egypt and were you concerned about the people that wanted you dead?"

Moses: "I hadn't thought much one way or the other about returning to Egypt. However, when God asked me to return to Egypt, I asked God, 'What about the people who want me dead?'

God then said to me, 'All the men that were looking to kill you are dead.' I was aware that after a Pharaoh dies, anyone who had been accused or convicted of a crime, including capital murder, was then acquitted. All charges are dropped from their name."

Abdullah: "So you packed up and left for Egypt?"

Moses: "We left for Mount Sinai. God wanted me to spend some one-on-one time with him before I left for Egypt."

Abdullah: "You said we, who's we?"

Moses: "It started out as a family trip. At Mount Sinai we realized that I would need all my concentration for God's work, so Zipporah and the boys headed back to live with Jethro. We'll be back together when I have finished here."

Marissa: "You said you needed all your concentration for God's work. You're not capable of concentrating on your God and spending time with your family? People in the audience, I told you Moses has a very low brain capacity."

Moses: Zipporah and I realized that God would be requiring a lot of one-on-one time with me to explain how to accomplish the task at hand.

Marissa: What do you mean that God would need a lot more one-on-one time with you? Moses are you are really that mindless?

Moses: "I'll not try to explain something about God that you cannot understand. You'll see in the next few days what I mean. Marissa, you go and spend time in your temples praying and talking and performing rituals to your different gods, is that not what you do?"

Marissa: "What kind of a question is that? Yes!"

Moses: "When you leave, you feel like a different person, more confident, more alive?"

Marissa: "Of course, spending time with our gods, lets us refill with inner peace and calm. We feel as if no harm can come our way."

Moses: "Yet with all your praying do they speak back to you with an audible voice?"

Marissa: "Well... no."

Moses: "If they can hear you, why do they not respond to your prayers? No gods made from stone and wood can answer prayer. They are idols and images that can't breathe or respond to your prayers. Our God is a real, living, and breathing Spirit; he speaks with a voice and he answers our prayers."

Marissa: "Your story gets crazier by the minute. Our gods do not speak to us because there is no need to. They hear us and answer our prayers."

Moses: "Our God, the God of Abraham, Isaac, and Jacob, are going to show you how your gods will answer your prayers in the near future, Marissa, you remember that."

Abdullah: "Marissa if I may interrupt, I have a question for Moses."

Marissa: By all means, ask your question Abdullah."

Abdullah: Moses, you were forty when you left Egypt, and how old are you now?

Moses: "As I left forty years ago, I am now eighty." Moses looked at Abdullah as if to say, "Did you really ask me that?"

Abdullah: "Moses, you are too old for your God to be sending you on an assignment like this, are you not?"

Moses: "Abdullah, how old is God?"

Abdullah: "He is older than the earth I guess, why?"

Moses: "That old and still able to work, so why do you think it is that I cannot get my job done?"

Abdullah: "What were you really sent by God to do?"

Moses: "I have told you as much as you need to know for now. If you want any more information, follow us and witness what is about to happen before the Israelites leave Egypt."

Abdullah: "Well, Moses, it seems that you are not going to answer any more of my questions. I can say that I have had the most exciting time with this documentary. Moreover, you have given us a lot to think about."

Marissa: "Moses, I want to thank you for taking the time to be on our show. You can be sure that this is not over, and I'll be following you everywhere you go. You are about to make a big mistake, and when you do, I'll be there with the TV crew to show the world how you have misled us all."

Moses: "The pleasure was mine."

Marissa: "People of Egypt, can you not see that even Princess Bithiah was unable to help a baby born to an Israelite woman become an Egyptian Prince? I feel sorry for Princess Bithiah, since she is the real victim in this whole story.

It is my hope that this documentary has helped you to realize that this Moses, the one here today, is the Moses of the past. I hope you saw with your own eyes that after spending so long in the desert, Moses is just another nut running around trying to cause us more trouble. His trouble, however, is more than that of an ordinary troublemaker.

For some reason, everything he says and everything he does is toxic to those around him. They run around like drunks; drunk on everything he has to say about his God. Addicted to his every move—his every word.

How do we get rid of this poison? The only thing I do know is that Pharaoh will not fall so easily into the trap that Moses and Aaron and their God have planned for him. We'll be keeping a close eye on Moses and Aaron.

I invite our viewers to let us know what they thought about this documentary. Contact us at ET NEWS Station, News Street, Rameses, Egypt. Until next time, this is Marissa saying 'May the gods of Egypt protect you.'"

As Moses, left, Marissa almost hissed, her words, "Moses, this battle is far from over—I have my eye on you."

Moses having heard Marissa, turned, looked her in the eye and spoke, "This battle, as you call it, is not between you and me; however, this is your time. I expect to see you again soon and until then, peace be with you, Marissa." Moses then turned and with sadness in his eyes said to Abdullah, "Peace be with you." Marissa and Abdullah both stood speechless as they watched him walk away into the sunset.

Chapter 8
Egypt

Goshen

Having heard that the Council Elders of Goshen called a community meeting at the Tent in Goshen, Jair was looking for a good spot to hear what was being said without attracting attention to himself.

Finding a spot in the corner to stand, Jair was ready to hear what the elders had to say. As his eyes scanned the area, he noticed that the chief elders, Thaddeus, Dan, and Asher were present.

There were a lot of people, more than Jair thought would be there. Moving next to the door, just in case he had to leave quickly he said, "Joshua and Johnathan are here, this could be a very interesting meeting."

The meeting already in progress, Thaddeus was speaking, "People, People, we must have quiet. Continue with what you were telling us, Tomer."

"Like I said, Pharaoh gave a decree and addressed us like he was our god. He is my God, but he needed not to be so nasty about it."

"Well! What did he say?" asked Dan.

"'How many times do I have to say it?' Pharaoh said, 'I shall not give you straw!'" answered Tomer.

An outraged crowd started shouting, "What!"

"How can he do this to us?"

"It is because of Moses and Aaron!"

"That's what we get for listening to them!"

"How are we going to get the straw now?"

Tomer interrupted, "Will you let me finish? Pharaoh said, 'You are to get the straw wherever you can find it, and you are commanded to keep the same quota of bricks as before.'

As Tomer finished giving his message from Pharaoh, the crowd once again erupted with barely controllable anger, "Why have we listened to Moses!"

"Pharaoh shall kill us all yet; you wait and see!"

Not wanting to be noticed and having all the information he needed, Jair quietly slipped out the tent door.

Thaddeus shouted, "Quiet! I'll have silence! That is better. There is nothing we can do about this situation at the moment and we solve nothing if we start shouting and making accusations. Thank you to Tomer for reporting to us as a subordinate official.

We have a lot to consider. People, I am telling you to go back to your homes. Get some sleep as tomorrow could be a long day, I declare this meeting adjourned."

As the crowd started leaving, Thaddeus asked Dan and Asher, "Do either of you know if Moses has heard about this?"

"No Thaddeus, we were wondering the same thing. Have you heard how the interview went?" asked Dan.

"With the events of the day I forgot about Moses' interview with ET NEWS. I guess the best thing would be to take our advice and get some sleep; tomorrow is going to be a long day I think. Shalom Dan, Shalom Asher."

Dan and Asher replied, "Shalom, Thaddeus."

That night some of the Israelites went to bed and fell asleep from exhaustion; others went to bed too full of worry about tomorrow to get any sleep. How would they ever be able to survive Pharaoh's new command?

Rameses

Menachem, one of many overseers of the Egyptian slaves, was having a rough day. "How are you going to get these people to stay at the same quota of straw as they had before Pharaoh told us there would be no more straw given to them? Yesterday was hard enough and today has not been any better. Moses, has been nothing but a pain in my side since he got here. Making Pharaoh unhappy with us is just stupid. God in heaven, where are you?

Yesterday was hard enough and today has not been any better. Moses, has been nothing but a pain in my side since he got here. Making Pharaoh unhappy with us is just dumb. Aaron is rude to Pharaoh in court, and it is not very intelligent either. God in heaven, where are you? Lord since Moses and Aaron have claimed to be hearing You, we have had nothing but trouble.

Menachem said to himself, "You need answers, stop filling yourself up with more questions and get back to work."

Throwing his arm, causing his whip to lash, more in fear of the taskmaster, who might have him punished for going softer on the work crew than anything else Menachem yelled, "Come on people- you need to have the same amount of bricks made today as before Pharaoh gave his new command. Yesterday was terrible, and I am warning you, you had better not be that slack today or you'll suffer the consequences.."

"Menachem!" Turning around, he found Maor his taskmaster calling to him. Trying hard not to shake in fear Menachem asked, "Maor, what can I do for you?"

"Masud said you are to meet him at his headquarters. I would hurry if I were you."

Palace

I hope the information I have is correct, Jair thought, waiting to meet with another snitch who worked for him at times. Standing in the back area of the palace's outer court, Jair spotted Moses and Aaron, "Well, well, this should be interesting."

Masud, chief of the slave driver program, had requested some of the slaves' taskmasters to make an appearance before him. Moses and Aaron heard about this and decided to wait in the back area of the outer court gates, expecting to hear from some of the men. They sat next to the watering troughs, as a group of Israelite slave drivers caught sight of them and headed straight for Moses.

Bitterness filled their voices as they angrily shout: "Moses! May God see what you have done and judge you because you have made us stink before Pharaoh and his servants! You put a weapon in his hand that is going to kill us all!"

Moses startled and confused, asked, "What has happened?"

Menachem answered, "Pharaoh's taskmasters were angry, so Chief Masud had us beaten and said, 'You had yesterday and today to get your quota to be the same as before, and it has not happened. Maybe this beating will remind you that I do not permit slacking.' After that I went with Tomer, Maor, and Thabit to appeal to Pharaoh."

We said; "Pharaoh, why do you treat us this way? You give us no straw and scream at us 'Make bricks!' Pharaoh said that it was he who issued the order to have us beaten, and that he'll not tolerate slackers. He had no reason to have us beaten except he likes to see us suffer. It is his officials that are at fault, not us!"

"Calm down, Menachem, what else did Pharaoh say or do?" asked Aaron.

"It was terrible, he screamed at us again, 'Lazy, lazy you are just lazy! That is the reason you continue to beg for me to let you go and make sacrifices unto your God.' Then he told us all to get back to work. He still refuses to let us have any straw, and we are to fill our daily quota. We'll all be dead in a very short time, and it is all your fault! Come on guys, we have work to do. I hope you are happy, Moses! Thanks a lot, Aaron!"

Jair, now on his way to report to Marissa for ET NEWS, said, "This is great! Wait until Marissa hears about this. I'll get a free meal from her tonight! I just hope she's at her office and not out somewhere when I get there."

As they walked back to Goshen, Aaron asked, "Why does God allow this to happen to the people? God told us the people shall leave for the Promised Land soon?"

"Aaron, you need to learn to trust God, and I need some time to speak with Him. I'll see you later," replied Moses as he headed to his solitude: his tent out next to the water where he went for rest and to speak with God.

Moses and God Argue

Moses arrived at his favorite alone spot, the spot where he spent his time praying, talking, if you like, with his God. It was a private, yet comfortable spot next to the water.

Thinking about the events that had taken place lately, Moses argued, "How can you allow Pharaoh to continue to mistreat your people? Why did you send me here if all you were going to do is let them keep being abused like this?

From the moment I arrived and met with Pharaoh in your name, he has become more and more abusive. Today I gave Pharaoh your message, and now he has become more brutal to them, and you have not delivered them at all! Help me to understand this!"

Then the Lord said to Moses, "Now you shall see what I'll do to Pharaoh. I will show him my power, and he will let my people go. I will show him my power, and he will throw them out of his country. I am the Lord.

I appeared to Abraham, Isaac, and Jacob, as God Almighty, but I didn't make myself known to them by my name, "The Lord." I also set up my covenant with them, to give them Canaan, where they lived as immigrants. I've also heard the cry of grief of the Israelites, whom the Egyptians have turned into slaves, and I've remembered my covenant.

Tell the Israelites, 'I am the Lord. I will bring you out from under the oppression of the Egyptians, and I will free you from slavery. I will rescue you with my powerful arm and with mighty acts of judgment. Then I will make you my people, and I will be your God.

You will know that I am the Lord your God, who brought you out from under the forced labor of the Egyptians. I will bring you to a land I solemnly swore to give Abraham, Isaac, and Jacob. I will give it to you as your own possession. I am the Lord."

"Yes, God, I'll do as you say, but you know that they shall not believe me. Their work has been hard, and they have lost their hope. When they look around them, all their eyes see is death. I feel very conflicted right now; however, I'll do as you say," replied Moses.

Moses and Aaron Spoke to the People

Moses listened while Aaron spoke the words given to Moses of God for the people of Israel. "God has just told you, 'He is Your Lord.' God is the one who shall take you from these harsh Egyptians, and God shall redeem our nation from it's sin.

God said, 'I'll make you my people; you will be my friends. I'll be your God; we'll have a one-on-one relationship. I'll bring you to the land of Canaan, the Promised Land that I promised to Abraham, Isaac, and Jacob. Why is that so hard for you to believe?"

The crowd responded in anger, "Why should we believe? Ever since you came to Goshen to give us good news, things have only gotten worse."

"If things only get harder every time you talk to Pharaoh, why should we believe that what you say is true? Moses, do not talk to God anymore!"

Aaron replied, "People, please, you must listen!"

"No! We are not listening to you any longer, we are going home!" shouted one from the group of listeners. An outraged, tired and confused people slowly left for home.

Moses encouraged Aaron, "It is alright—leave them alone. God knows what is going on with them, and he has not left them. When the judgments start to happen their eyes shall begin to open, and their hearts will start to melt toward God. Come, let us have some dinner."

God and Moses

Early the next morning Moses was praying when God spoke. "Moses, I want you to tell Pharaoh, the one I made to be the King of Egypt, everything that I say to you."

"Okay. However, in all the times that I have been before him he has not listened so why should he be any different now?"

"Moses, look at me. I have made it so that Pharaoh will deal with you as though you are God. You are to declare my will and purpose to him. Your brother Aaron, I have made to be your prophet.

I want you to speak everything I command you to your brother

Aaron and he will tell it to Pharaoh. Aaron will tell Pharaoh to let the people of Israel go out to another land.

I'll cause Pharaoh to have an unreasonably obstinate heart toward the people. Expect this, for you have been forewarned. I'll do this so that I can perform numerous signs and wonders in the land of Egypt.

Of course, Pharaoh will continue to ignore the messages that you give him. Then, I'll let go of the power of my right hand, and I'll use it against Egypt, and freedom shall come to my stupendous armies.

My people, my children of Israel, I'll free from Egypt with sudden and surprising acts of judgment. When I use my powers against Egypt and take the Israelites out of that land, they will know beyond a shadow of a doubt that I am the Lord."

Pharaoh Meets God's Power

Aaron spoke, "Moses it is by the grace of God that you and I are as healthy as we are. You are eighty, and I am eighty-three and yet we are as fit as someone in their twenties."

"Yes, Aaron it is only by the grace of God."

"How do you think Pharaoh will handle this intrusion today?"

"God told us Pharaoh is not going to like us very well." Moses spotted Marissa and Abdullah. Marissa proud of her upper hand, walked up to them and said, "Moses, I heard that you are on your way to talk to Pharaoh. I know the people would like to know what is going on, so I made arrangements to go in with you again and let the people see what you are up to."

"I'll not stop you Marissa, just stay out of my way."

"I would never get in your way Moses," Marissa purred while she thought I need not be in your way we have Pharaoh to take care of you.

As Marissa left to make sure things were done properly, she said, "I'll see you shortly Moses, we'll watch as you cower down to our great Moses."

Abdullah tried very hard not to break out laughing as he said to himself, "I feel for you Moses, it shall be interesting to see how that remark will come back to bite you."

At the palace, Moses and Aaron approached a palace guard. "You are Kamenwati?" asked Moses.

"Yes and you are Moses and Aaron if I remember correctly."

"Yes, we are, you remembered our names." answered Aaron.

"How could I forget them, you two are the talk of the palace. Are you by yourselves today?" asked Kamenwati.

"Yes, it is just the two of us."

"What can I do for you today?"

"We are here to speak to Pharaoh."

"You, John, come over and keep an eye on Moses and Aaron for me. I need to go find Vizier Jibade."

Walking in the area of Vizier Jibade's office Kamenwati said, "I hope the Vizier is not too hard to find, I hate walking forever." He paused a moment to look around, "There he is, Vizier Jibade!"

"Yes, Kamenwati, what is it you want?"

"Moses and Aaron are outside requesting an audience with Pharaoh again."

Walking together Vizier Jibade replied, "Again? Alright show them to the waiting room."

"Oh, you should know that Marissa is with them."

"It is alright; I told her she may enter and film whenever Moses comes, just assign one of the guards to keep a close eye on her crew. We do not need them snooping into something that is none of their business."

While waiting Moses and Aaron were humming to God, and Marissa gave her introduction to the public. Kamenwati approached them and waited for Marissa to conclude her introduction, "Moses, you, and Aaron may enter now.

Marissa, you, and your crew may enter; I'll be assigning a guard to you to keep you out of trouble."

Marissa replied, "Thank you, Kamenwati." At the same time thinking, 'Just what kind of trouble does he think we'll get into?'

Upon entering the court, Moses and Aaron bowed to greet Pharaoh.

Pharaoh gave a wave with his right hand, as if they were a burden he did not want to deal with, "Moses, what is it you want of me this time?

Wasn't your last visit enough, have you come for more punishment? At least you paid attention and brought only Aaron with you."

"Yes, Pharaoh it is just Aaron and me today."

"Well? I am a busy ruler, what is it that you have to say today? Another message from your God?" Pharaoh chuckled.

Aaron prophecies, "Thus says the Lord our God, 'Let my people go, so they can go down and worship me in the wilderness.'"

"How many times are you going to bring this request to me? Prove your God exists, show me a great sign, and I might let your people go."

Moses instructed Aaron, "Take your staff and throw it down on the ground next to Pharaohs' feet; then it shall become a cobra snake." Aaron threw the staff to the ground very close to Pharaoh's feet, as it touched the ground it became a cobra.

Because of Jair's warning Pharaoh's counselors, sorcerers, and magicians were on the alert and prepared for Moses and Aaron's tricks. Jambres intently looked around and said, "Just as we thought Jannes; they decided to pull the snake in the sand routine."

Pharaoh asked, "Moses, are you trying to threaten me? You think your little cobra can stand against Wadjet? Where are my counselors, sorcerers, and magicians?"

"We are here My Pharaoh."

"Tell me about this snake that Aaron has thrown at my feet."

While Pharaoh and Moses had been conversing, Pharaoh's men were having a conference of their own. Jannes, one the magicians answered, "We prepared our rods for this so if me and my men may be allowed to throw down our rods we can settle this matter."

"Then by all means do so."

"Alright Jambres on the count of three we shall throw our rods, one, two, three." As they all threw their rods in together Jannes spoke with authority, "Moses and Aaron you shall know that Pharaoh's power reigns supreme in the land. Pharaoh is the god of the land of Egypt."

All the eyes of Egypt were watching very carefully to see what would happen next. As Jannes and Jambres rods fell to the ground; they also became cobras. Everyone was eagerly anticipating Pharaoh's cobra's killing Moses' cobra.

Marissa whispered, "Finally! People Moses shall get what he has due to him, and the whole of Egypt shall see it! Pharaoh will once again prove that he is the Supreme Ruler of Egypt."

With the voice of an excited child about to win his first game of Hounds and Jackals, Jannes said, "Pharaoh should be especially happy with us after today. Look, our cobras are poised to strike; the victory is ours at any moment."

The two cobras, came up in front of Moses' cobra. After what seemed like forever, Pharaoh's cobra's reared up and spread their hoods to let the enemy know they were about to strike.

Moses' cobra, in a defensive pose, gave one quick glance at the enemies, then with lightning speed struck and swallowed Jannes and Jambres cobra's. It happened within the blink of an eye.

The whole place went silent; no one dared to move for fear of Pharaoh's reaction to this terrible loss of a battle. Waiting and watching for what seemed an eternity, everyone held their breath waiting for Pharaoh's response to what had just happened.

Pharaoh, unfazed by Moses' tricks said, "Moses you have become an eyesore to me this proves nothing! My answer is no, get out of my sight!"

Moses and Aaron acted as though they were expecting Pharaoh to react that way. They just turned around and silently walked away from Pharaoh's presence.

Marissa was not quiet, she talked to the people with mixed emotions. "People of Egypt, I hope you saw what just happened, the snake belonging to Moses jumped up with lightning speed, opened his mouth wide and had a double snake appetizer, unbelievable!

Not only that, Aaron then picked it up by the tail, and it is once again nothing more than a staff. A staff that looked just the way it was as though nothing ever happened. We have not heard the last of this, stay tuned, we will be on the air as further developments arise. Until then this is Marissa saying "May the gods of Egypt protect you.'"

Marissa and Abdullah followed Moses and Aaron out of the palace, a little unsure of what to make of this great tragedy. Marissa found herself asking why Pharaoh's snakes were eaten by Moses' snake.

She mused that perhaps it was something that Pharaoh planned in order to bring Moses back to him again. Feeling puzzled no longer, Marissa snapped her fingers and whispered "Of course it is, Pharaoh you are such a sly fox!"

Out by the donkey and camel parking area Marissa sent Abdullah ahead to bring Moses to her. She needed to hear what Moses' thoughts were with the outcome of the snake incident. After a few minutes of thinking and looking around trying to clear her head, Marissa saw Moses approaching her.

Moses saw that Marissa's eyes were sparkling with anticipation of something, but what he was not sure. "Moses, thank you for taking the time to answer a few questions I have. Abdullah you may leave to go get your work done."

As Abdullah left, he whispered, "I wonder if Pharaoh is the sly fox or if it might be Moses' God who is the sly fox."

"Moses, I am on air live and I believe that our viewers would like me to ask you about your cobra, how could it just swallow up Pharaoh's two cobras? What kind of sorcery did you use?"

"How do I answer your question so that your audience shall understand? The cobra that is supposed to help and protect Pharaoh is like a crown that Pharaoh wears on his head. His crown has a symbol on it; that symbol is nothing more than an idol, Marissa.

It is a symbol of power, but has no powers of its own. It is a symbol of authority, but has no authority of its own. That symbol even has a name, Wadjet.

Those two cobras that came forth from the staffs of Pharaoh's men came forth as representatives of the false goddesses symbols Wadjet and Nekhbet, her sister. Not under their self-will, for they are not living and breathing beings. However, under the authority of Satan himself and his magic.

1) Pharaoh's sorcerers gave your magician's the knowledge of how to produce the cobras, but the Cobras had no authority, no power over God's appointed cobra.
2) The cobra that came forth from my staff came forth as a representative of the God of the Israelites. That cobra was

real, not some idol some symbol like the one that Pharaoh wears on his head.

3) God spoke to his cobra and granted him the knowledge of how to defeat the enemy's cobras; nothing and no one has higher authority than the one true God.

God showed the people that he, the God of the Abraham, Isaac, and Jacob, is the God of the Israelite people, the God over all."

Marissa no longer tried to keep her calm, "Enemies of God indeed! You are right in saying that you are an enemy to Pharaoh. We are far from finished with this Moses; Pharaoh shall succeed in showing you for the trouble maker you are!"

"Marissa, I pray God to open your eyes to the truth of the matter here at hand."

"You heard first-hand people of Egypt, how Moses is trying to fill our land with poison. Until further developments arise, this is Marissa for ET NEWS saying 'May the gods of Egypt protect you.'"

Marissa more frustrated than she was before she talked with Moses headed straight for her prayer temple. "I will pray to Ma'at that Pharaoh shall succeed and Moses and his God will meet with doom. Then I and all of Egypt will have a party such as the world has never seen before.

Feeling refreshed after her time of worship Marissa was back at her office and ready to get to work. "Kebi, has Abdullah found Jair yet?"

"Abdullah just reported in; they'll be here in a minute or two."

"Thank you."

Marissa closed the door to her office and looked around. Her favorite spot in her office was her lounge chair, covered with a pillow the length of the lounge itself. The lounge chair was made of stone, her body pillow to lay on being one of the most important things in her office. It was red, one of her favorite colors and filled with goose down feathers.

Along with her desk, Marissa also had two other slab chairs for guests. One chair with blue silk covered pillows on it and in the corner on a rock table sat her miniature idol known by the name of Hapi. He was a typical household god worshiped by all. However, when Marissa had more troubling issues, she went to worship Ma'at.

Looking around her office with satisfaction she took her sandal's off and laid upon her lounge chair. Relaxing for that small moment in her office, she pridefully whispered; "I want my Emmy, I must have that Emmy, but more than that, I must help Pharaoh get rid of the enemies that have slithered into Egypt. ET NEWS will shine after I get done with Moses and Aaron."

In the middle of a pleasant dream Marissa was awaken by Kebi on the intercom system, "Marissa; Abdullah is here with Jair."

Hurriedly getting up from the lounge she answered, "Send Jair in and tell Azad, he may start getting ready for our next broadcast." As Jair opened the door, Marissa was purring like a kitten, "Jair how good to see you, what have you been doing with yourself?"

"Spying Marissa, spying what else would I be doing?"

"Of course Jair, I am sorry. What information do you have for me?"

Jair reported while heading for his favorite spot, "Moses and Aaron plan on meeting Pharaoh at his bathing and worshiping spot early in the morning."

"These two are no longer spotted goats. I believe they are python snakes that have come to try to squeeze the life out of Pharaoh and Egypt. Do you know what they have planned?"

"No, but I am sure they'll give another plea to let the people leave as that seems to be their primary concern."

"At least the palace magicians must have taken you seriously when you sent word explaining to them what Moses and Aaron had planned. They were prepared for them today; I need you to keep working and finding out what you can for me."

Marissa seated now rose and headed for the door, "Right now, I need you to go find Abdullah and let him know we are to be at Pharaoh's bathing spot next to the water at dawn. Thank you, that is all for now." Jair barely rose from his seat as Marissa came to him and shoved him out of her office. Closing the door behind them both she took off walking down the hall in pursuit of answers.

Chapter 9
Plague 1: "Water Turned to Blood!"

"I hope Pharaoh is in a good mood this early in the morning. I see Marissa and Abdullah are hiding around the corner. Is Marissa going to bulldog us until we leave Egypt?" asked Aaron.

"Marissa is not our concern; we knew ahead of time that the whole world would be watching. Let us just concentrate on our message to Pharaoh, shall we?" replied Moses.

ET NEWS: BREAKING NEWS: "Suicide Assignment."

"Marissa with ET NEWS. For you viewers who are up bright and early, Abdullah and I are at the palace. We have followed Moses and Aaron on what seems to be a suicide assignment. We are just outside the outdoor temple; it is here that Pharaoh conducts his morning bathing and worship to the Nile gods on behalf of his people.

Moses and Aaron plan on walking into this area and delivering another message to Pharaoh. Because Moses and Aaron are entering Pharaoh's bathing spot and worship area, we are not allowed to film what is about to take place between Moses and Pharaoh. However, I have sent Abdullah to accompany Moses and in this way you'll be able to listen to the conversation. Abdullah, are you set up? Do you see Pharaoh?"

One of the men called to Pharaoh, "Moses and Aaron are across the way." He then yelled over to Moses, "Moses, you are not to be here, this is a sacred place."

An agitated Pharaoh demanded, "Moses, why are you and Aaron here? You are in my sacred spot used for cleansing and for the worship of the Nile gods, why are you disturbing me?"

Aaron spoke, "God, the God of the Hebrews, sent me to you with this message, 'Release my people so that they can worship me in the wilderness.' So far you haven't listened. This is how you'll know that I am God. I am going to take this staff that I'm holding and strike this Nile River water: The water will turn to blood; the fish in the Nile will die; the Nile will stink; and the Egyptians won't be able to drink the water."

Moses said to Aaron, "Take your staff and stretch out your hand over the waters of Egypt—over its rivers, canals, ponds, and all its reservoirs—so that they turn into blood. There will be blood everywhere in Egypt, even in the wood and stone containers."

Before Aaron could use his staff, Marissa appeared. "Abdullah! Get this on camera! We are no longer listening; we are live on camera. We're here to let you see what happens when Moses' God threatens Pharaoh, in his worship spot no less.

We are witnessing Aaron as he tries to make the Nile River turn into blood! It appears that Aaron is waving his staff in the direction of the tributaries and ponds. Look how slowly he is moving toward the swimming and bathing pools. I do not believe it! The water looks like it is turning into blood!"

Looking intently at the water Pharaoh called for his counselors, sorcerers, and magicians.

Marissa spoke, "People, it appears to me that the magicians are in a huddle conversing with the sorcerers. I am unable to hear what is being said; however, I think they are chanting something to the Nile gods."

"Jannes, we have to do it now, Aaron has almost completed the circle," said Jambres.

"Have we all found our spot on the water to turn to blood?" asked Jannes. "Yes, do it!"

Just as Aaron was about to complete his circle in obedience to God, Jannes, Jambres and Jabr, went to different pools of water and turned them into blood.

Jambres laughed and called from across the way, "Aaron, are you just performing another cheap trick? We have also turned water into blood!"

"Yeah! A goat has more common sense than Moses and Aaron!" laughed Jabr. The three laughing and mocking magicians yelled, "What a joke!"

"Hey! Where did Pharaoh go?" Jannes asked.

"He must have gone back inside," answered Jambres. Puzzled by Pharaoh's sudden departure the men went back inside the palace.

"It is apparent that Pharaoh feels his magicians, sorcerers, and counselors have a plan to take care of this situation before sundown.

In the meantime, we will all just have to drink our Zytum and our wine. I have every faith that Pharaoh knows what he is doing. So for now, this is Marissa for ET NEWS saying 'May the gods of Egypt protect you.'"

Full of anticipation that Pharaoh had a plan to rid Egypt of Moses and his God, Marissa and her crew headed back to the ET NEWS office.

Goshen

On the walk back to Goshen, Aaron asked, "Moses this affects *all* people, Egyptian and Israelite alike, does it not?"

"Yes, Aaron, we'll all suffer this one, God has a lesson to teach all people. No water for seven days, completion, perfection, effectiveness."

"What are you talking about?"

"I am sorry; I was just thinking how interesting it is that the number seven—as in seven days—has the same meaning in the Hebrew language as it does in the Egyptian language," answered Moses.

"And that is the completion, perfection and effectiveness?"

"That it is, and it is a number used by God to show completion and perfection. God declared that he completed the making of the world in seven days, and also called the seventh day 'Holy.'

God said anyone who killed Cain would suffer God's vengeance seven times. God also spoke to Noah and told him to take seven pairs of every animal with him on the ark. My wife is one of the seven sisters, I had a choice of marrying. Do you understand what I am saying, Aaron?"

"I am beginning to understand the meaning of God's seven. However, how is it that the Egyptians consider the number seven the same as our God does?"

"Egypt suffered a famine for seven years. The Egyptians believe their god Hapi was responsible for releasing seven cubits of water, just the number needed to relieve the famine. In Egyptian the pool symbol representing water contains seven zigzag lines.

The Egyptian goddess Isis was guarded by seven scorpions when she went looking for her husband's body. Also, it is believed by the Egyptians that the number seven stands for perfection."

"I wonder if Pharaoh, or any of his men, shall pick up on that since they have no idea this shall last seven days?"

"They would not admit it, but I believe that the wise men and counselors shall pick up on it. Aaron, trust me they will."

"Why is God afflicting all the people with this plague and not just the Egyptians?"

"God is punishing all people for worshiping and relying on other gods."

"What have we made an idol out of that we have brought this upon ourselves?"

"Aaron, the Israelite people, are just as guilty of worshiping the Nile River as the Egyptians, even though we do not worship the river in the same way. We do not take food and animals to the different gods to appease them.

We do, however, rely on the Nile for our staples: leeks, lettuce, cabbage, and for our meat. We also rely on the Nile's water for drinking, cooking, bathing and cleaning.

When it looks like we may be running low on these things, do we ask our God, the God of Abraham, Isaac, and Jacob to replenish the waters of the Nile? No! We hope that the Egyptians shall soon appease their gods, so everything shall be alright.

We are just as guilty of worshiping the Nile gods as the Egyptians are; we just do it in a different way. We do not do it on purpose, but still we have forgotten about God.

God is reminding us that he is the one who provides for us, and he is the one who loves us. It is time we remember who our God is and what our God has done for us.

You and I must help our people to understand this. We need to help Thaddeus, Dan, and Asher, make sure they get through the next seven days without getting mad at God."

ET NEWS: BREAKING NEWS: "Three Days of No Water."

"Hello everyone, this is Marissa for ET NEWS. Today marks the third day of bloody water. People are being forced to dig holes around the Nile to find water, and it still comes up as blood. Every time they smell dead fish they ask Hatmehyt why she has allowed all her sacred fish to die.

I spoke with some of the locals, and they think all shall be back to normal in the next few days. I am out here on the streets with some of our viewers who would like to give their opinion on Moses. Your name is?"

"I am Ghada, Moses I do not know how you managed to imitate Pharaoh's magicians. However, I wish you had not caused them to make the water in our vessels to become as blood. You created the water problem without even warning us. We are living in an awful mess! How could you do that to the people who treated you with nothing but kindness?"

"Thank you, Ghada, I like that question. Moses, care to answer that question the next time we see each other? You are Mahdi?"

"Yes, I am Mahdi. Moses you cannot hurt us; Pharaoh is worshiping our Nile gods, so by the end of the day the water should be back to normal. We have three Nile gods: Hapi, Khnum, and Heket. It probably took them some time to get together to give Pharaoh an answer, but by tonight all should be normal. Who do you think you are? You shall not beat us and cause us to give up on our Pharaoh!"

"Wow! Thank you, Mahdi that is very encouraging to hear. We have time for one more, and your name is."

"Rahim, Moses may you and Aaron, and all the Israelite people suffer ten times over for the problems you have brought upon Egypt."

"Thank you, Rahim, it looks like you are having trouble with your Egyptian fan club, Moses. That is all the time we have for now. Until further developments arise, this is Marissa with ET NEWS saying 'May the gods of Egypt protect you.'"

Marissa made her way back to her office in time to find Jair waiting for her. "Kebi any messages while I was gone?" Kebi looked up from her paperwork long enough to say, "No messages." Marissa opened her office door, "Jair come in and tell me where Moses and Aaron are, what are they up to?" She closed the door and hung up her shawl as Jair looked for his favorite chair.

"I have not seen them; it seems that they have had private meetings with Thaddeus, Dan, and Asher."

Walking back and forth to get rid of frustration Marissa prods Jair, "And... what about those meetings? What are they saying? They have to be planning their next move!"

Jair sat straight up in his chair and shouted, "I cannot get into those meetings! They have those meetings in a private spot with no way for someone uninvited to get in; there is no way I cannot get close enough to find out what is going on. The talk around town tells me that Moses and Aaron are having trouble with keeping the approval of their people right now. It seems they have had to suffer the same as the Egyptians."

With satisfaction on her face Marissa looked Jair in the eye and said, "Good, they are getting what they deserve." Back to pacing Marissa questioned, "How can Moses, expect to promise the people freedom, and then bring this cursed blood for water on them and not be hated by the public?

At least they are smart enough to know that their liberty from Pharaoh is not going to happen. Maybe if the people of Goshen, rebel against Moses and Aaron, they'll just leave. As to all the slaves of Egypt, they are slaves and not good for anything but hard labor. They should be made to suffer more than their owners!" Feeling righteous, Marissa went and sat behind her desk.

Jair feeling totally unappreciated got up from his seat and

declared, "Not all of us are stupid, there are some of us that are made to live a really good life."

Marissa got up from her seat to comfort Jair, "Of course, of course, what was I thinking? I am sorry Jair, for a moment I forgot you came from the land of Goshen. You are a great help to me." She purred, apologizing and not meaning a word of it.

Leading Jair to the door, Marissa said, "Hopefully tomorrow you'll have a solution to this problem. I am going home, keep in touch." As Marissa opened her door, she said, "Kebi go home it is getting late." "Thank you, Marissa."

Talking to herself, Marissa said, "I think I'll stop off and spend some time at the temple worshiping Ma'at. I need some more answers."

ET NEWS: BREAKING NEWS: "Five Days, Still No Water To Drink."

"Hello everyone, this is Abdullah for ET NEWS. Today is the fifth day that we have had blood for water. I spoke with community members, and people are concerned that all the gods of Egypt have abandoned us.

During this attack of our waters, the crocodiles seem to have left the area. We have not heard a word from Sobek, the protector of the Nile. Therefore, the people are vulnerable to attacks from other predators.

The religious community is very insulted by this whole incident. Marissa, I have been told by a messenger of the priests, that the priests are unable to clean themselves as directed by the law of the gods.

As the priests are unable to perform their daily cleansing, they cannot pray to our gods. The Nile, that is the lifeline of the Egyptian people and the land, seems to be full of death. The priests are not allowed to have anything to do with this death. They too appear to be waiting for Osiris, Khnum, and Hapi to come to our rescue. Marissa, can you hear the cry of the people? Abdullah held the microphone out for Marissa to hear the people's cry.

"Where are you, Osiris?"

"We need you to respond to our crisis, Khnum."

"Why won't you save your people, Hapi?"

"When can we have food again?"

Marissa: "Abdullah have you found anyone who wishes to speak into the camera?"

Abdullah: "Not today. People say that because of the unclean state they are in, they'll only talk to me, away from the cameras, but that is all"

Marissa: "Well, it is the custom of any honorable and noble Egyptian to be clean and this blood in the water situation is unacceptable. That is why I have you out in front of the camera."

Abdullah: "A few weeks ago the crop farmers gave thanks to the god Hapi, for bringing in the inundation, so that the ground would have enough water for the plants to grow. Their concern now is that the blood or blood like water might smother the newly planted seeds. Could anyone have known such a problem would have come to the people of Egypt?

In talking with the Livestock and Cattle Association Official, it seems that drinking the blood or blood like water, in place of regular water is not acceptable for the animals, and some have died because of it; others are weak from thirst. Dead livestock creates another problem to the livestock farmers.

Marissa: "How are the people able to cook their meals and clean themselves?"

Abdullah: "People have been digging holes for water around the Nile, and those holes also had bloodied water. However, since it does not smell like death, people say they are using it for cooking and drinking—if they have no Zytum or wine left to drink. Cleaning and bathing are still a major problem.

Some people have oils and perfumes to clean their

bodies—however that is only good for a while; and no one wants to use bloodied water for bathing."

Marissa: "Have you heard anything about the harm to the environment?"

Abdullah: "People have been complaining about air pollution. Dead fish are a problem; when fish are rotting they contaminate the water and make it undrinkable. Rotting fish are also causing a terrible stench. The wind blows the smell of the dead fish across the land, causing some to wear cut linen material around their noses so they can breathe."

Marissa: "Abdullah, this is another strike against Moses in the case that Pharaoh is building against him. Pharaoh has the right to have Moses killed if he can prove to the gods that Moses is blaspheming against the gods and the kingdom.

I am sure I speak for the Egyptian people, in general, when I say I hope that happens real soon. That is all the time we have for now. Until further developments arise, this is Marissa for ET NEWS saying 'May the gods of Egypt protect you.'"

Goshen

Moses asked, "What is on your mind Aaron?"

"I am saddened that no one from Goshen has come to you and asked what they have done to cause this plague of the water. No one has asked you if you would make the water clean again."

"Aaron without the knowledge that you have, would you be thinking about coming to me and asking, "What have we done to cause this plague? Would you have asked me, a common person, to take the plague away?"

"You are right Moses, I would not be thinking that way."

Moses instructed Aaron, "The suffering of God's people shall not last as long as that of the Egyptians. In the meantime, we need to pray and teach Thaddeus, Dan, and Asher how to pray for the people."

"Thank you brother, I needed to hear that. Hey, tomorrow is the big day? The day when the bloodied water shall be drinkable water again?"

"That is why we need to get some sleep; tomorrow is going to be another big day. I am going home, Shalom Aaron."

"Shalom," Aaron said as he shut the door to his house.

Egypt

At the ET NEWS building, Marissa was in her office conferencing with Jair. "This is getting old! Jair, have you done everything possible to find out what Moses and Aaron are up to?"

"All is quiet out in the land. Everyone is busy digging holes to find drinkable water. They are attempting to find water that is not full of dead and smelly fish. Are you aware that this plague has caused the crocodiles to leave? And have you seen the land, it is a mess out there!"

"What do you mean have I seen the land? I am out there everyday reporting on this situation. Of course, I have seen the land! Enough of this, let's get to the root of the problem!" The intercom system beeped, "What is it, Kebi?"

Kebi winced in pain from Marissa's screech, "Abdullah is heading your way."

"Thank you. I wonder what Abdullah has found?" questioned Marissa, as she slowly paced the floor.

"Looks like we are about to find out."

A very excited and out of breath Abdullah opened the door to Marissa's office and shouted, "Marissa!"

"Calm down and tell me what is going on!" demanded Marissa.

"I got here as fast as I could. The water is water, the blood has disappeared!"

"What?" exclaimed Marissa and Jair at the same time.

Jair quickly got up from his seat and asked, "When? Have you seen it for yourself?"

"Yes, I was on my way to work when I decided to take a detour to go look at the Nile, you know, just in case. That is when I saw it—the Nile is normal again, no more bloodied water!"

Marissa asked, "Are you sure it was not a hallucination?"

"No! I mean, yes; I am sure. I looked around and all the people were jumping for joy, they all saw it too!"

"What are you waiting for? Get out! Get out and go cover this great miracle from the gods! Jair, you go and track down Moses and Aaron, I want to talk to them."

"On my way," replied Jair. Marissa left with Abdullah and her crew, shouting, "We'll be out in the field with breaking news regarding the water issue—if you need us while we are out."

Kebi absent-mindedly said, "About the water? What about the water? She is getting nuttier by the day."

ET NEWS: BREAKING NEWS: "WATER!"

"Hello, everyone out in Pithom, Rameses, and Succoth. I am Marissa with ET NEWS. After seven days the Nile River water is no longer blood; it is drinkable, usable water.

As you have probably already experienced, there appear to be no more traces of blood in the water. It is totally back to normal, praise to Pharaoh and the gods of Egypt for that.

Abdullah and I are in Goshen waiting to speak with Aaron. Unfortunately, Aaron is not here today, but we do have Moses with us and he is ready to answer our questions."

Marissa: "Moses, you and Aaron have been quiet these past seven days, were you hiding from us?"

Moses: "We were not hiding as you put it. There simply has been no reason for us to be in your land."

Marissa: "Now that the water is back to normal, would you explain to us what the point was for us having to suffer for seven days with this blood plague? I think we can call this a plague, it sure felt like one."

Moses: "Marissa, you and I know the Egyptian people worship many gods and goddesses. Let me place them in order to make sure everyone understands what I am saying:

1) Ptah, you acknowledge as being the creator of all creation.
2) Amun, is a god who was given authority by Ptah to create the universe. Then you also have the fourfold deity, representing the four elemental gods.
   A) Ra, your god of fire.
   B) Shu, your goddess of air.
   C) Geb, your god of earth.
   D) Osiris, god of the water.

You worship Pharaoh as a god—he is the son of Amun-Ra, is he not?"

Marissa: "Yes of course he is, what is your point?"

Moses: "Marissa, I have just shown you six gods and goddesses that the Egyptian people worship and what they represent. Now your people also add to the mix the Nile River— which is worshiped as the lifeblood of the people and the land. Three main gods are attached to the Nile River.

1) Khnum, the creator, and ruler or guardian of all water, not just the river's source. This is the same god you, claim forms every human body on his potter's wheel. His wife, Heket, you acknowledge as the one who breathes life into your body before being placed in the mother's womb.
2) Hapi, the spirit of the Nile River. He is the one whom you say floods your land with water and brings rivers of life to the land and the people for another year. You acknowledge him as being the giver of life itself.
3) Osiris, who is acknowledged as the life's bloodstream of the Nile River. Real Egyptians are to become like Osiris so they may be save from the devourer when they die. Osiris is the

god who judges the living and the dead. You say he is the one who judges your soul when you die. If your soul is found to be pure and sinless, he'll allow you to enter the kingdom of bliss. If your soul is weighted down with any sin or crime, then he throws your soul down to the pit with Ammit, the Devourer of Souls."

Marissa: "Yeah, yeah, we know that, answer my question!"

Moses: "Marissa, the Israelite people worship one God, the God of Abraham, Isaac, and Jacob. *He* is the God that created the world and gave life to all animals and plants.

Our God gave birth to *all* people, even the Egyptian people. Anything that has breath, our God gave that breath of life to. Our God, the one true God, formed man from the dust of the earth and blew the breath of life into his nostrils. It is our God who gives the water of life to the people and the land through the Nile that he created.

It is our God, the God of Abraham, Isaac, and Jacob, who judges the living and the dead. It is our God that threw Satan out of the Heavenly Kingdom and opened the earth to swallow him up in his kingdom called Hell.

We have *one* God to do what the Egyptians say at least ten of their gods and goddesses do! The God of the Israelites showed all people that not one of the Egyptian gods and goddesses were able to do anything about the water situation. Why? Because they are not a living, breathing being like our God. They are wood and stone—something that has no capability of seeing, hearing, tasting, or touching anyone or anything."

Marissa: "I do not know who this Satan is, and you still haven't answered my question! What's the matter, are you not able to tell me? Not enough brain function left to give an intelligent answer to my question?"

Moses: "It is you who is not able to hear what I am saying, let me try it again. When our God's cobra had Egypt's cobras for a snack, it demonstrated our *one* God's supreme power over your many gods' so called power. So before you say anything, this leads to step two, the blood. Pharaoh's refusing to acknowledge God's power, required God again to show himself as the Supreme Ruler of all.

He did this by causing the Nile River, the life source of Egypt, to become as death. None of your gods stopped this process. As a matter of fact, the whole country watched as Pharaoh's magicians helped to turn more water to blood. However, did any of them bring the water back to normal? No! Our one true God waited a full seven days, reminding each and every person of his supreme authority. Does that answer your question, Marissa?"

Marissa: "Who do you think you are? You are telling me that all our gods are dead gods. Your God is not the Supreme Ruler of the world! Pharaoh has to be close to building his case for a full-blown death sentence for you, Moses. Your God, Supreme God over all our gods, indeed! Moses, I am done speaking with you!

There you have it people, you heard it!" shaking her head in disgust and beginning to wrap up her broadcast, "Moses and Aaron are thorns that Pharaoh needs to pluck from the land. I think we'll all do well to stay away from them while Pharaoh builds his case against Moses and his God. The evidence will then show them guilty of blasphemy against the gods of Egypt and against Pharaoh; Moses and Aaron will then be rightfully put to death.

We have not completed our journey with Moses and Aaron. We'll be reporting events as they come in or as the facts develop. Until then, this is Marissa for ET NEWS saying 'May the gods of Egypt protect you.' Abdullah! Let's get out of this Goshen land and back home where we belong!"

As Moses and Aaron watched Marissa and Abdullah walk back toward Rameses, Aaron asked, "How would they react if they knew that this is just the beginning?"

"The same way as they are now, Aaron, the same way they are now. They are not capable of understanding what is coming. Come on, let us find something to eat."

Chapter 10
Plague 2: "Frogs?"

Marissa was in her office having a conversation with Jair. "All I know is that Moses and Aaron are spending time with their God, getting refreshed is how they put it. Just shows you that they are wearing themselves out trying to make Pharaoh look bad." replied Jair.

"I do not like this; things have been to quite for too long, men like Moses do not try to make Pharaoh look bad and then just disappear. He is planning something for us, get out there and find them and do not come back until you do!" ordered Marissa.

Palace

At the palace, the magicians were in their conference room talking over the events of late.

"What do you think Moses is going to try next?" asked Jannes.

"I am not sure, but you can bet your cat, they are conjuring up something with their God. They'll not be satisfied until they make us look bad again," answered Jambres, lying about on his concrete bleacher seat.

"I know that, we better come up with something. Pharaoh was not pleased that we made water to blood. Not being able to reverse the spell made things even worse. Moses is going to try and give Pharaoh a case of leprosy or attack Heket somehow, and we need to be ahead of him," observed Jabr, who was pacing back and forth.

"Why in the world would he want to give Pharaoh a case of leprosy? This is just not feasible; however, it would make sense for him to blame Heket," replied Jannes, who was leaning on the wall.

"Yes, it would make sense. He went after Khnum, Sobek, Hapi, and Osiris last time, and they are all Nile gods. Yes, let's go find Wamukota and see what we can do with frogs," said Jambres.

Jabr stopped pacing and laughed at the thought of getting even with Moses and his god, "I can't wait; we'll be ready. What a goat!"

The intercom system in Marissa's office beeped. "Jair is here." Busy reading a competitors' news article Marissa replied, "Send him in." The door opened, and Marissa's face lit up with anticipation, "Ah, Jair since I said not to return until you saw Moses or Aaron, I assume they have crawled out of their hole?"

"They have shown up, and my informant says they are about to have another confrontation with Pharaoh," answered Jair.

Licking her lips Marissa asked, "When?"

"They were heading for the palace's outer courtyard when I left them,"

Marissa spoke into her intercom, "Kebi, get me Abdullah! Tell him to meet me out front." Marissa went over and grabbed her linen shawl off the hook, opened the door and said to Jair, "Well, what are you waiting for, Egypt to have snow? Let's get going!" Marissa walked by Kebi's desk and said, "Kebi, we'll be at the palace with Moses." Kebi, who was busy trying to get a message to Abdullah, answered, "Thank you, Marissa." Then whispered, "Oh brother, here we go again."

ET NEWS: BREAKING NEWS: "Pharaoh's Outer Court."

"Hello everyone, this is Marissa for ET NEWS. Everyone should know by now that this would have been our ninth day without water. However, the water came back to us yesterday morning. It feels so good to have pure water back in our lives.

We give thanks to our God Hapi for taking care of his people! He provided the water we needed so that the land may give us food for another year. That water was receding when the blood came into the water. Therefore, the receding water helped to eliminate the blood faster than it might have otherwise.

We are still unsure how long we'll have to wait before we have fish to eat. The palace officials were kind enough to let us know that it was simply a case of *red tide* that came from the mountains around the Nile, due to the rains. As we all know, that happens on occasion; a red algae comes in and causes our life to become miserable. We are just thankful to the gods that the Palace's Water Management Officials, were able to find out for us what happened. With this information, we have proven that Moses and his God are liars.

I am at the palace's outer courtyard, where Moses and Aaron are about to confront Pharaoh again! Should be very interesting; it seems they never know when to quit. Abdullah, have they arrived?"

"Moses and Aaron have arrived at Pharaoh's outer court, apparently, with another message from their God. Let's see if we can see what is taking place."

"Moses, what is it that you want this time? I grow tired of you and your God," asked Pharaoh.

Aaron spoke: "Thus says the Lord, 'Let my people go out to the desert to worship me. If you refuse to let my people go, I'll bring upon your whole country a plague of frogs. The Nile River will be overrun with frogs. You'll have frogs in your palace, in your bathing spots, in your bedrooms and your beds! I shall not spare your officials; they too will be afflicted with the frogs.

They'll be in your servants' houses. All the people of the land will suffer the frogs. They'll be in the ovens, and they'll leap into your mixing bowls while your bread is being made. The frogs will jump on you, and jump on your people, and they'll also jump on your officials, not one living thing will be spared.'"

Moses turned and spoke to Aaron; "Hold your staff over the rivers, canals, and ponds. This will bring the frogs onto the land."

Abdullah exclaimed: "Frogs! The frogs are only tadpoles at this stage—where will he come up with frogs?"

"Here we go again, Jannes it seems that Moses will never learn.

Jabr, watch as we teach you how to bring forth frogs onto the land," instructed Jambres.

"We can handle anything Moses, and his God, decide to dish out," replied Jannes. Aaron held his staff over the Nile.

"Marissa, I can see frogs coming-they seem to be riding in on the waves of the Nile. Wait! Now they are coming in as tall and broad as the waves themselves. If I did not see this for myself, I would not believe it. People, do you see this? Marissa do you see this?"

"I see it, I just don't understand why Moses would want to give us more frogs. Frogs are a blessing to the people, a blessing of fertility, why would he want to bless us?" asked a confused Marissa.

Pharaoh shouted, "Magicians! Sorcerers! Counselors! Do your job!"

"Yes, O Pharaoh," they all replied at once.

"Marissa, the magicians are standing together with the sorcerers. It sounds like they are calling forward frogs from the ground here where we stand. I cannot quite hear what they are saying; however, it must be working. Look! The frogs from Pharaoh's magicians seem to be coming up from the ground. What are we going to do with all these frogs?"

Pharaoh, rose from his seat, "Moses, I have told you '*no*!' My slaves are not going anywhere, and you may leave."

Laughing and taunting Jannes shouted, "What are you going to do now, Moses? You just do not seem to understand, there is nothing you can do that we cannot also do."

Jambres taunted Moses also while laughing hysterically, "You keep acting more like a diseased goat every day."

"Aaron it is time to leave." said Moses, not giving the time of day to Jannes or Jambres.

"But the frogs, how do we not step on them?" asked Aaron.

"They are sacrificing their lives as God has asked them to; we'll have to step on them when we leave. Let's just make sure they are dead and not wounded, so they do not have to suffer," said a saddened Moses.

"Marissa, are you seeing this? The frogs came in so thick that Moses and Aaron had no choice, they had to step on the frogs killing them when they left the palace. It is a crime to cause harm to these frogs in any way. People you have just witnessed a most peculiar happening. Moses and the palace magicians have produced frogs. However, they have produced too many frogs. It is a death sentence to kill a frog accidentally-how are we going to keep our frogs safe? How are we going to keep ourselves safe?" asked Abdullah.

"Frogs, the symbol of our Goddess Heket. People, I cannot say why Moses chose to use the frogs against us. Moses just placed capital punishment upon himself and every person in the land of Egypt!

We need to pray that Heket puts capital punishment for the death of the frogs, upon Moses, and that she tells Pharaoh to pardon his people for the involuntary killing of frogs. I hope Pharaoh's men find a quick solution to the problem of frogs overtaking the land of Egypt. This story is not over, we'll have more for you as it comes to us. Until then, this is Marissa for ET NEWS saying 'May the gods of Egypt protect you.'"

Moses and Aaron

About half way home, tired of watching himself step on frogs, Aaron asked, "Suffice to say this affects the Egyptian and the Israelite people, right?"

"Yes it does. God is using the frogs to invade our homes, reminding his people that we have been holding Heket, the Egyptian's goddess of fertility, as the one who nurtures us from conception, and not God himself."

"Why is the goddess of fertility worshiped?"

"It is believed that before being laid in our mother's womb Heket breathes the breath of life into our body. They worship her because, they say, she blesses our midwives and stands beside a mother and guides her in childbearing."

An astonished Aaron replied, "Moses are you serious! I have never paid attention to such things. Wow! How stupid can you get, they really believe that it is some woman with the head of a frog; that breathes the breath of life in them before being laid in their mother's womb? They believe that she blesses them and keeps them safe while being carried in the womb? If that is not enough, they believe that this goddess watches over their mother when she gives birth?"

"Not just that, Aaron, some of us Israelites have bought into this form of worship as well, brought on because we became tolerant and allowed inner marriage.

God is saying to his people, 'You really want to worship a frog over me? I'll send frogs to you and remind you what a frog really is, an animal that I made! By the time, I place a death upon these frogs you will remember it is I, the great I Am, who breathes life into every person, into every animal or plant. Anything that breathes air to live is given that breath by the one true God, not some idol.' It's a lesson I hope we learn and never again forget."

"Do you think our people will get the point? I wasn't aware of this going on."

"I think they will start to wonder what is going on, but more to the point, will Pharaoh get the point? God said he would understand it enough to see the sin that he is causing; not liking what he sees he will refuse to bow down. I am thankful that God is on our side."

"Do you think that the people will ever realize that worshiping a statue of an individual who has the head of a frog is foolishness? Do people really believe that this frog goddess controls the fertilization of their food as well?"

"It makes me more and more thankful that my eyes are open to God; that he leads me in the path of righteousness."

"Let's head to the house, Elisheba should have something prepared for us to eat. I do not know about you, Moses, but I'm starving."

"Me too, let's go and find some breakfast, Ha Ha!"

"Ha Ha! To you too, you are hysterical. With our food being covered in frog slime, I think I'll be going on a fast," replied Aaron.

Rameses

Jair sat in his favorite chair and day dreamed about spending the money coming to him. Meanwhile Marissa paced back and forth ranting and raving about the whole frog situation and how unfair Moses and his God were being to the Egyptians.

Having finally calmed down Marissa walked over and sat down, "Jair what have you been able to find out?"

"What?" replied Jair, "Oh, well the whole of Egypt is just now beginning to fill up with frogs. It seemed when Moses said the whole of Egypt, he meant the whole of Egypt. There is not one house, hiding spot, or cave that isn't filled up with frogs. You can't walk, sit, or move without frogs being there to haunt you."

Marissa stood up and slammed her hand down on her desk, "This is not acceptable. You must go out and get more information on Moses and Aaron. It has been three whole days of this chaos. I need to know how Moses is coping with all these frogs. I need to know what he plans on doing to get rid of these frogs! Just go out and get me some dirt on Moses and this frog situation. Jair, you better not let me down. Abdullah and I had better go out and make an appearance to the public—the people have a right to know what is going on."

Jair went and opened the door to make a swift exit, "I'll get back to you as soon as I hear something." Marissa followed Jair out of her office, "Kebi, Abdullah and I'll be out giving an update, call me if you hear anything."

"If I can find a calling system that hasn't been slimed by these frogs!" she replied in disgust.

ET NEWS: BREAKING NEWS: "Three Days With the Frogs."

"Hello everyone, this is Marissa with an ET NEWS update. It has been three days since Moses, and the palace magicians, brought frogs upon the land. The whole country has become overrun with frogs. There is not one house, hiding spot, or cave that isn't full of these frogs. You cannot walk, sit or move without frogs being there to haunt you.

We thought that the frogs would have settled down by now; however, I have every faith in Pharaoh and his men, they'll have everything back to normal soon.

People, do not lose faith-do not lose hope. The priests must be able to make contact with Heket very soon, and then her frogs shall go home. We are a stronger people than Moses, and his God, think we are. Abdullah, I understand you are about 100 meters away listening to some of the women and they are not very happy; care to let the people see what is going on?"

"Marissa, I am over with a group of women who are trying to perform their daily tasks among the frogs. Ladies, I am Abdullah with ET NEWS. Would you mind telling us how you are coping with the frogs?"

"My name is Aziza, Abdullah, have you ever tried to make bread while you have frogs jumping in with your dough?"

"My name is Jamila, Abdullah, have you tried baking the bread in our earth ovens? I opened the ground where I made our oven and was planning on heating it up, I found so many frogs in my oven hole that I wondered how they could breathe." Abdullah tried to cut in, "Well that..."

"My name is Suma and I am not very happy, let me tell you! No bread for days! How long can we go without baking our bread?"

"You think that is bad I have frogs in my bath water, in my dishwater, in my toilet. How can I take care of my children that way?" asked Aziza.

"I know. I can't sleep, can you?" asked Jamila. Abdullah once again tried to cut in, "I know..."

"It is hard to go to sleep with frogs in my bed and on my sheets. How am I ever going to get my sheets clean again?" asked Suma.

"If I can get into bed then my husband and I are surrounded by frogs!" complained Aziza.

"I know, there's frog dust and frog slime everywhere!" complained Jamila.

"We are eating, sleeping and drinking with these frogs!" complained Suma.

"I sure hope Heket, finds her frogs and takes them home soon," commented Aziza. Abdullah tried one more time to cut in, "I don't..."

Suma spoke, "I know! With the children, it is hard not to have accidentally harmed one of the frogs. I do not think it would be right if families were to be punished by death because they harmed a frog.

Especially when they had no control over the environment. Time for me to get back to work, if I can find a spot worth cleaning that is." The other two women also said their good-byes to each other and left without acknowledging Abdullah at all.

"There you have it Marissa those women were so upset they forgot I was even around." "Fortunate for you I think, until further developments arise, this is Marissa and Abdullah for ET NEWS saying 'May the gods of Egypt protect you.'"

Marissa waited, "Abdullah, I need you to help me walk, I do not want to trip on these frogs."

"I hope I do not trip, trying to keep you from tripping."

Marissa replied sarcastically, "Oh, great!"

Goshen

Jair finally found a clog of bulrush to hide behind so he could listen in on the conversation that Moses and Aaron are having. "Frogs! Move over I need to be in this spot," ordered Jair.

"I wonder how Pharaoh feels about his bed being filled with frogs—the very animal worshiped to help produce children?" asked Aaron.

"He does not seem to be too concerned or he would have called for us by now. I continue to remind myself that it is all in God's good timing," answered Moses.

There was a knock at the house entrance. "Gentlemen, come in, what do you need?" asked Aaron.

How much longer is this going to go on... this frog business? My wife fell down last night and killed a bunch of frogs. Have you ever smelled a bunch of dead frogs? Everything is frogs or frog slime! How do we clean up? Also, the food is terrible!" complained Thaddeus.

I have been fasting; it is better than trying to eat bread that has frog residue, and drinking out of cups that have had frogs in them," said Dan.

"How about you, Moses, how does it feel to you every time you go to sit, and you drop on frogs? When will this end?" asked Asher.

"This ends when God says it ends, and he has not said anything about it ending recently. Until he does, it is our responsibility to show the people that God is in control. The people are suffering; this to have their eyes opened to the fact that they also have sinned, and to repent of the wrong they have done.

God is working with us to help them remember who he is; that all power belongs to him. As for sitting down, you should know by now that you are in control of your environment. You have the authority to tell the frogs to move before you sit. You did not invite them into your space. Let us remind the people that as long as this goes on, they do not have to work the mud pits; they should be thankful for that," answered Moses.

"This is information I can use to help Pharaoh's magicians! I'll go fill them in on this conversation," said Jair as he scurried off toward the palace.

ET NEWS: BREAKING NEWS: "Five Days In a Row!"

"This is Marissa with an ET NEWS frog update. It has been five days! How long can Pharaoh let these frogs be in control? We just got our water source cleansed, and now it is polluted again, this time with slime. Our Agriculture Department Official, Luzige is here to give us an update. Thank you for taking the time to be with us. Could you tell us how the crops have been affected most recently by the frogs?"

"Our crops have been hit hard twice in the past month. Without the help of Heket, I am not sure how our crops will survive this year. The frogs themselves are not the problem. It is the sheer number of them that has been our biggest problem. They have no choice but to be on top of the crops. The crops have not benefited from the constant pressure on them either."

"Thank you for that report, Luzige, we'll have you back with further updates as needed. We now turn to our Official of the Livestock and Cattle Association, Maskini. Thank you for taking the time to be here, what can you tell us about your situation?" asked Marissa.

"I am on my way back from a livestock producer meeting and

we are all experiencing the same thing. Our livestock is forced to stand or sit on frogs. Do you know how many livestock producers have lost livestock due to falling on frogs? Some of us are losing livestock because they have a hard time finding water; when they do, it is full of frogs!

Barely having time to recover from the blood, now our livestock suffer from frog residue and slime. What's next—a swarm of flies to fill our water once again with filth? Where is Pharaoh? These frogs are a direct attack on Heket and Hapi—so where are they in all of this?"

"Thank you, Maskini, for that report; we'll have you back with further updates as needed. Some of the women in the city of Rameses are here to voice their concerns."

"I do not want to be held responsible for the death of any frogs! I found them dead when I opened the ground oven to put my bread in!"

"That is right! They are impossible to keep away from; it is frog pollution I tell you!"

"Tell the Israelites' God to take his frogs back, we do not need them!"

"What did you mean when you said that the Israelites' God can take his frogs back?" asked Marissa.

"Marissa, I believe these frogs are not from Heket. These frogs are acting like they have been brought in from someone else trying to invade our territory. The only one with that kind of magic is Moses' God."

"That is a very interesting thought, thank you for that information. Thanks to all the people who have gathered together with us today. You were a great help. You have been watching Marissa with an ET NEWS update. Until further developments arise, 'May the gods of Egypt protect you.'"

Palace

"Jair, I assume that Marissa has sent you to us with an update?" asked Jambres.

"Yes," Jair informed the men, "I was able to listen in on a conversation between Moses, Aaron, and the three mountain goats. They seemed just as upset about the frogs as we are. They demanded to know when the frogs shall leave."

Jannes declared, "This proves the Israelite people are no different than we are; they know who they are and want to stay living the way they have been. Moses is forcing this other God upon the people."

Jair went on to explain, "Moses said this ends when God says it ends. He went on to tell them it is their responsibility to show the people that God is in control. He tried to say that the people are suffering these frogs so that their God can open their eyes to the fact that they also have sinned.

Moses then told them that they are to repent of the wrong they have done. I think the craziest thing I ever heard was when Moses told those men that it was up to them to control their environment. Moses said, and I quote: 'You have the authority to tell the frogs to move before you sit. You did not invite them into your space.'"

Jabr laughed and asked, "Moses really told them they had control of their environment? Oh boy, Moses is crazy!"

"Crazy or smarter than we realized," commented Jambres, deep in thought.

"Moses reminded them that as long as this frog situation goes on, they do not have to work the mud pits, and they should be thankful for that," declared Jair.

"Yes, that does bring up a concern for Pharaoh—his progress in the city has stopped because of all this nonsense. Did Moses say anything about his next plan of action?" asked Jannes.

"That was all I heard," replied Jair.

Baraka knocked and opened the door. "Baraka, how can we be of your help?" asked Jabr.

"Pharaoh is requesting the presence of all his counselors, sorcerers, and magicians," answered Baraka. "Tell Pharaoh we are on our way," replied Jambres.

"Jair, we look forward to hearing from you again. Would you like to walk with us as far as the meeting room?" asked Jannes. "Thank you, I think I will," replied Jair.

As the men approached the meeting room Jambres remarked, "Sounds like it is getting intense already—we had better get in there. See you later, Jair."

As Jannes and Baraka closed the door behind them, Jair looked around and saw no one. I think I'll stick around and see if I can find out what Pharaoh is up to; I had better be careful since there seems to be no easy spot to hide at." As Jair was concentrating on the conversation going on behind closed doors, a palace guard shouted his name: "Jair, what do you think you are up to!"

With a firm grip he takes Jair by the arm and says, "I'll escort you out... do you want me to lose my job?" The guard continued speaking to Jair while he escorted him to the outer court area. Jair is busy saying to himself. "Good going, Jair, you were not able to even hear what was going on... oh well, time to go snooping around elsewhere." Jair was so busy in his thinking, it took him a minute to realize that he was standing alone outside the palace entrance door.

Back in the palace, the officials were busy telling Pharaoh enough is enough. "We cannot take this anymore, frogs, frogs, everywhere frogs! Do you want to know what the peasants are singing when they think no one can even hear what they are singing?" asked Osaze.

"Frogs! Frogs! We thought we loved the frogs.

Now all we breathe, eat, sleep and dream is frogs!

Frogs! Frogs! We thought we loved the frogs.

Now we hear the loud crunch of death in every step we take.

Frogs! Frogs! We thought we loved the frogs.

We need some peace, and we need some food, what will Pharaoh do?

Frogs! Frogs! We thought we loved the frogs."

"That is what the people are singing?" shouted an outraged Pharaoh. Those attending the meeting, Aamir, Baraka, Courtier Obaid, and Osaze tried hard not to show their frustration at this whole situation.

"The people are losing heart. We are not supposed to kill a frog because they are sacred; yet every time we are forced to walk we hear the sound of, crunch, crunch, crunch. I did not know frogs could make such a loud noise." complained Courtier Obaid.

"Yeah, I hate to sit because when you sit, you are sitting on a bunch of frogs. If you are lucky enough to have them jump off, you are sitting on slime," complained Osaze.

"Pharaoh, have you not noticed how hard it is for us to bathe you with frogs jumping all over you and sliding down because of the oils we use? How about trying to bathe in a pool that is full of frog slime?" complained Baraka.

"How upset do you think the other gods are? We cannot give them the proper time of day because the frogs get in the way," commented Aamir.

"Enough! You all complain like a bunch of old ladies. Waugh, Waugh, Waugh. I'll not ask you to call the frogs home because I know you are not capable of doing so. I do not need to call for Moses; I'll contact the gods and goddesses on my own.

Tell me my counselors, magicians, and sorcerers, what good are you if you cannot do what I need to have done? Get out of my presence, or I will not be responsible for my actions!" Pharaoh shouted.

ET NEWS: BREAKING NEWS: "Seven Days, Will It Ever End?"

"Hello everyone, this is Marissa with an ET NEWS update. Today is the seventh day that we have spent with the frogs. I never knew frogs could be so loud; there is no silence. Everywhere you go, all you hear are frogs. How many of you have tried to have a conversation around these frogs?

We are at the palace's outer court awaiting the arrival of Moses and Aaron. Pharaoh requested an audience with them, and we are here to make sure all of Egypt sees what takes place. Here they come now… it appears as though Moses is going to speak this time."

"Moses, how nice to speak to you and not Aaron. To what do I owe this honor?"

Moses bowed and spoke, "I was instructed to speak this time. What can I do for you?"

"I challenge your God, to see if he can get rid of the frogs. I grow tired of them—I want them gone! I say to you, pray that the Lord would take these frogs away from me and my people. Then your people can go to offer sacrifices to the Lord."

"You have the honor of choosing when I should pray for you, your officials and your people. Then the frogs shall leave you and all your homes. The only frogs left will be those in the Nile where they belong."

Marissa whispered, "It appears that Pharaoh is thinking about when to have Moses pray. He must have a plan."

Pharaoh replied, "Pray for me tomorrow."

"Tomorrow you shall have the answer you have asked from God. God shall do this so that you'll know there is no one like the Lord our God. The frogs will leave you, your homes, your officials, and all your people. The only frogs you'll find will be those in the Nile. Enjoy the rest of your day, my Pharaoh."

"We have just witnessed something very interesting—Pharaoh has a most unusual plan. Will Moses pray to his God for us tomorrow? Will his God be able to do as Pharaoh has asked?

"We'll see you bright and early tomorrow morning with the results from today's court appearance. For now, this is Marissa for ET NEWS saying 'May the gods of Egypt protect you.'"

Later that day Pharaoh's palace official and others were in a conference going over Pharaoh's meeting with Moses. "Why would Pharaoh want to wait a day to get rid of these frogs?" asked Baraka.

"He must believe that Heket and Hapi shall show up and bring their frogs home," said Osaze.

Jambres, deep in thought tried to remember Moses' every word, "Moses promised that the frogs will leave, but how is he going to do it? He never told us how it would happen, did he?"

"I believe tomorrow will be a very exciting day one way or another," said Jannes.

Goshen

Moses ended his songs of morning worship to God with, "Great and precious is our God. The only one who can fix anything. Great and mighty is our God, the one who holds us dear. Great and powerful is our God, the one who gives and takes away. You are precious to each of us. May we always sing praises to you, our God.

Moses was praying to God, "Pharaoh finally asked for help from you to get rid of the frogs. On your behalf the frogs were brought into Egypt. At Pharaoh's request, I ask that you would take the frogs away.

Let Pharaoh and all people see that it is the great I AM that holds supreme power over all the land of Egypt. I ask that you would let the frogs die in their homes, in their yards, anywhere that they are at this moment in order to remind people of your mighty power.

Death to all the frogs wherever they are! Do this so that the people would witness your greatness, your great signs, and great wonders. God, I ask that the frogs may be piled in heaps and cause the land to stink with death. I ask that the people choke on the very symbol of what they have worshiped. Thank you for all you do. Amen."

God responded, "Yes, Moses, I am honoring your prayer and answering you as you have asked. Go out and be with the people. Continue to persevere and take courage that you are doing well in my sight."

ET NEWS: BREAKING NEWS: "Death of the Frogs!"

"Good morning everyone, this is Abdullah with an ET NEWS frog update. When you got up this morning, your first thought was: 'Are we going to have to endure another day with the frogs?' Looking around you realized that sometime while you slept, the frogs died.

No visible reason for their deaths—it is as though they just went to sleep and never woke up. Marissa said to remind you to be praising Pharaoh, Hapi, and Heket for sparing us from suffering an eighth day of frog infestation.

I also need to bring to your attention that according to the gods of Egypt, seven is the number of completion and perfection. Marissa wanted me to remind you that Pharaoh endured the frogs on behalf of his people for seven days in order to show perfection and completion of the war against Moses and his God.

Pharaoh has instructed the people to stack the dead frogs up into heaps. Then they'll be burned and covered with dirt. Because this land is full of air pollution once again, we need to go and get our linen patches to put over our noses. How will it take for the slime to clear itself out? I wish I knew. 'Until further developments arise, this has been Abdullah in for Marissa with ET NEWS.'"

Palace

"Jibade, I find that I can once again breathe. What a delight to enjoy peace and quiet and to be able to bathe and worship the gods undisturbed. However, I am glad that I was able to endure the frogs for the sake of the gods; I believe now that the war is over between me and Moses. Our gods and goddesses have won because of me. How do you feel about the whole thing?" asked Pharaoh.

"Ah yes, to eat without the taste of frogs on my food and to sit without them climbing all over me. Speaking of that, do you think the slaves can get back to building the city again soon?" asked Vizier Jibade.

"You are right!" Pharaoh slapped the table with the palm of his hand, "Yes, Jibade, you are right. Why should I give up the slaves? They are my slaves after all! Now that I can breathe again why should I let the slaves go? They belong to me and not some made up god. My slaves must stay with me. Jibade, I have decided the slaves stay with me in Egypt; they are not allowed to leave. Send a messenger to Moses stating what I have just said."

Vizier Jibade bowed before Pharaoh, "Yes, Pharaoh, it shall be done."

ET NEWS: BREAKING NEWS: "The Slaves Stay!"

"Hello everyone, this is Marissa with an ET NEWS update. Pharaoh sent word to Moses stating that the slaves are to stay in Egypt; they will not be allowed to leave at this moment in time. I wonder how Moses reacted to this news. Let us turn now to other news.

For health reasons, the Department of Health has required the piles of dead frogs to be burned. Our air quality is in jeopardy due to the fumes in the air brought about by the death odors of the frogs. The health department is advising everyone to pull out their linens to wear over their nose. We hope to have a live broadcast with Moses and Aaron soon. For now this is Marissa for ET NEWS saying 'May the gods of Egypt protect you.'"

Goshen

Moses was experiencing a quiet moment on the back porch of Aaron's house. Moses thought about how nice it had been just to relax for a moment. Aaron walked up to Moses and said, "Thaddeus told me that Marissa and Abdullah will be here any minute."

Moses wanted nothing more than to continue relaxing in his chair under the canopy and so he said, "You go and answer her questions and may God be with you." Moses then closed his eyes and leaned back enjoying the peace and quiet.

Aaron not wanting to meet with Marissa either said as he was leaving,

"Thanks, Moses—you are no help at all sometimes, you know that?"

"Yeah, I know," laughed Moses. "Life is hard and sometimes I just need to be able to pick on my brother."

ET NEWS: BREAKING NEWS: "Frog Update."

As Aaron walked toward Marissa, he mumbled to himself about how unfair Moses could be at times. "He was gone for years and yet it is like he never left. Baby brothers." Since he was now close enough for Marissa to hear what he was saying, Aaron turned his thoughts to the job at hand. "Marissa, how nice to see you again. Moses sent me to meet with you today. What can I do for you?"

Marissa looked at Aaron with disgust, "We are here to get some answers; our viewers have a few questions about the plague of frogs that we just went through. I was hoping that you or Moses could help our viewers with some of those questions." Aaron responded, "Absolutely! When?"

Abdullah shouted, "Marissa, we are on in five, four, three, two, one, go."

Marissa primped her hair and looked into the camera, "Hello everyone, this is Marissa with an ET NEWS update. We have made a special trip to Goshen where we have Aaron ready to answer a few of your questions. I would like to remind our viewers that there are those who say they felt like this attack by the frogs was more of a plague than an attack.

However, Pharaoh made it known that what happened was meant to give us a time to prove our loyalty to our gods and goddesses. We have succeeded; please remember that Pharaoh endured on our behalf and has won the war between him and Moses. I would like to thank you, Aaron, for agreeing to this interview."

Aaron greeted Marissa, "Nice to be with you again, Marissa."

"Thank you, Aaron, nice to be with you. Viewers, I want to remind you that the questions Abdullah and I ask are questions you have already submitted. We will use these to show the stupidity of Moses and his God—not to give them credit.

Aaron, now that the frogs have all died, would you care to explain to our viewers why we had to endure this plague and for what reason your God, placed this upon us? I can see why he would do that to his own people—but we are not his people, so why us?"

Abdullah had a hard time keeping the camera still as he was laughing at the shocked expression on Aaron's face.

"Let me ask you a question, Marissa. Do your people believe that Hapi is the god of the Nile, that he controls the soil deposits, and that he therefore gives life to Egypt's soil?"

"Hapi is the one, yes."

"Heket is your goddess of fertility; the goddess that you acknowledge as helping your women have a safe and successful birth, is she not?"

"She is one of the top worshipped for that reason."

"Isn't she also the wife of Khnum? The Khnum that the Egyptians worship as the one who created them from a potter's wheel. The one who you say creates the souls of all beings? Don't Egyptian's also claim that Khnum's wife is the one that blows life into every soul, before one is placed into the womb?"

"Yes, Heket is the wife of Khnum and the breath giver of all life, so what?"

"Your statues of Heket portray her as a person with the head of a frog! Your statues of Khnum also portray him as a person with the head of a goat. My God, the one true God, made all people in his image.

MyGod, used the frogs to show all people that he is God over everything and everyone, including the frogs and the goats. God— for those who choose to see—used the frogs to show the people that nothing is made by someone that is depicted with the head of a goat.

Nothing receives the breath of life, its first breath, by someone with the head of a frog. The only one who forms people or animals and breathes life into them is the one true God. That was the point of all this.

My God, wants people to see how foolish it is to worship these idols over the one true God. So will you continue to worship Heket now that you know she is not now, nor has she ever been a living being?

As Marissa squirmed and tried to find the right answer, she replied: "I did not make her the way she is but I worship her anyhow. What does this have to do with the frog overload we suffered?"

Aaron's facial muscles tightened as he tried hard not to say: "Hey stupid, what does it take to make you understand?" Instead, he responded: "Our God, the God of Abraham, Isaac, and Jacob showed all people that Hapi has no control over the soil and the fertility of the land. Did you see Hapi anywhere around taking care of the frogs during that seven-day ordeal?"

Marissa plenty agitated by now responded: "No! I didn't see our god Hapi; however, I am just an average person so he would not show himself to me!"

Aaron gave Marissa a duh look and then said: "Okay, how about Heket? Did she seem in control of all those frogs when they were here for seven days? When the frogs were being killed or suffering from being stepped on or sat on, did Heket stop it? Talk about a brutal way to die! Come on, Marissa, any god that is real and alive wouldn't have stayed hidden while that was going on!"

By now Marissa was quite upset and she tried hard to resume control of the interview. "Aaron, you are avoiding my question, what was the point of this mess?"

"Did either of your gods call their frogs home—back to the Nile? Obviously not! If they were living, breathing gods, they would not have let the frogs die, now would they? Not only that, but none—not Pharaoh, his sorcerers, or his magicians—could call the frogs home or they would not have summoned Moses to get rid of the frogs."

"It was just a test, part of Pharaoh's plan."

"Marissa, Pharaoh asked Moses if he would pray to the God of the Israelites to get rid of the frogs! He promised that if Moses prayed to our God and the frogs left, then he would let the Israelites leave. Pharaoh promised to let us go out into the desert and worship our God as soon as the frogs no longer existed. Moses agreed, went out the next day, and prayed to our God on behalf of Pharaoh and all the people.

Our God took all the frogs away; the only frogs left are back in the Nile where they belong. This proves once again that the God of the Israelite people is the one true God! Another thing, our God never goes back on his word or breaks a promise. Pharaoh made a promise to release the people to go to worship our God, if our God got rid of the frogs as Pharaoh asked. God did that expecting his people to come and worship him. Pharaoh, the minute he was comfortable, reneged on his promise."

By then Marissa was very frustrated, stunned, and tongue-tied. Suddenly she announced, "This interview is over! My people of Egypt, it seems that once again Aaron is trying to fill us up with lies and cause confusion among the people. I have stopped this interview before Aaron and the Israelite God so poison some of you that you start siding with them. For now, this is Marissa for ET NEWS saying 'May the gods of Egypt protect you.'"

Chapter 11
Plague 3: "Microscopic Bugs!"

Moses was singing in morning worship to God. "Great and precious is our God, the only one who can fix anything. Great and mighty is our God, the one who holds us dear. Great and powerful is our God, the one who gives and takes away. You are precious are you to each of us, our Great and Mighty God. May we always sing Praises to you our God."

Praying Moses said, "Glorious God, what would you have for me to do for you on this day? I pray for the people who are in this time of trouble; may they make it through with love in their hearts for you. Open their eyes that they might see your glory and come to understand that you are fighting this battle. Let them see that you are victorious, and that you win the battles for them. Help me to help Aaron in his understanding of you in this journey we are on. May we make it through this day with a stronger love for you. Thank you, God, for this day. Amen."

God responded: "Tell Aaron to hold out your staff and strike the dust on the ground. All over Egypt the dust will turn into lice [gnats]."

Moses replied, "As you say, Lord."

Moses and Aaron were at their favorite spot in the field next to the Nile, not too far and yet not too close to the houses in Goshen. They sat on large, smooth rocks and relaxed in each others company.

"God has placed a plague of tiny flying insects upon all people and all the animals of the land, right?" asked Aaron.

"Yes, God has one final lesson for his people, and then he will separate his people from the Egyptians. God is reminding us that the gods of Egypt are nothing more than idols made of stone and wood. He is letting his people see that he is fighting the battle against Pharaoh for us, and he is always the winner."

"I hope that our people remember that God is the supreme power and that to worship or rely on Pharaoh or any of his gods is nothing more than sheer foolishness," commented Aaron.

"Yes, and it is our responsibility to pray for and to educate the council elders. I do not know about you, but I am hungry; let's go have some breakfast before the insects get here, Ha!"

"Ha! Ha! to you too, brother! Ha! Ha! to you," said Aaron.

ET NEWS: BREAKING NEWS: "Invasion of Insects?"

"Good morning, this is Marissa with an ET NEWS update. It seems that Moses and his God have hit us again. Without warning! The palace guards have spotted what looks like a swarm—a huge black dust cloud of insects coming our way. People, prepare yourselves for a war against insects. Pharaoh said that the war between him and Moses was over.

However, it looks like Moses and his God are not ready to concede defeat. This insect attack is unfair, and there are too many kinds of insects to know how to prepare ourselves. We have warned you; now go and prepare the best you can. Until further developments arise, this is Marissa with ET NEWS saying 'May the gods of Egypt protect you.'"

Palace

Pharaoh had completed his morning worship and was busy preparing for the rest of his morning routine. His servant announced Vizier Jibade's arrival. "Jibade, come in. What has come up that you hunt me down?" asked Pharaoh. "It has been reported that a swarm of insects seems to be coming straight for us. Kamenwati first reported the swarm, and now Yamanu is tracking its progress." So far there seems to be no way to divert them, and sooner or later they'll be upon us."

"Moses! I'll get you for this!" screamed Pharaoh.

ET NEWS: BREAKING NEWS: "Are You Covered Up?"

"This is Marissa with an ET NEWS update. I hope that all people are wearing their linen breathing material, as well as, some linen material over their heads. Even now it is hard for me to talk to you. We have had to endure three days with these insects attacking us.

Recently we heard from Aaron, and he explained to us that the God of the Hebrews told Moses to have Aaron hold out his staff and strike the dust of the earth. That is how Moses' God produced these miserable insects. How rude! In the past, we were warned when Moses' God would strike us, why the sneak attack?

These insects are: biting, stinging, impossible to see, vermin. The presence of vermin is against our laws and customs to have around. We are experiencing the same problem we had with the blood and the frogs. We cannot communicate with our gods this way; they can have nothing to do with us!

Remember to use your Ben oil for the insects. If you are out of Ben oil, I suggest some Tea Tree Oil or some Peppermint Oil. I see people seem to be cutting off their hair. I have with me Enna, one of the temple priest's messengers, who has agreed to give us an update. You may speak to the people."

Enna spoke, "The temple priests asked me to let you know that they are gravely concerned about the life of their community. For the third time in less than a month, they have not been able to perform proper temple rituals. As the sacrificial animals are contaminated by this insect attack, we have had to quarantine them.

It has been impossible to communicate with Geb, our god of the earth. We have had no earthquakes lately, and so it appears that Geb has not been laughing. The priests have received no word from Seth, our god of the desert. It is from Seth's land that these insects have come, and Seth's a fierce warrior, one can only wonder what we his people have done to justify such a vicious judgment upon us.

The priests are doing the best they can, please know they'll continue to do what they can for the people."

"Thank you for that report. Until further developments arise, this is Marissa saying 'May the gods of Egypt protect you.'"

In the conference room of the palace magicians, Jambres, Jannes, and Jabr were discussing their current crisis. "We have had five days with these insects and I do not think we are getting anywhere. All our attempts to get rid of them have failed!" complained Jabr.

"That is of little concern to us, Jabr. Right now Pharaoh is mad at us for not being able to get rid of the frogs. He had to summon Moses to get rid of the frogs, and he blames us for it," complained Jambres.

"Jambres, you know that was Wamukota—that left handed ninny-he got the formula for that spell wrong. The sorcerers come up with the spells; we just make them come alive," replied Jannes.

"You had better not let Wamukota hear you say that! Pharaoh was pleased with our production of the frogs until all his officials started complaining," complained Jabr.

"You must admit I was beginning to get cranky myself. I wonder why Heket or Hapi did not come to help Wamukota with that. Do you suppose Pharaoh has displeased the gods somehow?" asked Jambres.

Jannes scolded, "Jambres you are talking yourself into big trouble, and keep your tone down—you do not know who might be listening in."

"That is what you think, Jannes. I think it is time we go and have a talk with the counselors. Jair has not left any messages lately, and we have no idea of Moses' next move," said Jambres.

"An excellent idea," replied Jannes.

ET NEWS: BREAKING NEWS: "Devastation by Insects."

"Hello everyone, this is Marissa with an ET NEWS breaking news, moment. We are suffering the fifth day with these insects; although it is hard to do, I am here in my office. It is my duty to keep you informed of all that is going on. Abdullah is out and about via satellite, Abdullah, are you there?"

"Thank you, Marissa. It is very hard to see all the devastation that has happened because of the insects. People are telling me that the insects carry a very painful and irritating sting. They have had trouble with them creeping into their eyes and nose. It is a difficult thing to witness this insect invasion, and no one seems to be immune to these insects. I have Maskini here with me; he is the Official of the Livestock and Cattle Association. I believe he has an update on this situation, Maskini."

"Thank you, Abdullah, I have just come from attending another livestock meeting with the palace's overseers of livestock. A common problem we found with all our livestock is death. Our animals have been traumatized: first the blood, then the frogs and now the insects. I am not sure, but I think the insects are a type of lice and yet others feel they are a gnat.

Either way they are driving our livestock crazy. So many are dying, and the insects seem to have no mercy. They climb into their noses; they buzz in their ears, and there are some that are sucking the life's blood from our animals. As they go to yawn, the insects dive into their mouth. It must be painful when they enter the mouth because they always make such a scream.

Do you know how hard it is for you when all you hear day and night are your animals screaming in pain? It echoes through the night. When you think you are about to get a break, one of your family members begins moaning from the pain that the insects have caused them.

It is worse for the children because they are not able to understand what is going on. Our elderly are not able to fight off the pain, and they succumb to death. Another problem we have is not being able to bury our dead. Every time we disturb the dirt the invasion of insects is too much for us to handle. Pharaoh, we need you to pray to Geb, and get this straightened out for us!"

"Thank you, Maskini, for that scary, but truthful report. Luzige, the official of our Agriculture Department, is with us to give an update on how our farmers are coping."

"Thank you, Abdullah. Most of us have been so devastated that we have no concern about the future of our food; however, I am here to tell you we should. It all started just as the Nile was giving life to the land for one more year. The crops we planted have experienced attacks by blood, frog dust, and frog slime. Now it is insects attacking our soil, our plants—all in less than a month. Every time we try to hoe the dirt or walk on the dirt, the soil seems to produce more insects. Consequently, proper soil care is out of the question!

I make this plea on behalf of all farmers in Egypt. Pharaoh, where are you? Please put this to rest! I do not know how long we can survive this war."

"You have all heard straight from the horse's mouth, so to speak. The devastation that this war has caused is beyond words. Now back over to you, Marissa."

"Thank you, Abdullah. I believe we can think of this as an all-out war. However, this is not like any war we have ever fought before. Our very hope is in Pharaoh and his priests to put a stop to this and soon. When we have further updates, we'll let you know. Until then, this is Marissa for ET NEWS saying 'May the gods of Egypt protect you.'"

Off camera to the public, but still able to talk to each other, Marissa spoke: "Abdullah, I am exhausted; I am going home. I think you should take the rest of the day off too. See you tomorrow."

Abdullah said, "Thank you, Marissa, I think I will."

Goshen

"Moses, what are we to do? Our people are suffering tremendously, and they have had to cut their hair! It is a bad thing when we are forced to cut our sacred hair," complained Thaddeus, who was sitting in the corner.

"Thaddeus, God knows the hard time you are experiencing. We pay this price because of the others that have done wrong. Our season of suffering is almost over; do not trip at the finish line. Go out and teach the people to sing praises to the Lord. When you sing praises to God, even in your sorrow, you win every time. Encourage them. Soon it shall be finished."

Dan, who had been listening up until now asked, "My wife has some Ben oil, [see glossary] and a few homemade remedies; this is so hard on the children. What can we do for the little ones?"

"There is not much we can do. Keep putting the salve on and give them some broth. Play with them and do whatever you can to take their minds off what they are suffering. As they grow, never let them forget what they have experienced at this time. This you do so that they may not make the same mistakes as their ancestors," answered Moses.

Asher, who was pacing asked, "I have tried hard to calm my people; they are starting to get very cranky with me. You realize we have had a few elderly that have died from the insect bites in my area of Goshen, don't you?"

"I am aware of this; tell the people that when the time of mourning is over they'll be burying their loved ones in peace. No more suffering, pain, or sorrow is going to be on them due to the plagues yet to come.

The Lord has told me that after the insects leave, his people shall receive grace and mercy. They'll have God's favor while they remain in Egypt. Very soon the insects shall also be gone. Now go and be encouraged, this war is almost over," answered Moses.

Palace

"Wamukota, have you had any success with contacting Imhotep? I need medical healing, and I need it now!" shouted a very sore and cranky Pharaoh.

"O my Pharaoh, I know not why, but I have had no response from Imhotep. Here—try some of this special tea I have made with the help of the sorcerers. It'll help with the pain."

"Help how? I want the pain gone and gone for good."

Wamukota handed Pharaoh, his tea, "I have consulted with other sorcerers in the palace; we found a book of spells, and they are making a salve that shall heal your wounds at this very moment."

Pharaoh waved his hand at Wamukota, declining the tea, "I want you also to make contact with the priests and tell them to contact

Sekhmet. These insect bites hurt, Ouch! I'll contact Renenutet; my guardian should he be able to help me. Where is that salve?"

There came a knock on the door; Wamukota yelled: "Come in, and hurry with that salve. You, chamber servant rub this salve on Pharaoh. Gently, I warn you, as he is very sore. I'll be going about my business and check in on you later, O my Pharaoh."

"Yes, yes, leave me in peace."

Sorcerers and Magicians

"Seven days—we have had to contend with these insects for seven days! Why has Pharaoh not asked to have the insects taken away?" asked Jabr.

"That is why we are all gathered here—to come to a conclusion about the insects. Come and sit down, Jabr, pacing cannot make you feel any better. Pacing back and forth only attracts more insects and misery to us all. What are we going to tell Pharaoh? He should be here any minute," stated Jambres.

"Whether we want to admit it or not, this is *"The Finger of God"* and only he can get rid of them. Who wishes to be the one to tell Pharaoh when he gets here?" asked Jannes.

Wamukota volunteered, "I'll tell him; it is my responsibility."

"I appreciate that, but I am the chief of the counselors; I'll do it." replied Yamanu.

The door opened; it was Pharaoh, and he was in a foul mood. "What have you my counselors, sorcerers, and magicians come up with to get me out of this jam? It had better be good, and you better do it quick!" ordered Pharaoh.

"Pharaoh, after much time and ...." "Stop the tab dancing!" shouted Pharaoh. Yamanu stated, "We have come to the conclusion that this is *'The Finger of God.'*"

"'Finger of God! The Finger of God!' Are you trying to tell me that you think the finger of the God of Moses brought these insects to *my* land?" asked Pharaoh.

"Yes!" they all replied at the same time.

"Out! Out! Now, all of you out! What a bunch of spotted goats!

How did I come up with such poor counselors? Moses, you can take your insects and do all you want; I shall not let my slaves go!"

ET NEWS: BREAKING NEWS: "Finger of Moses' God!"

"This is Marissa with an ET NEWS update. I have just received word that Pharaoh's counselors told Pharaoh that this was brought on by the 'Finger of the God' and to call Moses for help. Pharaoh has refused to ask Moses for help and declared that he shall not let the slaves leave.

People, I say to you do not lose hope—remember Pharaoh is a good and righteous man—if he says he'll not ask Moses for help, he has a good reason.

Until further developments arise, this is Marissa for ET NEWS saying 'May the gods of Egypt protect you.'"

Goshen

Moses and Aaron were walking home from relaxing at their favorite spot. "Why is God hardening Pharaoh's heart? I am still a little confused," asked Aaron.

"God explained it to me this way. He is not hardening Pharaoh's heart by changing who Pharaoh is in his natural tendencies. He is not forcing Pharaoh to act against his will. Every time that God displays himself with the signs and wonders he has been performing, Pharaoh sees something about himself that he does not like.

It reminds him of some sin, he is committing which he does not want to stop committing. If Pharaoh were to change for the better, he would have to stop the practice of sin and admit that he has been wrong.

Pharaoh is not about to do that, so instead he hardens his heart against God. God has created each man in his own image; therefore, each man has free will. In having free will we turn to the good of God or we turn to the evil of self and the devil.

When evil sees good it turns bitter toward the good; if it wants no part of the good it sees. Enough with the lessons, Aaron; when everyone wakes up in the morning, there shall be no more insects. Therefore, Marissa is going to be hounding us for an interview. I need some sleep—how about you?" asked Moses.

Shalom, don't not let the bed bugs bite," laughed Aaron.

"Ha-ha! Shalom, my brother."

ET NEWS: BREAKING NEWS: "Insects: Gone!"

"This is Marissa with ET NEWS. Good Morning, Egypt, what a glorious day! How many of you realize that sometime in the night the insects left? I did and let me tell you I feel wonderfully blessed. Geb must have gotten back from vacation, and when he realized what was going on he called his insects back to the ground.

I have sent Abdullah out to get a response from Aaron via satellite. Pharaoh was right; we needed no assistance from Moses' God, after all. Abdullah, are you with Aaron?"

"Yes, I am. Aaron, the insects went back home last night. Pharaoh did not summon Moses to ask your God to intervene. Your God looked bad; can you tell us what you think happened?"

"The people shall believe what they want to believe. I have high hopes that there are some Egyptians that are beginning to ponder about a few things, and it is to those that I'll address my answer.

Our God said many years ago that he formed a man's body from the dust of the earth; because of the sin of Adam, we'll all return to dust. This plague of insects was against the Egyptians' god, Geb, the one you credit with making the earth. Our God, the God of Abraham, Isaac, and Jacob, is the true God that created the world.

By using me to strike the dust of the earth, God was showing you that your god Geb is not the supreme power you thought him to be. Once again, God used a time span of seven days—the days of completion and perfection. Whether you believe it or not, our God was the one to call the insects back last night while you slept. That is all I have to say."

"You heard what Aaron had to say, and now it is time for you to draw a conclusion on your own. Marissa, back to you."

"People, I tell you that Moses and Aaron are only trying to

confuse you. Pharaoh is a wise and righteous man. Pharaoh shall prevail over the Israelites' God. We'll keep you updated. Until next time, this is Marissa for ET NEWS saying 'May the gods of Egypt protect you.'"

Marissa, met Jair back at her back office, "Why would Moses try to make another move on Pharaoh?"

"Moses' God seems to be attacking Pharaoh and the gods. I do not think he is done with trying to make Pharaoh and the gods look like fools. You of all people should know that," answered Jair.

"What do you mean—I should realize that? Yes, I realize that! What I do not understand is why? When is Moses' next meeting with Pharaoh?" asked Marissa.

Jair sat in his comfortable chair and sipped on tea, "Tomorrow morning when Pharaoh goes out to the Nile to worship."

Marissa went to her door, opened it and said, "Abdullah and I'll be there; go and see what else you can find out about tomorrow. I'll be waiting to hear from you."

Chapter 12
Plague 4: "Flying Insects?"

"Hello everyone, this is Marissa with ET NEWS. We are just outside the entrance to the outdoor temple, where Pharaoh conducts his morning worship to the Nile gods on behalf of his people. Moses and Aaron should be here at any time.

For those of you unfamiliar with the rules of royal temples, by law, no one is allowed to enter. Sacred rituals and ceremonies to the gods occur in this pool area in secrecy. To come here as an unauthorized person is to place a death sentence upon one's self.

Due to this privacy issue at the palace worship pool, we'll not be filming this morning. I have sent Abdullah to walk up as close to the temple as he can, so we can listen in on the conversation that is about to take place. Abdullah, are you set up? Do you see Pharaoh?"

"I have spotted Moses, and he seems to be alone. He is standing in the path leading to the cleansing ceremony. Is he crazy? It looks as though Moses is blocking Pharaoh's ability to proceed to the Nile! We shall see how well this goes over as I see Pharaoh and his men are approaching Moses now."

"Moses you did not bring your brother with you, and why not? Did he grow a brain and decide to leave me alone? Get out of my way!" commanded Pharaoh.

"Not until you hear what God has to say." replied Moses.

Pharaoh, on the brink of becoming livid with being interrupted by Moses, stated: "If it means I can get you to leave me alone to worship my gods, then by all means let me hear it."

Moses prophesied, "God has spoken: 'Release my people to go on a three-day journey out into the desert, and let them go to worship me. If you refuse, then I'll send swarms of flies upon you, your officials, your people and your houses. I'll fill every house belonging to an Egyptian with flies, even the ground outside shall be filled up to overflowing with swarms of flies.

On the day I fill the land with flies, I'll separate the land of Goshen from the land of the Egyptians. No flies shall touch the land of Goshen, where my people live I'll do this so that you, Pharaoh, will realize that I am the Lord, and I am right here in my land with my people. The land of Goshen and my people are not to suffer the flies. In this way, you'll know that I am God in this land. I shall make a sharp distinction between your people and mine. This miraculous sign will happen tomorrow."

"Whatever... you may leave my presence." Moses stepped aside and Pharaoh continued on toward the pool.

Abdullah spoke, "You heard it people; Moses gave another warning and Pharaoh acted as if he never even heard him. That means that Pharaoh has no concern, and you should not either. We have until tomorrow to see how things turn out. Back to you Marissa."

"Moses and his God have given us until tomorrow to get ready for an invasion of flies. I refuse to believe that the slaves in Goshen are not to have to suffer this plague. After all, they are mere slaves. If our land becomes filled with flies, I know that it shall come to nothing.

Pharaoh acted as though Moses is a pimple that he is about to squeeze. Pharaoh's magicians or sorcerers must already have a remedy for these flies, if they appear. Until tomorrow, this is Marissa for ET NEWS saying 'May the gods of Egypt protect you.'"

Council Meeting in Goshen

Thaddeus announced, "This meeting shall come to order! We have asked you all here that we may hear a word from Aaron. Please respect what he has to say. Aaron you may proceed."

Aaron stood in front of the men, "Thank you, Thaddeus. First and foremost, we'll open this meeting with prayer. "God our Father, we thank you that you are with us, we thank you that you have not forgotten us, and we ask for your continual guidance. Amen." Aaron informed the men, "God has called Moses to speak to Pharaoh again."

"What! What does this mean for us! Not again!" the men shouted.

"Quiet! Quiet! Let Aaron speak," ordered Thaddeus.

"I have been sent to let you know that from here on out all God's people who live in Goshen are to stay in Goshen. God is separating us from the plagues that he is now sending to the rest of Egypt. However, we are only immune to them if we stay in Goshen unless otherwise directed by God.

God is showing us, and Pharaoh, that he has chosen us as his own people. From now on we are to remember that God has chosen us; we are to act like we are his children. Remember Abraham, Isaac, Jacob, and Joseph.

There is going to be a swarm of flies, vicious flying insects. They'll be attacking all the people and the animals and the land of Egypt. God says he'll produce this sign tomorrow. He has given to everybody, including Pharaoh ample warning. We'll end this meeting with praise and prayer."

[In song]"Praise to our God, who has not forgotten us. Praise to our God, who shows us his love. Praise to our God, who sends help our way." Aaron went straight into prayer. "God our Father, I ask now that you would be with each and every one of these men. Remind them that they have been spared the troubles ahead. I pray that each of these men would have the strength and courage necessary to complete the assignment that you have given them for their part of the land. Amen."

Thaddeus spoke, "Men, it is your responsibility to go and tell the people in your area of Goshen what you have just heard; you are responsible to make sure that they behave accordingly. Have a blessed day, this meeting is adjourned."

ET NEWS: BREAKING NEWS: "Flies Arriving!"

"We were warned yesterday by Moses that a swarm of flies would be here today. I have just received word that a big cloud looking like a fly filled dust cloud is heading our way. People, you need to prepare yourselves.

Flies are such pests; get out your linen face covers and protect your children. I suppose you had better cover all your food areas as well. Pharaoh has not spoken a word, so I am still hopeful that he has a plan; otherwise he would have warned us.

I have no idea how long these flying insects shall be around. We Egyptians have endured before, and we can endure this time, also. Until further developments arise, this is Marissa for ET NEWS saying 'May the gods of Egypt protect you.'"

Palace

"I'll not bow down to Moses or his God! I do not care what his God is doing to the land. I am the God of Egypt, not some god that cowers before those slaves!" shouted Pharaoh.

"It is just that these flies are... ouch... vicious! Can't your counselors, sorcerers, or magicians come up with a way to get rid of these flying, biting insects?" asked Vizier Jibade.

"Vizier Jibade and I cannot get our work done, and the people cannot pay your kingdom taxes if they cannot function!" said a very frustrated Courtier Obaid.

"You are both crying way too soon; it has only been three days. I have instructed the priests to make offerings to Khepri. We have to give him time to find out what is going on and to respond to our request. You may leave my presence." commanded Pharaoh as he angrily motioned them to leave.

ET NEWS: BREAKING NEWS: "No End in Sight."

"This is Abdullah in for Marissa with ET NEWS. It has been three days, and we are all miserable. Ouch! Flying insects are worse by far than the gnats. I was able to find some of the town's people to see how they are doing. However, because of the severe swollen skin and disfigurement that the flies are causing, they refused to appear on camera.

The God of Moses has been very accurate. I'll thank the God of Moses that these flying insects seem to be leaving the livestock alone. Yes, Marissa would not be happy I said that, but it is the truth from my eyes.

People are another issue. These things seem to be like a Hercules fly. They dive bomb you with javelin speed and precise accuracy, and they love your eyelids. The only suggestion I have is to cover your children's faces completely to protect them. I understand these flies are sucking the very life-blood out of the people.

A word from our farmers is that these flies are reproducing at an alarming rate in the vegetation of our land, contaminating some of our newly planted food. Word from the sanitation department is: 'Please do not leave food lying around and make sure it gets into the disposals as fast as possible.'

Due to the severity of this mixed bag of flying insects, we'll have no more updates until this war with the flies is over. Until then, this is Abdullah in for Marissa with an ET NEWS Special Report."

Palace

Vizier Jibade begged, "It has been six days, Pharaoh, six days the land is devastated! Have you taken a good look out there!"

"Very well, but I do not like it. I'll only give Moses what he needs for the moment. You may tell the others and send word to Moses and Aaron that I need to speak with them. When Moses and Aaron arrive, lead them to my court chamber. You are dismissed."

A relieved Vizier Jibade answered, "Yes, O Pharaoh, as you have asked."

Looking around Pharaoh shouted, "Servant! There you are, send a message to Wamukota, telling him I need medical attention before Moses arrives. When Wamukota has finished covering my wounds, I'll need you to help dress me; then help me to my chamber court to meet with Moses."

The servant bowed and said, "It'll be done according to your needs, my Pharaoh."

Vizier Jibade walked down the business section hallway looking for Chigaru, "I'm in luck, there he is, Chigaru!"

A startled Chigaru replied, "Yes, my Vizier, how may I help you?"

"I need you to deliver this message to Moses immediately."

"As you wish, my Vizier," answered Chigaru.

The Vizier back in his office was busy reading important court documents. Hearing a knock on the door, he said, "Come in."

Chigaru informed Vizier Jibade, "I thought you might want to know that Moses and Aaron have arrived."

"It's about time; I have spent all afternoon trying to appease Pharaoh. You may leave now," replied Vizier Jibade. Thinking to himself: "I had better get my thoughts together before they get here—things could get bumpy when I take them to meet with Pharaoh." A palace guard knocked and opened the door, "Vizier, Moses and Aaron are here for you."

The guard left as Moses and Aaron walked into Vizier Jibade's office. "Moses, it is good to see you, I hope your walk here was pleasant. As you probably already know, I have been instructed to bring you to Pharaoh's Court Center."

"Yes, we had a pleasant walk from Goshen to the palace," replied Moses.

"Come right this way." Opening the door, they found Pharaoh awaiting their arrival.

With a very pleased and satisfied look on his face Pharaoh said, "Ah, Moses, come in! Come in! I wanted you and Aaron to know that I have decided that you may go and sacrifice *here* in this country."

"The animals we use for sacrifices are animals that your people worship. They would stone us to death for that, and you know it. God has said that we need to travel for three days into the desert to make our sacrifices, and that is what we'll do!" commanded Moses.

Determined not to let Moses get the best of this situation, Pharaoh compromised, saying, "I tell you what, I'll let you go, but I do not want you to go very far. When you make your sacrifices to your God in the desert, I want you to pray for me."

Moses reprimanded Pharaoh, "As soon as I leave your premises, I'll pray to God. Tomorrow the swarm of flies that has caused so much harm to you, your officials, and your people shall leave. It'll be as though they were never here. However, you have to stop tricking us. Stop saying we can leave when you do not mean it. You say 'yes,' and then when you get what you want, you say 'no'."

As Moses and Aaron left, Pharaoh remained sitting in his lounge chair in his chamber. Frustration that was buried deep in Pharaoh's soul starts to appear, "This court is dismissed!" he commanded. "All of you leave me!" By now Pharaoh was seething. He tried to find comfort from the infected bites on his skin, while at the same time he contemplated the demise of Moses and his God.

On his way home, just outside the city of Rameses, Moses prayed to God, "Great and precious is my God. Great and mighty you are. I hold you dear to me. Great and powerful is my God. The one who takes good care of his people. Glorious God, I ask that you would call your swarm of flies away from Pharaoh and all of Egypt. Pharaoh has promised to let us go and asked me to pray for him.

I ask that you would take the swarm away from them tomorrow as Pharaoh requested. Thank you for separating and sparing your people from this awful plague. Amen."

ET NEWS: BREAKING NEWS: "Relief at Last!"

"This is Abdullah in for Marissa. She was sickened by the flies and has asked me to give you an update. Moses was true to his word and prayed to his God. While I was getting up this morning, I noticed the flies were thinning out. It is noon, and there is no sign of the flies at all. However, I was told by a messenger of Pharaoh to inform Moses that Pharaoh has changed his mind; the slaves are not allowed to leave to go worship Moses' God.

These blood sucking, skin-tearing, flying insects, have disfigured our people. The people look like they have been through a bloody battle and took a severe beating. We are tired of being sore and miserable. The very land has been devastated; when we look out over the land of Egypt, all we see is a devastated war zone. By a war zone,

I mean it paints a picture of an army of monstrous insects that came into our homes and wreaked havoc!

All of Egypt, except Goshen, is full of microscopic holes. These insects left their waste everywhere—on the ground, in our food, on our tables.

Anywhere and everywhere you look, there is waste that we'll need to clean up. I am too tired and sore to go find Moses and Aaron. Sadly, we'll be left to wonder why these flies have so savagely attacked us. As the land heals and we can function normally, we'll be giving updated reports, so stay tuned for further developments. This is Abdullah, in for Marissa, with an ET NEWS Update."

Goshen

"This attack order was given by our God and was directed at the Egyptian's god Khepri. Do you think the people of Egypt will ever come to that realization?" asked Aaron.

"I do not. The people are too sore and too miserable to consider that right now. As time goes by, people tend to forget the reason things happen or else history could not repeat itself. Pharaoh, however, is a different story. He knows that this is a war against the many gods and goddesses the Egyptians worship." answered Moses.

"What exactly is this Khepri supposed to do for the people?" asked Aaron.

Moses informed Aaron, "He is the God that they associate with the scarabs (dung beetle). In our teachings, we were told that one day the Egyptians were watching a scarab roll her dung into a ball and then push it to her home. Their conclusion was that the sun must move in the same way. So they decided that their god Khepri must push the sun across the sky."

Those are the same thoughts we would have if not for the grace of God—we must always remember that. Without God in our lives, we are not capable of understanding the one who created us. And without his help, we are not able to withstand and resist temptation, or refrain from evil and sin. These are reasons that we should be consistently giving thanks to God."

Chapter 13
Plague 5: "Diseased Livestock!"

"Thanks to Pharaoh and all the gods of the land, for the hard work it has taken them to get things back to normal. All has been quiet, so we can assume Moses and Aaron have finished harassing us. We have succeeded people, and we should all be proud. We can breathe again.

We have had a tough go of it; however, we are Egyptians, and we can persevere. I look forward to a break; I'll be with you as we get the information on the restoration that we expect to take place soon. Until then, this is Marissa for ET NEWS saying 'May the gods of Egypt protect you'".

Marissa felt like taking a casual walk back to the office and sent Abdullah off to run some errands. Basking in her glory over Moses Marissa was startled back to reality when she heard her name being called. Marissa turned her head just in time to see Abdullah running toward her.

Irritated at being disturbed Marissa asked, "Abdullah, what is your problem? I sent you on an errand, why are you here?"

"He is at it again!"

Marissa gave Abdullah one of her I am about to claw your eyes out, looks and said, "So much for my casual walk. Who is at it again, Abdullah, what are you babbling about?"

"Moses! He is headed this way with a message for the Pharaoh!"

143

"Moses? Are you sure, did you see him coming?"

"No, Jair ran me down and told me to let you know."

"Moses what are you up to? Let's get over to the palace and get ready to go live, Hurry!"

ET NEWS: BREAKING NEWS: "Will Moses Ever Let Us Rest In Peace?"

"This is Marissa with an ET NEWS update. We are live at the palace; Moses should be in front of Pharaoh again at any moment. Will Moses never let us rest in peace?"

Pharaoh tired of this thorn in his side said, "Moses you are becoming dung to me. What do you want this time as if I did not already know?"

Moses replied, "This is what our God, the God of the Hebrews says: 'Let my people go out to the desert to worship me. If you refuse to let them go and continue to hold them in slavery, then I'll bring a terrible plague on your livestock. That means your horses, donkeys, oxen, camels, cattle, sheep and goats. However, I'll distinguish between Israel's livestock and the livestock of the Egyptians. No animal belonging to the Israelites shall die. I have chosen to do this tomorrow.'"

Pharaoh gave a wave of his arm in dismissal of Moses, "I have Amun-Ra, Apis, and Hathor by my side. You think your God concerns, me? Leave—me, I grow tired of you."

There you have it people—Moses' God has once again told Pharaoh that he plans to attack us and this time he says it'll be our livestock. Moses' God said that this will be against us, and nothing will touch the Israelite slaves or their animals.

However, Pharaoh reminded Moses of our backup from our gods Amun-Ra, Apis, and Hathor. I have every confidence in our gods; therefore you should not be concerned with Moses' threat. For you doubters out there, go and prepare your livestock for whatever you think might be coming your way. When we have more details, I'll let you know. Until then, this is Marissa for ET NEWS saying 'May the gods of Egypt protect you.'"

Council Elders of Goshen

Thaddeus spoke, "Aaron called this meeting due to new information that needs our attention."

Aaron addressed the council, "Council Elders, let us open this meeting with praise to our God. 'Praise be to our God. Praise you God for you show us grace and mercy. Praise be to our God, who cares and provides for us. Praise be to our God, who fights and wins the battles that we face. Praise be to our God.'

Men let us now pray to God. "Most Holy God, we ask for your guidance and wisdom. We ask you to show each of us how to do the things you have assigned for us to do throughout this day. Help us to help those we are to care for and protect. Amen."

Aaron went on to explain; "Council Elders, God sent Moses to give Pharaoh another message. This time God is placing a terrible plague upon the livestock of the Egyptians. We'll need to keep a close eye on our livestock—but not because of the plague. God has said our livestock is not to be affected by this plague; however, we think that when their livestock start to die, the Egyptians shall come to spy on us. Remember this plague only affects the Egyptian livestock that are in the fields. Now that you know what is to take place, we advise you to take precautions accordingly."

"Aaron, how do we handle them when they come to take our livestock?" asked Thaddeus.

"Pharaoh is inclined to send spies out to see if any of our animals have died. If they take some of the animals, then let them take what they need. In allowing them to take the cattle, it should humiliate them more than if we put up a fight. They'll see, our God is providing for us, and they'll see that their gods are leaving them helpless."

ET NEWS: BREAKING NEWS: "Livestock, Cattle, Sick, and Dying."

"This is Marissa with ET NEWS. Yesterday our livestock were stricken with an illness, so I have brought in Maskini with a livestock update."

"Thanks, Marissa, for being live at the palace yesterday. If you had not been there, we would not have had any warning. Since Moses only said that, his God's hand would place a severe pestilence upon our livestock, we were not entirely sure how to prepare for this war. After some time with the veterinarians, it was discovered that our livestock came down with Murrain. The vets say it is a type of distemper.

Thank the gods that it is only hitting the livestock in the fields. However, this is devastating and there is no way to stop it. Those in the fields shall die, and how do we work with so few livestock? This is the ruin of our country! I am not sure Pharaoh understands the gravity of the situation! People, this is horrible!

We do not have enough oxen and donkeys to handle loads of vegetables to take to market. Without the required camels and oxen needed for the transportation industry, they'll have a hard time delivering the goods ordered from other areas. We shall be sorely lacking in the milk department due to this loss of cows, sheep, and goats. The only livestock available for meat are those that were under shelter, therefore, again we are lacking.

Pharaoh has very few horses and donkeys for his chariots. There are few animals that qualify as clean for worship ceremonies. The gods are letting us down, and we do not know why, I am sorry, I cannot talk anymore."

"People, I do not understand what is happening right now. I think we should all do what we can to appease the gods and appeal to Pharaoh. Until further developments arise, this is Marissa for ET NEWS saying 'May the gods of Egypt protect you.'"

Palace

Pharaoh and his men were at the council chambers discussing the current events in Egypt. "It has been five days and all the livestock out in the fields appear to be dying. Pharaoh, you own cattle that are dying," reported Vizier Jibade.

"What is your definition of livestock?" asked Pharaoh.

"Our horses, donkeys, oxen, camels, cattle, sheep and goats! Gone all gone!"

"How many were not in the fields?"

"Not many, but that is not the point..."

"Point!" interrupted Pharaoh. "You think I do not get the point! Jibade, we still have livestock—maybe not as many as we would like, but we still have some. This God of Moses' cannot defeat me!"

"I think what Vizier Jibade is trying to say is..."

"Don't you say it, Obaid, not if you want to live a minute longer," declared Pharaoh. "I am telling you now; I shall not back down! I shall not put my tail between my legs and run! Send some spies into Goshen and find out how many of their livestock are dead. That is all. You are all dismissed!"

"Yes, Pharaoh, as you ask, it shall be done." answered Courtier Obaid.

After they left Pharaoh's presence, Courtier Obaid asked, "Jibade, what are we going to do? We cannot keep this up. It seems our gods have abandoned us, and we need to know why!"

"I know—we also need to figure out how to make Pharaoh a little more cooperative with Moses. I think it is time to have a conference with the counselors," said Vizier Jibade.

ET NEWS: BREAKING NEWS: "Cleanup Procedures."

"This is Marissa with ET NEWS. We have some devastating news! It seems that this Murrain has claimed the life of our bull, the one that represents our god Apis' life. Striking our cattle was bad enough, but for Moses and his God to personally attack the very representation of our god Apis, it is like attacking Apis personally. I cannot wait to see how Apis retaliates against Moses for this attack.

There will be a mummification and proper burial ceremony in the next few days. The word coming from Maskini is that the livestock families are doing the best they can to clean up after the horrible disaster that has taken place. The burning and burial of the animals have begun. Stay tuned for further updates, until then, this is Marissa for ET NEWS saying 'May the gods of Egypt protect you.'"

Palace

Courtier Obaid was busy giving Pharaoh an update on the livestock situation. "Pharaoh, it appears that things have turned out just as Moses said they would. It seems that none of the livestock belonging to the Israelites has suffered anything—not even a scratch. The spies knew you would want a more in-depth report, so they waited one more day to see what was going on. They came to the same conclusion, not one animal in Goshen has suffered."

Pharaoh fell into a fit of rage, "Moses! Moses! I am growing to hate that name. Who do you think you are? Send a message to Moses stating that he cannot win that easily! I shall not let my slaves go! You are dismissed."

ET NEWS: BREAKING NEWS: "The Slaves Stay!"

"This is Marissa with ET NEWS. Pharaoh has, once again, sent word to Moses that he is not letting the slaves leave. There are a few questions on everyone's mind: Where is our goddess Hathor? How could she allow a malady to be brought on by an unknown someone who claims to be the god of the slaves? She is many things to the Egyptians. She is the mistress of heaven, the one who welcomes us into the next life.

Hathor is our goddess of foreign lands, patron goddess of the miners. She is our protector, helping women in childbirth; our producer of love, music, dance, and joy. Surely, she sees the devastation we are experiencing. Surely, she sees that love and joy are becoming harder to find in her people. We must not lose hope in Hathor; she shall come and help us through our troubled times.

People on the street said they have begun to have some doubts about who shall win this war between Moses and Pharaoh. I tell you, Pharaoh shall win; he is our number one god, and he has a plan. Stay tuned for further developments. Until then, this is Marissa for ET NEWS saying 'May the gods of Egypt protect you.'"

Chapter 14
Plague 6: "Boils!"

Palace

Vizier Jibade and Wamukota were in a secret meeting discussing some concerns they had about their gods and Moses.

"What is going on here? How did we end up in a war between Moses and Pharaoh?" asked Vizier Jibade.

"Come on, Jibade, you do not know what happened?" answered Wamukota.

"No, I do not know, so help me out here, will you?" asked Vizier Jibade.

"Moses left for a foreign land and while there, he was poisoned by the God of the Hebrew people. He studied up on this God and now he knows how to perform his magic," replied Wamukota.

Vizier Jibade complained, "That is just great. What are we going to do about it? Moses' God, the Israelite's God, is the same God that has been a pain to our people for years. It is that same God's magic that has done a pretty good job of causing ruin to us and the world as we know it. What do we do? How do we survive? Pharaoh was doing a good job in the beginning, but now I think that he is determined not to stop until everything is dead around here."

"I know what you mean, we have tried all we know to do. I must keep communicating with our gods. During the plagues, our priests were not able to communicate with the gods because the filth of the plagues left them ceremonially unclean. Now our hope lies in the priests becoming clean enough to stand before our gods and pray for our desperate needs," observed Wamukota.

"I never thought much about our priests. You are right; all shall start to get better as the priests can now do their job. Thank you, Wamukota I feel better," said Vizier Jibade.

"Anytime, Jibade, anytime," laughed Wamukota.

Marissa was at her desk when her intercom machine beeped. "Yes Kebi, what it is?"

"I have a message from Jair, he said to tell you to get over to the palace right away. Moses and Aaron are due to arrive there any minute."

"Get a hold of Abdullah and tell him to get everything rounded up and meet me at the palace," ordered Marissa as she headed for the door.

ET NEWS: BREAKING NEWS: "Another Confrontation at the Palace!"

"This is Marissa with ET NEWS. We are live at the palace, where Moses and Aaron are meeting with Pharaoh yet again. Another confrontation with Pharaoh—Moses has had too much couscous and wine!"

Abdullah interrupted, "Marissa..."

"What is it Abdullah? We are on the air."

"I need to talk to you for a moment."

"What? Oh!.. Go to a commercial! Abdullah, you are so dead what is it?"

"Moses and Aaron are not here. They are meeting Pharaoh at the outer court. That is where Pharaoh is at this time of day. I thought you would want to know we are in the wrong spot."

"We are heading for the outer court!" Marissa shouted to her crew.

On the way over Marissa chewed on Abdullah. "How could you let me do such a thing, just wait Abdullah you'll pay for this."

"Marissa, we are here," said Abdullah.

"Yes of course we are," replied Marissa as she tried to gain her composure. "This is Marissa once again, sorry for the inconvenience, Abdullah has just found out that Moses and Aaron are meeting Pharaoh at the outer court. I'd say Moses has been on a wine binge! Look, they've stopped at the entrance and are reaching their hands into the furnace! Both of them have scooped up handfuls .. black ashes?"

"Moses! What are you doing here? Did you decide it was time to take in the lovely scenery of my palace garden or did you decide to play nice and have a swim?" Pharaoh asked sarcastically. "Moses, how much longer do you think you can just come around and be a pest and not get smashed? Moses, why are you not speaking to me? You came with another message so tell me, what it is!"

Marissa broke in, "I said Moses has had too much wine. It looks like he is throwing the ashes from his hand up into the air toward the heavens. Now he is taking the ashes that Aaron had in his hands and throwing them into the air. He has lost it, do you see this? When the ash hit the air, it became a very fine dust. Not just a little dust—this dust is spreading like a bad disease. The wind seems to be carrying it around and dropping it. It is falling like it has a particular assignment to follow. The men looked like they were developing bumps. He has put a skin disease on the people!"

"What is happening?" asked a very excited Jannes.

"Moses has struck us with a skin condition!" shouted Jambres.

"A wicked skin condition, let's get out of here! declared Jabr.

Pharaoh, not amused and visibly frustrated with this whole show, spoke: "What are you doing? What do you have in your hand? You threw some ashes up to the heavens, so what? Moses, what are you doing? Counselors, sorcerers, magicians!"

"We cannot come out, O my Pharaoh, we are unclean; Moses placed a horrid skin condition upon us," shouted Wamukota.

Pharaoh who was starting to show the signs of boils on his skin shouted, "Moses! Why do I always get stuck with you and Aaron, what has happened now? Guards, throw them out!"

"What has Moses and his God done? Why were we not warned! Moses and his God just let Pharaoh watch it happen! Oh... oh, I do not feel so well. For now, this is Marissa for ET NEWS saying 'May the gods of Egypt protect you.'"

ET NEWS: BREAKING NEWS: "Skin Condition."

"This is Abdullah with ET NEWS, stepping in for Marissa who is taking some time off. I have received reports that this skin condition has hit the beasts, as well as the people. How awful for these poor animals to endure so much pain. Marissa wanted you to know that the priests have been declared unclean and therefore cannot pray to the gods.

Because of the unclean conditions of the priests, they are not sure when anyone might hear from Sekhmet, Thoth, or Isis. Pharaoh and all his cabinet members, counselors, sorcerers and magicians have been affected by this disease.

There is no one ceremonially clean enough to communicate with the gods. Imhotep, our high priest the mentor of magicians, seems to have been afflicted as he no longer communicates with anyone. Until this disease has passed no more updates, this is Abdullah in for Marissa with an ET NEWS update.

Goshen

Moses and Aaron were resting at Aaron's home. Hearing a commotion, Aaron walked over and opened the door to see what was going on outside. "Moses, it looks like one of the palace messengers is here," observed Aaron.

"Open the door."

"Is Moses here with you?"

"Yes? I am Moses, what message do you have for me?"

"This is an official message from Pharaoh; 'You can keep up your little tricks, and I shall not let my slaves leave.'"

"Thank you, you may tell Pharaoh I have received his message. Aaron, did you hear that?" Moses said with a chuckle. "We can keep up our little tricks, he shall not let his slaves go." "I wish I could say I was surprised. I hope that the plans God has for Egypt are almost complete, and we can all leave this place soon."

Chapter 15
Plague 7: "Thunder, Lightning, Fire, and Hail!"

ET NEWS: BREAKING NEWS: "Enough Already!"

"Good morning to our viewers, this is Marissa with another ET NEWS update. I am at the palace out by the path that leads to Pharaoh's early morning worship. Moses and Aaron are expected to be here with another message from their God. Moses does not seem to know when to quit. I think we shall find this interesting, as I am sure Pharaoh has had enough of Moses, Aaron, and their God by now—here they come."

Pharaoh exclaimed, "Moses, you are standing in my path, get out of my way! Moses refused to move and said not a word. "Alright, what is your message this time?"

Moses spoke, 'God, the God of the Hebrews, says: Release my people so they can worship me. This time I am going to strike you and your servants and your people with the full force of my power so you'll get it into your head that there's no one like me anywhere in all the Earth. You know that by now I could have struck you and your people with deadly disease and there would be nothing left of you, not a trace. But for one reason only I've kept you on your feet: To make you recognize my power so that my reputation spreads in all the Earth. You are still building yourself up at my people's expense. You are not letting them go. So here's what's going to happen: At this time tomorrow I'm sending a terrific hailstorm—there's never been a storm like this in Egypt from the day of its founding until now. So get your livestock under shelter roof—everything exposed in the open fields, both people and animals, will die when the hail comes down.'"

Pharaoh responded, "And when is this threat to take place?"

"Tomorrow, God shall bring this upon you tomorrow," answered Moses.

Pharaoh, now bouncing from one foot to the next with impatience said, "Whatever! I grow tired of you and your God, Moses. I'll not let your people go! Now leave me in peace!" Moses stepped off the walking path and Pharaoh continued his walk to perform his daily rituals.

"Oh, the nerve—did you hear that! Moses has not just threatened Pharaoh again, he has threatened you and me! Who does he think he is? And by the way, I wonder why Aaron did not accompany Moses this time? People, I shall be out on the streets with an update during our noon broadcast, and I will be getting your reactions to this latest development. Until then, this is Marissa for ET NEWS saying 'May the gods of Egypt protect you.'"

Council Meeting in Goshen

Thaddeus opened the meeting, "Order! Let's come to order! That is better, now I call this meeting to order. Aaron, you have a word for us."

Aaron spoke, "Thank you, let us open with prayer: 'God, we ask that you would help us to listen and understand the message you have for us here today. Amen.'

Council Elders, Moses wanted me to let you know that God spoke to him last night. Once again, God has given Moses a word to give Pharaoh. God is angry, and shall strike Pharaoh, his people, slaves, and the land with a hail storm. God said this storm will be one that has never been seen before, ever. Goshen shall not suffer the devastation the rest of Egypt shall suffer.

We need to let the people know that they are safe only as long as they are in Goshen or under cover in the spot where God has placed them. Our animals and anything else we have must be inside Goshen. This storm shall take place tomorrow morning. That is all."

"Aaron?" asked Dan.

"Yes?" "How long is this storm going to last?"

Soberly Aaron replied, "Until God tells it to stop."

ET NEWS: BREAKING NEWS: "Storm Preparation."

"This is Marissa with ET NEWS. Moses' God has threatened us again. His God claims that this storm shall be stronger than any storm ever seen before—he says even our ancestors never saw a storm as awful as the one about to come upon us. If there is hail, then expect rain also. Doesn't this God know that we consider any rain to be a gift from the gods? Doesn't he know that we have a party when it thunders because we know we have pleased the gods?

However, when we see hail, it is because we have done something to upset our gods. We have done nothing to offend any of the gods, so I do not think they plan to leave us unprotected. What plans are you making for this event? Remember, it is scheduled to start so early tomorrow morning that most of us shall be in bed.

I thought you might like to hear from Luzige, our Agriculture Department Official. Luzige, have you heard from Pharaoh? Is he doing anything to protect his fig trees and his vine groves?"

"Nothing, he says to leave them alone; there is nothing to worry about."

"What plans do you and the other agricultural farmers have for this warning?" asked Marissa.

"One of the palace advisers informed us about the threat from Moses' God. I am so glad he did; otherwise we would not have known. The majority of the men who attended the agriculture meeting concluded that our only choice was to rely on Seth and Isis to protect our crops from this storm. They are the god and goddess that protect our crops.

How else are we going to protect our crops from a hailstorm? That is, if we see a hailstorm. We are going to the temple to pray and then we are going to get ready to party tomorrow. The vineyard growers are of the same opinion. Why would the gods want the grapes, olives, dates, figs, and pomegranates to be destroyed?"

"Thank you Luzige, go to the temple and may the gods hear your prayers.

I also have with me Maskini, our Livestock and Cattle Association Official, what do you have to tell us?"

"Pharaoh is not concerned at all and has no plans to call in his livestock, cattle, or slaves. None of us want to believe that this storm shall happen. However, how many of us can afford not to take precautions? We have been hit hard lately by these plagues caused by Moses' God.

Some of us are beginning to wonder if this God of Moses' is the most powerful of all the gods. About fifty percent of the livestock and cattle owners are taking this seriously. They plan to gather their livestock, cattle, and slaves under roofs before this storm hits us tomorrow. I just hope we have enough time to get them all to safety. Excuse me, Marissa, I have a lot to get done; I need to leave."

"Thank you, Maskini. Let's find a viewer from out on the street, perhaps one of them may speak with us. Let's see... you are?"

"My name is Akram; thank you for this program. If not for this program, we would not have known about the coming storm. Pharaoh has not announced anything to the people. I'll have all my animals and my children in the house. I shall also be praying to Shu for my house. Shu can keep my house and family from harm."

"Thank you Akram, I believe we have time for one more... you are?"

"My name is Sharifa, and I want to thank you for your coverage of this event. My father is the slave keeper for one who owns a vineyard. If my father had not informed his boss of the threat, the slaves would have died. Instead, he told my father to go and gather all the slaves from the field before tomorrow. If not for ET NEWS, we would be in trouble. I have to hurry to the temple."

"Thank you, Sharifa. People seem to be at a loss as to who is going to win this war. My faith is in Pharaoh. Until tomorrow, this is Marissa for ET NEWS saying 'May the gods of Egypt protect you.'"

God Spoke to Moses

God said to Moses: "Stretch your hands to the skies. Signal the hail to fall all over Egypt on people and animals and crops exposed in the fields of Egypt." Moses lifted his outstretched hands holding his rod toward the skies. By the way of his warring angels, God sent down the lightning bolts, the clash of thunder and the hail. The hail is sizzling with violence against the fireballs that God ordered placed inside the hail—which were made specifically for this moment in time—begin to erupt within their icy walls. What a sight, what a sound and what a mess!

Goshen

"Aaron, what was that?" shouted Asher.

"It has begun. The lightning is striking so hard that the ground is shaking under my feet."

"The hail, thunder, and lightning, it is horrible!" observed Dan.

"Moses! You made it back in quick time; we only just heard the storm," said a startled Thaddeus.

"I did not have far to walk."

"This is very scary. I am thankful that I am not in Egypt right now," replied Thaddeus as he watched the storm from afar with shivers running down his spine.

Moses explained, "God is outraged and has told his warring angels of heaven to wreak havoc on the people, animals, and land with thunder, lightning, fire, hail, and ice. You must never forget that the people suffered this because Pharaoh would not release God's people to go and worship him.

They have suffered this also because they have refused to acknowledge God as the one true God. They chose to put their faith in gods of stone and wood. They are not real! They cannot breathe, they cannot feel, they cannot hear, and they cannot answer prayer! You must never let your families forget what our God is doing here right now in Egypt."

"It is terrible, I cannot even hear myself think!" shouted Dan.

"How would you like to be the people not in the safety of Goshen or under cover right now?" asked Moses.

"Why would God spare the animals if they are under shelter?" asked Dan.

"God still loves the people and is showing favor to those who show they are beginning to believe in him. God is giving people, who choose to hear and heed God's warning, his protection from this storm. He has warned the people; now he is looking to see who chooses to trust and obey him and those who do not.

To God, it matters not if they are Hebrew or Egyptian. Obey and be protected—disobey and die. Thaddeus, Dan, and Asher, I want you to go out and spread the word to the other elders that they are to comfort their people. Tell them to remind the people that by obeying God, they have received favor, mercy and grace instead of the hardship that looms ahead for others.

Let the people know that they are to worship God and remember that it is God who has blessed all the people who stayed where God told them to stay. Men, some of the people cannot understand, however, I need you to understand that this is a test for all people. Those that obeyed, passed; those who ignored the warning, failed. Now go and do as I have asked you to do," ordered Moses.

Palace

Pharaoh, rudely awoken by the thunder, shouted: "What's that racket!" Courtier Obaid came into Pharaoh's bed chamber. "It is thunder, lightning, hail, and fire! I was just coming to see how you were doing."

"I was sleeping like a baby until that racket woke me up. Why were you coming to check on me?"

"I wanted to be sure you were safe! The storm out there is so bad one cannot leave a building. You cannot get next to any of the balconies."

"Cannot get next to any of the balconies, why?"

"Come see for yourself," replied Courtier Obaid. Pharaoh got up, and Courtier Obaid helped him put his robe on before they walked to the other side of the room, "What is this!"

"Moses warned you about this hailstorm. Do you realize all your livestock, cattle, and slaves out in the field are dead? Look at that fire! It comes down as hail the size of melons—when it hits the ground fire shoots out and runs along the ground. How can water sizzle so loudly and turn to fire at the same time? The storm looks to be the work of a Supreme God. Where are all our gods? Where is all our protection? Where is Nut?" asked a frightened Courtier Obaid.

"Get me the priests! Obaid, you have nothing to worry about; this storm cannot last very long."

"Are you trying to convince yourself or us?" asked Courtier Obaid, as he stormed out of the room.

ET NEWS: BREAKING NEWS: "Thunder, Lightning, Freezing Hail, and Fireballs!"

"This is Marissa with ET NEWS. I am stuck in my office, so we decided to go on the air with an update. People, I suggest that you get down on your knees and beg for mercy. Moses' storm seems to be upon us. It is so bright outside from the lightning that I had to shut my curtain to keep from going blind.

I did see what looked like fire in the hail as it was coming down. The thunder is so loud I am not even sure you can hear me. How can water turn to fire and burn? I want to encourage each of you; this cannot go on for very long. Our gods shall respond—stay inside and be safe. Until this storm has passed, this is Marissa for ET NEWS saying 'May the gods of Egypt protect you.'"

Palace

Pharaoh asked, "Jibade is in Pithom? I had you send a messenger to bring him back. Why has he not returned?"

"I sent messengers out three different times—each one was killed by the hail and burned by the fire before they made it six steps! Burnt flesh is horrible to smell," answered a nervous Barak.

Why is the floor so hot?"

"When the hail hits the ground, it turns into fireballs that look like someone is playing hockey. Those fireballs make the ground sweltering and dusty," answered Aamir.

"This has gone on for almost two days. Barak, send a message to my men—they are to meet me at the inner palace court; it is time for intense prayer to Seth, Nut, and Seshat. They shall come through for me."

Goshen

Dan spoke, "Those poor people and animals caught out in this storm, the fire and smoke, the constant thunder, and the lightning strikes are horrific. Thank God he has done what he said he would do. We are so close to this storm, and yet nothing has come near us. Thaddeus, have you noticed that not even the smell of smoke or the cloud of fire has come our way?"

"God really is a wondrous and gracious God, isn't he?" remarked Thaddeus.

"Moses, it has been almost two days, why hasn't Pharaoh sent for you?" asked Aaron.

"He is fighting the fact that he'll have to surrender this time. In Pharaoh's mind, he is the one who is supposed to be the power of all. We wait upon God."

Palace

Pharaoh was in his council chambers discussing the storm. "It has been almost three days—what's the plan, guys?"

"We need to find a way to trick Moses into stopping this storm," answered Osaze.

"Really! Any serious suggestions!"

"How about a confession? You tell Moses that your people have sinned, and that you need him to go back to his God and plead your case." answered Aamir.

"I like that—yes, Aamir, send Chigaru to bring Moses and Aaron back here. I expect to talk to them."

"As you command, O Pharaoh, ask and it shall be done," answered Aamir.

Rameses

Marissa, walked to her office, and found a wrinkled piece of paper on the floor. She bent over to pick it up, and began to read. "In case I do not make it through this storm, here is a note for you, Marissa. I have never seen hail like this before! Lightning and hail are mixed together, and the hail has fire in it! Appearing to be the size of a melon. This storm has no mercy! I see it killing any animal or person that is outside! Too awful!

All the plants have been beaten to the ground. It looks like a giant went outside and jumped on them for the fun of it. Decimated! The trees here in the yard have no more leaves, no more branches. The Lord God of the Israelites said he would do this, and yet I cannot seem to wrap my mind around this horrific devastation. It feels like a bad nightmare. I wish I were in Goshen right now. Born to Israelite parents, I declare that I have decided to stay with Moses and his God. You can keep your gods and Pharaoh; I want no more to do with them!" Yours, Abdullah.

After reading the note, Marissa continued walking to her office. She thought to herself: "Abdullah, you were just scared. It was the storm that made you think those things. He did not mean a word of it or I would not have found this note crinkled up and on the floor. I must remember to keep a close watch on him for a while. Abdullah, you are not to become a casualty of this war."

Palace

Moses, as he arrived to meet with Pharaoh, thought, "this should be interesting." The guard, kept watch out for Moses, as Moses approached the guard opened the entrance door to the palace. "Welcome Moses, you are a miracle from the gods—making it here alive."

"I am a living testimony to our God's power; he is in control of all," replied Moses. As Moses stepped into Pharaoh's side room,

Pharaoh said with a disheartened voice: I have sinned this time; the Lord is right, and I, and my people, are in the wrong.

Entreat the Lord, for there has been enough of this mighty thundering and this hail [these voices of God]; I will let you go; you shall stay here no longer.

Moses said, As soon as I leave the city, I will stretch out my hands to the Lord; the thunder shall cease, neither shall there be any more hail, that you may know that the earth is the Lord's.

But as for you and your servants, I know that you do not yet [reverently] fear the Lord God."

When Moses left the city, he lifted his hands as he had told Pharaoh he would. "God, I ask you to stop the thunder, the lightning, the hail, and the fire, so that Pharaoh and all of Egypt might know you are God. Amen."

ET NEWS: BREAKING NEWS: "Storm Has Passed!"

"This is Marissa with an ET NEWS update. Abdullah is out in the field via satellite. As you can see, the storm that Moses warned Pharaoh about, came to pass. It'll be some time before we can get accurate numbers of how many people and animals are dead. However, we do know that a vast number of individuals and animals died in the storm. I find this a hard pill to swallow. Pharaoh and the priests did all they could.

"Abdullah, I understand that when Pharaoh sent for Moses and Aaron, they came from the land of Goshen and were not hurt. They did not even smell like smoke. The messenger sent to get Moses, was not touched either. A palace official informed us that at least three messengers were sent to get the priests and each messenger was killed by the hail before he took six steps. What should we make of that?"

"You'll not like this answer Marissa, but it shows us that the God of the Israelite or Hebrew people has supreme power over the gods of Egypt."

"You are right, I do not like that answer! You have been listening to the wrong people! Abdullah, I have breaking news from the palace. Courtier Obaid says that anyone owning animals should contact the Office of Health and Welfare for assistance. The palace is going to have a person on every corner waiting to help with the death of family members. The Office of Health and Welfare workers are wearing badges to identify themselves.

The Official's of Health and Welfare is in need of help with the accumulation and incineration of the dead animals. Burials for the families of the dead are to be as soon as possible." Marissa, struggled to compose herself, but continued the broadcast. "It could be quite a while before we identify the bodies, some we may never be able to identify. The damage to them from the storm was extreme. Abdullah, is Luzige with you?"

"Yes, he is. Luzige, as the Official of our Agriculture Department, can you give us an update on the storm damage?"

Some of our most important crops were ruined by the storm. First of all, the barley had already started to form heads. Without barley, how will we make our Zytum? Next, the flax was in bloom when the storm hit and the blossoms were demolished. Now we have no way to make our clothes or thread. The wheat and the wild grain are okay. To see all this devastation makes my heart hurt too much. I am unsure what we have done to make the gods mad enough that they have refused to protect us.

As for the trees, they were badly smashed, but they'll survive; however, do not plan on receiving a crop from them this year. Badly damaged was the Papyrus grass, which means we cannot make boats, baskets, or paper. Unbelievable!

Our trees: the Tamarisk, the Acacia trees, our precious Cedar and Pine trees are not faring very well. The Sycamore trees were killed by frost! Yes, I said killed by frost! There was frost in this storm! We'll have no dates, figs, or pomegranates for the year. The vines of our grapes are not repairable; we will have to look around for transplants. I have no idea how long before we will have grapes for wine again.

No honey for a while—the flowers needed to produce honey were taken out by the storm—we have no idea where the bees have gone. It'll take days to assess all the damage. I have no more to say."

"Thank you, Luzige. People, we need to hear from you—how are you doing and where are you turning for help? The ordinary people are better off than Pharaoh and the palace. We also have Maskini, the official of the Livestock and Cattle Association, to speak to us."

"Abdullah, I am sorry to say that Pharaoh has very few animals left. It'll prove difficult to replenish the livestock, and there are not enough to feed off of for very long. He did not take Moses' warning seriously and left the grazing animals out to die. Do we have enough donkeys and oxen to get our product to the shipping yards? Remember, people, we need the few cows we have left and the few sheep to keep things going.

Anyone caught trying to steal or cause harm to these animals shall be dealt with severely. There are also the goats, pigs, ducks, geese, and pigeons to consider. They need time to reproduce. I am sad to say that it has been reported to us that the pet crocodiles around the pools died in this storm.

People, if you have pet monkeys, we need you to keep them well fed: otherwise we are required to put them down. We do not need anyone's pets causing problems. Does this God of Moses' really have power over our gods? I am sorry—I do not feel very well."

"Thank you, Maskini, I realize that this is hard on all of us. You should go and spend some time meditating. Moses' God does not have supreme power over our gods. Our gods have a plan for what has been happening; you'll see. Abdullah, do you have anyone around you that you could interview?"

"I see many people, but they seem to have blank stares on their faces. I am sure it is the shock of the whole thing. I'll see if someone would like to talk to me. Sir? May I speak with you for a moment?"

"What? What do you want?"

"Abdullah with ET NEWS, I was wondering if you could tell me where you are going and how you are doing?"

"Where am I going? I am not sure; I was going to work, but this storm has taken that away. I've heard that the Doom trees have received massive damage. For this reason, we cannot continue with construction of the bridge that was to replace the old one at the end of town. My wife also has no job—no trees to make ropes or baskets.

What are we to do? Where are we to go? Do you know where we should go? Do you? We need help!"

"Sir, I think you should walk to the corner where you can see someone from Health and Welfare. Marissa, it is no longer safe out here; I am coming in."

"People do not fall into the depths of despair; we are safe under the watchful eye of Pharaoh. I expect Pharaoh to make an announcement of comfort anytime now. Until further developments arise, this is Marissa for ET NEWS saying 'May the gods of Egypt protect you.'"

Palace

Pharaoh was in conference with his men discussing the day's affairs.

"Barak, send a messenger to inform Moses that I am not allowing my slaves to leave this land."

"Excellent, Pharaoh, who does this man think he is? It shall be as you have asked," answered Barak.

"And how about you, Courtier Obaid? You asked me if I was trying to convince myself, as I remember. What do you have to say now?"

"I apologize, Pharaoh, I was wrong; you should make the slaves stay," answered a humbled Courtier Obaid.

Chapter 16
Plague 8: "Locusts?"

Moses and Aaron were on their way to the palace because God said it was time to give Pharaoh another visit. Along the way Aaron spoke, "I know Pharaoh felt trapped when he begged to have that hail storm stopped. How is he going to react when we approach him today? How is all this going to play out?"

"God told me that he has hardened the hearts of Pharaoh and his officials. He did this so that he might show his divine power to Pharaoh. God also said I am to tell my children and grandchildren exactly how God has treated the Egyptians and about the miraculous signs he has performed among them. In this way, we shall all know that the great, I AM, is Lord."

"So God is using Pharaoh to show everyone his sovereign power, so that all may know our God is the one true God?" asked Aaron.

"Pharaoh acts as the sovereign God of the Egyptians. The people have a blind love for him and for the Egyptian gods—the idols, which do not indeed exist. Because of their choices, God is playing them for the fools that they are. They have acted fatuous and self-important, the very things that shall bring them to ruin. How shall it all play out? I am not sure except that God has a plan for everything. Here we are at the palace gates."

ET NEWS: BREAKING NEWS: "Moses At It Again!"

"This is Marissa with ET NEWS, breaking news. We are at the palace waiting to see if Pharaoh finally has enough on Moses and Aaron to okay their death warrants. Moses and Aaron are here to harass Pharaoh again!"

Pharaoh glared at Moses like a snake that had enough with being threatened and was about to lunge forward with a strike meant to kill. "Moses, let me guess another request to let your people go?"

Aaron said, "This is what the Lord, the Hebrews' God, says: How long will you refuse to respect me.

Otherwise, if you refuse to let my people go, I'm going to bring locusts into your country tomorrow. They will cover the landscape so that you won't be able to see the ground. They will eat the last bit of vegetation that was left after the hail. They will eat all your trees growing in the fields. The locusts will fill your houses and all your officials' houses and all the Egyptians' houses.

Your parents and even your grandparents have never seen anything like it during their entire lifetimes in this fertile land."

Marissa observed, "Moses and Aaron are leaving. Pharaoh never even got a chance to reply!"

Pharaoh enraged at what he had just heard, tensed every muscle in his body and sat himself up higher upon his throne. Making his finger resemble a venomous Cobra about to strike, Pharaoh pointed it toward the door and shouted; "Get out of here! You and the threats of your God are nothing to me! Out! Out of my sight!"

"As you just saw, Moses has been here making threats again, not just upon Pharaoh, but upon all the people and all the land of Egypt! How did this start out as a war between Moses and Pharaoh, and then become a war between Moses and all of Egypt?

Once again, Moses is making promises to finish us off with the total collapse of our life as we know it. Who does this man think he is? He is threatening us with locusts!

Nobody in their right mind messes around with locusts! How do you think Pharaoh and his officials plan to deal with these rabble-rousers this time? Until further developments arise, this is Marissa for ET NEWS saying 'May the gods of Egypt protect you.'"

Palace

Pharaoh and his men were in a conference regarding Moses and his threats. "How much longer, Pharaoh, how much longer is this man going to keep entangling us with his trickery?" asked Barak.

"Let the slaves go worship their God!" begged Courtier Obaid.

"Don't you get it yet? Egypt is being destroyed right under your nose!" declared Vizier Jibade.

"The people are about to riot on us and then what?" asked Courtier Obaid.

Vizier Jibade frustrated said, "I don't get it? Pharaoh, you know that all paths lead to the underworld. No one can escape Anubis the gatekeeper of the underworld. Once Anubis lets Moses into the underworld, his soul is then placed on a scale opposite Ma'at's feather where he will be deemed full of wrongful deeds. After that, he goes to Osiris; there Moses will be judged and prosecuted by Thoth who records the verdict. Moses is then thrown to Ammit (the Devourer) where he'll spend eternity in the darkest pit of the underworld. So why are you fighting him so hard? Let the slaves go out and worship their God; they'll be back in two or three weeks."

"You are sure about that, Barak? Well, are you?" questions Pharaoh.

"You are the one who has authority over judgment and death. You have a say in what happens to them," answered Vizier Jibade.

"You are right! I do have that authority. Send a messenger to bring Moses and Aaron back to me."

ET NEWS: BREAKING NEWS: "Pharaoh Sent For Moses and Aaron."

Responding to Pharaoh's call, Moses and Aaron were back at the palace. When they walked into Pharaoh's chambers, they found Pharaoh in a remarkably cheerful mood. "Moses, I have decided you can go worship your God. Tell me, who exactly is going on this journey with you?"

"Everyone! We'll be taking our young and old, our sons and daughters, our flocks and herds. For us, it's a pilgrimage festival in the Lord's honor," answered Moses.

Pharaoh's cheerfulness turned to sudden and instant rage. His face looked older and wickeder: "The Lord would have to be with you, if I would ever let you take your women and your children along. I know you're up to no good! No! Only the men may go to worship the Lord—since that's what you've been asking for."

Pharaoh continued: "Throw them out, now! Let them know, I am the Ruler of my slaves and not their so-called God! Guards! Make sure that Moses and Aaron leave my palace! Now!"

"You heard it fellow Egyptians, Pharaoh is not about to tolerate any more of Moses' tricks. My question is, how long before Pharaoh has a solid case against Moses and can have him and Aaron put to death? I am so tired of Moses always being in the way and spoiling our fun. What do you say? Will the threat of Moses' God come to pass? Tomorrow promises to be an exciting day. Until then, this is Marissa for ET NEWS saying 'May the gods of Egypt protect you.'"

God Spoke to Moses

God said to Moses: "Stretch your hand over Egypt and signal the locusts to cover the land of Egypt, devouring every blade of grass in the country, everything that the hail didn't get."

"As you ask." As Moses held his staff out over all the land of Egypt, God made a wind come in from the east.

"I want you to send for your elders. When they arrive, this is what you and Aaron are to tell them."

ET NEWS: BREAKING NEWS: "Strong East Wind and Locusts?"

This is Marissa and Abdullah for ET NEWS. All of Egypt is experiencing a very strong east wind. Abdullah was out looking things over, Abdullah?"

"Marissa, it looks and feels like an east wind. I'll walk to a more open area to get a better idea of what is going on. Marissa!"

"Abdullah? Abdullah? We seem to have lost Abdullah for a minute, wait, Abdullah?"

"I am back; the wind is strong out here! I'll tell you that."

"Abdullah, have you found out anything?"

"I have. The locusts Moses warned us about are coming in by way of the east wind. If you have not prepared yourself already, you had better do it now."

"People, go out and party or go to a temple—whatever you want to do. We'll be back with further updates. May this war, which we are about to experience against the locusts, be declared ahead of time to be victorious for our gods! Until then, this is Marissa for ET NEWS saying 'May the gods of Egypt protect you.'"

Goshen

Aaron instructed the people: "Elders of Goshen, God has spoken to Moses, and I am to inform you that God has sent locusts to devour everything the Egyptians have left in the land. If you step outside the boundary of Goshen, you won't be protected. Go out and remind the people that God has shown them much grace and mercy.

The people are to write these things on their hearts and to repeat all that has happened to their children and grandchildren. The elders are to let the people know exactly how God treated the Egyptians and the miraculous signs he used. By the retelling of God's miracles from one generation to the next, God's people should never be able to forget that our God is Lord. Thank you for coming."

As the elders left, Dan came up to Aaron and asked, "I was wondering about the Egyptians? They'll have nothing left to survive on, will they?"

"Only what is stored and protected from the locusts and that cannot be much."

"How much more can those people take?" asked Thaddeus.

"You mean, how much more will God punish them? God has said everything is about to come to completion. In the next few days, we are to prepare everyone to leave for the land of milk and honey. There is one thing that concerns me," replied Aaron.

"What is that?" asked Thaddeus.

"Can we retell the stories of what has happened here well enough to keep our future generations from suffering the same as the Egyptians are suffering now?" stated a very somber Aaron. Startled Thaddeus replied, "Why would you ask such a question? None of us are about to forget what is happening here."

Palace

Pharaoh commanded, "Courtier Obaid! I want the Agriculture Department Official and the Livestock and Cattle Association Official in here with damage reports. No excuses! I want to see them now!"

ET NEWS: BREAKING NEWS: " Dark Cloud, Heavy Wind upon Us."

This is Abdullah with ET NEWS. Early this morning an east wind brought in a dark cloud of locusts unlike anything anyone has seen before. It looks as though someone held the locusts by a string and suddenly cut the rope as thousands at a time just dropped to the ground. Moses' God has made good on his threat once again. Nothing like this has ever happened.

How long before you people wise up and realize that Moses' God is a real living, breathing God. From this day forward the God I was born under as an Israelite, is my one and only God.

The ground may be black, but have you looked, I mean really took a good look at the locusts? They have come in as a nation (of insects) waging war upon us. The babies seem to be just as vicious as the adults, and they have the teeth of a full-grown lion! Their teeth—in the mouth of baby locusts—are like the signature of a death arrow aimed straight at our hearts! The adults and the older locusts are working together like a well-disciplined army!

It is as if their assignment is to devastate our world. These locusts wear the badge of a mighty warrior. They make a noise of war with their loud trumpet that never seems to shut-off; there is a constant irritating noise that comes from their wings. They somehow communicate in a language foreign to me. The babies stay on the ground while all the others are in the air. Locust, locusts, locusts—everywhere!

They have caused great harm to Egypt's sons and daughters. They devoured our food and do not allow us any restful sleep or any place to sit—how are we supposed to walk? There is nowhere to go to get a break. Our storage bins of food shall be empty very soon. The locusts act as though each of them has been assigned to specific targets by a God.

We are living an evil nightmare; it reminds me of a movie in my mind that keeps rewinding and never goes any further. Bloodied water, frogs, gnats, flies, diseased livestock, boils, hail, and locusts... Just a moment people—Maskini, Official of the Livestock and Cattle Association, is here with an important update."

"Pharaoh requested I update the people. Due to being harassed by the locusts, our cows, sheep, goats, and pigs are showing signs of extreme exhaustion, with fearful behavior. It is a repeat of the frogs again!

The locusts have eaten all the food for our livestock and cattle. Our horses, donkeys, oxen and camels are going crazy. Pharaoh warns that anyone seen trying to steal or harm any of the palace animals shall suffer the stiffest of punishments available by law."

People from the crowd shouted, "Yeah, you think that matters to us?"

"We are starving to death!"

"First come first serve is what I say!"

Maskini nervously replied, "I am leaving, it is not safe to be here anymore. I need to get back to the animals."

Someone in the crowd yelled out, "Our crops are wiped out. The locusts have completely eaten our wheat, spelt, and emmer crops; and we have no way to make food for livestock or cattle!"

Another from the crowd screamed, "How about food and shelter for us? Every bit of food that we were growing no longer exists. All our shade trees have been devastated! We have no trees to make the products necessary to live! Tell Moses' God to get out of here and leave us alone!"

Another from the crowd said, "The lush gardens filled with leeks, garlic, melons, squash, beans, and lettuce, have all been destroyed!"

Another from the crowd expressed his concern, "I am a bee farmer and all the bees are gone. I had hoped that the bees would find their way back. However, as the flowers are dead and gone, that is not going to happen anytime soon. What am I going to do? Tell me, what am I going to do?"

Abdullah was visibly shaken as the crowd got noisier and became more agitated by the minute; as the crowd began to push in closer to where Abdullah was standing, he made the decision to wrap up the newscast. "People, you can see how the crowd is quickly getting out of hand. I am going to leave here now while I still have my life. You have been watching Abdullah with ET NEWS; I shall have further updates for you when more news comes in... if it is safe."

Palace

Courtier Obaid entered the palace quarters and introduced Maskini, Official of the Livestock and Cattle Association, to Pharaoh. "Yes, yes, Maskini, do come and sit; I need a damage report, so what can you tell me?"

"My Pharaoh, the locusts have harassed our cows, sheep, goats, and pigs so much that I think they are going schizophrenic. The goats are looking scared, and the cattle are suffering, I think they are in shock. How much more can our animals can take? It is a wonder we have any left.

The locusts are under their feet all the time, and they cannot sit—it is just like the frogs and the gnats. The locusts act like they were told to devour all the crops used to make food for our livestock and cattle. Our horses, donkeys, oxen and camels are wandering around confused; if I did not know better, I'd say they are war shocked.

Unsure how much more he would be able to report to Pharaoh without risking a prison sentence Maskini went on, "We have to find a way to feed and water them. I'll be warning the public again that anyone seen trying to steal or harm any of our animals shall receive the stiffest penalty allowed by law. I also need more men; we lost a lot of them to the gnats, flies, boils, and hail."

Pharaoh paced back and forth, "So if this lasts much longer, then we have nothing; is that what you are saying?"

Maskini said with a big sigh, "Yes, I guess that is what I am saying." "You are dismissed." As soon as Maskini left, Courtier Obaid opened the door and Luzige, Official of the Agriculture Department, came and gave his report to Pharaoh.

Pharaoh sat in his royal chair and showed no signs of what he felt earlier, "What kind of damage do we have out there—are we able to last a while longer?"

Luzige tried hard not to show how nervous he was, "My Pharaoh, our agricultural economy has been wiped out. No more trees of any kind. The saplings are no more. No lotus trees or reeds. The locusts consumed anything that was green. We have no way to make clothing, or to build bridges, or to make baskets. Even our wines for trade are no longer in existence. The olive trees and grapevines are in utter ruins. Lastly, we have no way to make anything to drink.

Luzige knelt before Pharaoh and spoke, "Devastation! Widespread devastation! My heart hurts—it is almost more than I can bear. There is nothing left to make bread and Zytum. The gardens have all been gleaned by these locusts. With having no more flowers for a while, there shall be no more honey or wax."

Pharaoh deep in thought, his chin in his right hand and his elbow on the arm rest now spoke, "I need to know about our sacred trees. How about Ished, the tree of life through Thoth and Seshat? How about the Acadia tree that belongs to Osiris and Isis? How about our sacred Sycamore tree that belongs to Nut and Isis?"

Luzige was greatly distressed by his great Pharaoh's question's. Why so much concern about these particular trees? Didn't he realize that so many other things were ruined, destroyed? Luzige wished that he could look his Pharaoh in the eyes. That Pharaoh would then come to realize the gravity of the situation. "Devoured, Pharaoh! They were completely devoured by an army of ruthless locusts." Pharaoh disgustedly dismissed Luzige and walked out on his balcony, where he stared out at the horizon as though he could magically find his answers there.

As Luzige left, Baraka arrived and said, "Pharaoh, we have a mob of people coming to the palace looking for food and clothing. They are the few who have not lost their faith in you. Let me send a messenger to Moses and Aaron."

Pharaoh, weary from the storm and looking for some peace, said, "Send a messenger to Moses and Aaron, we need to talk."

In the time it took for the servant to find and bring Moses and Aaron to the palace, Pharaoh stayed in his chambers and contemplated what he would say to Moses. Having dismissed all people from his chambers, he was deep in thought and prayer. Pharaoh was startled when Vizier Jibade walked in and announced, "Pharaoh, Moses and Aaron are here for you."

"Bring them in Jibade." As Moses and Aaron entered, Moses bowed before Pharaoh and asked, "How may I help you today, my Pharaoh?"

A truly humbled Pharaoh turned to Moses and begged, "I've sinned against your God and against you. Overlook my sin one more time. Pray to your God to get me out of this—get death out of here!"

Moses and Aaron looked Pharaoh in the eye, turned and walked out. The time for talking was over; it would not change the Pharaoh's mind.

Confused and upset Pharaoh raged at his men, "What was that about, Obaid, did you see that? Moses just turned around and left me! I did as you men asked me to, and Moses just leaves?" Pharaoh, having had enough with trying to please everyone, left the room muttering to himself and shaking his head in bewilderment.

Goshen

When they had returned to Goshen, Moses prayed: "Lord you heard Pharaoh, I ask that you would take this plague of locusts away from Pharaoh and the land of Egypt. Take the locusts away from all the inhabitants of Egypt. I ask you to call your army of locusts home.

May Pharaoh and his people learn from this tragedy. Thank you, Lord, for all you do, I thank you for who you are; for your goodness, kindness, and mercies. Thank you for taking such good care of us. Amen."

ET NEWS: BREAKING NEWS: "Forgive Me!"

"Marissa here with ET NEWS, it is good to be with my viewers today. Pharaoh spoke to Moses and Aaron at sunrise. Pharaoh asked Moses to ask their God to forgive us for our sins, and to pray for the death plague of locusts to end. Another ploy from Pharaoh to get Moses and his God off our back. I believe it worked as some of you may have noticed the wind seems to be blowing very strong and from the west. That is very strange. Look!

Do you see that cloud, it looks like the locusts are being picked up in a wind cloud and heading to the Red Sea? The locusts are leaving! Praise to our gods the locusts are being escorted out by a high wind cloud! Every locust, I see, is wrapped up in that dark cloud of death and leaving our country. Until further developments arise, this is Marissa for ET NEWS saying 'May the gods of Egypt protect you.'"

Palace

Pharaoh watched as the locusts were swept by the wind from his balcony; the locusts disappeared into the heavens heading to the Red Sea. With a voice of triumph, he laughed and commanded: "Baraka! Send word to Moses and Aaron, I am keeping my slaves right here with me where they belong!"

Chapter 17
Plague 9 "Darkness!"

Three Days and Three Nights: Terrifying Darkness, Heavenly Light.

ET NEWS: BREAKING NEWS: "Courtier Obaid Makes Announcement."

"This is Abdullah with ET NEWS; Marissa is taking time off. I am in the outer court of the palace where at any moment Courtier Obaid will make an announcement. We could sure use some good news—so much unrest—people have turned into wild beasts. Meanwhile, the wild beasts of the land have come to the cities looking for food, killing anyone who crosses their path. There is no such thing as a safe house or safe cave anymore. It looks like Courtier Obaid is about to speak."

"To the common people of Egypt, I have a message from our great Pharaoh. He wishes to let you know that it shall be some time before we'll be able to help any of you economically.

You are still required by Egyptian law to come and do your work so that we can get our nation back into a routine and the economy back on track. Pharaoh says not to concern yourself with this; it is only a temporary setback. As we all work together, the gods can help us recover what has been taken by the locusts."

The crowd began to yell, "How is this only a temporary setback!"

"Sounds like he wants to turn us into slaves!"

"The god's have not been helping us with these plagues, you think they are going to help us now?"

Courtier Obaid commanded, "Order, order, I demand order!"

Abdullah spoke, "The crowd here seems to be showing signs of becoming violent."

Courtier Obaid decided it was time to show his authority, "Civil unrest is never acceptable. Guards! Arrest those people for causing civil unrest. Pharaoh has heard rumors that the political arena is about to change. That is not true, and anyone caught speaking against Pharaoh or the Egyptian government shall suffer according to the laws of Egypt! Pharaoh is doing the best he can to keep Egypt as the number one country.

You cannot expect this to happen tomorrow, so give it some time. We encourage you to go and to worship your home gods as this can help get things back to normal sooner rather than later. It is Pharaoh's greatest prayer that we are done once and for all with the thorn in his side called Moses! Thank you, that is all for now."

The crowd responded: "You think that is all you have to do!"

"We need help and we'll get help—even if we have to invade the palace!"

"Come on, I bet the palace has food that they are hiding."

"Guards, stop them!" commanded Courtier Obaid, as he ran back into the palace.

"There you have it, people, once again, everything bad is blamed on Moses and his God. After all that has happened, perhaps you Egyptians should think about listening to Moses' God. What has Pharaoh been able to do for you lately?

Yes, I am in big trouble with Marissa and ET NEWS for saying what I am saying. I am an Israelite or Hebrew as some call us, by birth. I can see that our God is the most powerful God—the one and only true God—and I think it is time to listen to what our God has been trying to tell us.

Let the Israelite people go and worship their God. Pharaoh, please listen, let the Israelite people go and worship their God before there is nothing left!

For ET NEWS, this is Abdullah—with what might be my last broadcast with ET NEWS—saying, "Don't you think it is time to listen to Moses and his God?"

God Spoke to Moses

God said to Moses: "Stretch your hand to the skies. Let darkness descend on the land of Egypt—a darkness so dark you can touch it."

"As you say, my Lord," answered Moses.

Moses stretched out his hand to the skies. Thick darkness descended on the land of Egypt for three days. Nobody could see anybody. For three days nobody could so much as move. Except for the Israelites: they had light where they were living.

Then the Lord said to Moses, "Yet I will bring one plague more on Pharaoh and on Egypt; afterwards he will let you go. When he lets you go from here, he will thrust you out altogether. Now this is what I want you to do."

Goshen

"Moses, look! What is that upon the land around us? It looks like a thick circle of pitch-black that goes from the sky to the ground. Eerie—that is what it is, eerie. Has anyone ever seen such an eerie darkness before? How can anyone see?" asked Aaron.

"God spoke to me and said: 'Stretch out your hand to the skies, and a darkness that all souls shall feel will cover all of Egypt, except Goshen.'"

"No warning! How long do they have to be in that darkness?"

"Three days and three nights."

"Three days and three nights? I would be going crazy before three minutes were up. Why did God place such a darkness upon the people?"

Moses explained, "God said this represents his separation from people when they refuse to believe and obey him. He has given them a tiny taste of the never ending darkness that occurs at death—for those who worship false gods and goddesses. He has reserved this darkness, especially for those who continue to serve anyone or anything that is not of God himself. I feel for those people, Aaron. If this darkness does not open their eyes to the one true God, I fear nothing will."

Horror and Blessings Begin — First Twelve of Seventy-Two Hours

People were standing around talking about how upset they were with Pharaoh and the circumstances that had evolved. What were they going to do about it? Kamenwati and Hanif, the palace guards, were walking over to gather up the prisoners arrested for causing civil unrest. Suddenly, a blanket of darkness fell upon them all.

A sudden solar eclipse perhaps? No, this darkness had covered not just the sun, but the moon and stars as well. It would take a god or goddess to bring in this kind of darkness. Why would they do that?

Maybe Seth—it would be just like him to be causing chaos and mischief. Seth had never gone this far in his dealings with other gods. He usually left the people out of it. Eerie—that is what it is, eerie. Not only was it dark but there also seemed to be a feeling of complete evil in the air. Panicked, people started to scream.

"Help!" "Help me!" "What has happened to the sun?"

"What is this blanket of darkness and where did it come from?" yelled Kamenwati.

"Help? Why would I help you when I can't even see you?" yelled Hanif, the other palace guard.

The shrill cries of a terrified little girl were heard above and beyond the rumblings of the panicked crowd: "Mommy! Mommy! Where are you?"

Omid answered her daughter's cry with the comfort only a mother could give; "I am right here my little Hannah, just hold out your hand, and mommy will find you."

Hannah, feeling deep abandonment and loss, screamed out: "Mommy I can't see you! Someone did something with the light! Something happened to the sun, and something won't let me find your hand!"

Trying to keep herself calm for the sake of her daughter, Omid spoke words of comfort to little Hannah, "I'll reach out my hand to you."

"Hanif, can you see the prisoners?" shouted Kamenwati.

"How am I supposed to see them in all this darkness, and why has the sun been covered up?" asked a frustrated Hanif.

Kamenwati trying to keep his composure answered, "One of the gods must be in a playful mood—this can't last for long."

Abdullah and Osher — First Twelve of Seventy-Two Hours

Abdullah was startled by the sudden bubble of bright light that surrounded him, "What is this? I have never seen this kind of light before!" Looking around, he spotted another person, "You were standing next to me at the conference, what is your name?"

"My name is Osher, and you are... Abdullah?"

"That is me, co-anchor of ET NEWS. Well, Osher, it seems that my God must be up to something again. We appear to be in a bubble of light. I wonder if everyone is in their own bubble of light?"

"I am not sure, one minute the conference is over and I am thinking about heading home, and the next I am in this realm of light with you. The light has an unusually comfortable feeling."

"Yes, it does, I have never experienced anything like this before. Just one thing—we seem to be cocooned in this light, and I have no idea how to get anywhere. It looks like God has something going on, and he is protecting us from it. So until he decides it is time to release us from this cocoon, we'll just have to make the best of it. Since I am a reporter, do you mind if I interview you?" asked Abdullah.

"Not at all, what would you like to know?" replied Osher.

"Why were you at the conference this afternoon?"

"My father is the overseer of the sheep for Pharaoh. He has not been the same since the Murrain struck the herd. Father struggled intensely with the pain of seeing his sheep suffer so much from the disease. He had just become fun to be around again, when the hail struck us and right after that, came the locusts. We just never had a break. I decided to check out the news conference to see if the Pharaoh had something to say that would help my father." explained Osher.

Pharaoh — First Twelve of Seventy-Two Hours

Pharaoh shouted into the darkness. "Magicians, sorcerers, counselors! Why is everything so dark? Servants! Where are my servants? Amun-Ra, what has happened, where are you?"

Goshen — First Twelve of Seventy-Two Hours

Aaron spoke to the people, "Some of you have been wondering what is happening to our surroundings right now. Let me explain, God spoke darkness into all the land except Goshen. The people of Egypt are not under God's favor, they are experiencing a thick and threefold darkness.

I realize this is hard for you to understand; however, we are experiencing God's heavenly light. The light that surrounds us is God's pure love, not the natural sun. Just as for the Egyptians, who at this moment in time are experiencing God's fury, not the darkness that comes from having no moon, no stars.

Enjoy and relax in the pleasant warmth of his love for the three days that it is to last. After the darkness that has settled in our surrounding area has lifted, the Lord shall place one final plague upon Egypt. In a few days, the Lord shall be sending a plague of death to Egypt.

This plague shall kill the first-born of any male, human or animal, and that includes a household pet, which is in the land of Egypt." Aaron tried to explain further, but the people interrupted and shouted out their indignation and bewilderment."

"What! How can God do this?"

"Why would God do this?"

"Quiet! Quiet! Listen to all that I must tell you before you jump to any conclusions. God has instructions telling us how we, his people shall not suffer from this death. I'll explain more on that later. We are to be spared the death angel visit if we listen to all God has to say and obey his instructions.

During these three days, we must be preparing for our departure to the promised land. God has told me that Pharaoh is going to be pushing us out of Egypt when the next plague is over. In the meantime, God has called for us to prepare for what is to be called the Passover Meal. He has given it this name because the death angel that is coming through the land shall pass over us.

As I instruct you in these things; pay attention to what I say; otherwise, there shall be severe consequences. The things you must know; are as follows:

1) God has instructed us to have you pick out a lamb or a young goat for your families. This animal is to be our Passover Sacrificial animal. On the tenth day of this month, which is tomorrow, every man shall take the best lamb or goat from his flock, and pen it up in the sacrificial pen. The animal is to be a one-year-old and to have no deformities, no spots or blemishes. He is to be a perfect animal, and have no broken bones.

2) You are to take care of this animal and keep it separated until the fourteenth. On that day, we are to slaughter our animals simultaneously at the entrances of our homes. Make sure you hold the blood of the animal in a bowl and do not let any drop to the ground. Take a bunch of hyssop plant, dip it in the blood, and mark the right and left side of your doorposts looking similar to the symbol of a cross; you shall mark your lintel's [see glossary] in the same way. As soon as you have finished, no one is allowed to leave your house until morning.

All of you are to report back here on the morning of the thirteenth for further instructions. You have a lot to do and little time to do it in, that is all for now," said Aaron. The people knelt, bowing with their faces touching the ground, in reverence to God. The Israelites did as the Lord commanded them.

Rameses — Twenty-Four of Seventy-Two Hours

"How long can this continue? Shouldn't the moon and stars be shining by now? Where is Ptah?" shouted Kamenwati.

"If not Ptah, what about Thoth?" shouted Hanif.

The people's restlessness had now turned to panic. "I need some light!"

"It's getting hard to breathe!"

"Can somebody hold my hand?"

"I am scared! Help! I want to go home!"

"What has happened to my wife and children? Bring my family to me!"

"Horus! Horus!"

Hannah's cries had become more desperate, "Mommy! Mommy! Where are you?"

"Honey, I am right here, trust me. You are going to be alright; Mommy won't let anything happen to you," shouted Omid. And yet she had begun to wonder how she was going to find her little girl. There seemed to be no way to reach through the heaviness of this impenetrable darkness.

Abdullah and Osher — Twenty-Four of Seventy-Two Hours

"Have you noticed that we are surrounded by a bright light, yet there is no sun? God is doing something; I am just not sure what. You said your father currently is the overseer of the shepherds for Pharaoh, are you not Egyptian?" asked Abdullah.

Proud of his ancestry, Osher replied to Abdullah's question, "We are Israelites from the line of Jacob; Dan is my great, great grandfather. When my people first came to this land during the great famine, the Pharaoh of that time noticed that our sheep were healthier than his sheep. None of Pharaoh's people knew how to take proper care of the sheep. So Joseph sent for the best sheep herder [shepherd] of the Israelites to come and care for the palace sheep. It seems that I am next in line to be the overseer, if we have any sheep left, that is."

Abdullah asked, "You are what, about eleven or twelve years of age?"

"Just turned thirteen and had my Bar Mitzvah a few months ago," explained Osher proudly. "Why did you come to live in Egypt?"

"I was out wandering around here in Rameses while mother and father were busy. You do not go to Rameses alone; my parents would warn me. Did I listen, no! I was wandering around and bumped into Marissa, who was a news reporter for ET NEWS. She was in need of a grunt worker and decided that I could become her property for use at ET NEWS. My parents needed the money, not able to control me, so they gave their consent. I've been with Marissa and ET NEWS ever since," explained Abdullah.

"How old were you when that happened?" asked Osher.

"I was ten, it seems so long ago," answered Abdullah.

Pharaoh — Twenty-Four of Seventy-Two Hours

Pharaoh prayed, "Great gods of wisdom, Seshat, and Thoth, I ask you to send the word out to the other gods—ask them to help me. Ask Ra, Khepri, Horus, and Amun as there must be war raging in the realm of the gods. Is Seth causing trouble again and this time it is affecting us? What is this weight upon me? I cannot seem to find a way to get out of this chair. What is this heaviness I seem to be wearing? Wadjet, I ask you to protect me from the eerie things that are in the darkness of this night."

Goshen — Twenty-Four of Seventy-Two Hours

"Dan, we have completed twenty-four hours of the seventy-two hours, and I am glad that we have God's favor, that we are in his light. Although, I cannot help but wonder why the sun never goes down?" observed Asher.

"I know what you mean. It feels good, and the sunshine has caused everything to grow and the crops are about ready for harvest. The sun seems to feel different somehow, but I cannot explain the difference," said Dan.

"I've had a hard time sleeping with all this sunlight, how are we expected to sleep? Having sunlight twenty-four seven is not something we are accustomed to," Asher wondered out loud.

Dan responded, "I think this light is so peaceful that the question should be: 'How are we going to get any work done?'"

Laughing Asher replied, "You are right." Asher caught Moses from the corner of his eye, and cried, "Moses! You startled me. How long have you been standing there?"

"Long enough to hear your conversation, and frankly, I am surprised that you still do not understand what is happening here."

"What do you mean?" asked Dan.

"Dan, you were at the meeting where Aaron explained what was going on, were you not?" asked Moses.

"Yes, I was," answered Dan.

"And at that meeting, did Aaron not explain that the light we are experiencing is not the sun, but God's pure love?" asked Moses.

"Yes, he did, but what does that mean exactly?" asked Asher.

"Men, right now we have no need of the sun, or the moon or the stars. We are experiencing what the atmosphere is like when God is present. The sun, the moon, and the stars did not exist until God spoke them into existence," answered Moses.

"Asher! Edna is looking for you, come it is time for the evening meal. Moses, it is an honor to see you. Would it be alright to steal my husband from you for the evening meal?" asked Abigail, Dan's wife.

"But of course, remember what I explained to you. I want you to help the others to understand. Shalom."

"Shalom, Moses," they all replied.

"And you, Dan, get moving if you want me to serve you your evening meal, understand?" teased Abigail, her eyes twinkling.

"My adorable young lady, I'll get moving as you put it, but only if you walk me home." replied Dan.

Abigail blushed as she replied, "After all these years, you are still a hopeless flirt." Smiling with pride at his Abigail, Dan continued: "Only for you, my wife, only for you." Turning toward Asher, Dan said, "Shalom, Asher, have a good meal and a restful sleep."

"Shalom, Dan."

Rameses — Thirty-Six of Seventy-Two Hours

The people Courtier Obaid commanded the guards to take as prisoners, were now causing a commotion from within the darkness. They started to threaten the guards and others around them.

The people screamed, "How long has it been?"

"I need to go to the bathroom." "I'm hungry!"

"I want my family!"

"You had better let me out of this darkness, do you understand! You have no right to hold me like this!"

"Who are you talking to out there? You think that we put everyone in this darkness as a joke? If we were able to do that, we would not be in the darkness with you! Hanif, can you move around?" asked Kamenwati.

Hanif shouted, "Now that you mention it, no; I can't even sit down. This darkness is starting to bug me!"

"How much longer is this going to stay with us? I want to get back to the palace, drop these prisoners off, get home to my wife, and have some Zytum, what about you Hanif?" asked Kamenwati.

"Sounds real good to me—maybe some fish and bread—suppose we might get some cheese? I love Zytum with fish, bread, and cheese," replied Hanif.

Sarcastically, the crowd began shouting: "Listen to him, will you? I love Zytum with fish, bread, and cheese. So what!"

"We cannot have any and neither can you!"

"Yeah, you think you are someone special?"

"Hanif, it sounds like we've got ourselves a court jester out there. That is funny, real funny. Keep it up and you'll find out how funny you are when the sun comes back," shouted Kamenwati.

A desperate little Hannah yelled, "Mommy! Mommy! I can't see you, help me mommy!"

The forced calm voice of a very upset Omid spoke, "Hush, my little Hannah, Mommy's here; you are okay." Omid continued with a whispered prayer, "Please help us, Bastet, for you are our protector, you are the one who cares about us!"

Abdullah and Osher — Thirty-Six of Seventy-Two Hours

"How hard was it to have a Bar Mitzvah in the middle of Egypt?" asked Abdullah.

"It might have been hard if father had not put in extra time and gotten permission to take us to visit relatives in Goshen. But fortunately, we were able to have my Bar Mitzvah in Goshen with family. How about you, did you have a Bar Mitzvah?"

"No, I have not seen my family since the ET NEWS station bought me. I should say, 'Marissa bought me'... she put me to work at the station. I had almost given up on the God of the Hebrews until now."

Filled with curiosity, Osher asked, "What has happened to change your mind?"

"I've been in with this war between Pharaoh and Moses' God—our one true God—since the very beginning. From what I have seen and continue to see, our God is the only God that truly is alive."

Pharaoh — Thirty-Six of Seventy-Two Hours

Pharaoh spoke to himself, "Why did this happen when I had no wife with me! It sure would have been nice to have at least one of my wives next to me; yes, in this darkness a good companion would be an excellent help. Why can't I move? I want to stand up, walk, *anything* but sit!

This darkness is unbearably thick. Ra, what is this heaviness that does not allow me to move, and would you explain it to me, please? Wadjet, when will you help out of this mess? Moses' God has something to do with this, and I'll make Moses pay for what they are doing to me!

Great gods of the Sun: Ra, Amun-Ra, and Horus, I ask you to come and show the face of the sun to us again—for you, and you alone, can do this for me. I am the son of Amun-Ra; do not forsake me. Ptah, I have every happy thought that you'll appear at any moment and let the light of the sun and the moon cover me, and my country, again. I know not what has happened, but I give you glory and thanks."

Goshen — Thirty-Six of Seventy-Two Hours

"Good morning, Thaddeus, how are you this fine day?" asked Asher.

"Blessed by our God... I think." Thaddeus continued, "Did the sun go down last night?"

Dan looked around, "The sun went down I am sure, but remember Moses said that the light we are experiencing is not the sunlight, but the atmosphere of God's presence. When I look out beyond Goshen, I see a darkness so thick that one probably can't breathe in it. I am thankful God's love spared us from suffering that darkness."

Asher spoke, "Another day of total darkness out there, this is just eerie..."

"Eerie it is, Asher, but is it eerie enough to keep you from ending up where the Egyptians are at this moment in time?" asked Moses.

"Moses, you startled me! What do I know? However, I could not end up out there in the dark because I am an Israelite—a descendant of Abraham, Isaac, and Jacob," boasted Asher.

"You think that just because you are an Israelite you are exempt from the punishment that the Egyptians are receiving? It is only by the grace of God that we are not out there with the Egyptians. Have you so quickly forgotten that our people suffered for four hundred years because of disobedience to our God? God is showing what his grace looks like, and more of who he is to us.

God is also showing us what he can do, and shall do, to those who choose to ignore him. He also instructed us to tell our children and our grandchildren the stories of the miracles we have seen, so that they also may live in the proper fear and wonder of who our God is. Never forget that it is only by God's grace that we do not end up the way of the Egyptians. Come, we have work to do." scolded Moses.

The men followed Moses as he headed out to show them what still needed to be done in the next few days. There was much work to do preparing for their departure to the land of milk and honey. Parting to go to their assigned sections of Goshen, each man had a different thought on his mind. Some were excited and couldn't wait to leave Egypt. Others were not so sure about leaving Egypt, but if

Moses would lead them, they were willing to give it a try. Still there were others who just wanted out to do whatever was needed to get out of their current situation.

Rameses — Forty-Eight of Seventy-Two Hours

"I do not understand it." complained Hanif.

"Hathor, I am asking you to bring back the sun!" yelled Kamenwati.

The cries of the people were becoming more desperate: "Light, I need light!"

"Hard to breath!"

"What's that noise? Who's out there?"

People heard the sound of someone being slapped and then an angry voice piped up, "Stop touching me!"

They were starting to freak out when they heard what sounded like a very screechy, eerie voice that spoke with authority: *I'll touch you all I want!"* Then the voice gave an evil laugh and dared, *"Try to stop me!"*

In the suffocating darkness a voice yelled, "Help! I want to go home!" They heard what sounded like a slap that came from another direction and then another angry voice piped up, "Stop breathing on me!"

Another loud, raspy voice gave an eerie laugh and spoke with authority, *"I'll breathe on whom I want, anytime I want!"*

Kamenwati, tired and irritated, shouted with the authority of a palace guard, "You had all better pray you are dead before I get my hands on you, now shut up!"

Hanif, Kamenwati's second in command, chimed in and said, "Yeah, and if Kamenwati does not get you, then I will. There is no help for the likes of you people. So shut up!"

Hannah yelled, "Mommy! It is too dark—bring back the sun, Mommy! What happened to the moon and the stars? I cannot see you, help me, mommy!" Omid, at her wits end, spoke, "Mommy's here! I shall pray for help." With desperation in her voice she prayed, "Bastet, what happened to you? Please help us!"

Abdullah and Osher — Forty-Eight of Seventy-Two Hours

Osher said, "I hope that our God changes the way things are very soon. It has been scary living here in Egypt this past year."

"The weird events that took place in Egypt, this past year is the only reason I was allowed to become co-anchor for Marissa," replied Abdullah.

"Why do you say that?"

"Marissa and the board decided to do a documentary on Moses and she wanted protection from the Israelites. She decided I could protect her because many of the Egyptians are afraid of the Israelites. So, the only reason, the Egyptians are afraid of us, is because there are so many of us; that they think we shall revolt against them. Now that Moses and God are with us they are right."

Osher responded, "The Egyptians just do not understand who we are and who our God is."

Pharaoh — Forty-Eight of Seventy-Two Hours

Pharaoh prayed," Thoth, I ask you to show me your wisdom to help me end this raging war. Help me to be rid of Moses and his God. Let the light of the sun and the moon cover me and my country again. Do you hear me, Thoth? Have you any concern for us—your people?" By now, because of the constant darkness, Pharaoh had become a little crazy and while holding his head up with his hands in desperation shouted, "What is happening! Ra, when will this nightmare stop?"

Rameses — Sixty of Seventy-Two Hours

An exasperated Kamenwati shouted at the prisoners, "What is your problem? We cannot do anything about your circumstances! If you say one more thing, I'll feed you to the crocodiles!"

The people, equally exasperated, responded back with threats and sarcasm of their own. "You've got to find one first, buddy! The crocs are all dead by now."

"Help!" "I want out, do you hear me, *out!*"

Hanif questioned, "Have all the god's of Egypt lost this war against Moses' one God that the sun and the moon and the stars have been swallowed up by death and darkness?"

Hannah became more panicked by the minute and in her anguish yelled, "Mommy! I need you! I want to see you *now!*"

Time spent in this heavy darkness wore on Omid. Hearing and feeling the evil around her, her mind was no longer clear enough to remember Hannah. And Hannah was too small to understand what was happening. Omid's voice, raised with irritation to her circumstances, spoke, "Hannah, I have not gone anywhere!" Suddenly Omid heard that eerie laugh from somewhere next to her, "Shut up, I wasn't talking to you!"

Unable to understand that the darkness was making her mother go a little crazy, Hannah, full of terror and with a trembling lip cried, "Mommy! Why did you tell me to shut up? Father, where are you?"

Omid heard the cry of Hannah and spoke, "I am right beside you, Hannah." As her voice weakened, she said once again, "I am right beside you, Hannah."

Abdullah and Osher — Sixty of Seventy-Two Hours

Abdullah explained, "The Egyptians seem to have a god or goddesses for every purpose, every occasion. They started out worshiping one or two gods and goddesses. From there they started a family of them. It did not take long before they had over one hundred different kinds of gods and goddesses to worship.

Did you know the people worship an idol that represents anything that exists? They have a God for the grass, dirt, the wind, water, the sun, the moon." Abdullah shrugged his shoulders and shook his head as he finished his explanation, "Too many, too many gods."

It's hard enough for me to learn about our one God, how do they keep track of over one hundred gods?"

"I believe that is why they are in such a mess; there is no possible way to learn about that many gods. I have been with Marissa long enough to tell the god she worships the most is Pharaoh—even with all that has happened—Marissa continues to put her trust in him."

"Really?" Osher thought for a moment and observed, " I see their frustration with Pharaoh and their desire for him to let us leave or to kill us. Now that you mention it, there does seem to be a few that still side one-hundred percent with Pharaoh."

Pharaoh — Sixty of Seventy-Tow Hours

Pharaoh prayed, "Where are you, my great and glorious God, Ptah— the one who created the moon, the sun, and the earth? Come back to me and help me to overcome this thorn in my side."

Goshen — Sixty of Seventy-Two Hours

"I cannot get past this light. It should be the sun, just plain sun, but it is not somehow," mused Thaddeus.

Dan, was deep in wonder as he replied to Thaddeus' statement. "I know what you mean, I have heard complaints about the light staying around for far too long at a time. How can people look over the land and not see the darkness that has encircled itself around Goshen and that engulfs the rest of Egypt? How can they complain about too much light?"

"They are looking at it as the sun, it is not sunlight, it is the light that comes directly from the realm of God's pure love," answered Moses.

Dan asked, "What do you mean by the realm of God's pure love?"

"The realm of God's pure love is the area that exists around God. It is a touch of warmth and comfort that comes from being in the same zone. It is what his people shall experience when they die. We are not used to it because we have never experienced it before. We live our lives separated from God because we live in a world full of the darkness of sin. One cannot experience the full feeling of God's pure love until you give your whole life over to him."

Rameses — Final Seventy-Two Hours

The people were showing signs of being in the darkness for too long. They were suffering, they heard voices, they were feeling things that were not there. Moreover, they seemed to be confined to their own little prison spaces. By now they did not care about anyone or anything except escaping their prisons.

"I want to go home!"

"It's very hard to breathe."

"Then shut up and don't waste your air!"

"Don't touch me anymore or I'll...!"

"Stop! Stop breathing on me!"

"Sleep, peaceful sleep would be nice."

Hannah, her mind no longer able to comprehend, was heard yelling, "Father, something has happened to Mommy. Father, help me! I want to go home!"

Omid had gone crazy with fear because of the time spent in this wholly evil darkness. "Hannah, I have not gone anywhere! You do not need your father! I am right here! Do not touch my little girl!"

In the eerie, bleak silence of the total darkness, a stifled sob is heard. The intense darkness lingered on and on as little Hannah, with her mind almost gone, had one last thing to say: "Mommy, I cannot feel you!"

Abdullah and Osher — Final Seventy-Two Hours

Abdullah asked, "Whenever Moses and Aaron have appeared before Pharaoh, they ask Pharaoh to allow God's people to go out and worship. When Pharaoh finally gives his consent for the Israelites to leave, will you and your family go?"

"Oh yes!" exclaimed Osher. "My parents have been talking about little else. They have wondered why it is taking so long for this to happen and have become discouraged because of all the devastation. Through it all, they have refused to give up! When Pharaoh does release us, we are gone!"

"Do you think that Moses would allow someone such as me to go along with the Israelites?"

Abdullah, you were born to Israelite parents, why would you not be allowed to go? I guess maybe the bigger question would be: Even if Marissa and the news people said you could not leave, would you leave without their consent?"

"I've thought about that very thing. Yes! Yes, I would leave; maybe, just maybe I shall find my family again." Abdullah's answer left him with a feeling of joy that he had not felt in a very long time.

Pharaoh — Final Seventy-Two Hours

Pharaoh was fervently praying, "Ra, I thank you that I know you'll come and show your face again—you'll come and show your face again, won't you?" He repeated the prayer as fear, doubt, and confusion started to creep into his mind. "Wadjet, bring to me your all Seeing Eye and protection back to me. I repent of any wrong that I gave done and I ask you to place your favor back on me. Take your eye and find Moses and his God, that thorn in my side, and let me be free again. Servants! I want a drink; I am dying of thirst!"

Goshen — Final Seventy-Two Hours

Asher wondered, "Trapped for three days and three nights in that darkness, what are those people feeling? If I were them, I would feel as though my God had abandoned me. In feeling abandoned by their God, maybe they will start to ask questions about our one true God."

Thaddeus replied, "I would probably go crazy not being able to see anything for all that time. Just imagine how many times they must have bumped into each other. That darkness looks evil, scary!"

Moses spoke, "Reject the great I Am when you are alive in the world and the great I Am will reject you when your soul passes from this world to the next. Think of it this way. Why would you invite someone to live with you for all eternity if they continually talked bad about you? Or if they consistently tell you that others are better than you, and frequently say they do not need you?

If you were God, would you do that? God is showing us *all* that there is a difference between believing and worshiping our God and believing in and worshiping idols, deities, and other so-called gods."

"They seem to be convinced that their idols can take care of them completely. That they are somehow a living, breathing person," observed Dan.

"Dan, do you believe that way about our God?" asked Moses.

"Yes," answered Dan.

"Then why should they believe any differently about their gods? I grew up as a member of the Royal Egyptian family, and I know they are reacting in the only way they know. God is now showing them that he is the only living, breathing God. There are some people that shall come to understanding that about our God. Those that do not come to that understanding, shall suffer the consequences of their unbelief.

God is still a merciful God. Have any of you noticed that even though the Egyptians are going through these awful plagues, God is still treating them with kindness?" The three men looked at Moses with the same expression an old dog has when he thinks you are about to feed him a bone and instead, he sees you throw it in the garbage. Their total confusion and disappointment was evident.

"Well, I can see by the looks on your faces that you do not have a clue what I mean."

"Moses, the people of Egypt have suffered more than any people that I have ever seen. We, the Hebrews, in all our years of slavery have not suffered as the Egyptians are now. So what do you mean by saying that God has been showing them kindness?" asked Thaddeus.

"Men, we are leaving in the next few days, and when we leave we'll take with us only what we have prepared to take with us. Correct?" All three responded, "Correct."

"The food that is ready for harvest here in Goshen shall be available to the Egyptians; in this way, God is showing mercy and kindness. You need to keep your eyes open. Keep yourself close to God in prayer. God always finds a way to blend good in with the bad. Now we had better go see how the others are doing."

As they walked off in different directions, each one was thinking hard about what Moses had just said. The men were unaware, that in the near future they, too, would be challenged by circumstances that would require them to have their eyes wide open as Moses had just warned them about. And to succeed in that circumstance they would need to be close to God in prayer.

Let There Be Light

When the darkness came upon the people, it was with the swiftness of a bird stalking its prey. The darkness had quickly and totally smothered out light of any kind. It was with that same swiftness the light was returned.

Only this time there was not a cloud in the sky. The sun was bright and high as on any regular hot and sunny day. Three days in total darkness caused temporary blindness when the darkness left.

Kamenwati exclaimed loudly, "Wow! My eyes! The light—it is back! The sun is so bright it is hard to see and my eyes hurt!"

"The light is hurting my eyes too. Thanks be to Ra, nice to have you back. Are you able to see yet, Kamenwati?" asked Hanif.

"I am adjusting, but my eyes are still stinging."

After what seemed like forever, yet was probably only a few minutes of adjustment, the crowd shouted "Light! Praise be to our Sun God Ra, he is back!"

"Seth was unable to conquer our Ra!"

"Do you think Ra had help from the other gods?"

"I do not care; he defeated Seth and that is all that matters!"

"I can see a little bit, but I can see!"

"I can breathe!" "I can move!"

"My eyes hurt and my vision is blurry, but I can see!"

Hannah shouted, "Mommy! My eyes hurt. Mommy?"

"My dear Hannah, I am right here. Do you feel my hug?" Hannah shook her head yes and melted into her mother's arms. "As soon as I can see better, we'll go home and find your father, sisters, and brothers."

"Well, well, look—see what we have here, Hanif. I think my eyes see well enough to take care of some prisoners, what do you say?" asked Kamenwati.

"Like we said, you've got to catch us, pigs!" responded two of the prisoners.

"Let's start rounding them up—after you," said Hanif. "We know who they are, and they'll be around; let us go and find some of that Zytum, fish, bread, and cheese we were talking about," replied Kamenwati.

"Sounds like a good idea—they'll be easy to find later," said Hanif.

"Abdullah, our cocoon has opened, and the world is back to normal. Were all these people so close to us the whole time?" asked Osher.

"We must have been right beside them the whole time, and we did not even know it. We had not a clue about what went on with them while we were in that bubble of light. I feel we have experienced some special protection from God, but others were left vulnerable," answered Abdullah.

"What are you going to do? I know I need to go find my family to see how they are," asked Osher.

"I guess I had better go and see if I can find Marissa—look for me when Pharaoh says we can go worship our God. I would like to stay with you and your family until I can find my own. Do you think your family would mind?" asked Abdullah.

"I do not think they'll mind, especially when they hear that you and I spent time together in a cocoon of light for however long it was. Shalom, Abdullah." "Shalom, Osher."

Palace

A gleam of sunlight bounced from the gold on the palace doors. However, the picture was not pretty. The walls made of gold normally shined with pride in its splendor. However, when you looked at the gold, it had lost its shine. It had become broken, chipped, and cracked. The sunlight shined and showed the damage brought to the heart of the land of Egypt.

There was nothing left to look new. The gardens had nothing in them to come back to life. No trees to stand proud, just beaten poles trying to recover from war injuries. The palace crocodiles happily spending time in the pool, no longer existed. All the crocodiles that protect the royal Egyptian's world, were dead.

With much room for improvement, the sun was a welcomed sight for that battle-torn land. The bright, wonderful, and glorious sunlight had returned once more to the land of Egypt.

Inside, Pharaoh was expressing his great joy over the presence of the sunlight and the absence of darkness. Turning toward the heavens, Pharaoh reverently spoke to his spiritual father, the Sun God Ra. "Praise to Amun-Ra. You are my mighty, powerful and glorious god! Thank you, for bringing the sunlight back to my land.

Turning his attention now to immediate concerns, Pharaoh loudly declared, "It is time for Moses and his God to leave my country! Servants! Come and make me presentable, it is time to worship the great gods of Egypt." Courtier Obaid knocked on the Pharaoh's door, "Pharaoh? Pharaoh?" The doorman opened the door, and Courtier Obaid walked into Pharaoh's waiting room.

An utterly exhausted and stressed-to-the-max Courtier Obaid, dropped himself onto his favorite lounge. As he sat back—enjoying doing so in the sunlight—he thought to himself: "I hope Pharaoh knows how to handle this situation we are facing. When the sunlight came back to us, I realized that we are dealing with a much larger God than we realized. We have to give up those slaves!"

"Courtier Obaid, how did the news conference go?" asked Pharaoh, in a cheerful mood.

"You startled me!" complained Courtier Obaid, nearly jumping out of his chair.

Pharaoh chuckled, "I could not resist; you were resting peacefully like a baby. Now that you are awake, what do you request of me?"

"How can you be so calm? Did you not experience that horrible darkness?"

"That is over! The gods have taken care of it; now it is time to move ahead. Send for Moses, I wish to speak to him by the water."

"As you say," replied Courtier Obaid, in a hurry to leave Pharaoh's presence. Once out of the palace Courtier Obaid asked himself, "What is it with Pharaoh? He acts like nothing has happened!"

Goshen

"Moses, Moses, the sunlight is back! Funny—but our sunlight does not seem as bright now as it was during their darkness," observed Dan.

"I think it was because of the darkness around us; it trapped the sun and made it seem brighter to us." answered Asher.

"Yes, but why the sunlight all the time? We saw the moon, yet it was so dim because of the unusual light that was present. We saw the sunrise and the sunset, yet there was a constant light even when the sun had set." observed Thaddeus.

"Must I remind you again? The light you were seeing for three days and three nights, was not the natural sun and the moon. The light which comes from God himself and from his very presence, is the light that we were experiencing. While Egypt suffered three days and three nights of life *without* God, God, let the land of Goshen experience three days and three nights of life *with* God.

God gifted the Israelites with God's pure love, yet they were unable to comprehend it. That to me is sad; however, I have hope that someday real soon they'll grow to understand. Come on guys, we cannot stand around all day; we have work to do! Let's get ready so that we can leave this place! Suddenly everyone was full of anticipation for the journey ahead and speedily went out to get their work done.

Aaron walked up to the group of men and spoke directly to Moses. "Excuse me, Moses."

"Yes, Aaron?"

"A servant of Pharaoh has requested your presence at the palace. Pharaoh wants to speak with you."

"Thank you, Aaron I am on my way. Men, please excuse me while I go and find out what Pharaoh wants."

Chapter 18
Plague 10 "First Born Males Die?"

"This is Marissa with breaking ET NEWS from the palace. Pharaoh has called for Moses—unlike times in the past, only Moses shall appear before Pharaoh. It is my belief that Pharaoh and the gods have finalized a plan to get rid of Moses once and for all. Moses is approaching Pharaoh right now, let's watch the drama as it unfolds."

Pharaoh, felt good about the decision he made, and addressed Moses, "I am releasing you to go and worship the Lord! Even your women and children are going with you! However, I'll need you to leave your flocks and herds behind; they must stay with me."

"You know I need those animals, you must give permission for them to leave with us. I'll not leave a hoof behind. We need them to present as a sacrifice to our God, and we won't know what we need until we get there."

With the energy and volatility of lightening, Pharaoh flew into a fit of rage as he spewed: "Forget it! I have had it with you, Moses; you are not going anywhere! I have tried and tried to accommodate you and what do you do—spit in my face! Get out of my sight this very minute, do not ever let me see your face again! The day I do, *you shall die!* Do you hear me? You-shall-die! Guards, take Moses out of my sight before I have him killed!"

Moses, thoroughly disgusted with Pharaoh, clearly stated, "You are right Pharaoh, you'll never see my face again."

Kamenwati walked up to Moses, "If you want to stay alive, you had better come with us peacefully." Kamenwati took Moses by his arm intent upon him and another guard escorting Moses from the palace. Moses escorted by the guards took about ten steps from Pharaoh's presence, he then pulled away from the grasp of Kamenwati. Kamenwati was startled as Moses suddenly yanked his arm loose, "What are you doing, you just killed yourself!"

Moses turned to Pharaoh and said, "Thus says the Lord: About midnight I will go out through Egypt. Every firstborn in the land of Egypt shall die, from the firstborn of Pharaoh who sits on the throne to the firstborn of the female slave who is behind the handmill, and all the firstborn of the livestock. Then there will be a loud cry throughout the whole land of Egypt, such as never been or will ever be again. But not a dog shall growl at any of the Israelites—not at people, not at animals—so that you may know that the Lord makes a distinction between Egypt and Israel.

Then all these officials of yours shall come down to me, and bow low to me, saying, 'Leave us, you and all the people who follow you.' After that I will leave."

With that, an outraged Moses turned and left Pharaoh's presence.

"You heard it people. It seems that Pharaoh finally has enough against Moses to get rid of him for good. Pharaoh said if he sees Moses' face again, then Moses shall die. We know that Moses cannot help but show his face to Pharaoh one more time, so he is dead!

The Israelite slaves are not going anywhere; everything should be back to normal very soon. I hope that this gives you a renewed faith in Pharaoh and our gods.

We'll have another update for you before the midnight hour. We'll have at long last won the war between Pharaoh, Moses, and his God. Until then, this is Marissa for ET NEWS saying 'May the gods of Egypt protect you.'"

Marissa made her way through the crowd to tell Abdullah the exciting news, "Abdullah, Pharaoh did it! He finally found a way to get rid of Moses and his God. The Israelites have to come back and be the slaves they were meant to be. What a glorious day, Praise to all the gods of Egypt! I will have my Emmy very soon."

Abdullah stated with authority, "Very soon I'll be leaving with Moses and Aaron and heading to the land of milk and honey."

"What! I did not hear you right. Abdullah, do you believe that nonsense that Moses was spouting off in there?" Marissa raised her voice and pointed her finger to the palace court. "Abdullah! You have been away from your family long enough to know that what Moses said is nothing but garbage. You better be here with me for the late night program to complete our victory. If not, Moses is not the only one that shall be dead!" declared Marissa.

"Threaten me all you want, Marissa! I spent time in a cocoon of our God's light with a young Jewish boy. During that time, my God, the God of the Israelites, showed me that it is not too late for me. God has called his people to leave Egypt to go worship him.

I am an Israelite! I am going with them to worship my God! So, since I'll never see you again, goodbye, Marissa!" declared Abdullah. With a new found boldness and purpose in life Abdullah walked away from Marissa, and headed in the direction of Osher's house, he hoped.

Marissa watched in disbelief as Abdullah walked away from her, "Who do you think you are? Come back here, you belong to me! Get back here now or you'll not be alive by tomorrow!" It was too late as Marissa's shouts fell on deaf ears.

Goshen

"Cephas, the ninth hour is almost upon us, time to prepare to sacrifice our lamb. I'll go and get the lamb and bring him to the house. Would you prepare the butchering utensils?" asked Thaddeus.

"Dabi, go and gather the hyssop for us, will you?"

"Yes, Father."

Thaddeus instructed Moriah, "Go and tell your mother that I need the bowl to hold the blood. After you bring that to us, I need you to help your mother with the packing... hurry now."

As Moriah headed to the house, she found herself thinking: I wonder what tonight shall be like... It'll be a miracle just getting everything done before we leave, I know that.

"How is this bread going to taste with no leaven in it?" asked Martha.

"I know what you mean, this whole meal shall be different. We do want our last meal in this land to be unforgettable, don't we?" Libi said with a laugh.

"Mother!"

"What is it, Moriah? You do not need to shout."

"Father says he needs the bowl for the lamb's blood as it is time to prepare for the sacrifice."

"It is over on the shelf, what else did your father say?"

"He told me that I am to make sure I help you with the packing."

"Then you had better take your father this bowl and *after* he has it, come and help me." Moriah grabbed the bowl and ran out the door.

"That girl—to have her energy again. We have waited so long to leave, I never thought about how we would transport our things. I never dreamed that what we can take with us can only be what we can carry, or place on an animal."

"I had been thinking about that same thing all day; then it came to me, God is taking us to the land of milk and honey, and we shall have all we need—so who cares!" replied Libi.

"It is exciting to think that this will be our last meal here in Egypt. Did you know I heard that God has given this meal a name?"

"No! What does he call it?"

"The Lord's Passover meal."

"The Lord's Passover meal, what an impressive name. Is it because God shall be passing over us and not allowing the death angel to enter the houses marked by the blood of the lamb?"

Martha tried hard to imagine the meal about to take place, "I suppose so—imagine—we will be partaking of a meal prepared in a whole new way, a meal that we have never tasted before. And we are to eat it dressed to depart at a moment's notice, never to return again. There shall be no sleeping tonight.

Just think—the Lord told Moses that this meal and this night are to be *remembered forever* because of what the Lord is doing for us, for his people. We have been told to prepare a meal that will consist of lamb roasted to perfection which will remind us of God's perfect loving-kindness, and to make unleavened bread in remembrance of our quick departure.

I expect the bread will be flat and probably taste bland, but it will certainly be memorable! We will have bitter herbs which we usually don't eat. But tonight we will eat them to remind us of the harsh slavery which we have endured.

We are making a paste of fruits and nuts to remind us of the mortar we used to build the storehouses for Pharaoh. Another food we don't normally eat. Sprigs of parsley to eat as a reminder that our hope is in God. Aaron said to dip the parsley into salt water, the salty taste will remind us of the taste of all the bitter tears we have shed during our many harsh years of slavery."

Libi nodded her head slowly as she responded: "It'll take me some time to understand how our God wants things done and why."

"Yes, Libi, I agree with you. However, I'll try; I shall certainly try."

ET NEWS: BREAKING NEWS: "Death Rumors, Not True!"

"Hello, everyone, this is Marissa with ET NEWS. Some of you may not have heard Pharaoh's and Moses' last conversation. Moses told us that his God is going to strike all of Egypt's firstborn sons with a plague of death!

The audacity of that man and his God; not only shall our first born sons die, but also our firstborn male animals right down to our family pets as well. What kind of god attacks men and their pets, and for no reason, except to make Pharaoh let the Israelites leave Egypt?

"Today we are at the palace with Vizier Jibade who has a message from Pharaoh. It is such a privilege to be here with you as you are usually busy out in another part of our great land."

"That is right, Marissa; the job of Vizier has me gone more than I am home. Pharaoh has asked me to speak to the people for a moment on this significant development with Moses and his God.

"People of Egypt, it is of great importance that you hear what I have to say. As you know, the kingdom of Egypt practices the Law of Primogeniture. Because of this law, each of you should know that the loss of the firstborn male in your family would be especially disastrous. If that were to happen, no surviving member would be legally eligible to receive the family inheritance.

There would be no surviving member left to take care of the family. As no survivor member would be able to be made executor, no one would have a legal right to any family inheritance or family headship. Therefore that legal right would be handed over to Pharaoh who would then decide the fate of each family's estate.

Another reason this shall not happen is because Pharaoh knows of no god that would want to take from our men their pride and joy. Our firstborn male is the first proof of our manhood; he is our strength, he is our family honor.

I am sure that you are all familiar with the fact that in each Egyptian family, the firstborn son is the son destined to be the controller of the power of the family name. Every firstborn son makes the gods look honorable. Which of our gods would ever allow every first born son to be taken away from us?

Losing the first born animals would likewise be very devastating. Our first born male animals have a vital role in our society, we offer them as first fruits to our gods. What possible reason would our gods have for allowing the destruction of the very symbols of our devotion to them! Again, what god would be so cruel as to ever allow that to happen to *his* Egyptian families? Foolishness, utter foolishness.

Egypt—the world for that matter—would be at a standstill; the world as we know it would no longer exist. Total devastation, chaos, riots, an uncontrollable mad house—that is what the world would be. There are no gods known to Pharaoh, who would allow such a thing to happen.

People, I am second in command. As your second in command, as your Vizier, let me assure you—this death threat to our first born males will not occur! You have my word on this. Our gods and goddesses shall not let us down. They'll protect us from anything that Moses and his God might try to do. Even our Pharaoh said: 'Sit back and relax, do not concern yourself with this foolish threat.'"

"You have now heard it from Vizier Jibade, himself—so what do you think? Are you concerned that come midnight your firstborn son or your firstborn male animals shall die? As our great and mighty Pharaoh has no concern at all about this, why should any of you?

I say this because it has been brought to our attention that there are some of us Egyptians who are going to stay with the Israelites on this night. Their brains have been badly confused by all the dramatic events that have taken place recently. They are weak minded people, and we are better off without them. It is time for all good and righteous citizens of Egypt to stand up with Pharaoh and get rid of this plague called 'Moses and his God.'

We'll be live at the Palace about a half hour before midnight for the conclusion of this long and drawn out war. This war started out between Pharaoh and Moses along with Moses' God. Somewhere along the line as with so many wars, the innocent became involved.

This war is now between the Egyptians and the Israelites. I am sure that you, my fellow Egyptians, are just as excited as I am to see Moses finally meet the death he so greatly deserves. I am excited to see the real Egyptian citizens get back to the superior life we were meant to live. Until tonight, this is Marissa with ET NEWS saying 'May the gods of Egypt protect you.'"

Goshen

"Sapphira, make sure we have enough fuel to roast the lamb. We'll need the fire to stay hot in order to have the lamb roasted before midnight. Once we have marked the door-post, we will be unable to leave the house until morning. Our master shall be unhappy with us if we do not follow the instructions for roasting the lamb. As God has instructed us not to eat the meat raw," instructed Peninnah.

Ira asked, "How about burnt? I like burnt meat."

"Well then, you may have some after the rest of us as we are going to eat lamb roasted to perfection." answered his mother, Peninnah.

Elisheba looked around and asked, "Where are Aaron and Nadab... I thought they were with you?"

"Aaron and the guys went with Moses when he went to meet with Pharaoh," answered Miriam.

The door burst wide open, Elisheba relieved threw up her arms and walked to greet them, "Finally, what took you so long? Phinehas, did you have fun with Uncle Moses?"

"Very much, however, I had better let Uncle Moses explain; he'll be in soon."

Jochebed asked teasingly, "Did he buy some special stuff to take on our trip?"

Phinehas walked over to his great-grandmother and gave her a hug, "He did not buy anything, but he did get something for you, great-grandmother."

Smiling, Jochebed said, "Now I am curious! Come tell your great-grandmother—what did my Moses do? Phinehas, come on and tell your sweet, adorable, great-grandmother."

Phinehas tried very hard not to give away his great-uncle's surprise, "great-uncle Moses will be in with your surprise any minute."

"Why all the suspense? He did not buy anything, so I cannot think of what it would be."

Phinehas took his great-grandmother by the hand and said, "You'll be surprised!"

Just as the door opened and Moses entered, Elisheba said, "I hope he gets in here soon—I think it is close to the ninth hour."

"Moses! Where have you been! I understand you have a surprise... Princess Bithiah?"

"Yes, mother, I brought you..." Moses took Princess Bithiah by the hand and gently walked her towards Jochebed and said ever so gently, "Bithiah." A little unsure of how to act on this new journey of her life and a bit unsure just how the household would feel about her showing up, Princess Bithiah whispered, "Hello, Jochebed."

"But how? Why? Oh, Bithiah!" Jochebed greeted Princess Bithiah and welcomed her with a big hug.

"Bithiah and I have talked from time to time since I came back, and she decided to give her life over to our God. Bithiah shall be leaving with us when we head out to the land of milk and honey."

Rameses

"Jair, I've been looking everywhere for you. I need you to do me a favor," begged Abdullah.

Jair tried to wiggle loose from Abdullah and head for his favorite hiding spot, "No, whatever it is you want, the answer is no. Marissa has not paid me a shekel; traitor, she said that there is no possible way she can pay me now. Unless you can show me payment, the answer is no."

Cornering Jair Abdullah continued to explain, "I need you to go and get some cameras for me from the Rameses News office. I have left Marissa and ET NEWS, however, I want to film the Passover meal, live from the house of Moses. I have made arrangements with the Rameses News to cover the Passover Meal. However, if I show up who knows what trouble there might be. When Marissa finds out, she'll hiss like that cat that she worships. Will you help me, pleeease?"

Jair thought about how much fun it would be to see Marissa burnt by Abdullah and on TV no less, "Ooh, that would scald Marissa but good! Just when her precious Pharaoh is having troubles all around her, you are showing everyone the power of Moses' God—and it is on the competing news channel!"

Abdullah afraid of the intruding ears around him whispered, "Jair, you need to have it to me before dusk; I'll not be leaving the safety of Moses house tonight."

"Sure, sure, no problem. So you are staying in a safe house? Are you the oldest male in your family?"

Abdullah stated sadly, "When I left the house, I was the only child."

"I am the oldest son also, however, all my family is dead, so I do not think I should be concerned by this death threat."

Shocked by such a statement, Abdullah asked, "You are not going to go to a safe house?"

"Why? I am from Israelite blood—no harm will come to me."

Abdullah informed Jair, "I too am a blood-born Israelite; however, God said he shall spare only those who are under the roof of a house whose doorposts and lentils show the bloody mark of the lamb."

Jair waved his hand in the air to wipe away the thought of such rubbish, "I do not believe that, and I am not going to one of the trouble making Israelite's houses, just to avoid some scare, I am safe."

"Then you, Jair, shall die just like the others. Now go and get that equipment for me."

"See you in a few hours." Jair started to leave when Abdullah grabbed him by the arm and whispered, "Meet me at the house of Moses."

"What! No way, they'll figure out that I am Marissa's snitch, and things shall go badly for me," declared a very irritated Jair.

Abdullah began to briskly walk toward Goshen turned his head and shouted, "I need that equipment and I need it at Moses', see you there!"

Goshen

In Goshen Moses was busy with the dinner preparations, "Mother, it is time to sacrifice the lamb. I need to make sure that the servants have everything ready. Bithiah, I'll be back soon," said Moses.

"Ira, quickly go and make sure that all the dogs stay out of the way," stated Elisheba.

"Yes, grandmother, may I bring my dog Sheba into the house? She is so old and could sit by the fire—she won't not be in the way, I promise."

"Yes, Sheba may stay inside all night with us for the Passover. Why don't you go and help her get her exercise while you make sure the other dogs stay out of the way of the men."

"Yes, grandmother, thank you, I sure will," Ira replied as he ran out to find his dog. While the men were out preparing the lamb for the evening sacrifice, Menahem, the overseer, caught sight of Moses, "Moses, Aaron, we are in the process of sacrificing the lamb. Would you like to make sure all is done according to your specifications?"

Moses, while glancing around, shook his head in approval,

"From what I can see, you are doing just fine. However, I don't see the bowl of blood."

"It is on the table over in the corner; I did not want anything to happen to it."

"Splendid, I'll be in need of it very soon. Aaron and I have a few other things to attend to—I shall be back."

Menahem shook his head in acknowledgment and went back to instructing the men, "Make sure the pomegranate wood pole is strong enough to hold the lamb—we must be sure there are no bones broken." A servant walked up and asked, "What am I to do with the innards?" "Just a moment... Timothy, be careful not to break the wooden spike that goes between the ribs. Now young man, what were you asking?"

"I need to know what to do with the innards?"

Menahem smiled at the man, happy that he asked and did not just try to take care of them on his own, "Place them on the top of the head of the lamb—every bit of this lamb is to be roasted and eaten."

Back at the house, Miriam was busy giving instructions for the meal, "Peninnah, start finding the people you are in charge of and bring them in, would you, please? Also, make sure they have dressed correctly and are ready to leave."

"How many extra people should we plan for?" asked Elisheba.

"Hard to say as we'll have whomever Moses and Aaron bring in off the streets," answered Jochebed.

Elisheba, finally saw her chance and walked over to Bithiah. Unsure if she was allowed to give Bithiah a hug, Elisheba smiled, extended her hand, and warmly said, "Bithiah! How nice it is to see you, welcome into the family—God's family."

Jochebed spoke, "I hope you do not mind, I have a meal to prepare. Please feel free to talk with me while the preparations are being cared for."

"I think just to watch you shall suit me fine for the moment; this is so different that it shall take me a while to get adjusted," replied Princess Bithiah.

"Sapphira, someone is knocking on the door. Be a good girl and answer it for me, would you?" asked Jochebed. As Sapphira opened the door, she found a stranger.

"Hello, my name is Abdullah; you are expecting me. Is it okay to come in?"

Elisheba came to the door and greeted him, "Abdullah, come in, come in! Aaron is expecting you—he'll be with us later." Looking past him she asked, "Who is this with you?"

"This is Jair, my cameraman," answered Abdullah, praying she would not catch on to his fib. Elisheba let the men in and went back to her business as Miriam welcomed the men to their home, "Take a seat young man, we are busy with the meal preparations."

The door opened suddenly just missing Jair. Aaron shouted, "Stand aside everyone, it is time to bring the lamb in and place it on the fire." As the men made their way through the door, everyone made a broad path.

Moses stepped in making sure everyone was ready for the night before, placing the blood on the door-post. Miriam asked, "Moses, are you prepared to mark the door-post with the blood of the lamb?"

"If everyone is in and accounted for, then I am."

"Do you think you should take a quick walk to see that no one is out on the street without a home to be in?" asked Aaron.

Moses slapped his hands together and rubbed them with excitement, "Good idea, anyone want to take a quick walk with me?"

"Sure," answered Ithamar and Abihu. As Moses, Ithamar, and Abihu closed the door, Aaron turned his attention once again to Abdullah.

"Abdullah, welcome to our house; you received the permission you needed to film the Passover meal?"

"I got the equipment and there shall be people all over Egypt watching your family as you eat your last supper here in Goshen. Where can I set up?"

"I hope you do not mind—I brought a friend with me to run the camera. Jair, this is Aaron, Moses' brother." Aaron shook Jair's hand as to welcome him to his house.

"Nice to meet you, I hope you'll feel welcome in our home. Jair was looking for a spot to set up his equipment when Aaron said,

"You look familiar; do I know you from somewhere?" Jair thought, I knew this would happen. What do I say? Yes, I am the one that was spying on you for Marissa? He quickly responded with: "I do not think so, maybe..."

Moses walked in and loudly spoke, "Look whom we found, Phinehas and Ira; they had their dog out for a run. I believe all are present and accounted for." Looking around he spotted Abdullah.

"Abdullah, you have someone with you."

"Moses, this is Jair. He has volunteered to be my cameraman for the night."

"Good, you must excuse me, I must now go out and mark the door-post with the lamb's blood," stated Moses. He then asked Eleazar, Phinehas, and Ira if they would like to come mark the door-post with him.

Phinehas asked, "Father, may we go with Moses?"

"I would be most interested to see this—are you coming, Nadab?" asked Eleazar.

"Let's go," stated Nadab.

Outside Moses explained to the men the importance of this new festival. "This is a new ordinance given to us by our God. Every year on this day we shall celebrate the Passover meal; God said this is to be done to remind us of how he brought us out of the land of bondage. Watch as I take the blood of this sacrificial lamb and brush it on our door-post. Phinehas, would you hand me the hyssop?" Phinehas carefully and reverently gave Moses the hyssop.

"Thank you, now I shall mark the right side of the door-post with a symbol similar to a cross." Eleazar and Phinehas watched with interest as Moses completed the right and moved to the left side of the door-post.

"Why do we mark both sides of the door-post with the symbol of a cross, using the blood of a sacrificed animal?" asked Phinehas.

Moses explained: "As part of their custom, the Egyptians carve the faces of the household idols they worship on the right and left side of the entrances to their homes.

Some of the Egyptians also have a miniature altar on the right and the left side of their homes. Their altars allow them to sacrifice a small animal to their God before they enter their home. The Egyptians believe that this sacrifice protects their household from any harmful spirit that may try to enter their homes; they call the god they make the sacrifice to the 'God of the Threshold.'

Boys, remember that God has told us that we are to take the blood of the sacrificial lamb with hyssop, and place a mark on the right, the left, and the lintel [top] of our door-posts.

This blood mark is a sign given to us from God, when he sees it then he will protect us. He has chosen us as his first born son. [see glossary] Also in obeying this command, God has chosen to spare us the judgmental death of the firstborn male (both humans and animal), which all others shall experience.

At midnight tonight, God shall go ahead of the death angel to see which door-posts have the blood of a lamb or goat on it. When God *sees the blood*, he shall then tell the death angel to *pass by* that particular household."

Breaking the silence Abihu walked over to Jair and asked, "Are you excited about leaving this place?"

Jair responded, "I am not sure how I feel—I guess I am excited and concerned at the same time."

"I think we all probably feel that way," commented Abihu.

Ithamar asked, "Do you plan to go with your family?"

Jair explained, "I lost my parents long ago, so I also lost communication with the rest of my family. Abdullah gave his consent to let me go with him while I look for them."

"How about you, Abdullah, will you leave with family?" asked Ithamar.

"My family sold me to Marissa when I was ten. I was more than they could handle, always running away. I plan to leave with some people that I know. In the meantime, I'll also look for my family."

Looking around and rubbing his hands together, Aaron broke into the conversation, "God shall help you find your family, of that, I am sure. I hope you are ready to leave since we shall not have much time to prepare when Pharaoh releases us for the Promised Land."

"I have been preparing since Moses gave the warning at the palace," replied Abdullah.

"I'll be ready," said Jair. What have I gotten myself into? he wondered.

Moses commented to the men as they entered the house, "So you see we have a lot to do and little time to do it in."

"Moses, is everything complete?" asked Aaron.

Rubbing his hands together as he entered Moses answered, "All are marked safe and sound."

Miriam shouted over the conversation going on in the house, "There's a knock at the door."

The men said simultaneously, "Open the door and let them in."

"Open the door and let them in—as if I did not have enough to do," Miriam muttered as she opened the door.

"Hello, my name is Okpara, and this is my wife Rahab and this is our baby Caleb."

Miriam motioned for them to come in, "Don't stand outside, it is not safe!" As Miriam hurriedly closed the door, a group of concerned people swarmed the couple with multiple questions as to how they came to be at their door.

Okpara, obviously shaken, begged, "No one would take us in. Please! Do not ask us to leave, please! You see, I am Egyptian, and my wife is an Israelite. We have been married not quite a year. Rahab holds our firstborn son, Caleb; he is six weeks old. When we heard about the expected death plague, we did not know what to do. I am a firstborn son, and this is our firstborn son. We have seen what your God can do, and we want to live. What must we do to live?"

Moses stepped forward to console the man, "You are in good hands; no one will send you away in this household. I am Moses, and this is my brother, Aaron. All who seek to know God and want protection are welcome in this house. The women are in the kitchen preparing for our Passover Meal. Let's find you a place to sit… how about here next to Bithiah. The one you hear shouting orders is my mother, Jochebed."

"Sapphira, make sure you put the leafy greens on the table."

"I'll place some at both ends, Jochebed."

"How's the bread coming along? We want lots of bread. I hope it turns out well, it cooks differently with no leaven in it." observed Jochebed.

Laughing Peninnah remarked, "Yes, this shall be interesting. Should we put three plates of bread on the table?"

Jochebed answered, "Two plates one at each end should be okay; we can pass it around. Do they have the wine ready?"

"The wine is in the wine skin and is ready for serving when needed," answered Miriam.

"Make sure that everyone is dressed as instructed and is prepared to leave at a moment's notice," instructed Jochebed.

Aaron gave introductions: "Okpara, you and your family have not officially met our other guest, have you?" Bithiah—the Egyptian mother of Moses. She has also committed herself to our God."

Bithiah replied, "We have been sitting here visiting, however, I did not tell them who I was. Thank you, Aaron. I am pleased to meet you and your family officially."

Okpara with a look of confusion on his face asked, "Why do they call you Princess Bithiah?"

"In Egypt I was Princess Bithiah, here in Goshen I am just Bithiah."

"You have given up the *royal bloodline* to be part of the Israelite family of God!" exclaimed Okpara.

"Yes, I got that from Moses, I think. I raised Moses in the royal palace and yet he chose not to become an Egyptian and live the life of luxury. As I watched Moses, I grew to understand that the life I lived in Egypt was not the life I wanted. I desired something more and was unable to find it. When I found Moses in the Nile, I found my something more."

Elisheba gave Aaron a look of: "Help! It is time for the meal, how do I interrupt this conversation?"

Bithiah continued, "When Moses left and we knew not where he went, I was crushed, and the royal family treated me severely for bringing a traitor into the palace. When Moses returned, my heart was filled with joy. I secretly met with him a few times and knew that my joy is in his God."

Okpara exclaimed, "That is so close to my story. I am of Egyptian blood and yet felt something was missing in my life. When the plagues came upon us, and the Egyptian gods were doing nothing, I kept thinking, someone is doing this and that someone is more powerful than our gods, but who? My wife brought me to my senses."

"Moses…" Aaron interrupted. "Yes, what is it?"

"I am sorry to interrupt this good conversation, but it is time for the Passover meal to begin."

Moses slapped his knees, stood up and replied, "So it is my brother. So it is."

Abdullah, who had been quietly enjoying the conversation and the wonderful cooking aromas, realized that the special meal was about to begin. He interrupted with a request: "I was wondering if I could go ahead and tune in the public, I really need to speak to my audience before you begin your meal."

Moses turned to Abdullah, "Yes, of course you can, thank you for asking." Then turned and instructed the rest of those in the house, "Family, it is time to partake of the Passover meal. Abdullah, is about to speak to his audience, and I shall instruct the new members on what is to happen as we partake of this meal."

The Passover Meal

"We are live in 5,4,3,2… Hello, everyone, this is Abdullah with Rameses News. You might be thinking, 'He is with ET NEWS, not Rameses News.' Well, for this night I am working for Rameses News. I am in Goshen at the home of Aaron, along with Moses and his household. They are about to partake of their evening meal. Tonight is a special meal, as the God of the Israelites has called it *'The Lord's Passover Meal.'*

This meal is to remind the Israelite people that God is showing them grace on this night of death. Those who have placed the blood of the perfect sacrificed lamb on their door-post and lintels, God shall have the death angel pass over them.

It has been explained to me, by Moses, that this night the God of the Israelites shall go through all the land of Egypt. As he does, he'll instruct the death angel to kill all of the firstborn males, both humans and animals. However, if you are in a home that has had the door-posts and the lintels marked with the blood of a kid (baby goat) or a lamb, then your life will be spared.

The God of the Israelites, or Hebrew people as some call them, are doing this personally to show everyone that there is no other God anywhere in the world that is a living breathing God. Not one of the gods or goddesses that anyone worships can control, defeat, or overthrow the Hebrews' one true God.

If you choose to stay tuned, you'll witness the meal and the interaction of Moses' household in obeying the words spoken by the Lord. So stay with us and experience the truth that our Lord, the God of Israel, is the one true God."

"People of Israel, God has decreed that this meal is one that will never be forgotten. Generations to come will be told of this meal and of this night and will recreate its uniqueness. This meal will be new to our taste buds; it is not a meal to taste and please the flesh, but a meal to remind us of the harshness we have been through and to never again allow ourselves to fall into slavery.

God has instructed us to eat this meal dressed to run out the door—never to return to Egypt again. I shall pray over each part of this meal as we come to it. Let us bow our heads to pray as we give thanks for the lamb:

Gracious and merciful God, we ask you to bless the food which we are about to receive. We thank you that you are our Father, our Leader, and our Guide.

We are thankful for those you have sent our way on this night. Grant that we may always keep our door open to those who choose to be part of your family. Bless this lamb, the symbol you have given to remind us of your perfection and of your loving-kindness.

Please bless our bodies with strength for the long journey ahead, and may we never forget the blood of these innocent lambs that is being used to grace us with your protection from the death that is about to take place. Amen."

With the prayer over the lamb completed, Moses continued, "Each of us will walk up past the lamb where it has been roasting over the open fire, and receive some of the meat from Sapphira.

Then, as the rest of the food is passed around the table, I'll explain what each dish represents."

Remember that as much as we are enjoying this meal, we are to eat it in haste; we know not when Pharaoh will call for Aaron and me. When he does, we'll have to leave quickly; therefore, we'll have no time to prepare a meal. Come now as I lead you to the lamb."

Aaron got up from his seat, "Guests first."

Rahab pointed at the piece of meat she desired," I would like that piece of meat right there."

"This one?" replied Sapphira. "Yes, that piece."

"Bithiah, show Sapphira what piece of meat you would like. Take only the amount you know you can finish, for God instructed us not to waste any of the lamb," instructed Jochebed.

"Grandma, come and sit here beside me, and you also Princess Bithiah," said Ithamar.

"Thank you, how nice to have a family meal. Who knows how our meals will be when we leave this place in the morning? We shall not have enough time to leaven our bread, and the lamb shall be all gone. It'll be interesting to see how we are to make our meals," commented Jochebed.

Bithiah asked, "Young man, why am I allowed to sit and yet you have to stand?"

"It is because you usually sit at a meal; my grandmother also sits at her meal. God told us we were to eat in haste wearing a sash around our robe, sandals on our feet, and (for those that have one) our walking stick in hand. That makes it a little hard to eat sitting down; however, I am right beside you and immediately ready to help you leave in haste," explained Ithamar.

"Bithiah, this will be a very different lifestyle for you. Do you expect to need help to adjust?" asked Aaron.

"I was very concerned about the differences in the way we live; however, my love for my new God outweighs any concerns I may have had. Moses assured me that my new God takes care of my every need, and no harm shall come to me," answered Bithiah.

"Everyone, it is time for me to pass the food around the table—let us bless this food together."

Moses took a piece of bread, blessed it, saying, "Bless this unleavened bread. It is the symbol you have given to us as a reminder that we shall leave this country because you have chosen to free us. We could not obtain freedom on our own, however you chose now to release us from this country and its bondage of slavery. For that, we are thankful.

We repent of any pride we have felt over the Egyptians and what has happened to them, may it be entirely left behind. Instead, let us focus on your favor and grace that you have given unto us. Teach us humility and may we never forget that you are our one true God. Amen.

Bithiah spoke, "Amen! I would like a small piece of that bread please."

"How about you, Phinehas, what would you like?" asked Elisheba.

"I want two large pieces as I am making a sandwich with mine!"

"Me too, burnt lamb in a sandwich!" exclaimed Ira.

"Ooh, yuck a sandwich made with unleavened bread, bitter herbs, sauce, and lamb!" exclaimed his father, Eleazar.

Naamah, Ithamar's wife, teased, "Eleazar, how do you know if a sandwich made that way will taste yucky, have you had one?"

"Ha, ha, you are so amusing, you eat one."

"I found some horseradish, and since we are cleaning the cupboards, I put it out. Would anybody care for some?" asked Elisheba.

"That should go well with my burnt lamb sandwich." "Ira!" everyone exclaimed.

Jochebed commented, "Peninnah found a bag of figs and nuts, so I had her put them on the table."

"Horseradish! I love horseradish, I wonder how it'll taste on my leftovers," said Abihu.

"Pretty disgusting if you put it on your figs like Ira," replied Nadab.

"What!" They all broke out in laughter.

Elisheba said, "Ira, if you are going to make a sandwich out of everything, then you should also include the greens."

"When the bowl comes around to me, I'll put some on my sandwich," said Ira.

Moses prayed a blessing on the Karpas. [Parsley Sprigs]

"God bless these greens that we now use as a symbol to remind us of hope and springtime growth.

Moses then lifted his cup and blessed the wine, "Lord bless this wine, the symbol of our freedom from slavery. Thank you, Lord, for this new freedom—the freedom to choose you as the only God we worship and for freedom to enjoy a happy life once again. Amen.

Family and friends of this household: eat, drink, laugh, and enjoy that which the Lord our God has provided, and be on alert for a sudden departure from the land of Egypt," declared Moses.

I am Abdullah reporting to you from the Moses' family home in Goshen. Anyone in Egypt, who may still be watching, some of you are experiencing the death angel at your house right now. Others of you, I am sad to say, will soon experience a visit from the death angel. Moses warned Pharaoh this would happen.

When this demonstration of God's power has come to its completion, all people shall know that the is a difference between the gods of Egypt and the God of the Israelites.

Tomorrow when this is over, the Israelites shall leave Egypt. I pray that you take to heart what is happening in Egypt as I speak. When we leave, anyone that wants to give their heart to the one true God is invited to leave with us. I do not think I'll see you again, as I shall be moving with Moses and the rest of the Israelites.

Thank you for watching us this evening, and thank you Rameses News for allowing me to broadcast this meal. I wish to leave you with this prayer, 'As the one true God makes his appearance tonight through the death angel, may each of you come to give your heart to him—the one true God of the world. Amen.' Abdullah here with Rameses News for the last time saying, 'Goodbye and God's peace.'"

Moses complimented Abdullah, "I am not sure anyone was around to watch your broadcast, but well done."

Naamah suggested to Rahab, "You may want to eat in a hurry so that little Caleb has adequate time to eat before we leave."

Rahab felt a little unsure about her new circumstances, turning to her husband, she asked, "Okpara, would you hold him while I hurry up with my meal; then I'll feed him while you eat."

"I was just waiting for you to let me have my son. You are right, Rahab; Caleb is so little sometimes I want to be the only one taking care of him. However, a man cannot feed his son properly. Hum?"

"Okpara, would you like me to hold him while you eat?" asked Eleazar.

"Thanks for asking, but I think I should enjoy my son for awhile," replied Okpara.

Ira announced, "Watch and see how I build my sandwich, the Last Goshen sandwich, that is what I'll call it."

"That is quite a creation you have, my son; are you sure you can eat all of it before morning and eat it quickly?" joked Eleazar.

"Just watch me."

"Bithiah, do you plan to come with everyone when we leave for the Promised Land?" asked Rahab.

Yes, I am; like Moses, did many years ago, I am walking away from my life in Egypt. I am stepping into a new life, a life with the God of the Israelites," answered Bithiah.

"What about you, Okpara? Are you and your family coming with us?" asked Bithiah.

"That is our hope; somewhere along the way we also hope to see the family flag belonging to Rahab's tribe. Then we can go with them," stated Okpara.

"What tribe are you from, Rahab?" asked Aaron.

"My family belongs to the tribe of Dan."

"That flag has the picture of the scales of justice; it should not take long to find," said Nadab.

Miriam walked over to the lounge area and asked, "As we are all together, would you like me to lead you in a time of praise and worship?"

"Yes, of course, could we?" they all responded. "I'll sing it the first time, and you can join in on the same words the next time, okay?" asked Miriam.

"I'll sing to the Lord, he has won the war to our delight. The Lord is my strength; The Lord is my song.

He is my Savior, and I shall praise him. The Lord is our warrior, The Great I AM is his name.

Praise and glory and honor are his. I'll sing to the Lord, I'll confess, I'll praise, and I'll give thanks to the Lord.

Blessed is he who comes in the name of the Lord. You are welcome here, at our place of rest. Oh, all you people, give thanks for his mercy.

Give thanks for his grace. Give thanks—for his loving-kindness is better than life itself.

The Lord is my strength, and the Lord is my song. He is my Savior, and I'll praise his Holy Name.

ET NEWS: BREAKING NEWS: "Death, HAH!"

"This is Marissa with an ET NEWS update. I am in the palace and it is about a half an hour before midnight; we are about to see the climax of this war between Pharaoh and Moses. Let me remind you that Moses tried to convince all of us that the deaths of our firstborn males would begin at midnight and continue on until all the firstborn humans and animals had died.

Well, it is almost midnight, and I refuse to believe that there shall be any deaths. The God of Moses shall not succeed and win this war; he shall not! As some of you know, Abdullah, my former cameraman and co-anchor of the 'A Man Called Moses' documentary, has foolishly defected to the other side. However, tonight I have a new and faithful cameraman, Sabri.

I am looking forward to a peaceful night of news reporting, something few of you have heard for quite some time. Tonight is the night I expect to announce the death of Moses and the victory of our honorable Pharaoh. As we await the glorious news to come from Courtier Obaid or possibly from the Vizier himself, I shall show you what the inside of the palace looks like as I walk through this section of the palace.

We are presently at the entrance quarters, also known as the visitor's area. Right here we are looking at the marble floors, high ceilings, and long dark halls. Every few feet there is a rack holding a cloth wick which is burning brightly to give us light.

There are a few pictures hung in this hall. This one looks like a long sleek black cat wearing a gold necklace. Magnificent to see, this must have been completed by a royal weaver. It is stitched with black thread and the necklace is made of gold dust. Exquisite!

Let us move further toward the living quarters of the palace subjects. We are not allowed into the rooms or private areas; however, we can walk the halls and take a peek at the life of the royal family. Later on I may be able to give you a peek at the lovely grounds outside, but for now we shall enjoy the loveliness of the palace itself.

"I see a guard, let's find out if he has heard anything. Guard, I am Marissa with ET NEWS and..." Just then a messenger interrupted them and spoke directly to the palace guard.

"Excuse me, sir, is your name Ghulam?" asked the messenger.

"Yes, it is, you have a message for me?"

"Your firstborn son has just died in his sleep," with nothing else to say the messenger turned and left.

"Viewers, what you have just heard has nothing to do with Moses or his God. It is just a coincidence." Refusing to admit that Moses may be right, Marissa tried to lighten the mood and continued on.. "Let us move on down the hall.

Wow, Sabri, show the viewers this beautiful lounge seat here in this hallway. Made of pure gold, I think. Here comes another guard, perhaps we can speak to him. Excuse me, guard, I am Marissa with ET NEWS and..." Marissa was interrupted again by a messenger. "Excuse me, sir, is your name Dana?" asked the messenger.

"Yes, it is, you have a message for me?"

"I am to tell you that your slave girl Carmel... her newborn son has just died. He was nursing, fell asleep, and never awoke. Do you have a message for me to relay, sir?" asked the messenger.

"No, yes, tell them I'll be home shortly." In a daze, Dana turned to Marissa and said, "You were about to ask me something?

"Yes, I was about to ask you what the good news from the palace is."

"Good news from the palace! You just heard the good news

from the palace. What is wrong with you? Can you not hear all the screams of death that started at midnight? You need help, and I have important business to attend to, Goodnight." As Dana left, Marissa started to allow the sounds she had shut out of her mind sink in and become reality.

"People, can it be, right? Are the noises we hear the noises of death, brought on by Moses' God? Where is Bes, the protector of our families? I refuse to believe he is on vacation. I refuse to believe Bes just does not care about what is happening here! Marissa looked around desperately trying to find a reasonable explanation to the horror around her.

Finally, she spotted someone to get a reliable answer from, she hollered out: "Vizier Jibade, I hear screams... what is going on? Surely Moses' prediction that Egypt's firstborn male sons and animals shall die this morning has not come to pass!"

"Yes, Marissa, there are people dying. I just lost my firstborn son, and now I am worried about my first-born grandson." Marissa looked at the Vizier as he started praying to his gods: "Apis, you are our strength, please help us! Heket you were there when my wife gave birth, where are you now? O Apis, please help us!"

Following his short prayer, he turned and said, "Marissa, I do not have time for you—I must go check on the others." She watched in disbelief as the Vizier walked away talking to himself. "What in the world is going on?"

About to go find Pharaoh herself, Marissa spotted Courtier Obaid, as he came walking down the palace hall, "Courtier Obaid, I just spoke to the Vizier, and he says there have been a number of unexpected deaths since midnight. He feels that these people have died in accordance with what Moses warned us about. Please tell the people Moses is wrong!"

"All I know is that the Vizier's firstborn son died not too long ago. My family has not experienced any of the deaths that others are experiencing. However, Marissa...." Right at that moment a palace guard came up: "Courtier Obaid, you have a message that you are required at home immediately." The color drained from Courtier

Obaid's face and he was visibly shaken. He turned and left without saying a word.

Marissa's rage turned to concern for those that she had come to know at the palace. With a voice that spoke with concern and disbelief, she asked, "You guard, what is your name?"

"Hanif, why do you ask?"

"I was just wondering if you know a guard by the name of Kamenwati. He is always kind to me when I come to the palace. Is he here? I would like to interview him for ET NEWS."

Hanif started to shake as he remembered how he and Kamenwati got to know each other when they were together with the prisoners. Together in the plague of darkness for those three days, they became friends. Looking like a war-torn warrior and with his voice full of sorrow, Hanif stated, "Kamenwati was a firstborn son…"

"Was a first born son…? You mean he is dead!"

Hanif weary from all that had happened said, "Died maybe an hour ago, I cannot keep track of time… too many deaths. Now if you would excuse me, I have work to do." With that Hanif walked away from Marissa.

"People, we are still stationed inside and walking the palace halls. As we walk along, I can hear awful noises, and I believe you hear them also. Bear with me as I walk around and look for someone who can give us further information on this phenomenon. Sabri, Moses said that the animals would also be experiencing the death of the firstborn.

Of course—Maskini! I need to go and see Maskini! As the Official of the Cattle and Livestock Association, he will be able to help us solve this mystery. Look over there—someone else is in the hallway. Excuse me, sir, I need some help."

"Yeah? Everyone in Egypt needs some kind of help, lady, what makes you so special?" asked Wamukota, the chief palace sorcerer.

"I am Marissa with ET NEWS, and I need to go outside to see Maskini, will you help me?"

"It just so happens I am on my way to see Maskini myself, you may come along if you'd like."

As they walked down the long hall toward the chariot, Marissa asked, "Why do you need to see Maskini?"

"He sent a message that his firstborn animals are dying or dead and asked for my help. I'll speak to the gods, and they'll bring them back to life." answered Wamukota as they stop at the palace exit door. Marissa, dazed and trying to take in the reality of the situation, asked, "Dead? They are dead?"

Wamukota said impatiently, "Maskini needs my help, are you coming or not?"

"No... No, I think I had better cover the palace news," replied Marissa as she turned and headed back down the hall.

Wamukota opened the palace door and said, "Suit yourself. If you ask me there's nothing, I mean nothing, anyone can do about the mess we are in except the gods."

In the room of Chatuluka, the Chief Servant of Pharaoh's firstborn son, there was a conversation going on between Chatuluka and Baraka, one of the palace officials.

A panicked Chatuluka spoke, "All this death has occurred just like Moses warned us. I fear for the life of Pharaoh's son. How long before we hear bad news about him? Oh no, this is too much for me! Baraka, I cannot do this on my own. I need to summon some assistance for what may occur.

Baraka, please go and tell Jannes, Jambres, Jabr and Wamukota to meet me at the Royal Youth Quarters as soon as possible. Please, go now!"

As Baraka headed out on his mission, he bumped into Marissa. "Marissa, why did you run into me like that? Such carelessness, what is going on with you?" A very drained and shocked Marissa asked, "Baraka, when, oh when will this nightmare end?" Baraka continued on and said over his shoulder "I do hope soon, very soon. I am in a hurry; we'll talk later."

After wandering the halls for what seemed like hours, Marissa was both emotionally and physically exhausted. She was hopeful and nearly convinced that her work tonight at the palace was nearly complete. "Sabri, I think it might be time to wind things up for tonight. The halls are empty, and it is hard to hear over the screams.

Wait a minute, what's this?" Marissa looked to the left and motioned for Sabri to look toward the left hallway. "The Palace magicians are heading this way with Baraka, hmm, let's follow." Marissa's reporter instincts were alive once again.

Baraka, who was able to find the men that Chatuluka requested, lead the men to the Royal Youth Quarters. Inside, he proceeded to announce their arrival,

"Chatuluka, I have Jannes, Jambres and Jabr. I sent a messenger for Wamukota." Closing the door behind him, Baraka left and said, "I want nothing more to do with what is going on."

Jannes with concern in his voice spoke, "Chatuluka, you have never called us to a private meeting with you before, what is it that you need from us?"

"One of you shall have to go and bring Pharaoh to me, and the rest of you I shall need to help me with Pharaoh when he arrives. The three men who had been looking at Chatuluka were now looking at each other with "what did he say expressions" on their faces. A totally frustrated Chatuluka continued, "Are you men not aware of all the death that has happened since midnight? The firstborn son of Pharaoh shall soon be dead!"

Simultaneously, *"Dead?"*

"Yes, somebody has to tell Pharaoh when it happens, and it shall not be *me*!" declared a very shaken and panicked Chatuluka. "I need you here so when we receive news that the Pharaoh's son has died, one of you can go directly and get Pharaoh. The rest of you can begin to pray for him and bring him back to the land of the living!" At that moment, as if on cue, there came a panicked knock on the door.

"Please, Chatuluka, open the door!" A very annoyed Jambres ordered, "Jabr, open the door before the whole world comes in on us!"

With the door open, Chatuluka could see that something was wrong, "Layla! What has happened to bring you here?"

Layla, head Mistress to the Queen informed the men, "It is the Queen—she has it in her head that her firstborn son has gone to be with the gods in the underworld. I have come to seek your assistance; I do not know what else to do."

The men all looked at each other and tried not to show the panic they felt. "How did she come to that conclusion?" asked Chatuluka.

"She came up to me and said, 'I am a mother, and I know when something is gravely wrong with my children. Layla, the gods and goddesses—for whatever reason—have chosen to take my firstborn son from me this night.' Then she became hysterical and began to yell, 'Help me, help me!'"

"Is she in her chambers?" asked Jambres.

"When I left her, she was, but who knows where she is now."

As he tried to keep calm, Jambres said to Layla: "Go back and comfort her the best you can…we'll be right behind you." Walking her to the door, he gave her a gentle push and said, "Go, it'll be okay."

Jannes, in a calm voice said: "Chatuluka, go check on the prince and get back here as soon as possible! We cannot do much until we know what has happened to the prince."

"Now what do we do?" they all asked as Chatuluka left.

Jannes was the first to gather some composure and voiced a plan: "When Chatuluka comes back and gives us confirmation, then I shall go and tell Pharaoh that Chatuluka is in need of him. I'll bring him back here with me—you guys figure it out from there."

Taking no time at all, Chatuluka was back. "As I was heading to check on the prince, a servant was coming to get me. I have received word that the prince died in his sleep, not that long ago."

Jannes opened the door to leave—his mission foremost in his mind—he must now persuade Pharaoh to return with him so that Chatuluka could somehow tell Pharaoh of the death of his firstborn son.

Sulking in his anger and cursing under his breath about this whole unbelievable situation, Jannes bumped into the news media. He simply could not believe the news crew was still snooping around for news. "Get out of my way!" He shouted as he shoved a very stunned Marissa out of his way.

"Sabri, did you see that? Jannes is certainly up to something; I can smell it." Marissa tried to catch up with Jannes, however, with the shoes she had on it was hard to run. The palace halls went forever and had many turns. "I must keep up with him," she said as her news reporter instincts kicked in and brought her back to life.

"I need to be able to hear! I need to be able to think! All this horrific noise, death, death, death! Turning around Marissa spotted another guard headed in the direction of the Royal Youth Quarters located on the east side of the palace. She followed the guard to the door of Chatuluka's office and watched as he knocked and entered.

As the guard entered Chatuluka's office, he immediately began to tell Chatuluka what had happened. "I was talking to one of our scribes, Hadi, and in the middle of a sentence, he dropped down to the ground dead! What do I do?"

"Don't bother us with that, we have bigger problems to handle," shouted Chatuluka.

"What bigger problems?" asked the guard.

"Jannes just left to bring Pharaoh to us, and then *we* must tell him his firstborn son is dead," answered Jambres.

"I think we had better be in the prince's room praying to the gods when Pharaoh gets here," said Jabr.

Marissa, being the reporter, she is, spoke, "Sabri, the people need to hear what is going on in that room, but how?" Suddenly the door opened and a group of men left. Marissa decided to follow them.

"When Pharaoh arrives at the Prince's bed-chambers, we need to look busy. Otherwise, he'll think we have not done enough for his son or haven't earnestly sought the gods." proclaimed Jambres. "Agreed," the men stated simultaneously.

Marissa whispered to Sabri, "Hurry, we cannot let them slip away this time! There's a story here—I just know it!"

When the men entered the bed chambers of the Prince, they were in for a shock. They found a very hysterical Queen, "No! No! I hate you—I hate you!"

Yamanu, the chief counselor of Pharaoh, looked upon the queen whom he had known for years. The queen is a woman of composure and grace, and most countries wish they had her for a queen.

Yamanu realized that someone must help her at least until Pharaoh arrived. Moving to the queen, he gently touched her hand as he knelt down to her, with compassion and concern, he spoke with a gentle tone, "My Queen, what are you doing here?

The sorcerers and magicians have arrived with me to help you and to pray to the gods on your behalf. All shall be well again, you'll see, and Pharaoh shall be here any minute."

The others walked over to the prince's cold, lifeless body and started to pray, "Amun-Ra, the creator of all gods... "Ma'at, you gave him the breath of life just before you placed him in his mother's womb. We ask you now to breathe life back into his body; place Pharaoh's son's soul back into his earthly body.

"Come, my Queen, be with me for a while." Layla spoke while trying to move the Queen from the bed of the prince, but the queen would have no part in it. She would only stay with the body of her son.

The queen continued with her hair-raising screams—screams that can only come from a mother who once labored to bring her child into the world and who now has had that child so rudely taken away from her. "I want my son back! You had no right to take him from me! My son is the future pharaoh, and you let him die. Why? I want him back!"

As Jannes and Pharaoh approached Chatuluka's office, Jannes was very aware that the Pharaoh's whole world was about to explode. Jannes tried to speak—struggling to find the right words to prepare Pharaoh for the death of his firstborn son. However, time ran out because the closer they came to the Prince's bed-chamber the more obvious it was that something was not right. The blood-curdling screams of the Queen were impossible to ignore or to explain away.

As Pharaoh heard all the commotion, he ran full-bore into his son's bed-chamber yelling, "What is all this noise about?" As his eyes canvassed the room, he noticed Lotus Blossom with Yamanu standing next to her with grave concern on his face, why? "What is wrong my Lotus Blossom?"

Lotus Blossom finally acknowledged someone. Getting up from her son's bedside, the Queen quickly walked to Pharaoh, "My beloved Acacia, our Seti, your firstborn son... He is dead!"

Pharaoh shouted in disbelief, "What!"

Lotus Blossom pleaded with Pharaoh, like a mother whose heart had just been torn violently from her body: "Why are the gods allowing this to happen? Is there nothing you can do?"

"Lotus Blossom, I need you to be strong for me. My men and I will pray that the gods give life back to our son, you need to go outside the room for me."

Pharaoh's precious Lotus Blossom looked at him with rage and confusion in her eyes and shook her head, for she no longer had the strength to utter a word. Pharaoh looked Layla in the eye and said, "You take good care of her."

"Come, my Queen, Pharaoh and the men need room to work and you need rest. Let us go into the prince's waiting room. You can lay on the lounge while we await word on your son." The queen, no longer able to respond, allowed Layla to help her from the prince's bed-chambers.

Pharaoh shouted orders, "Counselors, sorcerers, magicians! We'll pray over my son's body. One of you go and get the sacred oil." Jannes slipped out of the room to go get the sacred oil used for times like these.

As he left, he met Marissa in the hallway. "Marissa, if you interrupt what is taking place in there, you shall be one of the dead. Do you understand?" Not waiting for an answer, he walked off to complete his mission.

Marissa, unable to believe the commotion around her, nodded her head yes. As soon as Jannes left, Marissa motioned to Sabri to turn on the camera.

ET NEWS: BREAKING NEWS: "Trouble At the Palace."

Marissa here with an ET NEWS Breaking News report. I am still at the Palace. I do not know how to say this—and I am still in shock—however, it looks and sounds like death has visited the palace tonight.

How many are dead I do not know, but with the screams and the suffocating feeling in the air, it is obvious that death is all around. When things have calmed down and we are better able to comprehend what has just happened, I'll be here to give you the up to the moment news. Until then, this is Marissa saying 'May the gods of Egypt protect you.'"

"Sabri, I think it is time for us to find our way home. Let's head to the palace entrance and see whom we can find to give us a donkey ride back. I do not feel like I can walk home, how about you?" Marissa's voice sounded like someone who had just experienced a traumatic death scene in a horror movie. Sabri, too tired to care and too shocked at Marissa's kindness, replied, "Thank you, Marissa, I would like to go home by way of a donkey."

Prince's Bedchamber

"Amun-Ra, the creator of the gods of all the people, you fashion us from clay, and back to clay we shall go. Fight for Seti and bring him back to me—where is the sacred oil?" Pharaoh shouted just as Jannes handed the sacred oil to him. As he took some of the sacred oil and spread it on his son's body, Pharaoh began to pray again with the help of the magicians who stood in agreement with him.

I ask you, Ma'at, under the authority given me as the High Priest of Every Temple, to give the breath of life back to my son. I ask you, one god to another, to breathe life back into my son." Pharaoh prayed as he rubbed the oil used for healing purposes onto his son's skin.

Nekhbet, you are the protector of my family. I ask you to go find our son's soul, bring him back to us, and do not let him die. Renenutet, you are a protector of the kings, give me my first born son back." A very broken, shaken, and confused Pharaoh now turned to Jannes and yelled: "Send someone to bring Moses and Aaron to me, now!"

As Pharaoh realized that his mission was hopeless and that his firstborn son had gone to be with his ancestors in the underworld, he ordered "Stop! There is nothing more we can do for my son. You stay here until I return. I must go now and give the news to my Lotus Blossom."

Walking back to meet with his Queen, Pharaoh pondered upon how to handle this situation. Usually he would ask his counselors, but it seemed that they were all busy with the death of their sons.

As he walked into the outer chamber of their son's palace area, he saw her. As his eyes met hers, he found himself thinking: "How am I going to tell my first love, my precious little Lotus Blossom, that our pride and joy, the first real sign of our love, our connection to each other, has been taken home to be with the gods?

Lotus Blossom noticed that her dear Acacia, who once looked tall, strong, and powerful, now looked bent, weak, and war-torn. She said a silent prayer: "Wadjet, I need your help. Help me to stand strong, help me to help my husband with this life-changing loss." Lotus Blossom tried to take some of the burdens off of Acacia as she came to him and melted in the comfort of his embrace.

Her very core was so numb with shock that she wondered how she would find her voice. Suddenly she heard herself whisper, "Acacia, our Seti has gone home to be with the gods, has he not?"

Looking deep into her dark brown eyes, he found himself suddenly not ready to give up. He'll not let Moses and his God win this war, not yet! "I'll continue to ask the gods to bring him back, you must not lose hope, my Lotus Blossom. Allow me and the gods just a little more time."

Lotus Blossom quietly hugged her hero, her god, her husband, her king. She desperately wanted to show him how much she cared and how much she wanted to comfort him. At the same time she thought to herself, it is over my Acacia—for whatever reason the gods and goddesses have not helped you to win this war."

Goshen

On the road to Goshen, which was just a short one-hour walk from the Palace, Chigaru let his mind ponder on all that had happened lately. "This road is so dark tonight, although, as I walk closer to Goshen the road seems to not be as dark. The moon appears brighter, how can that be?" Tired and scared, he started grumbling to himself, "What am I doing in Goshen? Why do I have to bring Moses back? Where shall I find him? He is probably dead by now, and who cares what Pharaoh wants—Pharaoh is no longer the person he was. What god has attacked our great Pharaoh and caused him to become such a mess?"

Looking around, he suddenly noticed that all was quiet; not the eerie quiet that he had gotten acquainted with, but a peaceful quiet that he forgot existed. Wow, such a feeling of peace! How am I going to find the house of Moses? Just then, he felt the urge to walk in the direction of the north part of town. As he moved along, he was not sure where to turn, but decided just to trust the feeling he had.

Quite suddenly he found himself in front of a door. As he stood outside and wondered what to do, he heard the sound of laughter and singing from inside the home. Chigaru said to himself, "The world has been gloomy for so long that I forgot the sound of joy. Oh well, I had better see if they know where Moses lives."

The people inside who were unaware of Chigaru, sang. "God is good, God is great, God is the only God and he takes such good care of me." Miriam stopped the singing for a moment and asked, "Some of you seem to be having trouble keeping up with me. Do you want me to slow down? I forget there are people here new to this kind of singing."

"Moses, I think there is someone at the door. Do you suppose it is the messenger sent to ask you to go to the palace?" asked Elisheba.

Moses said, "Someone answer the door, and then we'll find out."

"Abihu, would you answer that?" asked Miriam. As Abihu opened the door, a medium height man who looked to be in his twenties asked, "Do you know where I can find Moses?"

"I am here, come in, come in. You have been sent to bring Aaron and I back to meet with Pharaoh?"

"I have been sent to bring you and Aaron back to the palace, yes, will you both come with me?" asked Chigaru.

"We are ready to go, lead the way. As to the rest of you, get things ready because we leave very soon—continue to give God praise and glory, we'll be back," instructed Moses.

As the door closed, everyone was giddy with excitement. At long last they were to leave Egypt. They are leaving for a land full of milk and honey. A land that has grapes the size of melons, wheat so thick you cannot walk through it, and bees so busy there is honey everywhere you look. No more worries, no more troubles.

Palace

As Moses and Aaron were ushered in by Chigaru, they were not surprised to find that Pharaoh would not be meeting with them. The Royal family was too consumed in the grieving process to be bothered with the likes of Moses, Aaron and the God of the Israelites.

Chigaru, as he lead them down the hall explained, "You are to meet with Aamir, one of the Palace Officials. He shall give you Pharaoh's message. Ah, here we are—Aamir, Moses and Aaron are here for you." Chigaru turned to Moses and said, "I hope to see you later."

As they entered the room a man introduced himself, "Moses and Aaron, I am Aamir, please sit." As Moses and Aaron settle into the chairs across from his desk, Moses carefully observed this man.

He was a fairly tall man probably in his forties. Moses thought he had seen him before, but could not remember where or under what circumstances. Aamir sat down behind his desk and continued, "I have been instructed to give you a message from Pharaoh. Please do not take offense as this edict comes from Pharaoh, not me.

Pharaoh's message said, 'You and the Israelites must leave me and my land at once, just leave! Leave me alone! I want peace! Just go, go away from me, go and worship your God. That is what you have been asking to do from the start, is it not? I say, take with you everything you have, take your flocks, take your herds, take everything that you have been asking to take! Just go and go now! Do not hesitate for I want you and your people gone! *Do you understand, Moses*, I want you gone!'

Relieved to have gotten this far with the message of Pharaoh, Aamir took a deep breath and made one final request, "Pharaoh also asks that you bless him and pray for him before you go! Would you pray for him? Moses? Please pray for us."

Moses spoke not a word (what was there left to say?) he simply turned around and left, Aaron followed close behind.

Aamir shouted to Moses one more time, "Pray for Pharaoh, pray for Egypt, please!" Won't you *please* pray for us before you go?"

Palace

As they left the palace, Moses walked by Vizier Jibade and Courtier Obaid. They bowed down at the knee before Moses and said: "Moses you and all your people leave! Leave us before we are all dead! Leave us alone and let us live!" Due to the death of their firstborn sons, the people came to see Moses as a stronger and more powerful god than their Pharaoh.

Aaron answered them, "We'll leave with all our people, all our animals, and with all our supplies—as soon as we can get the word to all the Israelites."

On the way back to Goshen, Moses and Aaron informed the Israelites that were living in Rameses that it was time to leave. They also reminded them that God had told them to go and ask the Egyptians for their silver, gold and clothing. Moses hoped that the Egyptians freely giving their possessions to the Israelites would ever be a reminder to the Israelites that God gave them favor. What a gift from God to receive that kind of favor from those who once treated them with so much cruelty.

Chapter 19
"Leaving at Last!"

Moses spoke to the members of his household before he left to lead the people to Succoth. "Mother, it is time to gather up the food supplies and the blankets and all the other necessities—we are about to leave. Aaron, make sure that any leftover meat and bones are burned in the fire, will you?" asked Moses.

"Already done my brother, already done," answered Aaron.

Moses replied, "Good, you and I need to get out there and lead the people out of here. Ira, take good care of my household and that includes Bithiah."

"You know I shall... all except Miriam, she is on her own," Menahem said with a twinkle in his eye. Aaron chimed in teasing his sister, "Do not concern yourself with her, she can take care of herself—you know how those bossy types are."

Miriam pretended to be shocked and whined, "I heard that! Whom are *you* calling bossy? I would rather be bossy than the highfalutin authoritarian you seem to be, ha-ha!"

Moses said with a light-hearted laugh, "Come on sister, we love you, you know that. You cannot help it if you are as stubborn as a mule with a toothache. I am leaving to lead us out to the Promised Land." As he left, Moses heard Miriam playfully whine: "Mother, did you hear that? I am not a mule with a toothache!"

Jochebed playfully scolded all her children, "Really? It is as though you were little children at home playing your war games that ended up with one of you declaring, 'Foul, you did that wrong, and

I am not dead!' I did my best to stay out of it then, although *you,* my dear Miriam, were old enough to know better. You think I'll come to your rescue now when you are in your nineties?" As Jochebed turned to work on some more provisions for the trip she threw up her head and laughed. "Hah!"

Moses, headed toward the door, stopped and gave Jochebed a kiss on the cheek, "Love you, mother of mine. Aaron and I must now leave, if you have any questions, send one of the servants to find us. Tell them to look for the front flag, I'll be there."

Moses took a few steps outside when suddenly he heard, "Moses!"

"Miriam, I have to get to work!"

"I forget to tell you that Abdullah is with another family; he'll be living with them until he can find his tribe. That other man with him, what is his name...?" Moses interjected, "Jair." "That was it; he went with Abdullah and the young couple, they will be traveling with the tribe of Dan. Allon said he's concerned about the feed for the animals, just in case he says something to you."

"Sounds good, now I have to be gone."

As Moses and Aaron left, Miriam turned to Sapphira with an armful of clothing and said, "That Moses, I have not seen him in years and he is just as bad as Aaron! Help me with these clothes, we need to get them on a donkey."

Rameses

Moses walked the streets of Rameses to make sure there were no complications for the journey to the Promised Land. As he turned to check on another couple, he found Courtier Obaid coming his way. Courtier Obaid bowed before Moses and asked, "Moses, as you leave our country, is there anything I can do to help you?"

"Yes there is, Courtier Obaid. I would like you to tell your people to give the Israelites all the silver, gold, and clothing they can as a token of appreciation for our departure. Would you do that for me?"

"Is that all you and your people need?" asked Courtier Obaid.

"That is all we are in need of, thank you, Courtier Obaid."

A very humbled Courtier Obaid said, "I'll put my people to work on it right now."

Okpara's eyes scanned the crowd in hopes of seeing his parents one more time, in hopes of helping them change their minds. He just wanted his parents to come and accept the one true God as he had before taking his family away from Egypt, never to return. Finally spotting his parents, Okpara walked over to them as they would not come near his wife and child. In their eyes, they were the ones taking him away from them.

"Goodbye, Mother. Goodbye, Father… it is so hard to say good-bye with the knowledge that I shall never see you again."

Okpara's mother, bitter and disgusted with the whole situation, voiced her opinion: "Why you married an Israelite woman and decided to side with her people, I shall never know. You get what you deserve, I hope you'll be happy."

"Mother, father, won't you at least say goodbye to Rahab and Caleb?" Okpara's mother, unable to feel anything but anger and gall towards those taking her son away, answered: "Why should we? Rahab and the baby are the reason you are leaving us—no you just go, and we shall try our best to forget you." With that, Okpara's mother walked away from him and did not look back to see if he was watching her.

Okpara's father, in pain caused by his son, shrugged his shoulders and said, "I will not say good-bye as I hope you come to your senses some day and return to us." Okpara watched his father catch up with his mother and walk out of his life without even turning back to get one last look.

Okpara returned to his wife, many were there to say goodbye and watch them leave, "Goodbye, we'll miss all of you. May you find the one true God someday."

Their friends responded, "We'll miss you, too, I wish we could understand why you have decided to leave with Moses and his people, you are an Egyptian Okpara, not an Hebrew."

"Simple. After all the plagues, my eyes were opened to the fact that Egypt's gods are not real. Rehab and I stayed in a house where the mark of the lamb's blood was on the door, and we were spared death—both me and our son. Why can't you see that Moses' God is the real God? How can you say that the God of the Israelites is not a powerful God?"

One of the neighbors said with anger in his voice, "We'll think of you and pray to our Egyptian gods that you may return safely to us. Goodbye for now, my friend."

Sure that they would never see each other again, the families gave each other goodbye hugs. The Okpara family was on a new journey; it was the start of a new chapter in their life. Okpara for the first time in his life had confidence that he was on the right path, and that he was about to lead his family from a dangerous situation into a good one.

Still not sure why, this new adventure made him feel as though nothing could ever go wrong in their life again. Oh, for the moments of refreshment that blot out what lies ahead.

Families Preparing to Leave with Moses

Peleg, an Israelite who married an Egyptian, had decided to take his family and follow Moses. He was speaking with his in-laws, "I'll miss you all so much, and I wish you would come with us, after all you are my wife's parents and the grandparents of our children."

Thamir asked, "Is there still time, I mean it is not too late to go with you?" A very hopeful and excited Peleg replied, "Father, we are still here—all you have to do is gather up your clothes, your animals, your food; we'll help!"

"What do you say, my dear wife? Should we try something new and go with our daughter and her husband? We know that her husband lived when he should have died the same awful death of so many others."

"Yes, oh Thamir, yes!" "Come, we must hurry."

Another spoke to his son, "Nahum, my son, why after all that has happened would you want to stay behind and live in Egypt? Do you not realize how they'll treat you? Can you not understand that our God is the only way to go?"

"Father, you lectured me all my life about the one true God and I am tired of it. I do not see how we are that much different than the Egyptians. Do you not see how they have suffered?"

"There is a difference and you must choose the way of life you want to live. Do you want a life with the God of the Israelites, the only living, breathing God? Or do you want a life spent with gods and goddesses made of stone and wood and not able to do anything for you? My son, I wish you would come with us, but ultimately the choice is yours."

"Father, I'll stay here with my wife and children where I belong. Very soon we must put our oldest in the ground."

Overcome by emotion, a very sad father embraced his son, "Goodbye my son, I'll not see you ever again."

Nahum, sad and unsure about the decision he had to make, said, "Mother, I love you, and I hope to see you again someday."

Nahum's mother came forward with her arms outstretched to her son whom she knew she would never embrace again. "My son, my son, I'll always pray for you— give me one last hug to remember you by." Her heart grieved as she reached out to hug her daughter-in-law and grandchildren one final time.

One of the children asked, "Mother, why does it have to be this way? Why can't we all be together as we were before?"

Her mother replied, "Hush my child enough with the questions." Someday she will try to explain all that has happened to the children. However, for this moment in time, it'll have to be enough to say her goodbyes and say her prayers-that soon their life would get back to some normalcy.

Everyone leaving with Moses caravan was required to register at the information station in Rameses. This was required so that all would know what tribe to report to and where that tribe was located. Also, it would be easier for the head of each tribe to keep track of their families within their tribe.

A man named Ziya was at the registration booth, "My family is so excited, we never thought you would let us leave with you!"

Abidan, assigned to help Ziya and his family, spoke "Moses told us God's instructions are that any person, Hebrew or Egyptian that wants to leave with us, is allowed to leave with us. However, later on you and your family must meet the requirements set by God to become a part of the family of God. Your family can camp with the tribe of Asher—remember their tribal flag has the symbol of a tree on it. You must be ready when the trumpet sounds; it is our signal to leave."

Another family prepared to leave, "Martha, we are to leave any minute! Keep the bread dough in its kneading trough; we do not have time to add your leavening, just wrap it in a cloth, and I'll carry it."

"What about the possessions given to us by the Egyptians, what do I do with them?"

"Wrap them in a cloth, and I'll put it on one of the donkeys. I can lead the packed donkeys, and you can lead the donkey with the twins—I do not want them to wander off and get lost."

"That is fine; I have the baby to carry on my back and between that and leading the donkey, I shall have my hands full."

"Who would have thought we would get enough silver, gold, and clothing from the Egyptians that we would need an extra donkey to carry it all? Turning suddenly, he asked "What's that sound? I think I heard a trumpet blast, did you?"

"Yes! It is time—the others have already started walking away—let's go, let's get out of here! I wonder where we'll be tonight?"

"Who cares? We'll not be here, and that is all that matters to me," Mary's husband replied.

"Do we have everything in order?" asked Moses.

"I'd say yes, we have Joseph's bones, and all the animals are with the tribe they belong to. You'll lead out the whole procession—about 2,500 cubits wide (approximately a half mile) and forever in length. We have everything ready; Moses, lead us to the Promised Land."

"We are a strong, healthy looking people, are we not?"

"Yes, we are. Dan, I am to lead two million or so people out of Egypt, and there is not one person lame in the whole of us," answered Moses.

A proud Dan observed, "Have you noticed that we also have strong and healthy animals? We are taking every animal that belongs to us from this land, and that includes every dog, sheep, goat, cow, camel, donkey and the one or two chickens."

"Yes, Dan, as God instructed. I need you and Aaron to keep an eye out to make sure that no one has taken any animal that belongs to the Egyptians. We must take nothing more than that which God has instructed us."

"As you wish... do you think it is time to leave?"

Overcome with emotion for what God was about to do, Moses exclaimed, "The Lord is great! Yes, Dan, daylight does not last very long when we have this many people to journey from here. Aaron, *blow your trumpet!*"

Aaron blew the lead trumpet, followed by the eleven other trumpets, the signal that they were finally on their way. They were now on their way to the land filled with plenty, filled with grapes the size of nuts, filled with lush grasses, grains, and honey so sweet that others would be full of envy.

Never again would they have to struggle for food. Never again would they be under forced labor. Never again would there be sad and unhappy times. This was the happy thought the people had on their minds as they left Egypt; this land, that for them, was the land of misery, toil, and trouble.

ET NEWS: BREAKING NEWS: "Going, Going, Gone!"

"Marissa here with ET NEWS, I have my co-anchor Azad with me. Before we get started, I would like to say hello to all you wonderful people out there in Egypt. We are live in the middle of Rameses. What a grand and glorious day this is! Together we'll be watching Moses lead his people out of Egypt. The crowd of people here sending them off is incredible. Azad is out in the crowd, Azad, can we hear some of the conversations?"

"I'll stick the mike out and let you listen."

The comments came from the crowd, "Thank you, Pharaoh, these people are finally leaving!"

"Thanks to Pharaoh we'll have no more cause of grief from these Israelites."

"We'll all sleep tonight without the fear of Moses!"

"They are leaving! Good, it cannot be soon enough."

"Moses, your departure is such a relief."

"There you have it, Marissa, the people here in front of me are relieved that Moses and his people are leaving. They say it could never have been soon enough; I agree, it is about time that Moses and his people leave our country. Sir, you have a comment?" asked Azad.

"Yes, I do; I say anytime a dirty, smelly, stiff-necked sheep herder leaves the country the better off we are! Never could stand the sheep or those who care for them; I have no use for them—give me a good old ram or goat any day."

"Thank you for your input. Marissa, Moses and his God have been the cause of misery long enough here in Egypt. If the only way to get Moses to leave is for him to take these slaves and leave the country, then hurry up! Let's help them gather together and leave Egypt, it cannot be soon enough! This is Azad, saying back to you, Marissa."

"Thank you, Azad. I've been instructed to give you this message from the palace: "Sixty-nine days from now we'll have the Egyptian funerary procession for the loss of the royal palace's future king, Seti. As you should know by now, the embalmers are overcome with bodies. Due to the extreme amount of dead people, they cannot provide all the usual embalming rights—the usual supplies are in short supply.

The palace has given word that due to such an unusually high death count of humans and animals, we'll be conducting a nationwide funeral rite ceremony in seventy days. We'll have more information in a few days.

Back to Moses, I have some nagging questions. Have you noticed that a lot of us are lame, sore, and unhealthy? When I look at Moses and his people, the slaves, it seems they are healthy. Look around at the people, not one of them is sick, no one has a limp, nothing!

Every Israelite man, woman, and child from newborn to one hundred and ten years of age appears to be in good health! Those slaves ought to leave this country broken and discouraged. How did this happen? How did they become so strong and healthy in the past few weeks?

Why are we the ones who have suffered so much with the locusts, darkness, and the death of so many fathers, brothers, sons, and animals? How did these people end up with all our worldly possessions?

Do you people realize that Moses is leading them out of this country through the front gate of Rameses? They have our silver, our gold, and our very best clothes! Even so, I still believe that our precious Pharaoh shall bring our Egypt, our country, our supremacy back very soon—I am sure of it.

I'll be on assignment this week; so for now this is Marissa with ET NEWS saying 'May Pharaoh, who is Egypt's one true god, protect you.'"

Palace

At the palace, Courtier Obaid updated Pharaoh as to the progress of the royal family's arrangements.

"Have you informed everyone, as to what is to take place with the funerary rituals for my son?" asked Pharaoh.

"The embalmers have been told that none of the dead are to be embalmed at this time. They're waiting until your son—your royal bloodline—is ready to be presented to the people after the customary seventy days."

"Excellent... and how is Lotus Blossom, how is my Queen?"

The queen is fine—Jannes gave her a potion, and she is able to sleep, thank the gods."

"Yes, thank the gods, that lovely woman needed some rest; she has been understandably hysterical. I want you to send some spies out to follow Moses and those people. I want to know in three days' time where they are and what they are doing, do you understand me?"

"I shall do as you ask, my gracious Pharaoh."

Rameses

"Marissa, you are to report to the Chief in five minutes," blurted Kebi over the intercom system.

"Five minutes? Why?"

"I was only told that you are to report to the chief in five minutes."

"Five minutes! What in the world, it is not Emmy time yet." She hurried to her walled mirror to examine her hair and make-up.

Marissa spoke words of encouragement to herself, "You are gorgeous as ever Marissa; you are fit to handle whatever the Chief dishes out. With the way the year has gone, you'll probably have to wait until next year for your Emmy.

I wonder, the Chief has no reason to pink slip me. Would he really do that to me? Marissa, you are just stirring up trouble for yourself. Ma'at, I ask for your favor, I thank you for your favor. Now breathe, Marissa, breath in the favor of Ma'at.

As she knocked on the Chief's door, she heard his familiar, "Get in here!" She hesitantly opened the door, "Marissa, you've been doing an excellent job on this whole Moses thing."

Marissa closed the door and asked, "Thank you, Chief, but why the..."

"Yes, yes, sorry to give you a scare—I just needed to talk with you in my office out of the reach of the daily tongue wagging. Marissa, I'll get right to it. I need you to go out on assignment and to keep up with Moses."

"I already told the viewers that I am to be on assignment, so what has changed?"

"You are riding on a camel along with Captain Sekani; Pharaoh himself recommended him to me. He'll be your guide and guard— your protector, if you like. You'll take a slave along; his name is Liron, and I have chosen him myself. He'll care for your camel and any other needs you may have. You need to leave now if you want to stay current on the news. This time you are not to broadcast live."

"What! Then why go if I cannot go on the air live?" Marissa's cat-like hiss could be heard loud and clear; her cat stance of anger started to make her hair fall out of place, her sparkly hazel eyes became piercing darts of death.

"Marissa, Marissa, stop," laughed the chief. "Pharaoh made a special request. When you are on assignment, you are to report to Vizier Jibade via satellite to the palace."

"Pharaoh's... request? Oh wow! Me, he asked for me?" Marissa could not believe her ears, Pharaoh asked for her.

Laughing at Marissa's reaction to the news, the Chief asked, "Does that mean you'll do it?"

"Yes! Oh yes, of course, I'll do it! Whatever Pharaoh needs me to do." As Marissa replied, her answer had a purring sound to it, and her playful glee was back. She now had the look of an Egyptian cat about to eat the mouse she had longed to catch.

"Great, go to your house and get packed for a desert journey. You need to be back here before the seventh hour," ordered the Chief.

"I'll be back before you know it! Thanks, Chief," yelled Marissa as she ran purring with the excitement she was feeling over the honor of such an assignment.

"That girl of mine... one of these days I am going to have to marry her." Chief, alarmed by what he had just said, quickly looked around his office to make sure no wagging tongues were around to hear what he had just said.

Succoth, Egypt

Aaron asked, "How long do we get to rest?"

"Just as long as it takes to pick up the rest of our stragglers and eat a quick meal," answered Moses.

"The people are doing, especially well on this journey. I find it interesting how God is disguising himself as a pillar of cloud by day to keep his people at just the right temperature for this desert journey," observed Aaron.

"Did you catch on to the fact that God is also a pillar of fire at night that we may have light to move both day and night?"

"I think God's as excited for us to get to our destination as we are."

Moses said, "I think you are right, hopefully people will use this rest time, to find their clan and be where they belong. For the moment, I need to spend some alone time with God, and then we'll leave."

"I'll see that you are not disturbed."

"Bithiah, how are you doing? We only have enough time for making quick meal and then back on the road we go," said Jochebed.

"I am doing better than I thought I would be; as a matter of fact, I cannot ever remember feeling this good! What happened to that nice young couple, I have not seen them for a while?"

"I heard that they found their tribe and are very thankful to be with family again."

"Jochebed, I have wanted to ask you for some time… how does it feel to be reunited with Moses after all these years? You hid Moses, nurtured him for me, and then lost him. How have you managed to stay so healthy and sound of mind?" asked Bithiah.

Jochebed replied, "You know that Moses is my youngest child, he was a gift to my husband and me from our God. All children are a gift from God, we as parents tend to forget that. I learned the hard way that God only places a life, a soul on the earth when he has a plan for that child.

The only thing that can get in the way of that plan is us. God has given each of us free will—free choice, if you want—over our lives. We decide on our own if we wish to be part of him and part of his plan. I wonder if sometimes in the excitement or disappointments of life, we do not somehow get ahead of God's plans or fall behind with his plans for our life.

Either way, Bithiah, it still boils down to the only one that stands in the way of what we do in life—right or wrong—is us. We want to blame someone or something else, but it comes down to us.

I have stayed healthy and sound of mind because I have learned that lesson. I trust God with my life, and I try the best I know how to stay close to God. We had better go and see how soon before we leave." As Jochebed turned to go on her errand, Naamah walked up and said, "It is time to move on, we should hear the trumpet blow any moment."

"Thank you, Naamah... Bithiah, we'll have to finish our conversation later."

"Yes, we will, and it was just getting interesting," said Bithiah feeling more comfortable than she thought was possible.

Marissa

"Courtier Obaid, this is Marissa with ET NEWS. Moses seems to be taking a break at Succoth. I talked with some Israelite people, and I understand that he is to pick up some of his people from the Succoth area. My informant said that this shall allow the others to replenish some food supplies for the journey. They are to be here for six to eight hours and then on the road again."

"Splendid Marissa, do remember that Pharaoh wants no one to know that he has Moses under surveillance. Let me know when you are at your next stop. That is all for now," replied Courtier Obaid.

Sekani, since you are my protection, you'll come with me. Have you ever been to Succoth?"

"I have, and yes, I'll show you a good and safe place to eat," answered Sekani. Inwardly Sekani wondered how *he* got stuck with such a sheep herder's assignment—Pharaoh either trusts me or hates me.

"Liron, take care of my camel and make sure no one touches anything!" ordered Marissa. As Marissa walked away, she shouted, "If you're a good boy, I will bring you back something to eat."

Israelite Camp

"Jair, how are you?" asked Abdullah.

"We should be in the land of milk and honey by now, right?"

"No, I understand that the whole trip should take about three more days."

Jair, who felt like he was back in Egypt on a case stated, "I am getting the feeling that something is about to go bad on this journey."

Abdullah felt elated with the journey, and was not about to let Jair burst his bubble, "How can anything go wrong? We are being led out by Moses! Our journey has just begun."

Jair concerned for his friend warned, "I am telling you Abdullah; something does not feel right."

"Patience, my friend, patience. All is well, we ate that lamb, we survived the night of death, and I feel better than I have in a long time."

"Moses, how was your time with God?" asked Aaron.

"It was great; we are being told to go to Etham at the edge of the wilderness and camp to await further instructions. The trumpet blasts are signaling that it is time to march, let's get these people moving."

Allon called out, "Come on you lovely sheep, keep together and move along. Men, keep your sheep moving—we do not want them to stop once they start, or we'll be in trouble."

"Come children, now is the time to head to our new home, not play tag. If one of you falls, you are going to get stepped on," one mother scolded. Another father called out, "Stay in line like I placed you, or you'll be sorry when you get lost in this crowd of people."

Someone made the comment, "I understand that the cloud and the fire are forms of God, how amazing that he has not left us—not for a millisecond."

"I just want to know how many days we are to be on this journey to the Promised Land?" spoke another from the crowd.

Etham, Egypt

Aaron gave orders to each of the twelve tribal leaders, "We shall set up camp for the day. Take the time to rest up and be ready to leave at this time tomorrow unless told otherwise. Now go and tell the people what Moses has spoken."

With a quick look at Moses, Aaron asked, "Should we help our women folk set up the tent for a day?"

"No, they have the servants to help; you and I need to walk around and make sure everyone behaves themselves. You head south and east, and I'll take the north and west—meet me here in three hours."

Miriam looked around observing all the activity that was going on around her. The women were busy starting fires to cook their meal. The children were running, playing kick the rock, and having fun. "It sure is nice to see the children play and not have a worry in the world—children able to be children; we have not had that for some time. It sure feels good to rest again and to make a meal for the men. Finding a sleeping spot makes one feel right at home," she said with joy once again in her heart.

I suppose you are right; however, it'll take me some time to learn all these things. I hope you are not going to run out of patience while you teach me," said Bithiah.

Miriam hoped to encourage Bithiah, "Mom and I—even our servants—are at your service to help you learn all the fundamental homemaker skills. You are a fast learner and in a few days when we get to our new land you'll feel comfortable with your new life."

"I am glad you think so, where's your mother?"

"She heard one of the servants call for help; they think one of the women in camp is having labor pains."

"Labor pains! I never thought about women having babies on this trip," replied a startled Bithiah.

Miriam laughed, "Forgive me, I just now realized how different palace life is from the common Hebrew's life. I can imagine that when you lived as the princess of Egypt you would not have given much thought to babies being born or how children experience daily life. No matter what we do or where we go life continues to provide us with the ordinary everyday experiences."

"Moses, Aaron, it is time for a good meal; won't you sit and eat with us?" asked Miriam.

"That sounds like a wonderful idea—where's Elisheba and Phinehas?" asked Aaron.

"The mother in the tent next to us is in labor and I think they went to check on how she is managing."

"Father, you are back—great to see you!" exclaimed Eleazar.

"It is nice to see you too, is your mother coming?" asked Aaron.

"Mother is at the neighbor's, but she'll be here in a few minutes. The neighbor's wife is in labor so mother will quickly eat with us and then return to assist with the birth. Uncle Moses, are you going to have a meal with us?" asked Eleazar.

"I am going to eat with the family, yes."

Upon entering the tent, Elisheba spotted Aaron, walked over and gave him a kiss on the cheek, "Jochebed and I have to eat and go back over to help the neighbor. She is in labor, and since this is her first child, it may be a while before the baby comes."

"Let's sit for a meal before it gets ruined by this heat," said Miriam. As they all bowed their heads to give thanks for the meal, Moses prayed: "God bless this meal onto our bodies, grant us the nourishment that is needed to continue our journey. Help each of us to stay revived and ready to do what you need us to do, when you need us to do it. We pray for the safety of the mother as she delivers her first baby. We pray for the safety of the new baby as it comes into this world. What an exciting time for this one to arrive! Thanks be to God."

"Pass me the bread—so do we have anything to make a sandwich?" asked Ira.

"Ira!" They all tease at the same time. "I like sandwiches—what can I say?"

Jochebed asked, "Moses, have you heard from God where we are to go next?"

"The only thing I have heard from God, is that we are all to have a good night's sleep and be prepared to leave the same time tomorrow as we stopped today."

"Well, that is as good a plan as any and as God said to have a good night's sleep, that is what I'll do," Bithiah said to everyone's surprise.

With everyone startled Moses spoke, "Why Bithiah, that is the most you've said since you came to us, you must be feeling comfortable with us."

Jochebed concerned for her neighbor spoke, "I pray that the baby comes and that the mother receives some rest before we need to leave."

"I hope we have only one more day in this awful wilderness, or I'll go crazy," complained Jair.

"Jair, you really need to get a hold of yourself, can't you see where God is leading us to?" asked Abdullah.

Sarcastically and with eyes rolling Jair replied, "No, where?"

"We should be in Gaza by tomorrow and into the land filled with all that is great and good! Can't you see how easy it is?"

"I know that the wilderness of Shur takes us to the Philistine land, and that is not good."

Abdullah said, "My friend, you need more faith in our God. Why would he send us where the people would attack us?"

"I have been under Egyptian rule too long I guess. I just don't trust this God of ours."

"What! God is taking us to the land he promised to Abraham.".

"Yeah! It still is a land filled with violent people!"

Abdullah exasperated with Jair, threw up his arm and moved it around the land stating, "Why would God allow us to have to fight so many people to get to our promised land? No, I refuse to entertain such a thought. I am going to get some sleep while I can. Shalom Jair."

Jair walked away from Abdullah, not sure where he was going, just needing some space, Jair shouted, "Shalom Abdullah. I hope you are right, because I feel like something big is about to happen." After he walked a short distance Jair stopped and stared at the sky trying to figure out what his next move should be. Jair spoke to himself, "You had better get some sleep while you can."

Marissa

Marissa made a satellite call to update Courtier Obaid on the progress of her assignment. "Courtier Obaid, this is Marissa with ET NEWS."

"Yes, Marissa, what do you have for me?"

"Moses and his people left Succoth, and are camped at Etham at the edge of the wilderness. I do not know how long they'll be there; however, they have set up their tents. What would you like us to do?"

"Stay put, and if they prepare to leave that area, then let me know. Where's Captain Sekani?" asked Courtier Ubaid.

Captain Sekani brushed Marissa to the side as if standing in salute, "I am right here, sir."

"I need you to keep a close eye out; it is crucial that the minute you see them attempt to make a move, you track them. When you get a general idea of where they are going, let me know. That is all for now." Instantly they were disconnected.

Captain Sekani stood in awe, "It amazes me how we have communicated one second and with the flip of a switch it is cut off. I would like to know how this satellite works."

Marissa laughed, "Just the new way of communication Sekani." She stood and gazed out at the desert, mystified at how many Israelites there were.

Without realizing it Marissa spoke, "No wonder Pharaoh is so concerned about Moses trying to take control. Do you see how many Israelites are out there? I never realized how many Israelites there are; they seem to never end. I saw a vast number when they left Egypt, but out here in the wilderness you can get a better view of how many there are. They are as far as the eye can see, wow!"

Captain Sekani gently reminded Marissa, "Remember that not all of them are Israelites, there are some defectors of Egypt mixed in with them."

"From out here they look like a herd of animals out looking for food. All grouped into 12 armies. I hope I never see that many animals packed together looking for food," observed Liron.

Marissa said, "I am hungry; since we do not know when the slaves may be on the move again, let's figure out what to eat."

Captain Sekani looked at Marissa with a here-we-go-again look, "Eat?"

Marissa replied sarcastically, "Yes, food—surely you know what food is."

Sekani looked out over the horizon as if the Israelites might pack up and leave any moment when he knew that was not going to happen, he shook his head and complained, "I know what food is, but out here just how is the food supposed to keep? We only have bread and Zytum until our next city. Why do you think I told you last night to stock up when you ate? And you may address me as Captain Sekani! Women, they do not belong out here on assignment."

Marissa responded with her cat-like claws extended and her battle hiss coming through loud and clear. "If you are referring to me, I may not belong out here right now as I've never trained for this kind of area. However, if you mean women in general, then you are wrong mister, dead wrong. One of these days, you men shall come to realize how valuable women are! And I will call you Sekani if I want!"

"My you do have some spunk; I thought you were all fancy nails and make-up. What a pleasant surprise to find out that you have claws and venom and even some intelligence under your jet black hair."

Taken off guard Marissa tried not to show her embarrassment at misjudging Captain Sekani, "Thank you, but that still does not answer my question, is there any food?"

Captain Sekani walked over to the camel and pulled out a basket, "It just so happens I brought some bread and honey along with some leeks. There is Zytum to drink—warm, of course—I do not know how much longer any of our food and drink shall be available due to the recent storms we have had."

Marissa found that she was enjoying herself and smiled, "Thank you, Captain Sekani, this is a surprise. I would like a small piece of bread with honey—if you do not mind—and some of your Zytum."

As Marissa sat down for the meal she was looking for conversation, "I have never ridden on a camel before; this has been an experience, let me tell you. Every bone in my body hurts."

Captain Sekani tried not to speak in a way that would rile Marissa up again said, "Pharaoh instructed you receive only the best he had to offer for this trip, most people ride without a seat."

Jolted by the thought Marissa asked, "How would you ride a camel without a seat?"

"You sit on top of the first hump or between the humps; many people ride that way. Matter of fact, this is the first time I have ridden a camel with a seat… and that is a fact," declared Sekani.

Marissa not sure if Sekani was trying to pull one over on her or not said, "That is a fact, huh? I cannot see how anyone could ride that way; I'll have to see that someday." Trying to find a way to get comfortable as she needed to be wide awake when something happened Marissa commented, "I have never slept out in the open desert before and without as much as a tent. It is a good thing I brought my Bastet Amulet with me."

Just before she bedded in for the night Marissa picked up the Amulet and prayed, "Bastet, I ask you to keep me and the others with me protected from all that would want to harm us. O great Serqet, I ask protection from all scorpions and cobras on this night." Laying down she was sure she would get a restful night's sleep.

Israelite Camp

Moses with mirth in his voice said, "I slept like a baby last night, how about you old brother?"

Aaron teasing said, "Old brother is it? I'll old brother you!"

Miriam, not one to be left out threw her two cents in, "Boys, you are both just about ready to become a front door ornament while I am still in my prime."

Daringly Moses said, "What! Look who is talking—she is older than us by far and yet she thinks she is in her prime, what about that?"

Elisheba loved the relaxing time, she teased and scolded, "Children, children behave yourselves, or I'll have to throw you all outside and I'll be queen for the day."

Jochebed, unnoticed walked into the room and listened to the joyful teasing going on. How it brought back long forgotten fun times. She whispered, "Thank you God for the opportunity to have my children together once again." Jochebed decided it was time to get in on the fun, with a twinkle of humor in her eyes she said, "Good morning, how is everyone today?"

Startled Elisheba turned toward Jochebed smiled and said, "We are doing fine, mother, how about you?"

Miriam looked at her mother said, "It was a late one with the delivery of the new baby. Here come sit on the cushion while I get you some coffee."

Moses asked "How are mother and child?"

"Doing well—after some God time and some food, I'll go check on them. The others can take down our tent," replied Jochebed.

Moses deep in thought asked, "Mother, what did she have—a boy or a girl?"

Jochebed full of excitement for the future answered, "A healthy, bouncing baby boy, they named him Adriyel."

Aaron enjoyed his coffee and said, "How appropriate, it means 'God's flock.'"

God Spoke to Moses

Moses asked God, "Lord, what is your plan for taking the people through the Philistine territory?"

"You are not leading the people through the Philistine territory."

"I thought we were just a few days away from where we were supposed to go? How are we to get to our destination?"

"I know that you thought we would take the shortest route; however, I shall not lead the people by the road through the land of the Philistines. If these people encounter war, they'll turn tail and run—right back to Egypt."

"Are you sure that is what you want me to do?"

"Yes, I want you to turn their direction around and head to Pi Hahiroth. You'll be between Migdol and the Red Sea. I want you to camp opposite Baal Zephon. Pharaoh shall think the Israelites are lost and confused, that the wilderness has closed in on them. I shall make Pharaoh's heart stubborn again; he'll pursue the Israelites thinking they are an easy target."

"Alright, but then what?"

"I'll use Pharaoh and his army one last time to put my glory on display. The Egyptians shall finally realize that I am God."

"That is true. I know you have a plan, may I ask what it is?"

"That is all you need to know for now. I shall do to Pharaoh and his entire army what is necessary for me to receive the honor due me."

"Thank you, Lord, I'll do as you wish. Did you say between Migdol and the Red Sea?"

"Yes, Moses—Migdol and the Red Sea, and that is all you need to know for now."

Moses spoke as he left the presence of the Lord, "You are a good and gracious God."

Israelite Camp

Abdullah excited about the day spoke, "Jair, we are about to leave, one more day and we'll be in the Promised Land!"

"Yeah, yeah, I can hardly wait. I tell you, Abdullah, something is going on here; I can feel it in my bones", scoffed Jair.

"You have been a thief and spy for too long, my friend; you have to learn to trust our God. The trumpets are blowing; we must get in line, come on!" yelled Abdullah as he headed for the line.

"Being a thief and a spy has taught me to know when something is about to happen," Jair said to himself while he headed to his spot in the line.

Aaron spoke to the people, "Moses has heard from God. We are to turn our direction around and to set up camp in front of Pi-Hahiroth, between Migdol and the Sea. God told Moses to pay close attention to setting up camp across from Baal Zephon. That is all, now hurry, and we should be there within the day."

Jair smugly told Abdullah, "You see! Did I not tell you something was going on?"

Abdullah rolled his eyes, shrugged his shoulders and replied, "Okay, so God has us going in a different direction; I suppose he just wants to make sure we'll follow him no matter what." As Abdullah walked away, Jair spoke softly, "I do not like it, this is not over—not by a long shot."

As the first trumpet sounded, followed by the other eleven,

Moses shouted, "Aaron, I need you to help make sure everyone follows closely so that this journey runs smoothly."

"As you have asked, it shall be. I'll not see you for a while, Shalom Moses."

"Shalom Aaron."

Marissa

From her current desert quarters Marissa made contact with the palace. "Courtier Obaid, this is Marissa with ET NEWS."

"What news do you have for me?" Captain Sekani, stood beside Marissa and spoke, "The Israelites are packed up and ready to leave, I cannot tell you which way they plan to go; however, they are taking down the tents."

Leaving? Why hadn't Sekani told her before they called Courtier Obaid? Upset, Marissa asked, "Which way are they headed?"

Ignoring Marissa Courtier Obaid gave his orders, "As soon as you see which direction they head you are to let me know. You might get a hold of one of my assistants, so tell them I said they were to go and find me. I need to know firsthand the direction they go, that is all for now."

Sekani said to himself, "I thought that this job assignment was a punishment, *now I realize what Pharaoh is up to.*"

Marissa, ready to lay into Captain Sekani, changed her tune when she heard talking about Pharaoh. Slowly and deliberately she asked, "What is Pharaoh up to?

Startled, Captain Sekani answered, "What?"

"You said '*now I realize what Pharaoh is up to,*' what is he up to?" asked Marissa.

Captain Sekani, in deep concentration looked at Marissa, and yet looked through her more than at her. "I'll let you know later— for now I better concentrate on how to get an answer for Courtier Ubaid."

Sarcastically, and with a cat's hiss of surprise, Marissa responded, "Thank you, *Captain* Sekani, that would be very helpful… and if I can do something to help, just let me know." Who does he think he is, leaving me in the dark when this is *my* mission for Pharaoh!"

Palace

When Pharaoh first released the slaves to go with Moses to worship their God all his magicians, sorcerers and counselors were happy. They watched with excitement as Moses led the slaves out of Egypt. That was two days ago. Amazing how people's attitudes can change so fast.

After the men had time to survey the damage they were right back to complaining. It seemed that there were no slaves left to clean up the mess Moses and his God had left behind. So Pharaoh's counselors decided that they led Pharaoh to make an unwise choice by letting the slaves go and now wanted him to bring them back.

"Pharaoh, what have we done? Look at that mess out there, and we have no one to clean it up! Bring the slaves back!" whined Vizier Jibade.

Yamanu was fit to be tied, "How could we have let our Israel, our slave labor, leave like that? Moses, I hate you and your lowly, God."

Aamir threw a question out to the others, "We need those slaves back, but unless Moses is out of the picture, they are useless to us. How do we go about doing that? It seems that his god is more powerful than any of our gods."

Osaze walked up, bowed before his King and begged, "Almighty Pharaoh, we need those slaves back."

Pharaoh, sat on his royal court throne and paid no attention to what his men were saying, he was busy stewing over the events of the past forty-eight hours. Suddenly it came to him that with just a little more prayer, he would succeed in trapping Moses and bringing *his* slaves back to the place they belong.

His ears began to hear the men complain and he thought to himself, all through these blasted plagues I have given into these men and where has it gotten me? I have a kingdom in shambles, my first-born son is with the gods, I have been robbed of my peace, my calm. Enough I say I have had enough! Pharaoh suddenly stood up and waved his arm in authority.

The men didn't seem to notice until they heard him shout, "Enough! You men do not know what you want. First you say not to give in to Moses. Then you beg me to give into Moses. Now you tell me to find a way to kill Moses, so that you may have the slaves back. You know what I say! Quit your complaining and start thinking and working together like the men you are suppose to be. I will inform you when I have my plan fully developed.

You are to be ready for my order when it comes or else you'll be sleeping with the god's like my son!"

Pharaoh thought about the day the Israelites left his kingdom turned on the men again and stated, "Those Israelites left me and didn't even look back! They acted strong and proud—each of them walked, not one of them limping or hurting! They marched away from me like a well-greased army. Standing up straight and proud, they made a fool out of me! How dare my slaves do that to me, I'll show them! They shall come back to me! Not to you whiny men, but me! And when they do, I'll make them sorry they ever chose to leave me!"

For Pharaoh's men it had been a long time since they had seen Pharaoh carrying himself with that kind of authority and they all knew that it was time to leave his presence quietly and be ready for his order.

Marissa

At camp headquarters Marissa waited for Captain Sekani to return with news of Moses whereabouts. Captain Sekani dismounted from his camel and walked over to Marissa. "Marissa, I found out which direction, Moses is going, can you use your machine and make a call into Courtier Obaid?"

"Yes, Liron, help me to get this machine set up." Putting together the equipment was hard to do alone and there were pieces that had to go together properly in order for the machine to function.

"Ready?" Marissa asked after Liron stepped back. Liron nodded his head yes. "I'll give it a try." She flipped a few switches and spoke into the camera on the screen connected to the satellite equipment. "Marissa here with ET NEWS, Courtier Obaid are you there? No response—I'll try again; Courtier Obaid this is Marissa with ET NEWS, are you there?"

After what seemed like a minute, but was probably only a few seconds she heard, "Hello Marissa, what is it you need?" came the voice of an assistant to the Courtier.

"I was instructed to tell you to get Courtier Obaid immediately; we have some important information for him."

"He is in a meeting with Pharaoh, and I cannot..." Marissa interrupted, "If you do not go and get the Courtier right now, you and your family shall be living in the underworld!"

"I'll be but a moment," replied the assistant with a trembling in his voice.

"Good job, Marissa, I like your cat like actions more and more," laughed Captain Sekani.

Marissa puts Sekani in his proper place with, "Don't like them too much, our days together are short."

As Courtier Obaid's assistant walked down the hall to the conference room, he contemplated out loud, "Marissa or Pharaoh? Pharaoh is a safer choice by far. Here is the conference room—I better knock on the door and suffer the consequences. Knocking, he opened the door a crack and asked, "Pharaoh?"

"You are interrupting a meeting!" yelled Pharaoh.

Quivering with fear the assistant replied with a faint voice, "There is an ET NEWS call from Marissa for the Courtier."

Courtier Obaid jumped up and said, "Marissa! I need to take this—it might be the answer you are looking for."

"It had better be… get back here and let me know what she has to say," ordered Pharaoh.

Courtier Obaid got up from his chair and said while he bowed, "Yes, my Pharaoh." He then ran to the satellite station situated in the back section of the conference quarters. "Marissa, this better be good. I am in a meeting with Pharaoh, and he was very upset by this interruption."

Sekani responded, "I know the direction they are going, Courtier, they do not realize it, but they are trapping themselves. Moses is leading them into a trap."

Courtier Obaid anticipated the reward Pharaoh would have for him and said, "Don't keep me in suspense Captain Sekani, where are they headed?"

"They are heading to Migdol," answered Captain Sekani.

"Excellent! I'll inform Pharaoh. Meanwhile, you continue to follow Moses and call back in a few hours; we may have further instructions. That is all." With that Courtier Obaid was gone. "I really hate it when that machine does that."

Palace

Back at his meeting Courtier Obaid informed Pharaoh, "Captain Sekani said that Moses headed in the direction of Migdol."

"They are closed in on all sides by the desert. Moses and those stupid slaves are going around in circles, how much easier can it get?" remarked Jannes.

"You are right, Jannes, they are wandering around that desert like they have lost their way. The desert god Seth has sent them into confusion causing them to be swallowed up by the desert, which makes them that much easier to corner and capture.

Praise to you almighty Seth. Alert my chariots, alert my army! We leave as soon as we are suited up. Take me to my chariot house, I'll have my victory at long last—Moses, you are about to meet your destiny!" declared Pharaoh.

Marissa

Marissa jumped up from her blanket as if suddenly stung by a scorpion, "Liron, I can see it!" she shouted.

Captain Sekani who was busy thinking about the day ahead jumped up from his ground seat, looked expectantly in every direction and asked with disgust, "Can see what? Marissa I can't see anything. What do you see?"

Rolling here eyes dumbfounded that Sekani would ask such a thing. Marissa stated "My Emmy of course! At long last after months of hard work, I shall have finally earned my Emmy!"

"Your... Emmy?" Not willing to let Marissa know that he had no idea what she was talking about he continued, "Right.. what do you mean by that?"

Captain Sekani watched as Marissa showed her cat like irritation at his question.

"Where were you these last few months?" "It sure is interesting how her hair can suddenly look like it is standing on end and how her eyes narrow to look like a cat when she is riled Captain Sekani thought.

Realizing Marissa was waiting for an answer and not wanting her to have the upper hand, he said, "I have been on assignments for Pharaoh, too busy to know what went on with the rest of the world." Standing tall and looking every bit the military soldier he is just to get his point across.

Marissa not showing any sign of concern for anyone but her beloved Pharaoh decided to explain to Captain Sekani how she came to be with him on this assignment, "I imagine that when you are on an assignment for Pharaoh your concentration is on your assignment and not on what else is going on in the world.

Let me explain, When Moses came back to Egypt, everyone asked the question 'Is this the Moses of old? The one who was being groomed to become Pharaoh or is this some impostor?' After many meetings ET NEWS decided that we needed to let the public know who this man really is. The best way to do that was by producing a documentary on Moses. We had no clue at the time what was about to take place. And we are not about to let go until this story comes to completion.

After Pharaoh allowed the Israelite people to leave, he decided that he needed to know where they were going. That is how I ended up with you here in the desert following Moses and the slaves. Pharaoh requested I satellite spy for him as I have been in on this from the beginning. And he must trust you very much or he would not have assigned you to help me with this mission."

Captain Sekani looked at her suspiciously, "So you planned that Pharaoh would send you out here to spy on Moses?"

For the first time in a long time, Marissa found herself laughing, "No, I thought the assignment was over with for me when Moses took the slaves out of Egypt, and frankly I was pleased. I grew tired of chasing him around and was completely upset that Pharaoh had not been able to find a righteous way to get rid of him.

That day when I got back to my office, my chief-my boss-told me that Pharaoh requested *me* to follow Moses and the people out of Egypt. Said I was to satellite information back so Pharaoh could keep track of the slaves. I never dreamed I would be asked to do such a thing."

Marissa had paused for just a moment to ponder on how things had turned out so far. " However, I expect an Emmy out of this mission. I also expect to have a personal interview with Pharaoh when this is over, for *all* the world to see." Captain Sekani watched Marissa as she pretended she was interviewing Pharaoh and that all of Egypt was watching.

Captain Sekani said with a hint of laughter, "Well Liron, we have an assignment to concentrate on, and we do not want to lose Moses along the way or our little Marissa might lose her Emmy." Marissa shook her head and once again laughed like she had not laughed for a long time, "Hah-ha! Like that would ever happen." Marissa felt blissful even giddy, as she waved her arms in the air, and twirled around as if to wash away all the depression of the past.

She then decided it was time to take a short walk just to see what she could see. "Liron, come take a walk and enjoy ourselves while Captain Sekani concentrates on keeping track of Moses."

Chapter 20
"Let God Arise!"

Rameses Army Headquarter

Pharaoh prepared to meet the citizens and lead his men into battle to bring his slaves back to their rightful home. "Find General's Abasi and Runihura, tell them to meet me here at my Army Headquarters. Obaid, get my bodyguards together, wait… I have not lost any have I?"

"You still have your four: Lukman, Yafeu, Mahfuz, and Hondo."

"Tell them to meet me here, at my Army Headquarters."

ET NEWS: BREAKING NEWS: "Chariots Arise!"

"This is your news-anchor Azad with ET NEWS; Marissa is on assignment. I am at the Palaces' Chariot Headquarters along with Farah to give you an up to the minute news update.

We understand Pharaoh should come out of his Army Headquarters fully dressed in his chariot battle gear. As we all know, the Israelite slaves were given permission to go out and worship their God. Farah, what can you tell us.?"

"Pharaoh received word that the Israelites are on the move toward the Red Sea. Pharaoh granted the slaves permission to leave for three days to worship their God. However, it is believed that they are looking for a way to elude ever coming back to Ramses.

It appears that Moses has convinced them that they are not the property of Pharaoh. Those slaves do belong to Pharaoh and are needed here in our country to get things back in order. What we do not need is Moses and his God.

Pharaoh ordered his army and chariots together to bring the slaves back to us. During Pharaoh's morning prayer, he received permission from the other gods and goddesses to do away with Moses. With Moses gone, the slaves shall gladly come back to us.

There are four spearmen waiting for Pharaoh by his chariot. Two of the Pharaoh's bodyguards are waiting for him also. Here comes Vizier Jibade."

Vizier Jibade announced, "People of Egypt, I would like to present to you our God of the earth, Pharaoh." The crowd with great enthusiasm erupted with screams of joy, whistles and friendly jeering.

Farah continued reporting, "Azad, the screams of joy from the crowd are so loud it is hard to hear. What a sight! The people had not been pleased with Pharaoh since this whole nightmare started. However, they now seem very pleased with his latest decision.

What a glorious sight Pharaoh is as he make's his appearance. He is wearing a leather tunic and a waist-length robe covered with gold plating.

The leather tunic has rows that look ruffled, every other row consists of a very attractive dark blue color. Also made of leather with gold plating is his waist-length robe; it is decorated with that same dark blue color arranged in dots and circles.

To top off his royal battle look, he wears the blue crow helmet worn only in combat. It is made with the same blue coloring and of course, it has the Cobra symbol of protection attached to one of his protectors, Wadjet.

Not to be forgotten are the amulets worn on his waist shield. Normally Pharaoh also holds in his hand a good luck white water lily with many on his chariot as well. However, due to the recent weather, they were not able to produce the white water lily.

Pharaoh's chariot is gold plated with yellow leather and blue markings. He has two chestnut-colored horses, each attired in a very colorful blanket. Look at the colors—blue, red, green, and gold. I have never seen anything like it!"

The horses have head protection that matches the colored

marking around their necks, and they each have a decorative feather on top. "What a magnificent sight to see! I doubt we will ever see this again in our lifetime."

Azad spoke, "Pharaoh and his bodyguards seem to be in a light hearted conversation, I see them laughing and heads shaking. That picture just makes me feel like the gods are smiling on us today. Farah, I see that Hakim, is with you."

"Yes, I have Hakim top general and a military expert with me. Welcome Hakim, what a proud day this is for Pharaoh and all of Egypt."

"Yes, it is Farah, yes it is."

"Hakim, would you describe the military formation to us?"

"I would be glad to, Ziyad, a top-ranked infantry trooper, is out front to lead the way. Ziyad shall lead the whole unit out to the battlegrounds. Following him shall be rows of chariots. We have over six hundred chariots here today, each one is under the command of Pharaoh.

Every chariot holds an officer and a driver; most chariots lead by donkeys. The chariots cocoon the infantry soldiers, and by forming this cocoon, the chariots are placed to the north, south, east and west of the infantry."

Farah asked, "Would you explain to our viewers about the lions?"

"After some discussion over how dangerous Moses and his God could be, we decided to include some of the lions as a new defense strategy. The lions are wearing leather harnesses due to their powerful bodies. They will be walking to this glorious battle. What a beautiful sight it will be, seeing everything working together in unison. Pharaoh, of course, is leading the chariots."

"Thank you, you have been most helpful, would you stay for a minute and help us to understand more of the battle tactics?"

Hakim, with his eyes looking intently at the men and their chariots replied, "I cannot, I must join the men to go out to battle."

Azad said, "I am sure I speak for the people of Egypt, when I say 'May the gods of war protect you and our Pharaoh.'"

"Thank you, I hope so," Hakim said as he left for the battle line. As Azad watched Hakim walk off, he spoke, "I wish to remind you that I am Azad, news anchor and with me is Farah co-anchor for ET NEWS.

Sabri, I wonder if you would get a shot of the rest of the troops and chariots. The other chariots we see have a thin layer of gold with leather overlay. The donkeys are a type of chestnut and gray; they do not have the blanket cover the others do.

The men wear what I understand is the standard gear of men of that rank—simple chest protection and a helmet with feathers. Each chariot officer is donned with a white waist protective covering that has a front made from fiber for extra protection.

However, nothing is worn to protect the chest. The only way to tell who is who is that the officers wear a thin linen cloth over their heads with dark blue stripes. Quite the procession! That is it from me—back over to you, Farah."

Just in from Vizier Jibade, "As Pharaoh and his men soon go to the battle, this leaves very little protection at home. Should something happen, it would be devastating!"

"Farah, is that Pharaoh I see giving the signal to march?"

"Yes, it is, Azad—our great and fearless Pharaoh and his unit of chariots and troops are on their way to return our slaves to us. That is all for now. So people of Egypt, you shall not hear from us until our slaves are back. Azad and Farah in for Marissa with ET NEWS saying 'May the gods of Egypt protect you.'"

Palace

Courtier Obaid was in the satellite room conferencing with Marissa, "Marissa, Pharaoh and his troops along with the chariots have just left—heading in your direction." Marissa stood next to Captain Sekani when he asked, "What does that mean for my assignment, what do I do next?"

"You need to stay where you are; it'll be a day before they catch up with you. I need you to keep your eye on Moses in case he tries to make a run for it. Marissa, you are in on this until the great and glorious end. That is all for now."

Pi Hahiroth

Moses' family had set up camp and were resting. "It feels good to take a break, putting the tents up means we can have some rest time, don't you think?" said Aaron.

"I hope we do not camp too long, I'll feel better when we are in the land that God has promised us. You are right though the people need a rest. Knowing that God has covered us in his pillar of cloud, will give me a wonderful and peaceful rest." replied Jochebed.

Aaron turned his attention to Bithiah and asked, "Bithiah, how are you?"

"I think I'll take a nap, you do not mind, do you?" As she headed inside the tent Jochebed answered, "Of course not, this is so different from your old routine; I'll wake you when it is time for a meal."

"Mother, I need to check on Moses and make sure the guards are where they belong; you and the others shall be okay, while I am gone?" asked Aaron.

"Yes, my son, we are covered by our God. What more could we want? Now go." replied Jochebed who was looking forward to some alone time with God.

Meanwhile, over in the camp of Abdullah and Jair they were about finished with the setting up of their tent. While Abdullah pounded the last tent peg into the ground Jair decided it was time to voice his opinion again. "Why are we stopping here, is Moses lost? I'm telling you, Moses is leading us to the sea! I do not like it, not one bit—we are placing ourselves in a trap, something is going on here."

Abdullah, who was glad for an opportunity to rest and grew tired of listening to Jair's suspicions, said, "Take it easy, you are worse than an old woman! Moses has his guards in place, will that help you to calm down? I'll catch you later—I'll be napping should anything arise."

With that Abdullah went into the tent fully intent on a nap. Jair however, decided it would do him good to take a short walk and clear his mind. Murmuring to himself: "A walk? Yes, a walk is what I need to prove clear my mind. Why did I ever let myself get talked into coming out here anyway? The way Moses is taking us, we will all die for nothing, I could have done that back in Goshen. Everything is too quiet; maybe I *have* been a spy for too long. Jair, there is nothing to be upset and unsettled about, yet I cannot seem to relax."

As Jair stopped and looked around all he saw were people, people everywhere. Suddenly realizing that everything he did or said could be seen or heard he changed his tactic. He turned around and purposefully walked toward his camp whispering, "I need to go back and take a nap. What was I thinking anyway? All I did today was walk and my head never cleared so why would it now. A nap is what I need, yes, I will go and have some sweet dreams. Wake up refreshed and ready to meet the world again."

Marissa

Marissa spent the day with the hot sun beating on her and was beginning to think she would all die of heat stroke. It was different somehow being out in the desert verses being at home in the center of Rameses. I am tired of this heat, bored to tears and I will be hungry again soon. When will something happen! I have never been good at the waiting game. Marissa was talking to herself when she heard Liron shout, "Captain Sekani! I think I see Pharaoh's Army!"

Captain Sekani, who had been looking in the other direction with his spy glass and deep in his own thoughts spun his head around almost bumping into Liron, "What, where?"

Liron threw his arm up and pointed his finger, "Over there—is that not his army?"

Captain Sekani used his spyglass to get a closer look, "You are right, I think that is Pharaoh."

Marissa walked over to them to see if she could use Captain Sekani's spy glass. "Can I see with your glass?" Captain Sekani handed her the glass. "That was fast; it has not taken them as long as they thought. Should we inform the Courtier?" asked Marissa."

"That was our orders, better get a hold of him," replied Captain Sekani.

"Liron, the equipment is heavy. I'll hook it together." "Marissa, it is ready to hook up." "Thank you Liron, Courtier Obaid, Marissa here. I'm…" Courtier Obaid interrupted, "Marissa, I've been expecting your news call; I take it Pharaoh's army is in sight?" Marissa replied: "Yes, Courtier, he is."

Excitedly Captain Sekani broke into the conversation and asked: "May I go and join in on the conquest?"

Courtier Obaid gave his orders, "I know how you feel, Captain Sekani, however, for the sake of Marissa and the fact that we do owe her safe passage home, you had better not. What if something were to happen to you in battle? Continue to follow at a safe distance. And please, Marissa, news feed us live as soon as you feel you can. That is all for now."

"I hate it when he does that! Liron, begin to prepare the equipment for departure; we must be ready at a moment's notice," ordered Captain Sekani.

"I take it we need to ride and meet up with Pharaoh's army?" asked Marissa.

"We need to ride out for a short distance and then I shall leave you to rest until I catch up to Pharaoh and his army. Then I'll come back for you. For the moment, I need you to get on your camel and be ready to go. Liron, are we loaded?" asked Captain Sekani.

"Loaded and ready," answered Liron.

As Captain Sekani mounted his camel Marissa could see he was in his leadership role for he held himself as one that was used to authority. She watched as he instructed them, "When we leave follow closely and keep an eye out for Pharaoh and his army."

Israelite Camp

Meanwhile, back at the Israelite camp, Asher blew the trumpet with a warning blast, while a messenger ran toward the camp shouting, "Pharaoh, Pharaoh's army is coming after us! Get Moses!"

Moses, unaware of what was happening ate a meal with his family, "Great meal mother."

"Your welcome," Bithiah's eyes sparkled as she leaned against a blanket for support. For the first time in her journey she felt content.

She had a sense of total peace. "I have had such a wonderful time spending time with you, Moses. It has been such a long time since we could really visit. And this is the first time that your mother and I have had the chance to really get to know each other. It amazes me how much we have in common—even though we come from two entirely different backgrounds."

"People are the same everywhere, one way or another. With you and mother, first and foremost, you have me in common. Also, you both care about others, and your hearts lean toward the same things."

A messenger came running into camp shouting, "Moses! Moses!"

"What is all the commotion about?" asked Moses rising from his seat.

"Pharaoh and his army have just been spotted coming this way!" Suddenly, starting to shake and eyes pleading he continued, "What do we do? What do we do, we have nowhere to go!"

Moses, perturbed, spoke, "Relax, God has everything under control! However, I suppose I had better head out and try to keep the people calm. They are probably a bit crazy by now."

A crowd built around Moses' tent and started throwing accusations; "There are not enough graves in Egypt for all of us, is that why you brought us out into the desert to die?" "You promised us the Promised Land and yet here comes Pharaoh and his army!" "Some Promised Land!"

"He'll succeed in killing us all!"

"No matter how far we go, Pharaoh is always there—we should have stayed in Egypt."

The people were coming at him from every side, "We told you back in Egypt to leave us alone." "Yeah, and we also said we were just fine as slaves to the Egyptians, would you listen to us? No! Now look at the mess you got us into!"

"Moses, you do not care about us; it would have been better for us to stay as slaves to the Egyptians than to die out here in the desert."

Moses stood on a rock formation above the crowd and shouted, "*Enough*! That is enough, stop it, all of you! Shame on you for being so fearful, you are the people that have seen God perform plagues on the Egyptians. You are the people that have seen God place harm on the

Egyptians and spare you. So why are you acting this way now? Do you not have faith that what God has done once, he shall do again?

God has not left you; from the time we left Rameses until now, he has been with you. God's plan is to save you today. Today you saw the Egyptians for the last time. Take a good look at them for you'll never see them again, ever. God has done battle for you before, and he'll do battle for you today. However, if you do not calm down, you'll be too worked up to see what God is about to do for you.

Behave yourself—I'll be back in a few minutes." Moses looked around, this time he was smiling, "Good job, what a nice divergence!" Everyone could feel the calm that came over them once Moses put them straight. Sadly, that calm would not last for long. They stood quietly, and in deep thought, as they watched Moses walk to his meeting place with God.

Moses and God

Moses unsure and tired spoke, "God, I need your help here. You told me this would happen, but you did not tell me what I needed to do when Pharaoh and his army got here. What do I tell the people?"

God answered Moses: "Why cry out to me? Speak out to the Israelites. Order them to get moving. Hold your staff high and stretch your hand out over the sea: split the sea! The Israelites will walk through the sea on dry ground.

Meanwhile, I'll make the Egyptians keep up their stubborn chase. I'll use Pharaoh and his entire army—his chariots and his horsemen—to put my glory on display so that the Egyptians will realize that I am God."

"Thank you, God, as you say I shall do."

Israelite Camp

As he returned to the people, Moses had this to say: "God has just spoken and has given you a message. Now listen to what God has to say before you jump to any conclusions. You are to move ahead—now listen.

"I am going over and raise my hand and staff; the sea shall split and then we are to walk in the middle all the way to the other side.

You must do this by faith; God shall *not* let anything happen to you, but you have to make the choice to go because he shall not force you to go. Now go and get everyone ready to cross; we'll not stop until *all* have crossed the Red Sea."

After that, no one did a thing except intently watch Moses go over to the edge of the Red Sea and look up toward heaven. Moses then took his staff in his hand and lifted it high in the air. As he did this, God honored what he had told Moses to do, and the Red Sea began to split.

No one spoke a word—Moses just lifted his arm with his staff in hand, and the Sea began to open up—slowly at first and then it picked up speed. Then, as if to assist the process, there was a sudden East wind that came upon them.

Moses, finished with that job, turned around and said, "We do not have all day—as it is, we'll be up all night. Come on, let's leave this place!" With that said, excitement and awe filled the air as the people began their miraculous walk through the Red Sea.

In all the busyness of crossing to the other side, the people seemed blinded to the fact that God was still with them; God moved his position from the front guard to the rear guard.

In fact, if they had taken the time to look up with eyes wide open, they would have noticed the angel of God. He had been in the cloud of daytime shade in front of them.

God, moving to the back of the people, served as a bright light enabling them to see in the darkness. At the same time, he served as an impenetrable darkness to Pharaoh and his men.

The Egyptian army was being held back by God's pillar of cloud, which brought additional darkness in the night. It was so dark that neither Pharaoh nor his men could travel forward due to the extreme darkness and lack of visibility.

Marissa

Liron spoke, "We have almost caught with Pharaoh's army; it looks very dark that way. It might be another trick of Moses' God; we had better stay here until it is safe."

"That is fine by me; I am tired, and I cannot broadcast in this light. I am going to take a short nap," replied Marissa as she waited for assistance to dismount from her camel.

Liron sure that Marissa was being helped dismounted from his camel and replied, "I think I'll shut one eye also as it seems no one is going anywhere."

Israelite Camp

As the people obeyed Moses' instructions and traveled through the sea, the water walled up for them. "Mother, what happened to the sky? The water is too high!"

A father spoke, "Why worry about seeing the sky? When we get through, you can see the sky all you want, now move, my son, move on."

A child asked, "Grandfather, why do we have water on each side of us and yet it does not fall on us?"

Grandfather explained, "Our God has opened the sea, so that we can escape the evil man Pharaoh. God has provided this escape; he'll see no harm comes to us."

"My husband, have you noticed God's wind is making the ground dry and easy to march forward on?"

"Yes, my wife, I have noticed."

A husband asked, "Have you noticed that the wind makes a deafening noise as it whistles through this like a tunnel?"

His wife answered, "Huh?" "What did you say?" Frustrated, he turned to look at her and said, "I said... Hilarious, you are hilarious."

"Grandfather, can I touch the water when it is standing so tall and making circles?" asked his curious three-year-old daughter.

"I do not think you should, what if the sea decided to swallow you up, never to return you to me?" answered her grandfather.

The three-year-old replied, "That would make me very sad, grandfather."

"I would be sad also, granddaughter. Remember this day, my young one, no one can ever tell you that this never happened."

"Mother, have you noticed that the water churns in a continuous rolling motion. I wonder how God talks to the water and makes it move that way," asked her four-year-old son.

His mother in the wonder of it all herself answered, "I wonder myself, someday we'll have to ask him."

"Together—can we ask him together?" asked the four-year-old.

Laughing, the mother answered, "Yes, you and I together, I bet he would like that."

A father stated to his daughter, "My dear daughter, never forget this night. Promise me that when you get married you will tell your children so it stays fresh in their minds."

His daughter replied, "Father! How could I forget to tell my children about this night? Father, do you realize that you said I would get married someday? You always say that there is no man good enough for me."

Father laughed, "Slip of the tongue, daughter, slip of the tongue."

"Grandfather! Grandfather look in the water, there is something big!"

"What, my child, are you talking about?" asked Grandfather.

"Look—in the water I just saw something huge watching us, and I think it was smiling."

"You have a wild imagination my child," answered Grandfather.

"I want you to look, Grandfather—there is an animal, and I think it might be a turtle. I've heard of them but never seen one."

Grandfather sure his grandchild's imagination was working overtime turned his head to look and said, "Child, I shall look but… Wow, you are right! I think that might be a gigantic sea turtle watching us."

"Wonder what he thinks about us being in his territory?"

"Child, we have a story to tell others, don't we?" "Yes, Grandfather, we do."

ET NEWS: BREAKING NEWS: "Moses Dead!"

Marissa with ET NEWS, Breaking News, live from the Red Sea. Our great and glorious Pharaoh and his men have caught up with Moses and the Israelite people. It is almost morning—a little dark yet—so it might be fuzzy to you.

The God of Moses has done it again! Somehow the sea has opened up and is letting Moses and the Israelites cross over to the other side. The path is still open, so Pharaoh and all his men are in hot pursuit. Because it would be impossible to film from where they are, we'll stand on the shore and show this to you live for as long as we can.

I do not know how well you can see this. Can you see how the men with the lions struggle to keep them in control? It is as though the lions do not want to go out onto that road. They do not wish to walk through a tunnel that has walls of water on each side of them.

This is what it looks like… a straight and narrow road with a tall protective wall of water on each side. What a sight! I pray to you, Hapi, on behalf of all of Egypt that you keep Pharaoh and his men safe from harm as they cross the sea.

This wall of water that separated, making a path to walk through, is eerie, just plain eerie. However, Moses and his people are crossing over; so Pharaoh and his men should be able to cross without complications as well.

We are on location and able to see what happens when it happens. Right now Pharaoh and the rest of his men are chasing Moses, and at a good pace, I might add. However, I cannot see clearly—it appears that Pharaoh and his army are about halfway across—oh no, trouble!

What kind of trick is this? It seems as though an invisible hand swept by some of the chariots and pulled some of the wheels off. Yes, I said an invisible hand has pulled the wheels off some of the chariots. I am not going crazy, people. Could it be that Moses' God has powers that we have never seen?

Where the ground was dry, it now has started to fill with water causing the chariot wheels to lug down in the mud, and they are no longer able to turn. Can you hear the men? They are saying something. Liron, turn the volume rod on high." As soon as Liron obeyed Marissa's request, they heard the men, "Let's get out of here!"

"I am leaving and I do not care what Pharaoh does to me!"

"The God of Israel is fighting against us and for the Israelites!"

"Pharaoh, we are leaving… it is not worth it!"

A very disturbed Marissa commented: "I do not believe it! Just watch the men, they are abandoning Pharaoh! They are turning around and heading back to Egypt's shoreline."

Pharaoh shouted, "Get back here you cannot leave me! I am the god of the earth! You cannot leave me!"

The water and wind made so much noise that no one heard when God spoke to Moses, "Moses, it is time for you to reach your hand out over the Red Sea and then the water shall return to normal. As it does, it shall fall back over the Egyptians—including their chariots, the cavalry, the animals, and all men that came prepared for battle."

The Israelite people, busy making sure everyone made it to the other side, did not see what Moses was about to do. Moses without saying a word looked up toward heaven and stretched his hand over the sea. Fierce and ugly the sea was as a great and mighty wind caused the water to collapse within itself. The water came crashing down with the energy of an army, striking its foe, as the wind rumbled with a strength that rivaled that of a mighty hurricane.

In a matter of a few short minutes, the sea flowed normal again, burying any evidence that Pharaoh and his men were ever in that body of water. The one true God of the Israelites spoke many times warning people of the consequences paid for disobedience. Here again was another example of the price paid for placing their faith in a false god.

When the God of the Israelites was finished with Pharaoh, it was as though Pharaoh, his chariots, his cavalry, his animals and his army never existed.

Marissa shouted, "Moses, what have you done?" In total disbelief of what her eyes were telling her was true, Marissa began to shout: "Run!" Marissa desperately tried to warn Pharaoh and his men of the danger they could not see.

Liron, unable to rescue the men he watched drown, became concerned for Marissa and ran to her, "What are you talking about?"

Marissa pointed her finger at the sea and yelled, "Look! The water is falling! What is happening? Oh Pharaoh, what is happening?"

Before Liron could answer her, she gained her composure,

looked at the camera, and spoke: "People of Egypt, the men are trying to run; the Red Sea is closing in on them. It is closing down upon our army! Pharaoh! Where is our king? Liron, do you see Pharaoh anywhere?"

"No! I see nothing but the sea!" answered Liron.

Marissa cried in dismay, "Pharaoh, what has happened to you? He is alive, right? Liron, Pharaoh is alive? Liron, Pharaoh, and the men—this is just a nightmare! I need to wake up!"

"Marissa… people, this is Liron. I cannot explain what has happened here. It is your worst nightmare happening right before our eyes. Marissa is in shock as we all are.

You have just witnessed the showdown between Pharaoh and Moses. Pharaoh, our great leader, our almighty ruler, has lost this war. The gods have taken Pharaoh to be with them.

We heard the men right before they died. They were shouting that Moses' God was against us; they shouted it to the bitter end. They shouted that Moses' God has more power than *all* our gods combined."

Refusing to admit what had just happened, Marissa shouted, "But not more powerful than Pharaoh. He will show up… wait and see!"

Liron, concerned for Marissa tried to console her, "Marissa, the bodies of the men were swallowed up by the sea. There is no evidence they were ever there… not one of them is alive."

Captain Sekani made his way over to Marissa and took over for Liron, "People, this is Captain Sekani, I am Marissa's bodyguard. She is in extreme shock due to the events that just occurred before our very eyes. I am having a hard time believing it myself, but it seems that every man and every animal that left in pursuit of Moses and the Israelites is dead—drown when the waters of the sea closed in on them.

All people of Egypt, I do not know of an easy way to say this, but our Pharaoh is dead! Yes, I said Pharaoh is dead! Egypt is in total ruin. So as Egypt is in ruin, so the whole world is in ruin. We'll have more when I get Marissa back to the beaten and bruised country of Egypt."

Epilogue

There you have it, my lovely people of Egypt—the record of how many, many years ago, my lovely great aunt Marissa started to search for one answer never expecting to find another.

My aunt Marissa never fully recovered from the tragic loss of all she knew and loved. She did, however, live to receive the Emmy she so dearly coveted. All that time, all that work, all that ambition, just to accept her Emmy. Interestingly enough, when the day came and all applauded for her, cheered for her, and celebrated all she had done for the sake of Egypt, she said she felt an emptiness deep inside.

As Marissa lamented for Pharaoh, she admitted that she would give it all away to have her precious Pharaoh back again as the King of Egypt. It took the people many years to recover from the events that happened in the span of just one year. I believe that my generation, the third one down from that terrible period in history, is the first generation to finally start to mend from the bloody war.

It was a horrific war that Moses waged the day he stepped back into Egypt, bent on the destruction of our country of countries, our great and glorious country, our Egypt.

Some of us are of the opinion that as long as the Israelite people stay away from us we shall be okay. Others still think we did something wrong and that the people suffered severely because of it. There are still others that live here who believe in their great God of the Hebrews and the Israelites. They live life with the anticipation of the arrival of the new King... the Savior of the World, the King of Kings, and Lord of Lords."

Glossary

Aaron: Biblical, male, means "high mountain" or "exalted". Moses' Israelite brother

Abidan: Biblical, male, means "my father is judge".

Abigail: Biblical, female, means "my father is joy". Dan's wife.

Abihu: Biblical, male, means "he is my Father". One of Aaron's sons. 1 Chronicles 24:2.

Abraham: Biblical, Hebrew, male, means "father of many, multitude".

Adriyel: Hebrew, male, first born on way to the Promised Land in this book.

Allon: Hebrew, male, means "oak". Aaron's head sheep herder.

Amram: Biblical, male, means "exalted nation". A priestly tribe assigned to take care of God's Holy Place. Moses' father.

Caleb: Biblical, male, means "dog", "whole or all of heart".

Carmel: Hebrew, female, means "fruit garden, orchard, vineyard".

Cephas: Biblical, male, means "rock". Servant of Thaddeus.

Dabi: Hebrew, male. Thaddeus' son.

Edna: Biblical, female, means "pleasure". Asher's wife.

Eleazar: Biblical, male, means "my God has helped". Aaron's first-born son. 1 Chronicles 6:50.

Eliezer: Biblical, male, means "my God is help". Moses' second son. 1 Chronicles 23:15.

Elisheba: Hebrew, female, means "my G-d is an oath, pledged to G-d". Aaron's wife. Exodus 6:23

First Born Son: Reference Exodus 4:22.

Gershom: Biblical, male, means "exile, stranger and sojourner in a foreign land". Moses first-born son. Exodus 2:22

God: Leader of *all* Israelites, Hebrews, Jews and Gentiles. Names used for God at that time: I AM — I AM WHO I AM — WHAT I AM — I WILL BE WHAT I WILL BE. Ruler overall, including Satan himself. Adonai another name for God meaning "God of the Hebrews".

Ira: Hebrew, male, means "watchful".

Isaac: Biblical, male, means "he laughs".

Ithamar: Biblical, male, means "palm island". One of Aaron's sons. Exodus 6:23.

Jacob: Biblical, male, means "holder of the heel" or "supplanter".

Jair: Hebrew, male, means "he shines". He is Marissa's spy.

Jethro: Biblical, male, means "abundance". Midian Priest and Zipporah's Father.

Jochebed: Biblical, female, means "YAHWEH is glory". Moses' blood mother.

Johnathan: Biblical, male, means "YAHWEH has given".

Joseph: Biblical, male, means "he will add". Joseph's name means this according to the Bible Genesis 30:24.

Josephus: Hebrew, male, means "he will add".

Kohath: Biblical, male, means "congregational, wrinkle, bluntness". A son of Levi, Exodus 6:6. Moses' grandfather.

Libi: Hebrew, means "my heart".

Leah: Biblical, female, means "weary".

Levi: Biblical, male, means "attached". Moses' great grandfather.

Osher: Hebrew, male, means "happiness".

Menahem: Hebrew, male, means "comforter".

Moriah: Hebrew, female, means "seen by YAHWEH". Thaddeus' daughter.

Martha: Biblical, female, means "lady". Thaddeus' wife.

Melcha: Hebrew, Biblical, female, Genesis 11: 29.

Miriam: Biblical, female, original Hebrew form of Mary. Moses' Israelite sister.

Moses: Moshe (mo-SHEH): Biblical, male, meaning "I drew him from the water". Exodus 2:10.
1) Senmut: Moses' Egyptian palace name, meaning "mother's brother".
2) Beautiful: name given Moses by his birth parents Exodus 2:2 (God's Word Bible)

Moshe Rabbenu: Jewish, meaning Moses our teacher.

Naamah: Hebrew, female, meaning "pleasant". Ithamar's wife.

Nadab: Biblical, male, meaning "generous". Aaron's first-born son.1 Chronicles 24:2.

Nahum: Biblical, male, meaning "comforter".

Okpara: Egyptian, male, Family spent Passover with Moses family.

Peninnah: Biblical, female, meaning "precious stone". Eleazar's wife.

Phinehas: Biblical, male, meaning "serpent's mouth". Aaron's grandson by Eleazar. 1 Chronicles 6:50

Peleg: Hebrew, male, meaning "division, channel".

Puah: Hebrew, female, meaning mouth, corner, bush of hair. One of the midwives mentioned in Exodus 1:15.

Rahab: Biblical, female, meaning "spacious".

Sapphira: Biblical, female, meaning "sapphire" or "lapis lazuli".

Sheba: Biblical, female, meaning "oath". Name of the Dog in this book.

Shiphrah: Biblical, female, meaning "beautiful". One of the midwives mentioned in Exodus 1:15.

Thamir: Arabic, male, meaning "fruitful".

Zipporah: Biblical, female, meaning "bird". Moses' wife, Exodus 18:2.

Ziya: Arabic, male, meaning, "splendour, light, glow".

Chief Council Elders of Goshen

Asher: Biblical, male, meaning "happy" or "blessed".

Dan: Biblical, male, meaning "he judged".

Thaddeus: Biblical, male, is possibly derived from a word meaning "heart".

Other Locations and Cities in Egypt

Baal Zephon: Means lord of the north. Numbers 33:7.

Etham in the wilderness camp: Where they crossed the Red Sea. Exodus 13:20.

Goshen: Located in the northeastern Nile Delta area. The area of land that the people of Joseph were given to live in by Pharaoh during the famine in Egypt. Part of the Rameses region. Joshua 11:16.

Midian: Means strife. A people and an area of the Sinai. Exodus 2:15.

Migdol: Means the tower. Exodus 14:2.

Pi-Hahiroth: Means mouth of water, faces Baal Zephon. Exodus 14:2.

Red Sea: A long, narrow sea in which part of it is in the Arabian Peninsula. Exodus 15:4.

Mountains

Mount Sinai: Sinai means "thorny". (Strong. 2001. #05514). The mountain where Moses received the law from; located at the southern end of the Sinai Peninsula between the horns of the Red Sea; exact sight unknown. (Strong. 2001. #4614). Horeb means "desert" 1) Another name for Mount Sinai from which the LORD God gave the law to Moses and the Israelites. (Strong. 2001. #02722).

Shur: Is the wilderness that Mount Sinai is located in.

Symbols used by Moses and Aaron

Hand: Rod-Staff: Represents the power of God used to produce many signs and wonders. Genesis 49:10

Blood: Represents sacrificial, cleansing, worship to God. Exodus 23:18, Leviticus 9:18.

Serpent: Used to devour all the divine power of Egypt.

Other Names

Amen: Used to close a prayer, means so be it, or it is so. [So let it be said, so let it be done.]

Bar Mitzvah: Hebrew, Jewish celebration and ceremony of boys on their 13th birthday. Done to show their obligation to observe the commandments.

Firstborn of Israel: Exodus 4:22-23.

Hell: Kingdom made by God for Satan. Matthew 25:41, Revelation 20:10.

Hockey: Like ice hockey today only played on the desert sand.

Holy Ground: Ground where God addressed Moses.

Holy Land: God's land.

Karpas: Hebrew name for Parsley Sprigs

Lintel: Upper door frame on Egyptian huts.

Michael: Meaning "who is like God?" One of the chief angels of God. Daniel 10:13.

Nomads: People that have no permanent residence, desert people, tent dwellers. Jethro's people were considered Nomads. Genesis 13:3.

Papyrus: A plant common at this time that was used to make a type of paper and other things.

Pillar of Cloud: A form of God. Exodus 13:21-22.

Shalom: Used to say hello and goodbye in the Hebrew language.

Ten Plagues (In order of Bible placement)
1) Blood 2) Frogs 3) Lice 4) Insects 5) Diseased Cattle 6) Boils 7) Storm 8) Locusts 9) Darkness 10) Death of the first born.

Tribes outside of Egypt

Amorites: Tribe of warlike mountain people. Exodus 34:11.

Canaanites: Overall term used for the people of the land of ancient Israel. Exodus 34:11.

Hittites: Powerful warlike empire that warred against Lower Egypt. Exodus 34:11.

Hivites: A group of ancient villagers in Canaan. Exodus 34:11.

Jebusites: A nation of warlike people living in the mountains. Exodus 34:11.

Perizzites: A tribe of dwellers in the open country of Canaan. Exodus 34:11.

Twelve Sons of Israel (Jacob's sons in proper order of birth) 1)Reuben 2)Simeon 3)Levi 4)Judah 5)Dan 6) Naphtali 7) Gad 8) Asher 9) Issachar 10) Zebulun 11) Joseph 12) Benjamin

Egyptian Times News or ET NEWS Team

Abdullah: Hebrew, male, Arabic given name, means "servant of God". Marissa's co-anchor.

Azad: Persian, male, means "free".

Farah: Arabic, female, means "joy".

Kebi: Egyptian, female. Marissa's secretary.

Liron: Hebrew, male, means "song to me" or "joy to me".

Marissa: Latin, female, means "of the sea".

Sabri: Arabic, male, means "patient".

Sekani (Captain): Egyptian, male, means "laughs".

Pharaoh and Family

Seti: Means, "of Seth (2)" in Egyptian. The name was of two different Pharaohs of the 19th dynasty. Name this author used for Pharaoh's firstborn son, in this book.

Lotus Blossom: Egyptian, the female pet name for the queen, named after the sacred Lotus Tree.

Pharaoh: Egyptian, male, meaning that disperses, that spoils.

Other names and meanings for Pharaoh: God, God of the Earth, Lord of the two lands. Also: High Priest of Every Temple, God of the people. The people associated all Pharaohs with being the sons of Amun-Ra. Acacia was his Queen's pet name for him, named after Horus's sacred tree.

Pharaoh's Administration

Jibade: Egyptian, male. The Vizier, second in command under the Pharaoh.

Obaid: Muslim, male, means "faithful". The Courtier, Pharaoh's right-hand man.

Officials of the Palace

Aamir: Egyptian, male, means "stern".

Baraka: Egyptian, male.

Hadi: Arabic, male, means "leader, guide". One of the scribes.

Luzige: Egyptian, male, Official of Farm Agriculture Department.

Maskini: Egyptian, male, Official of the Livestock and Cattle Association.

Osaze: Egyptian, male, means "loved by God".

Tomer: Hebrew, male, means "palm tree". A subordinate official.

Pharaoh's Counselors, Sorcerers and Magicians

Yamanu: Egyptian Mythology, reconstructed Egyptian form of Amon. Chief Counselor to Pharaoh.

Wamukota: Egyptian, male, Sorcerer.

Jannes: One of two magicians who gave Moses a hard time in the Bible. 2 Timothy 3:8.

Jambres: One of two magicians who gave Moses a hard time in the Bible. 2 Timothy 3:8.

Jabr: Arabic, male, means "consolation, assistance". Apprentice Magician.

Pharaoh's Military

Abasi: Egyptian, male, General

Hakim: Arabic, male, means "wise". A top General and military expert.

Runihura: Egyptian, male, a General.

Hondo: Egyptian, male, one of Pharaoh's bodyguards.

Lukman: Egyptian, male, one of Pharaoh's bodyguards.

Mahfuz: Arabic, male, means "safeguarded". One of Pharaoh's bodyguards.

Yafeu: Egyptian, male, means "bold". One of Pharaoh's bodyguards.

Ziyad: Egyptian, male, means "growth". A top ranking infantry trooper.

Guards

Ghulam: Arabic, means "servant, boy".

Dana: Persian, male, means "wise".

Hanif: Arabic, male, means "true, upright".

Kamenwati: Egyptian, male.

All of the Palace

Masud: Egyptian, male, meaning "lucky". Chief of the slave driver program.

Menachem: Biblical Hebrew, male, means "comforter". An overseer of the Egyptian slaves.

Maor: Hebrew, male, means "light". Taskmaster.

Thabit: Egyptian, male, means "strong".

Palace Help

Chatuluka: Egyptian, male, Chief Servant of Pharaoh's oldest son.

Chigaru: Messenger for the Palace.

Layla: Egyptian, female, means "night". Head Mistress to the Queen.

Egyptian Names, Meanings, and References

Bithiah: Biblical, female, means "daughter of YAHWEH" in Hebrew. 1 Chronicles 4:17

Hannah: Biblical, female, means "favor or grace" in Hebrew.

Marinda: Latin, female, derives from the name MARIUS or from the Latin word marinus "of the sea". Marissa's niece who is telling this story.

Omid: Persian, female, means "hope".

Satan: Biblical, Biblical Hebrew, derived from the Hebrew meaning "adversary". Job 1:6

Cities in Lower Egypt

Goshen: The area of land in Egypt given to the Hebrews by the Pharaoh of Joseph. (Gen 45:9-10) The same land from which they later left Egypt at the time of the Exodus.

Pithom: One of the store cities built for Pharaoh by the Israelite slaves. Exodus 1:11.

Rameses: One of the store cities built for Pharaoh by the Israelite slaves. Exodus 12:37.

Succoth: An Egyptian city close to where the people of Moses first met after leaving Rameses heading to the Promised Land. Numbers 33:5.

Egyptian animals

Crocodiles: Worshiped and feared as water gods.

Hippopotamuses: Worshiped and feared as water gods.

Monkeys: Were house pets along with cats and some dogs.

Symbols used by the Egyptians

Rod/Staff: Represented the Egyptian Cobra, a symbol worn on one of the Pharaoh's crowns. Represents all the divine power of Egypt.

Egyptian Other

Ben Oil: Moringa oil from the Drumstick tree, also called Ben oil.

Boils: Bacterial infection of hair follicles.

Couscous [koos-koos]: Type of wheat.

Hounds & Jackals: Ancient Egyptian board game similar to chess.

Ished tree: Considered to be the god's tree of life by Thoth and Seshat.

Murrain: Did not refer to a specific disease at the time of history in this book, simply represent an unknown disease that results in death.

Nile River: This river was worshiped as the very lifeblood of the people and the land.

Primogeniture: Egyptian law of family order and inheritance at the time period in this book.

Pool symbol: The symbol for pool water contains seven zigzag lines.

Senet: Ancient Egyptian board game with rectangle board and small sticks.

Vessels: Anything used for holding liquids, such as a bowl, vase, wooden barrel.

Zytum: General name in the Egyptian language for ancient beer.

Gods and goddesses that Egyptians worshiped in this book:

Ammit (Ammut): Known as the goddess devourer of the underworld, shown with the head of a crocodile, midsection of a leopard and hind-end of a hippopotamus. Sometimes shown as standing by a lake of fire. Helps Anubis with carrying out the judgments of the Egyptian underworld by eating the heart out of those who do not pass Anubis scale test.

Amun-Ra (Amen-Ra, Atum): Known as lord of all things and creator of life to the Egyptians, depicted as a human. God of the air and the sun. For the Egyptians at that time, Amun-Ra had a role very similar to that of our Christian God. The name is combined with the sun god's name-Ra.

Anubis: Known as god of dead, gatekeeper of the underworld, ruler of the underworld. Depicted as human body head of a jackal.

Apis: Known as a bull god, protector of the dead and of pharaoh. Depicted and actualized as a bull.

Bastet (Baset, Bast): Known as a cat goddess. Protector of Ra, as his third eye. Bast household protector god. Wisdom, guard of perfumes, protector of Lower Egypt and women, children and cats. Depicted as a woman with the head of a cat.

Bes: Known as a dwarf god, a household god to protect, kill snakes, fight evil and watch over the children.

Geb: Known as an earth god, depicted at times as a man with a goose on his head. Allowed crops to grow, his laughter was the earthquakes, and he watched the weight of your heart in the afterlife.

Hapi (Hapy): Known as a Nile god or water god, god of fertility to plants. Spirit of the Nile, giver of life to all men. Depicted as a blue, green man.

Hathor: Called the Eye of Ra, goddess, mistress of heaven. Depicted as wearing a falcon on her head or a sun disk on her head. Also often times depicted as a woman with the head of a cow. Helped with pregnancy and with childbirth.

Hatmehyt (Hatmehit): Fish goddess. A water goddess who represented life and protection.

Heket (Heqet): Known as the frog goddess of childbirth. She gives the breath of life while in the womb. Credited with giving life to the flooding Nile River water each year. Germinates the corn. Depicted as a woman with the head of a frog.

Horus: Known as the god of war, sky, and protection. The symbol of the majesty and power of the Pharaoh. Depicted with a falcon head.

Imhotep: Known as the god of medicine and healing. Depicted with a papyrus scroll across his knees wearing a skull cap and a long linen kilt.

Isis: Known as the goddess of the throne. Goddess of magic, marriage, healing, and perfection. Depicted wearing a crown with a throne or disc and two horns.

Khepri: Known as the god of creation and the movement of the sunrise. The name means to create. Depicted as a man with the head of a scarab or dung beetle.

Khnum: Known as the third part of a god trinity. (Amen, Ra, and Khnum) Creator of the waters, the Nile River. Creator of the people on the potter's wheel, god of rebirth. Depicted as a man with the head of a ram.

Nekhbet: Known as a vulture goddess, patron of Pharaoh and of Upper Egypt. Sister of Wadjet. Depicted as a vulture with a white crown.

Nut: Known as the goddess of the sky and the night stars. Depicted as a blue skinned woman arching herself forward over the earth.

Osiris: Known as the god of the dead, and the ruler of the underworld and the afterlife. Also god of vegetation and fertility. It is said that the Nile is Osiris transforming life's blood. Depicted as a green skinned man, part mummy, wearing a crown of white and two ostrich feathers.

Ptah: Known as the god of creation, Lord of Ma'at.

Renenutet (Termuthis, Emutet, Renenet): Known as a goddess of fertility and children. Depicted as a woman with the head of a cobra, wearing a doubled plumed headdress or the solar disk. She gave newborn babies a secret name and her mother's milk. For fertility, protector of children from curses.

Sekhmet: Known as the Lady of Terror, Lady of Life. Goddess of lions, fire, and vengeance. Patron of physicians and healers. Depicted as a lady lion head, sometimes a sun disc on the head.

Serqet (Serket): Known as the scorpion goddess. For healing, stings, and bites. Woman with scorpion on her head.

Seshat: Known as the goddess of wisdom, writing, and management. Depicted as a woman wearing seven stars on her head.

Seth (Set): Known as the god of the desert and storms. Rival of Horus and Osiris. Protector of Ra.

Sobek (Sorbek): Known as the crocodile god of the Nile. Protects against the dangers of the Nile. Depicted as a man with a crocodile head.

Shu: Known as the god of wind, dry air and atmosphere. Depicted as a man wearing a feather headdress, the scepter and ankh, the sign of life. Is a protector of Ra and a god of punishment in the afterlife. In charge of killing the corrupt souls.

Thoth (Tehuti): Known as the god of the moon, magic, and writing. Lord of the holy words, scribe of the gods. Inventor of all arts and writing. Depicted as a man with the head of an Ibis.

Wadjet: Goddess, known as the protector of Lower Egypt and of the Pharaoh. Protected the women in childbirth and the lower land of Egypt.